THE WORDSWORTH
CLASSIC HORROR STORIES

The Wordsworth Book of
Classic Horror Stories

SELECTED AND EDITED BY
Christine Baker

Wordsworth Editions

This edition published 1998 by
Wordsworth Editions Limited
Cumberland House, Crib Street
Ware, Hertfordshire SG12 9ET

ISBN 1 85326 732 5

Typeset by Antony Gray
Printed and bound in Great Britain by
Mackays of Chatham plc, Chatham, Kent

ACKNOWLEDGEMENT

'Tarnhelm' is reprinted by kind permission of Sir Hugh Walpole's literary executor, Sir Rupert Hart-Davis.

The Publishers have attempted to trace and contact copyright holders prior to publication, but this has not always been possible. If notified, they will be pleased to rectify any errors or omissions.

CONTENTS

INTRODUCTION

Attempts to define the horror story invariably make much of the nebulous qualities of its form. The nature of horror itself is so hard to pin down. Undeniably, it has many common sources, elements that will provoke primal fear in most of us, yet our perceptions of horror change with the times. During this century in particular, the scope of terror seems to have expanded beyond measure. Moreover, horror, which is an emotion that can only spring from within ourselves, must intrinsically have some highly personal associations. George Orwell saw this clearly when he created the pervasive image of Room 101 in *Nineteen Eighty-Four*,[1] the ultimate, tailor-made torture chamber where each individual's worst fears are realised.

In the diverse selection presented in this volume, classic tales from two centuries have traditional elements in common yet feature material, supernatural, pseudo-scientific and psychological horrors. These are loose categories, overlapping and open to interpretation, but each story bears out the fact that whether the horror be real or imagined, its mystery ultimately explained or inexplicable, the success of the tale lies in the power of the sensation evoked. And this sensation may come suddenly, abruptly, or dawn slowly, creeping irrevocably towards its climax. Philip Van Doren Stern describes the high point in a good horror story:

> There is an actual physical response – the celebrated *frisson d'horreur* is no imaginary thing, as anyone who has experienced it will testify. The nervous system reacts as if it were being subjected to an electric shock.[2]

For many, the most intense kind of fear is that of the unknown, and hence the tenacious success of the supernatural or ghost tale. This instinctive, transcendental terror is a universal component of all early folklore, and its descent can be traced from ancient accounts of Druidic sacrifices and hideous fertility rites, through the lore involving magic and cabbalism in the Middle Ages, witchcraft and satanic practices in the sixteenth and seventeenth centuries, and the scientific dabblings of astrologers and alchemists. Belief in

---

1 George Orwell, *Nineteen Eighty-Four*, London, 1949. In Orwell's vision of an anti-Utopia, where all human values have been systematically destroyed, the ultimate punishment for those who defy the state is a visit to Room 101.

2 Philip Van Doren Stern, ed., *The Midnight Reader*, 1948 (Introduction)

the supernatural is a prerequisite of all religions, from East to West, and an acceptance of the forces of evil is entirely compatible with many, including Christianity, so that almost every culture has bred its own dark mythology and its own tradition of terror.

If horror of all sorts was a recurring feature in European literature from earliest times, a specific genre of horror writing did not really exist until the mid-eighteenth century. Until then, stories from an oral tradition tended to be incorporated into mainstream literature in primitive, anecdotal form. There was little development of these in their own right. The first signs in Britain that writing of such stories might be refined into an art form came in 1764 with Horace Walpole's novel *The Castle of Otranto: A Gothic Tale*. The word 'Gothic' here implied 'medieval', for the novel, and the Gothic School it spawned, drew on both the superstitious fears and the romance of the Middle Ages, exploiting all these afforded in terms of emotional thrills, glamour, supernatural fantasy and grotesque horror. The school had many followers. With the novels of Mrs Ann Radcliffe, a trend in public taste for macabre literature was established, and suspense fiction took on a new distinction.[3] Despite the mediocre qualities of much Gothic writing, and the mechanical explanations often indulged in by even the best authors, the school had a prevailing impact throughout Europe and America. Its stock trappings of gloomy forests, haunted castles, labyrinthine secret passages, sliding panels, dungeons, graveyards, and apparently supernatural incidents were deployed to produce extremes of lurid sensationalism.[4] The works of Matthew Gregory Lewis and Charles Robert Maturin tempered the Gothic with other European influences while William Beckford's exotic novel *Vathek* of 1787 plundered Arabian sources.

The turn of the eighteenth century saw the publication of many works that were to have a profound effect. There was a huge revival of interest in magic and the occult fed by miscellaneous works such as William Godwin's novel *St Leon* of 1799 and Francis Barrett's *The Magus* of 1801, a dissertation on occult practices. Godwin's story was one of the first to exploit the Rosicrucian theory of an elixir of eternal life,[5] a theme that was rich with terrible possibilities, while the effects of Barrett's book reverberate through later horror fiction in the works of Walter Scott, Bulwer Lytton, Godwin's

3 For a full discussion of Radcliffe's achievement, see Eino Railo, *The Haunted Castle. A Study of the Elements of English Romanticism*, London and New York, 1927.

4 The excesses of the genre were beautifully sent-up by Thomas Love Peacock in both *Nightmare Abbey* and *Gryll Grange*, and by Jane Austen in *Northanger Abbey*.

5 Purportedly founded by one Christian Rosenkreutz in 1484, the secret society of Rosicrucians or 'bretheren of the Rosy Cross' first came to light in 1614 and aroused interest all over Europe. Apparently based on the teachings of Paracelsus, its main concerns were mysticism and alchemy. Rosicrucians were alleged to have secret knowledge and various magical powers which gave control of the elements and elemental spirits, the ability to transmute metals and, most significantly, to prolong life.

daughter Mary Shelley (author of *Frankenstein*), and countless others who saw the potential for horror in the combination of mysticism and science. Charles Robert Maturin's *Melmoth the Wanderer* was also widely admired. Maturin showed especial sophistication in his communication of a sense of evil and what he called 'the passion of supernatural fear'.[6] His peculiarly deft use of suggestion points to the work of Edgar Allan Poe, and was to influence the writing of horror literature throughout the next century. Faustian themes and diabolic images abounded by 1830, when Walter Scott (whose Satanic masterpiece of 1807, 'Wandering Willie's Tale', opens this collection) published a synopsis of European witchlore, *Letters on Demonology and Witchcraft*.

Alongside all this, a curiosity about psychic phenomena and abnormal states of consciousness and their induction was resurging,[7] together with an interest in psychology and the dark side of human nature. Sheridan Le Fanu, who is generally regarded as the writer who perfected the short ghost story and 'mapped out the boundaries of supernatural horror in English fiction',[8] addressed all these themes. *In a Glass Darkly* of 1872 was Le Fanu's first collection of stories that were framed as case histories from the papers of Martin Hesselius, a scientific doctor investigating psychic phenomena in terms of mental illness. Each story begins with an explanation of the particular aspects of Hesselius's study that the case illustrates. Tension is built up by a slow accumulation of detail. Yet while this gives credence to the tales themselves, Le Fanu is generally ambivalent about the doctor's final elucidation of events. Disturbing questions invariably remain unanswered, and he creates a precarious world where a malign chaos swirls just beneath a surface which may be breached at any moment. His grim vision encompasses the psychological understanding of a dark side to all human nature that is shared by Robert Louis Stevenson. Stevenson's obsession with duality pervades his work and is best illustrated by his allegorical thriller *The Strange Case of Dr Jekyll and Mr Hyde*, while his supernatural horror story 'Thrawn Janet' conveys a stark terror that is worthy of Le Fanu. Le Fanu's horror is often intensified by humour, and his extraordinary manipulation of ambiguity, of dramatic irony, and of a complex system of narration that copes with both the actual and the imagined or supernatural in his stories, works to give his demons a powerful reality. In 'Green Tea', the story anthologised here

6 C. R. Maturin, *The Fatal Revenge*, 1807

7 The theosophical writings of Swedenborg, a Swedish philosopher, scientist and mystic who experienced visions and claimed to converse with angels, had engendered considerable interest in states of human consciousness. Promoted in England by William Blake, Swedenborg's work had been available in English since 1750. Strindberg and the French Symbolists were also much influenced by Swedenborg.

8 Jack Sullivan, *Elegant Nightmares: The English Ghost Story from Le Fanu to Blackwood*, Ohio University Press, Athens, 1978

and perhaps his greatest, Le Fanu forces the reader to see the apparition exactly as Jennings the fictional patient does, so that his shared terror is an authentic experience. In widely varying aspects, Le Fanu's work anticipates that of Henry James, of Bram Stoker whose *Dracula* was modelled on Le Fanu's vampire tale 'Carmilla', of Poe, Hawthorne, M. R. James, Ambrose Bierce and many more.

Almost contemporaneous with Le Fanu and equally important in establishing the form for horror writing was the American, Edgar Allan Poe. Like Le Fanu, Poe displays a curiously modern interest in human psychology. His peculiar understanding of the sources of terror and the ways in which an individual mind can be driven over the edge smacks of personal experience and informs all his narratives. Poe had an obsession with perversity or the self-destructive *alter ego*, and madness, coupled with alienation, is a theme that runs through his work. Other subjects, such as murder or live-burial, recur frequently enough to suggest personal fears. Two lines from a poem that features in the story 'Ligeia' epitomise his writing:

> And much of Madness and more of Sin
> And Horror the Soul of the plot![9]

Though there are Gothic overtones in Poe's work, his skill in reducing incidents to their bare essentials, sustaining atmosphere by means of subtle emphasis, and working towards one single climax of maximum effect, presented an economy that was entirely new at the time. The best of his work is allegorical, and though Poe's monsters are malignant and extremely potent, they are usually symbols of a more profound evil within the victim himself. Omens and prefigurings are used with these symbols and contribute to a pervasive sense of doom. 'The Black Cat' is a piece that combines his most characteristic traits, and shows the merging of nightmare and reality as he moves fluently between the conscious and subconscious mind of his tor- mented protagonist. Poe has had an enduring effect on the mainstream of horror writing, and on the very form of the short story itself. A contemporary of Poe and a fellow American, Nathaniel Hawthorne is a master of subtlety whose prime concern is with sin rather than madness. Hawthorne avoids the lurid, and his tone is melancholy and mildly didactic. He uses allegory to show evil as a very real, and almost inescapable force. 'Young Goodman Brown', the moral fable included here, illustrates this with appalling clarity as it reflects Hawthorne's insight into the hypocrisy of the human race.

By the late nineteenth century, serious investigation into paranormal phenomena was underway headed by the Society for Psychical Research, which had branches in both England and America. The society's

---

9 Edgar Allan Poe, 'Ligeia', in *Tales of Mystery and Imagination*, ed. J. S. Whitley, Wordsworth Editions Ltd, 1993

publications, which reported on sightings of ghosts, experiences of presentiment, communication with the dead through listed mediums, and other mystic occurrences, were subscribed to by some of the most eminent intellects of the time. Spiritualism of all sorts stirred the public imagination, and writers usually associated with other forms of literature often tried their hand at a horror story. Dickens, who encouraged many authors to contribute pieces on the supernatural to his magazine *Household Words*, turned out many a fine ghost story, the best of which, 'The Signalman', is anthologised here. Others who dabbled in horror fiction and produced occasional masterpieces were Stevenson, Kipling, Hardy, Henry James, Charlotte Perkins Gilman, F. Marion Crawford, Conrad, Saki and W. W. Jacobs.

Macabre tales were simultaneously flourishing in France, where Victor Hugo, Balzac, Gautier, Baudelaire,[10] Mérimée, Huysmans, Villiers de l'Isle-Adam and Maupassant all made their contributions. H. P. Lovecraft has pointed out that the French are 'more suited to a dark realism than to suggestions of the supernatural',[11] and it is true that the stories by Balzac and Maupassant presented here are in the mould of the *conte cruel*. These deal with material horror and are richly laced with irony and cynicism. Material or physical horror differs radically from supernatural horror, which is not to undermine it. The terror aroused in a good material horror story can be as profoundly felt as that produced by the evocation of something supernatural. These stories, which often have fantastic elements, require different narrative techniques. Tension is always crucial, but there is no need for ambiguity to create doubt, nor for indirectness or narrative distance. The writer who is dealing with only one level of reality can be more explicit. Conan Doyle's 'The Brazilian Cat' presents a fine example of material horror as does 'Vendetta', Maupassant's dark story of savage revenge. Balzac's 'The Mysterious Mansion' brilliantly treats one of Poe's most haunting themes, that of being buried alive; Wilkie Collins' story 'A Terribly Strange Bed' is the stuff of real nightmare. But as I have said, categories of horror are not always clear-cut. Some authors deal with several types of horror, and even mix them. H. G. Wells wrote both science fiction and material horror stories, the latter involving such fantasy that they are hard to classify. The sardonic American writer Ambrose Bierce produced some supernatural horror stories, but like James and Poe, he confessed to scepticism. Stories of the paranormal, such as his 'The Damned Thing', can be interpreted in the light of science fiction, and are most simply described as 'weird'.

Another rich vein of horror that departed from the Gothic tradition lay in

10 Baudelaire was a great champion of Edgar Allan Poe, who through Baudelaire's influence came to be seen as father of the Decadents in France, and for a long time was better appreciated there than in his native America.
11 H. P. Lovecraft, *Supernatural Horror in Literature*, New York, 1927. This is one of the most comprehensive accounts of the development of horror fiction.

the demonology of extinct cults. Michael Rhodes James initiated the antiquarian ghost story which derives from this, and twentieth-century writers such as Arthur Machen, Algernon Blackwood and H. P. Lovecraft adapted the theme to various ends. James was a most devoted admirer of Le Fanu, but he found his own form, and he has a huge following. He was to prescribe his method for constructing a ghost story in the preface to his collection *Ghosts and Marvels*, published in 1927:

> Let us then be introduced to the actors in a placid way, let us see them going about their ordinary business, undisturbed by forebodings, pleased with their surroundings, and into this calm environment let the ominous thing put out its head, unobtrusively at first, and then most insistently until it holds the stage.

M. R. James's narrative detachment is reminiscent of Le Fanu, but his spare style and simple plot structure are unique, and contrast dramatically with the hyperbolic excesses of Gothic fiction. He uses innuendo, understatement and wry humour, relying on a certain complicity with his readers, who, he seems to assume, share his scepticism. His tone is learned, but light and conversational as he writes of antiquarians whose bizarre fields of interest bring them into contact with ancient objects imbued with magical powers. In one of his most anthologised stories, 'Oh, Whistle, and I'll Come to You, My Lad', he shows, as Le Fanu does, that anyone can be prey to evil spirits. But the evil in James's world is dormant until inadvertently activated by the often bumbling, unsuspecting antiquarian. There is a sense in his stories that there is inevitably something unwholesome in the meddling pursuits and relishing of the past indulged in by his heroes. A stylist above all, James paces his stories with superb precision, controlling tension as he works towards the denouement. Jack Sullivan has noted that, in James's stories, 'his final revelation is less compelling than the means of arriving at it . . . the scene is horrifying, but interest lies in the eccentricity of the mode of perception'.[12] Many have followed James with antiquarian subjects or have emulated his approach to horror. His influence can be traced in the work of E. F. Benson. L. P. Hartley, Elizabeth Bowen, Robert Aickman and many more modern writers. In this collection Hugh Walpole's chilling story 'Tarnhelm' turns on the diabolic power of an ancient cap; the celebrated horror-classic 'The Monkey's Paw' by the humorist W. W. Jacobs suggests the magical properties of an old and curious talisman.

It is notable that the possessed objects in antiquarian horror stories often come from distant countries, and that many horror stories are set abroad. An exotic locale seems to enhance mystique and intensify a sense of menace. This suggests not only the extensive range of sources of horror as discussed

12 Jack Sullivan, *Elegant Nightmares: The English Ghost Story from Le Fanu to Blackwood*, Ohio University Press, Athens, 1978

earlier, but the exploitation of a tacit, instinctive suspicion of all things foreign. Linked to this feeling, and fostered by Christian prejudice, was a persistent identification of the devil with pagan deities.[13] Kipling's powerful tale 'The Mark of The Beast' treats a malignant sorcery that could not have happened in England, while the incantations of the child in Saki's 'Sredni Vashtar' would surely lose their potency if spoken in English. Yet the mysterious power of prayer or will is a commonplace in our national lore, too. Violet Hunt's 'The Prayer' and D. H. Lawrence's 'The Rocking Horse Winner' turn this topic to chilling effect.

The horror story has been denigrated in the past and is still regarded in some circles as a sub-genre, unworthy of serious critical attention. Yet, as Van Doren Stern insists,[14] it is a form that requires refined narrative skills. Many of its techniques are those of the short story, which was also largely an invention of the nineteenth century: a marked style, sound plotting, careful structure and selection of detail, the ability to create and sustain suspense and bring off a sharp climax. But in the horror story especially, 'atmosphere is the all important thing',[15] for its peculiar force is dependent on constantly rising tension. A thorough understanding of psychology is certainly necessary to the modern horror writer and specialist knowledge in almost any area can be useful. Subtlety, an instinct for the uncanny, and humour too have their place. The medium is in fact challenging for any writer, but the appeal of terror, if hard to explain, is impossible to refute. Recalling sentiments expressed by Schiller as he contemplated the achievement of Poe, Chauncey Burr wrote this in his *Memoir* of 1850:

> . . . it is an universal phenomenon of our nature that the mournful, the fearful, even the horrible, allure with irresistible enchantment.[16]

It is with this in mind that I have gathered the stories for this volume. Sadly, one is inevitably restricted, and there are fine tales by great writers that it has not been possible to include. My aim has been to illustrate the flexibility of the genre, and excellence has been the criterion for selection. I would like to thank Professor Warwick Gould of the Centre for English Studies, University of London, and Mr David Stuart Davies for their help in suggesting suitable material.

CHRISTINE BAKER
London

---

13 In much early Western literature, it was common for the devil to be perceived as a black man. In this volume see 'Thrawn Janet' by R. L. Stevenson.
14 Philip Van Doren Stern, ed., *The Midnight Reader*, 1948 (Introduction)
15 H. P. Lovecraft, *Supernatural Horror in Literature*, New York, 1927
16 Chauncey Burr, *Memoir*, 1850. A fuller extract from Burr is cited in David Galloway's Introduction to David Galloway ed., *Selected Writings of Edgar Allan Poe*, United Kingdom, 1967.

Wandering Willie's Tale

SIR WALTER SCOTT

YE MAUN HAVE HEARD of Sir Robert Redgauntlet of that Ilk, who lived in these parts before the dear years. The country will lang mind him; and our fathers used to draw breath thick if ever they heard him named. He was out wi' the Hielandmen in Montrose's time; and again he was in the hills wi' Glencairn in the saxteen hundred and fifty-twa; and sae when King Charles the Second came in, wha was in sic favour as the Laird of Redgauntlet? He was knighted at Lonon court, wi' the king's ain sword; and being a red-hot prelatist, he came down here, rampauging like a lion, with commissions of lieutenancy (and of lunacy, for what I ken), to put down a' the Whigs and Covenanters in the country. Wild wark they made of it; for the Whigs were as dour as the Cavaliers were fierce, and it was which should first tire the other. Redgauntlet was aye for the strong hand; and his name is kend as wide in the country as Claverhouse's or Tam Dalyell's. Glen, nor dargle, nor mountain, nor cave could hide the puir hill-folk when Redgauntlet was out with bugle and bloodhound after them, as if they had been sae mony deer. And troth when they fand them, they didna mak muckle mair ceremony than a Hielandman wi' a roebuck – It was just, 'Will ye tak the test?' – if not, 'Make ready – present – fire!' – and there lay the recusant.

Far and wide was Sir Robert hated and feared. Men thought he had a direct compact with Satan – that he was proof against steel – and that bullets happed aff his buff-coat like hailstanes from a hearth – that he had a mear that would turn a hare on the side of Carrifra-gawns* – and muckle to the same purpose, of whilk mair anon. The best blessing they wared on him was, 'Deil scowp wi' Redgauntlet!' He wasna a bad maister to his ain folk, though, and was weel aneugh liked by his tenants; and as for the lackies and troopers that raid out wi' him to the persecutions, as the Whigs caa'd those killing times, they wad hae drunken themsells blind to his health at ony time.

Now you are to ken that my gudesire lived on Redgauntlet's grund – they ca' the place Primrose-Knowe. We had lived on the grund, and under the Redgauntlets, since the riding days, and lang before. It was a pleasant bit:

---

* A precipitous side of a mountain in Moffatdale.

and I think the air is callerer and fresher there than onywhere else in the country. It's a' deserted now; and I sat on the broken door-cheek three days since, and was glad I couldna see the plight the place was in; but that's a' wide o' the mark. There dwelt my gudesire, Steenie Steenson; a rambling, rattling chiel' he had been in his young days, and could play weel on the pipes: he was famous at *Hoopers and Girders* – a' Cumberland couldna touch him at *Jockie Lattin* – and he had the finest finger for the back-lilt between Berwick and Carlisle. The like o' Steenie wasna the sort that they made Whigs o'. And so he became a Tory, as they ca' it, which we now ca' Jacobites, just out of a kind of needcessity, that he might belang to some side or other. He had nae ill-will to the Whig bodies, and liked little to see the blude rin, though, being obliged to follow Sir Robert in hunting and hosting, watching and warding, he saw muckle mischief, and maybe did some, that he couldna avoid.

Now Steenie was a kind of favourite with his master, and kend a' the folks about the castle, and was often sent for to play the pipes when they were at their merriment. Auld Dougal MacCallum, the butler that had followed Sir Robert through gude and ill, thick and thin, pool and stream, was specially fond of the pipes, and aye gae my gudesire his gude word wi' the laird; for Dougal could turn his master round his finger.

Weel, round came the Revolution, and it had like to have broken the hearts baith of Dougal and his master. But the change was not a'thegether sae great as they feared, and other folk thought for. The Whigs made an unco crawing what they wad do with their auld enemies, and in special wi' Sir Robert Redgauntlet. But there were ower mony great folks dipped in the same doings, to mak a spick and span new warld. So Parliament passed it a' ower easy; and Sir Robert, bating that he was held to hunting foxes instead of Covenanters, remained just the man he was. His revel was as loud, and his hall as weel lighted, as ever it had been, though maybe he lacked the fines of the nonconformists, that used to come to stock his larder and cellar; for it is certain he began to be keener about the rents than his tenants used to find him before, and they behoved to be prompt to the rent-day, or else the laird wasna pleased. And he was sic an awsome body, that naebody cared to anger him; for the oaths he swore, and the rage that he used to get into, and the looks that he put on, made men sometimes think him a devil incarnate.

Weel, my gudesire was nae manager – no that he was a very great misguider – but he hadna the saving gift, and he got twa terms' rent in arrear. He got the first brash at Whitsunday put ower wi' fair word and piping; but when Martinmas came, there was a summons from the grund-officer to come wi' the rent on a day preceese, or else Steenie behoved to flit. Sair wark he had to get the siller; but he was weel-freended, and at last he got the haill scraped thegether – a thousand merks – the maist of it was from a neighbour they caa'd Laurie Lapraik – a sly tod. Laurie had walth o' gear –

could hunt wi the hound and rin wi' the hare – and be a Whig or Tory, saunt or sinner as the wind stood. He was a professor in this Revolution warld, but he liked an orra sough of this warld, and a tune on the pipes weel aneugh at a by-time, and abune a', he thought he had gude security for the siller he lent my gudesire ower the stocking at Primrose-Knowe.

Away trots my gudesire to Redgauntlet Castle, wi' a heavy purse and a light heart, glad to be out of the laird's danger. Weel, the first thing he learned at the castle was that Sir Robert had fretted himself into a fit of the gout, because he did not appear before twelve o'clock. It wasna a'thegether for the sake of the money, Dougal thought; but because he didna like to part wi' my gudesire aff the grund. Dougal was glad to see Steenie, and brought him into the great oak parlour, and there sat the laird his leesome lane, excepting that he had beside him a great, ill-favoured jackanape, that was a special pet of his; a cankered beast it was, and mony an ill-natured trick it played – ill to please it was, and easily angered – ran about the haill castle, chattering and yowling, and pinching, and biting folk, especially before ill-weather or disturbances in the state. Sir Robert caa'd it Major Weir,* after the warlock that was burnt; and few folk liked either the name or the conditions of the creature – they thought there was something in it by ordinar – and my gudesire was not just easy in his mind when the door shut on him, and he saw himself in the room wi' naebody but the laird, Dougal MacCallum and the major, a thing that hadna chanced to him before.

Sir Robert sat, or, I should say, lay, in a great armed chair, wi' his grand velvet gown, and his feet on a cradle; for he had baith gout and gravel, and his face looked as gash and ghastly as Satan's. Major Weir sat opposite to him, in a red laced coat, and the laird's wig on his head; and aye as Sir Robert girned wi' pain, the jackanape girned too, like a sheep's-head between a pair of tangs – an ill-faur'd, fearsome couple they were. The laird's buff-coat was hung on a pin behind him, and his broadsword and his pistols within reach; for he keepit up the auld fashion of having the weapons ready, and a horse saddled day and night, just as he used to do when he was able to loup on horseback, and away after ony of the hill-folk he could get speerings of. Some said it was for fear of the Whigs taking vengeance, but I judge it was just his auld custom – he wasna gien to fear onything. The rental-book, wi' its black cover and brass clasps, was lying beside him; and a book of sculduddry sangs was put betwixt the leaves, to keep it open at the place where it bore evidence against the Goodman of Primrose-Knowe, as behind the hand with his mails and duties. Sir Robert gave my gudesire a look, as if he would have withered his heart in his bosom. Ye maun ken he had a way of bending his brows that men saw the visible mark of a horseshoe in his forehead, deep-dinted, as if it had been stamped there.

---

* A celebrated wizard, executed at Edinburgh for sorcery and other crimes.

'Are ye come light-handed, ye son of a toom whistle?' said Sir Robert. 'Zounds! if you are – '

My gudesire, with as gude a countenance as he could put on, made a leg, and placed the bag of money on the table wi' a dash, like a man that does something clever. The laird drew it to him hastily: 'Is it all here, Steenie, man?'

'Your honour will find it right,' said my gudesire.

'Here, Dougal,' said the laird, 'gie Steenie a tass of brandy downstairs, till I count the siller and write the receipt.'

But they werena weel out of the room, when Sir Robert gied a yelloch that garr'd the castle rock. Back ran Dougal – in flew the livery-men – yell on yell gied the laird, ilk ane mair awfu' than the ither. My gudesire knew not whether to stand or flee, but he ventured back into the parlour, where a' was gaun hirdy-girdie – naebody to say 'come in' or 'gae out'. Terribly the Laird roared for cauld water to his feet and wine to cool his throat; and hell, hell, hell, and its flames, was aye the word in his mouth. They brought him water, and when they plunged his swoln feet into the tub, he cried out it was burning; and folk say that it *did* bubble and sparkle like a seething caldron. He flung the cup at Dougal's head, and said he had given him blood instead of burgundy; and, sure aneugh, the lass washed clotted blood aff the carpet the neist day. The jackanape they caa'd Major Weir, it jibbered and cried as if it was mocking its master; my gudesire's head was like to turn – he forgot baith siller and receipt, and downstairs he banged; but as he ran, the shrieks came faint and fainter; there was a deep-drawn shivering groan, and word gaed through the castle that the laird was dead.

Weel, away came my gudesire, wi' his finger in his mouth, and his best hope was that Dougal had seen the money-bag, and heard the laird speak of writing the receipt. The young Laird, now Sir John, came from Edinburgh, to see things put to rights. Sir John and his father never gree'd weel. Sir John had been bred an advocate, and afterwards sat in the last Scots Parliament and voted for the Union, having gotten, it was thought, a rug of the compensations – if his father could have come out of his grave, he would have brained him for it on his awn hearthstane. Some thought it was easier counting with the auld rough knight than the fair-spoken young ane – but mair of that anon.

Dougal MacCallum, poor body, neither grat nor graned, but gaed about the house looking like a corpse, but directing, as was his duty, a' the order of the grand funeral. Now, Dougal looked aye waur and waur when night was coming, and was aye the last to gang to his bed, whilk was in a little round just opposite the chamber of dais, whilk his master occupied while he was living, and where he now lay in state, as they caa'd it, weel-a-day! The night before the funeral, Dougal could keep his awn counsel nae langer; he cam doun with his proud spirit, and fairly asked auld Hutcheon to sit in his room with him for an hour. When they were in the round, Dougal took ae tass of brandy to himsell, and gave another to Hutcheon, and wished him all health, and lang life, and said that, for himsell, he wasna lang for this world; for that every night since Sir Robert's death, his silver call had sounded from the state-chamber, just as it used to do at nights in his lifetime, to call Dougal to help to turn him in his bed. Dougal said that being alone with the dead on that floor of the tower (for naebody cared to wake Sir Robert Redgauntlet like another corpse), he had never daured to answer the call, but that now his conscience checked him for neglecting his duty; for, 'Though death breaks service,' said MacCallum, 'it shall never break my service to Sir Robert; and I will answer his next whistle, so be you will stand by me, Hutcheon.'

Hutcheon had nae will to the wark, but he had stood by Dougal in battle and broil, and he wad not fail him at this pinch; so down the carles sat ower a stoup of brandy, and Hutcheon, who was something of a clerk, would have read a chapter of the Bible; but Dougal would hear naething but a blaud of Davie Lindsay, whilk was the waur preparation.

When midnight came, and the house was quiet as the grave, sure aneugh the silver whistle sounded as sharp and shrill as if Sir Robert was blowing it, and up gat the twa auld serving-men and tottered into the room where the dead man lay. Hutcheon saw aneugh at the first glance, for there were torches in the room, which showed him the foul fiend, in his ain shape, sitting on the laird's coffin! Over he cowped as if he had been dead. He could not tell how lang he lay in a trance at the door, but when he gathered himself, he cried on his neighbour, and getting nae answer, raised the house, and Dougal was found lying dead within twa steps of the bed where his master's coffin was placed. As for the whistle, it was gaen anes and aye; but mony a time was it heard at the top of the house on the bartizan, and amang the auld chimneys and turrets, where the howlets have their nests. Sir John hushed the matter up and the funeral passed over without mair bogle-wark.

But when a' was over, and the laird was beginning to settle his affairs, every tenant was called up for his arrears, and my gudesire for the full sum that stood against him in the rental-book. Weel, away he trots to the castle, to tell his story, and there he is introduced to Sir John, sitting in his father's chair, in deep mourning, with weepers and hanging cravat, and a small walking rapier by his side, instead of the auld broadsword, that had a hundredweight of steel about it, what with blade, chape and basket-hilt. I have heard their communing so often tauld ower that I almost think I was there mysell, though I couldna be born at the time.

'I wuss ye joy, sir, of the head seat, and the white loaf, and the braid lairdship. Your father was a kind man to friends and followers; muckle grace to you, Sir John, to fill his shoon – his boots, I suld say, for he seldom wore shoon, unless it were muils when he had the gout.

'Ay, Steenie,' quoth the laird, sighing deeply and putting his napkin to his een, 'his was a sudden call, and he will be missed in the country; no time to set his house in order – weel prepared Godward, no doubt, which is the root of the matter – but left us behind a tangled hesp to wind, Steenie. Hem! hem! We maun go to business, Steenie; much to do, and little time to do it in.'

Here he opened the fatal volume. I have heard of a thing they call Doomsday-book – I am clear it has been a rental of back-ganging tenants.

'Stephen,' said Sir John, still in the same soft, sleekit tone of voice, 'Stephen Stevenson, or Steenson, ye are down here for a year's rent behind the hand – due at last term.'

Stephen. 'Please your honour, Sir John, I paid it to your father.'

Sir John. 'Ye took a receipt then, doubtless, Stephen; and can produce it?'

Stephen. 'Indeed, I hadna time, an it like your honour; for nae sooner had I set doun the siller, and just as his honour Sir Robert, that's gaen, drew it till him to count it, and write out the receipt, he was ta'en wi' the pains that removed him.'

'That was unlucky,' said Sir John, after a pause. 'But ye maybe paid it in the presence of somebody. I want but a *talis qualis* evidence, Stephen. I would go ower strictly to work with no poor man.'

Stephen. 'Troth, Sir John, there was naebody in the room but Dougal MacCallum the butler. But, as your honour kens, he has e'en followed his auld master.'

'Very unlucky again, Stephen,' said Sir John, without altering his voice a single note. 'The man to whom ye paid the money is dead – and the man who witnessed the payment is dead too – and the siller, which should have been to the fore, is neither seen nor heard tell of in the repositories. How am I to believe a' this?'

Stephen. 'I dinna ken, your honour; but there is a bit memorandum note of the very coins; for, God help me! I had to borrow out of twenty purses; and I am sure that ilka man there set down will take his grit oath for what purpose I borrowed the money.'

Sir John. 'I have little doubt ye *borrowed* the money, Steenie. It is the *payment* to my father that I want to have some proof of.'

Stephen. 'The siller maun be about the house, Sir John. And since your honour never got it, and his honour that was canna have ta'en it wi' him, maybe some of the family may have seen it.'

Sir John. 'We will examine the servants, Stephen; that is but reasonable.'

But lackey and lass, and page and groom, all denied stoutly that they had ever seen such a bag of money as my gudesire described. What was waur, he had unluckily not mentioned to any living soul of them his purpose of paying his rent. Ae quean had noticed something under his arm, but she took it for the pipes.

Sir John Redgauntlet ordered the servants out of the room, and then said to my gudesire: 'Now, Steenie, ye see you have fair play; and, as I have little doubt ye ken better where to find the siller than ony other body, I beg, in fair terms, and for your own sake, that you will end this fasherie; for, Stephen, ye maun pay or flit.'

'The Lord forgie your opinion,' said Stephen, driven almost to his wit's end – 'I am an honest man.'

'So am I, Stephen,' said his honour; 'and so are all the folks in the house, I hope. But if there be a knave amongst us, it must be he that tells the story he cannot prove.' He paused, and then added, mair sternly, 'If I understand your trick, sir, you want to take advantage of some malicious reports concerning things in this family, and particularly respecting my father's sudden death, thereby to cheat me out of the money, and perhaps take away my character, by insinuating that I have received the rent I am demanding. – Where do you suppose this money to be? – I insist upon knowing.'

My gudesire saw everything look sae muckle against him, that he grew nearly desperate – however, he shifted from one foot to another, looked to every corner of the room, and made no answer.

'Speak out, sirrah,' said the laird, assuming a look of his father's, a very particular ane, which he had when he was angry – it seemed as if the wrinkles of his frown made that selfsame fearful shape of a horse's shoe in the middle of his brow – 'Speak out, sir! I *will* know your thoughts; – do you suppose that I have this money?'

'Far be it frae me to say so,' said Stephen.

'Do you charge any of my people with having taken it?'

'I wad be laith to charge them that may be innocent,' said my gudesire; 'and if there be any one that is guilty, I have nae proof.'

'Somewhere the money must be, if there is a word of truth in your story,' said Sir John; 'I ask where you think it is – and demand a correct answer?'

'In hell, if you *will* have my thoughts of it,' said my gudesire, driven to extremity – 'in hell! with your father, his jackanape and his silver whistle.'

Down the stairs he ran (for the parlour was nae place for him after such a word), and he heard the laird swearing blood and wounds behind him, as fast as ever did Sir Robert, and roaring for the bailie and the baron-officer.

Away rode my gudesire to his chief creditor (him they caa'd Laurie Lapraik) to try if he could make onything out of him; but when he tauld his story, he got but the warst word in his wame – thief, beggar and dyvour were the saftest terms; and to the boot of these hard terms, Laurie brought up the auld story of his dipping his hand in the blood of God's saunts, just as if a tenant could have helped riding with the laird, and that a laird like Sir Robert Redgauntlet. My gudesire was, by this time, far beyond the bounds of patience, and, while he and Laurie were at deil speed the liars, he was wanchancie aneugh to abuse Lapraik's doctrine as weel as the man, and said things that garr'd folk's flesh grue that heard them – he wasna just himsel', and he had lived wi' a wild set in his day.

At last they parted, and my gudesire was to ride hame through the wood of Pitmurkie, that is a' fou of black firs, as they say. I ken the wood, but the firs may be black or white for what I can tell. At the entry of the wood there is a wild common, and on the edge of the common, a little lonely change-house, that was keepit then by an ostler-wife (they suld hae caa'd her Tibbie Faw), and there puir Steenie cried for a mutchkin of brandy, for he had had no refreshment the haill day. Tibbie was earnest wi' him to take a bite of meat, but he couldna think o't, nor would he take his foot out of the stirrup, and took off the brandy wholely at twa draughts, and named a toast at each: the first was the memory of Sir Robert Redgauntlet, and might he never lie quiet in his grave till he had righted his poor bond-tenant; and the second was a health to Man's Enemy, if he would but get him back the pock of siller, or tell him what came o't, for he saw the haill world was like to regard him as a thief and a cheat, and he took that waur than even the ruin of his house and hauld.

On he rode, little caring where. It was dark night turned, and the trees made it yet darker, and he had let the beast take its ain road through the wood when, all of a sudden, from tired and wearied that it was before, the nag began sae to spring and flee and stend that my gudesire could hardly keep the saddle. Upon the whilk, a horseman, suddenly riding up beside him, said: 'That's a mettle beast of yours, freend; will you sell him?' – So saying, he touched the horse's neck with his riding-wand, and it fell into its auld heigh-ho of a stumbling trot. 'But his spunk's soon out of him, I think,' continued the stranger, 'and that is like mony a man's courage, that thinks he wad do great things till he come to the proof.'

My gudesire scarce listened to this, but spurred his horse, with, 'Gude e'en to you, freend.'

But it's like the stranger was ane that doesna lightly yield his point; for, ride as Steenie liked, he was aye beside him at the selfsame pace. At last, my gudesire, Steenie Steenson, grew half angry; and, to say the truth, half feared.

'What is it that ye want with me, freend?' he said. 'If ye be a robber, I have nae money; if ye be a leal man, wanting company, I have nae heart to mirth or speaking; and if ye want to ken the road, I scarce ken it mysell.'

'If you will tell me your grief,' said the stranger, 'I am one that, though I have been sair miscaa'd in the world, am the only hand for helping my freends.'

So my gudesire, to ease his ain heart, mair than from any hope of help, told him the story from beginning to end.

'It's a hard pinch,' said the stranger; 'but I think I can help you.'

'If you could lend the money, sir, and take a lang day – I ken nae other help on earth,' said my gudesire.

'But there may be some under the earth,' said the stranger. 'Come, I'll be frank wi' you; I could lend you the money on bond, but you would maybe scruple my terms. Now, I can tell you that your auld laird is disturbed in his grave by your curses, and the wailing of your family, and if ye daur venture to go to see him, he will give you the receipt.'

My gudesire's hair stood on end at this proposal, but he thought his companion might be some humoursome chield that was trying to frighten him, and might end with lending him the money. Besides, he was bauld wi' brandy, and desperate wi' distress; and he said he had courage to go to the gate of hell, and a step farther, for that receipt. The stranger laughed.

Weel, they rode on through the thickest of the wood, when, all of a sudden, the horse stopped at the door of a great house; and, but that he knew the place was ten miles off, my father would have thought he was at Redgauntlet Castle. They rode into the outer courtyard, through the muckle faulding yetts, and aneath the auld portcullis; and the whole front of the house was lighted, and there were pipes and fiddles, and as much dancing and deray within as used to be in Sir Robert's house at Pace and Yule, and such high seasons. They lap off, and my gudesire, as seemed to him, fastened his horse to the very ring he had tied him to that morning, when he gaed to wait on the young Sir John.

'God!' said my gudesire, 'if Sir Robert's death be but a dream.'

He knocked at the ha' door just as he was wont, and his auld acquaintance, Dougal MacCallum – just after his wont, too – came to open the door, and said: 'Piper Steenie, are ye there, lad? Sir Robert has been crying for you.'

My gudesire was like a man in a dream – he looked for the stranger, but he was gane for the time. At last he just tried to say: 'Ha! Dougal Driveower, are ye living? I thought ye had been dead.'

'Never fash yoursell wi' me,' said Dougal, 'but look to yourself; and see ye tak naething frae onybody here, neither meat, drink or siller, except just the receipt that is your ain.'

So saying, he led the way out through halls and trances that were weel kend to my gudesire, and into the auld oak parlour; and there was as much singing of profane sangs and birling of red wine and speaking blasphemy and sculduddry as had ever been in Redgauntlet Castle when it was at the blithest.

But, Lord take us in keeping! what a set of ghastly revellers they were that sat round that table! – My gudesire kend mony that had long before gane to their place, for often had he piped to the most part in the hall of Redgauntlet. There was the fierce Middleton, and the dissolute Rothes, and the crafty Lauderdale; and Dalyell, with his bald head and a beard to his girdle; and Earlshall, with Cameron's blude on his hand; and wild Bonshaw, that tied blessed Mr Cargill's limbs till the blude sprang; and Dunbarton Douglas, the twice-turned traitor baith to country and king. There was the Bluidy Advocate MacKenyie, who, for his worldly wit and wisdom, had been to the rest as a god. And there was Claverhouse, as beautiful as when he lived, with his long, dark, curled locks, streaming down over his laced buff-coat, and his left hand always on his right spule-blade, to hide the wound that the silver bullet had made. He sat apart from them all, and looked at them with a melancholy, haughty countenance; while the rest hallooed, and sang, and laughed, that the room rang. But their smiles were fearfully contorted from time to time; and their laughter passed into such wild sounds as made my gudesire's very nails grow blue, and chilled the marrow in his banes.

They that waited at the table were just the wicked serving-men and troopers that had done their work and cruel bidding on earth. There was the Lang Lad of the Nethertown, that helped to take Argyle; and the bishop's summoner, that they called the Deil's Rattlebag; and the wicked guardsmen, in their laced coats; and the savage Highland Amorites, that shed blood like water; and many a proud serving-man, haughty of heart and bloody of hand, cringing to the rich, and making them wickeder than they would be; grinding the poor to powder, when the rich had broken them to fragments. And mony, mony mair were coming and ganging, a' as busy in their vocation as if they had been alive.

Sir Robert Redgauntlet, in the midst of a' this fearful riot, cried, wi' a voice like thunder, on Steenie Piper to come to the board-head where he was sitting; his legs stretched out before him, and swathed up with flannel, with his holster pistols aside him, while the great broadsword rested against his chair, just as my gudesire had seen him the last time upon earth – the very cushion for the jackanape was close to him, but the creature itsell was not there – it wasna its hour, it's likely; for he heard them say as he came forward, 'Is not the major come yet?' And another answered: 'The jackanape will be here betimes the morn.' And when my gudesire came forward, Sir Robert, or his ghaist, or the deevil in his likeness, said: 'Weel, piper, hae ye settled wi' my son for the year's rent?'

With much ado my father gat breath to say that Sir John would not settle without his honour's receipt.

'Ye shall hae that for a tune of the pipes, Steenie,' said the appearance of Sir Robert. 'Play us up *Weel hoddled, Luckie*.'

Now this was a tune my gudesire learned frae a warlock, that heard it when they were worshipping Satan at their meetings; and my gudesire had sometimes played it at the ranting suppers in Redgauntlet Castle, but never very willingly; and now he grew cauld at the very name of it, and said, for excuse, he hadna his pipes wi' him.

'MacCallum, ye limb of Beelzebub,' said the fearfu' Sir Robert, 'bring Steenie the pipes that I am keeping for him!'

MacCallum brought a pair of pipes might have served the piper of Donald of the Isles. But he gave my gudesire a nudge as he offered them; and looking secretly and closely, Steenie saw that the chanter was of steel, and heated to a white heat; so he had fair warning not to trust his fingers with it. So he excused himself again, and said he was faint and frightened, and had not wind aneugh to fill the bag.

'Then ye maun eat and drink, Steenie,' said the figure; 'for we do little else here; and it's ill speaking between a fou man and a fasting.'

Now these were the very words that the bloody Earl of Douglas said to keep the king's messenger in hand, while he cut the head off MacLellan of Bombie, at the Threave Castle; and that put Steenie mair and mair on his guard. So he spoke up like a man, and said he came neither to eat, or drink, or make minstrelsy; but simply for his ain – to ken what was come o' the money he had paid, and to get a discharge for it; and he was so stout-hearted by this time, that he charged Sir Robert for conscience-sake – he had no power to say the holy name – and as he hoped for peace and rest, to spread no snares for him, but just to give him his ain.

The appearance gnashed its teeth and laughed, but it took from a large pocket-book the receipt, and handed it to Steenie. 'There is your receipt, ye pitiful cur; and for the money, my dog-whelp of a son may go look for it in the Cat's Cradle.'

My gudesire uttered mony thanks, and was about to retire, when Sir Robert roared aloud: 'Stop though, thou sack-doudling son of a whore! I am not done with thee. Here we do nothing for nothing; and you must return on this very day twelvemonth, to pay your master the homage that you owe me for my protection.'

My father's tongue was loosed of a suddenty, and he said aloud: 'I refer mysell to God's pleasure, and not to yours.'

He had no sooner uttered the word than all was dark around him; and he sank on the earth with such a sudden shock that he lost both breath and sense.

How lang Steenie lay there, he could not tell; but when he came to himsell, he was lying in the auld kirkyard of Redgauntlet parochine, just at the door of the family aisle, and the scutcheon of the auld knight, Sir Robert, hanging over his head. There was a deep morning fog on grass and gravestane around him, and his horse was feeding quietly beside the minister's twa cows. Steenie would have thought the whole was a dream, but he had the receipt in his hand, fairly written and signed by the auld laird; only the last letters of his name were a little disorderly, written like one seized with sudden pain.

Sorely troubled in his mind, he left that dreary place, rode through the mist to Redgauntlet Castle, and with much ado he got speech of the laird.

'Well, you dyvour bankrupt,' was the first word, 'have you brought me my rent?'

'No,' answered my gudesire, 'I have not, but I have brought your honour Sir Robert's receipt for it.'

'How, sirrah? – Sir Robert's receipt! – You told me he had not given you one.'

'Will your honour please to see if that bit line is right?'

Sir John looked at every line, and at every letter, with much attention; and at last, at the date, which my gudesire had not observed: '*From my appointed place*,' he read, '*this twenty-fifth of November*. What! – That is yesterday! Villain, thou must have gone to hell for this!'

'I got it from your honour's father – whether he be in heaven or hell, I know not,' said Steenie.

'I will delate you for a warlock to the privy council!' said Sir John. 'I will send you to your master, the devil, with the help of a tar-barrel and a torch!'

'I intend to delate mysell to the presbytery,' said Steenie, 'and tell them all I have seen last night, whilk are things fitter for them to judge of than a borrel man like me.'

Sir John paused, composed himsell, and desired to hear the full history; and my gudesire told it him from point to point, as I have told it you – word for word, neither more nor less.

Sir John was silent again for a long time, and at last he said, very composedly: 'Steenie, this story of yours concerns the honour of many a noble family besides mine; and if it be a leasing-making, to keep yourself out of my danger, the least you can expect is to have a red-hot iron driven through your tongue, and that will be as bad as scauding your fingers with a red-hot chanter. But yet it may be true, Steenie; and if the money is cast up, I shall not know what to think of it. – But where shall we find the Cat's Cradle? There are cats enough about the old house, but I think they kitten without the ceremony of bed or cradle.'

'We were best ask Hutcheon,' said my gudesire; 'he kens a' the odd corners about as weel as – as another serving-man that is now gane, and that I wad not like to name.'

Aweel, Hutcheon, when he was asked, told them that a ruinous turret, lang disused, next to the clock-house, only accessible by a ladder, for the opening was on the outside, and far above the battlements, was called of old the Cat's Cradle.

'There will I go immediately,' said Sir John; and he took (with what purpose, heaven kens) one of his father's pistols from the hall-table, where they had lain since the night he died, and hastened to the battlements.

It was a dangerous place to climb, for the ladder was auld and frail, and wanted ane or twa rounds. However, up got Sir John, and entered at the turret door, where his body stopped the only little light that was in the bit turret. Something flees at him wi' a vengeance, maist dang him back ower – bang gaed the knight's pistol, and Hutcheon, that held the ladder, and my gudesire that stood beside him, hears a loud skelloch. A minute after, Sir John flings the body of the jackanape down to them, and cries that the siller is fund, and that they should come up and help him. And there was the bag of siller, sure aneugh, and mony orra things besides that had been missing for mony a day. And Sir John, when he had riped the turret weel, led my gudesire into the dining-parlour, and took him by the hand, and spoke kindly to him, and said he was sorry he should have doubted his word, and that he would hereafter be a good master to him, to make amends.

'And now, Steenie,' said Sir John, 'although this vision of yours tends, on the whole, to my father's credit, as an honest man, that he should, even after his death, desire to see justice done to a poor man like you, yet you are sensible that ill-dispositioned men might make bad constructions upon it, concerning his soul's health. So, I think, we had better lay the haill dirdum on that ill-deedie creature, Major Weir, and say naething about your dream in the wood of Pitmurkie. You had taken ower muckle brandy to be very certain about onything; and, Steenie, this receipt – ' his hand shook while he held it out – 'it's but a queer kind of document, and we will do best, I think, to put it quietly in the fire.'

'Od, but for as queer as it is, it's a' the voucher I have for my rent,' said my gudesire, who was afraid, it may be, of losing the benefit of Sir Robert's discharge.

'I will bear the contents to your credit in the rental-book, and give you a discharge under my own hand,' said Sir John, 'and that on the spot. And, Steenie, if you can hold your tongue about this matter, you shall sit, from this term downward, at an easier rent.'

'Mony thanks to your honour,' said Steenie, who saw easily in what corner the wind was; 'doubtless I will be conformable to all your honour's commands; only I would willingly speak wi' some powerful minister on the subject, for I do not like the sort of soumons of appointment whilk your honour's father – '

'Do not call the phantom my father!' said Sir John, interrupting him.

'Weel, then, the thing that was so like him,' said my gudesire; 'he spoke of my coming back to him this time twelvemonth, and it's a weight on my conscience.'

'Aweel, then,' said Sir John, 'if you be so much distressed in mind, you may speak to our minister of the parish; he is a douce man, regards the honour of our family, and the mair that he may look for some patronage from me.'

Wi' that, my gudesire readily agreed that the receipt should be burnt, and the laird threw it into the chimney with his ain hand. Burn it would not for them, though; but away it flew up the lum, wi' a lang train of sparks at its tail, and a hissing noise like a squib.

My gudesire gaed down to the manse, and the minister, when he had heard the story, said it was his real opinion that though my gudesire had gaen very far in tampering with dangerous matters, yet, as he had refused the devil's arles (for such was the offer of meat and drink) and had refused to do homage by piping at his bidding, he hoped, that if he held a circumspect walk hereafter, Satan could take little advantage by what was come and gane. And, indeed, my gudesire, of his ain accord, long forswore baith the pipes and the brandy – it was not even till the year was out, and the fatal day passed, that he would so much as take the fiddle or drink usquebaugh or tippenny.

Sir John made up his story about the jackanape as he liked himsell; and some believe till this day there was no more in the matter than the filching nature of the brute. Indeed, ye'll no hinder some to threap that it was nane o' the Auld Enemy that Dougal and my gudesire saw in the laird's room but only that wanchancy creature, the major, capering on the coffin; and that, as to the blawing on the laird's whistle that was heard after he was dead, the filthy brute could do that as weel as the laird himself, if no better. But heaven kens the truth, whilk first came out by the minister's wife, after Sir John and her ain gudeman were baith in the moulds. And then my gudesire, wha was failed in his limbs, but not in his judgement or memory – at least, nothing to speak of – was obliged to tell the real narrative to his freends, for the credit of his good name. He might else have been charged for a warlock.

The Ace of Spades

A. M. PUSHKIN

HERMANN SHOOK HANDS with himself. He had received a letter giving him the coveted rendezvous, a meeting that should further his desperate plan, and so bring him within reach of an easy fortune.

A young officer in the Engineers, he concealed beneath a cold exterior a flaming ambition, a passionate craving for wealth.

Two or three weeks back, he had heard a strange story from Naroumof, a lieutenant in the Horse Guards.

This story was concerned with Naroumof's grandmother, the Comtesse Anna Fedotovna, a former beauty, and now a redoubtable old lady of eighty-six.

Long ago, she had lost a big sum of money at cards in Paris. After vainly applying to her husband for assistance, she had appealed to the eccentric and notorious Comte de Saint-Germain.

Under a promise of secrecy, and on the condition that she would never play again after she had won back the money, the comte named three cards which she was to play in succession. The comtesse had played these three cards, and had more than regained the money she had lost.

Although many had tried to get from her lips the names of these three winning cards, she had held to her promise, with the exception of confiding the secret to a dearly loved son.

This story had haunted Hermann. He could not get it out of his mind. If he could but get acquainted with the comtesse, he might, by persuasion or force, obtain from her the secret of the three cards, and so win a large sum of money.

He had taken to watching the town house of the old comtesse, and here luck had favoured him. He had caught the eye of a handsome young woman seated at a window, a young woman who was presumably the old lady's companion. He had stared until she had dropped her eyes; but after a minute she had raised them, and then she had blushed.

This was the beginning of a silent courtship which Lisabeta Ivanova, aching to escape from the trying old comtesse, took seriously.

Then, when she was attending the comtesse to her carriage, Hermann, on the watch, had saluted her and pressed a note in her hand.

She had read this note on returning from the drive, a note that contained ardent protestations of love. Then, by the hands of a milliner who called at the house, she received frequent letters from Hermann.

These, at last, she answered, with a warmth that waxed with each letter.

She had ultimately given him a rendezvous late at night in the house, at the same time furnishing elaborate instructions on how to get into the place, and what direction to take when inside.

He must take every care to avoid the comtesse's apartments.

Hermann, like a tiger in sight of its prey, trembled in every limb. He saw himself wealthy, honoured. Somehow or another, he would face the comtesse, and by fair means or foul, obtain her secret.

It had been arranged that he should seek admission to the house while the comtesse and Lisabeta were absent at a ball. Everything went according to plan. Instead, however, of seeking the girl's room, he hid himself in the large bedroom of the comtesse.

In due course, the old lady returned with Lisabeta, and was attended by three old maids of honour to the bedroom. As the comtesse suffered from insomnia, she did not at once go to bed, but reclined in a chair.

In this room, lit only by the lights before the icons, the comtesse looked more dead than alive.

It was not until Hermann confronted her that she appeared really alive.

'You have nothing to fear – nothing whatever,' he said in a low even voice. 'But it was necessary that I should see you – alone. As I have told you, you have nothing whatever to fear, provided you tell me something that I must know.'

The old woman regarded him in silence, and as though she did not understand. Believing she was deaf, he put his lips to her ear and repeated his words. The comtesse still maintained silence.

'You are able to make me happy for life,' he continued, 'and in a way that will not cost you anything . . . For you know the secret of a certain three cards which . . . '

Hermann stopped short. She evidently understood what he meant.

'All that's merely a joke,' she said. 'I swear to you it was only a joke.'

'It was nothing of the sort,' he declared, with rising anger. 'You gave the secret to one of your sons – your favourite son . . . '

The comtesse was troubled. She took refuge in apparent stupidity.

'Won't you tell me the three winning cards?'

The comtesse was silent. Hermann fell on his knees.

'If you have ever known love, if you have ever tasted ecstasy, if you have any humanity, I ask, I beseech you, by the love of a husband, the love of a lover, the love of a mother, by everything that is holy in life, to do what I ask . . .

'You are old. You have not long to live. But I . . . young as I am, I am ready, eager to be responsible for all the sins you may have committed, and to be answerable for them before God, if you will tell me this secret.'

The old comtesse was obstinately silent. Hermann got up from his knees. 'Cursed old woman!' he cried, grinding his teeth. 'At least I have something that will open your lips.'

He brought out a pistol. At the sight of this weapon, the old comtesse came to life. Her face betrayed fear. Her head shook as though palsied, and as she stretched out her arms to defend herself from the pistol, she suddenly fell back in her chair and was still.

'Don't play the fool,' cried Hermann, seizing the old woman's hand. 'For the last time, will you, or will you not, tell me those three cards?'

The comtesse was persistently silent. Hermann perceived she was dead . . .

Hermann went to Lisabeta's room. He told her everything, including the death of the comtesse. She burned with shame. She recalled his passionate letters, with their warm protestations of love. She now knew these were false; that all he had wanted was money.

She had been the blind tool of a thief – the murderer of her protectress. She wept bitterly.

Her looks and her tears did not touch this man of iron will. He did not repent of what he had done. He knew no remorse for the death of the comtesse. He was torn by the thought that the secret he had coveted had permanently escaped him.

The long silence was broken by Lisabeta. 'But you are a monster!' she cried.

'There was no question of my killing her,' he coldly replied. 'The pistol wasn't loaded.'

'I must get you out of here,' she said. 'But you will have to go through the comtesse's room. I . . . I am afraid.'

After receiving a key and the necessary directions from her, Hermann again entered the room where the old comtesse still sat in her chair. He stared at her for some time, as though to assure himself of this stark reality, then found his way from the house.

Hermann had returned from the funeral of the comtesse.

On kneeling beside the body beforehand and regarding its face, he could have sworn that one of the eyes had mocked him, then winked. For the rest of the day, he was troubled with a singular depression.

On ordering his dinner in a restaurant, he found himself unable to eat, but drank far more than he usually did. He returned to his rooms in good time. Without undressing, he threw himself on the bed and fell fast asleep.

When he awoke, it was night, and the moonlight was streaming into his chamber. He looked at his watch. It was a quarter to three.

He did not want to sleep any more. He sat on the bed and thought of the old comtesse. Someone stared through the window, but he paid no attention. And presently he heard someone open the door of the sitting-room.

Believing that this must be the caretaker, who often came back drunk in the small hours, he took no notice, until he heard an unfamiliar footstep. Then . . . then the bedroom door opened, and a woman all dressed in white came into the room, and advanced to the foot of the bed.

Hermann saw the old comtesse.

'I have come to you in spite of myself,' she said. 'I am compelled to answer your appeal . . . Three – seven – ace will win all you want, if played in that sequence. But . . . but you must only play one card in twenty-four hours. And after, you must never touch cards again. As for my death, I will forgive you only on the condition that you marry Lisabeta Ivanovna, my companion.'

The old comtesse then quitted the room. Hermann remained dumbfounded, stunned. Later, on going to the sitting-room, he found the caretaker asleep on the floor and the key turned in the lock of the door.

Hermann went to the gambling-rooms kept by the famous wealthy Tchekalinski. He was introduced by Naroumof, from whom he had learned the strange story of the cards.

In one of the rooms, Tchekalinski presided, as banker, at a table where faro was being played. (In this game each player is dealt a card by the banker. The banker then deals two other cards on to the table. If the player's card is a duplicate of one of the two the banker has laid down, the player receives double the money he has staked.)

When Hermann was presently introduced, he asked if he could take one card.

Tchekalinski graciously gave the required permission. Naroumof laughingly congratulated Hermann for thus taking it into his head to gamble, and wished him good luck.

'There you are!' said Hermann, after having written a figure on the card he had taken.

'How much?' asked the banker, blinking his eyes. 'My sight isn't quite what it was.'

'Forty-seven thousand roubles,' replied Hermann.

All heads were raised at hearing this sum. Naroumof thought his friend had gone mad.

'Rather a large stake,' said the banker, with his eternal smile. 'Of course, I don't doubt your ability to pay if you lose, but I rather wish you'd back your card with some money.'

Hermann brought out a note. After glancing at this, the banker placed it on the card. He dealt two cards, a ten on the right and a three on the left.

'I win,' said Hermann, showing his card, a three. A murmur of astonishment arose from the crowded table. For a moment the banker looked glum, but soon recovered his smile.

'Shall I settle up now?' he asked the winner.

'If you wouldn't mind.'

The banker, producing a pocket-book, took out some banknotes and handed these over to Hermann, who pocketed his winnings and then left the table. He drank some lemonade, and went home to bed.

The next evening he returned to the gaming-house and sought the table where Tchekalinski was banker. The punters greeted Hermann with respect and made a place for him.

Hermann awaited a new deal, and then took a card on which he staked not only forty-seven thousand roubles, but also what he had previously won. The banker started to deal. He dealt a knave to the right and a seven to the left.

Hermann showed a seven.

There was a general gasp of astonishment, and the banker looked uncomfortable. Counting out ninety-four thousand roubles, he gave them to Hermann, who coolly accepted them, collected his stake and took his leave.

He came again the next evening. On seeing him, the players deserted their games and crowded round the principal table. They wanted to see if Hermann's astonishing luck would hold. Tchekalinski turned pale on recognising him, but somehow managed to smile as he braced himself for the play.

Taking a new pack of cards, Tchekalinski cut and dealt one to Hermann, who covered it with a pile of bank-notes. It was like preparing for a duel. He began to deal. His hands trembled. He threw a king to the right and an ace to the left.

'My ace wins,' said Hermann, showing his card.

'Your queen has lost,' replied the banker, triumphantly.

Hermann trembled violently. Instead of an ace he saw he held a queen of spades. He could not believe the evidence of his eyes. He could not understand how he had made a mistake.

His eyes were fixed on this fatal card. It seemed to him that the queen of spades winked, and looked at him with a jeering smile. He was stricken with horror at seeing that there was an uncanny resemblance between this queen of spades and the dead comtesse . . .

'Curse the old woman!' said Hermann, terrified, to himself.

Tchekalinski, using a rake, heaped up his winnings. Hermann seemed turned into stone. He did not move for quite a long time. When he at last left the room, conversation began.

'What a punter!' commented the players.

Hermann went mad, and is in an asylum. He does not answer if spoken to, but continually repeats to himself, 'Three – seven – ace! Three – seven – queen!'

Lisabeta is happily married.

The Mysterious Mansion

HONORÉ DE BALZAC

ABOUT A HUNDRED YARDS from the town of Vendôme, on the borders of the Loire, there is an old grey house, surmounted by very high gables, and so completely isolated that neither tanyard nor shabby hostelry, such as you may find at the entrance to all small towns, exists in its immediate neighbourhood.

In front of this building, overlooking the river, is a garden, where the once well-trimmed box borders that used to define the walks now grow wild as they list. Several willows that spring from the Loire have grown as rapidly as the hedge that encloses it, and half conceal the house. The rich vegetation of those weeds that we call foul adorns the sloping shore. Fruit trees, neglected for the last ten years, no longer yield their harvest, and their shoots form coppices. The wallfruit grows like hedges against the walls. Paths once gravelled are overgrown with moss, but, to tell the truth, there is no trace of a path. From the height of the hill, to which cling the ruins of the old castle of the Dukes of Vendôme, the only spot whence the eye can plunge into this enclosure, it strikes you that, at a time not easy to determine, this plot of land was the delight of a country gentleman, who cultivated roses and tulips and practised horticulture in general, and who was besides a lover of fine fruit. An arbour is still visible, or rather the debris of an arbour, where there is a table that time has not quite destroyed. The aspect of this garden of bygone days suggests the negative joys of peaceful, provincial life, as one might reconstruct the life of a worthy tradesman by reading the epitaph on his tombstone. As if to complete the sweetness and sadness of the ideas that possess one's soul, one of the walls displays a sundial decorated with the following commonplace Christian inscription: *Ultimam cogita.* The roof of this house is horribly dilapidated, the shutters are always closed, the balconies are covered with swallows' nests, the doors are perpetually shut, weeds have drawn green lines in the cracks of the flights of steps, the locks and bolts are rusty. Sun, moon, winter, summer, all in turn have worn the panelling, warped the boards, gnawed the paint. The lugubrious silence which reigns there is only broken by birds, cats, martins, rats and mice, free to course to and fro, to fight and to eat each other. Truly, here an invisible hand has graven the word mystery.

Should your curiosity lead you to glance at this house from the side that points to the road, you would perceive a great door which the children of the place have riddled with holes. I afterward heard that this door had been closed for the last ten years. Through the holes bored by the boys you would have observed the perfect harmony that existed between the façades of both garden and courtyard. In both the same disorder prevails. Tufts of weed encircle the paving-stones. Enormous cracks furrow the walls, round whose blackened crests twine the thousand garlands of the creeping plants. The steps are out of joint, the wire of the bell is rusted, the spouts are cracked. What fire from heaven has fallen here? What tribunal has decreed that salt should be strewn on this dwelling? Has God been blasphemed, has France been here betrayed? These are the questions we ask ourselves, but get no answer from the crawling things that haunt the place. The empty and deserted house is a gigantic enigma, of which the key is lost. In bygone times it was a small fief, and bears the name of the Grande Bretêche.

I inferred that I was not the only person to whom my good landlady had communicated the secret of which I was to be the sole recipient, and I prepared to listen.

'Sir,' she said, 'when the emperor sent the Spanish prisoners of war and others here, the government quartered on me a young Spaniard who had been sent to Vendôme on parole. Parole notwithstanding, he went out every day to show himself to the *sous-préfet*. He was a Spanish grandee! Nothing less! His name ended in os and dia, something like Burgos de Férédia. I have his name on my books; you can read it if you like. Oh! but he was a handsome young man for a Spaniard; they are all said to be ugly. He was only five feet and a few inches high, but he was well grown; he had small hands that he took such care of; ah! you should have seen! He had as many brushes for his hands as a woman for her whole dressing apparatus! He had thick black hair, a fiery eye; his skin was rather bronzed, but I liked the look of it. He wore the finest linen I have ever seen on anyone, although I have had princesses staying here, and, among others, General Bertrand, the Duke and Duchess d'Abrantzs, Monsieur Decazes and the King of Spain. He didn't eat much; but his manners were so polite, so amiable, that one could not bear him a grudge. Oh! I was very fond of him, although he didn't open his lips four times in the day, and it was impossible to keep up a conversation with him. For if you spoke to him, he did not answer. It was a fad, a mania with them all, I heard say. He read his breviary like a priest, he went to mass and to all the services regularly. Where did he sit? Two steps from the chapel of Madame de Merret. As he took his place there the first time he went to church, nobody suspected him of any intention in so doing. Besides, he never raised his eyes from his prayer-book, poor young man! After that, sir, in the evening he would walk on the mountains, among the castle ruins. It was the poor man's only amusement, it reminded him of his country. They say that Spain is all mountains! From the commencement of his imprisonment he stayed out late. I was anxious when I found that he did not come home before midnight; but we got accustomed to this fancy of his. He took the key of the door, and we left off sitting up for him. He lodged in a house of ours in the Rue des Casernes. After that, one of our stable-men told us that in the evening, when he led the horses to the water, he thought he had seen the Spanish grandee swimming far down the river like a live fish; when he returned, I told him to take care of the rushes; he appeared vexed to have been seen in the water. At last, one day, or rather one morning, we did not find him in his room; he had not returned. After searching everywhere, I found some writing in the drawer of a table, where there were fifty gold pieces of Spain that are called doubloons and were worth about five thousand francs; and ten thousand francs' worth of diamonds in a small sealed box. The writing said that in case he did not return, he left us the money and the diamonds, on condition we paid for masses to thank God for his escape, and for his salvation. In those days my husband had not been taken from me; he hastened to seek him everywhere.

'And now for the strange part of the story. He brought home the Spaniard's clothes, that he had discovered under a big stone by the riverside near the castle, nearly opposite to the Grande Bretêche. My husband had gone there so early that no one had seen him. After reading the letter, he burned the clothes, and according to Count Férédia's desire we declared that he had escaped. The *sous préfet* sent all the gendarmerie in pursuit of him; but I trust they never caught him. Lepas believed that the Spaniard had drowned himself. I, sir, don't think so; I am more inclined to believe that he had something to do with the affair of Madame de Merret, seeing that Rosalie told me that the crucifix that her mistress thought so much of, the one she had buried with her, was of ebony and silver. Now in the beginning of his stay here, Monsieur de Férédia had one in ebony and silver, and I never saw him with it later. Now, sir, don't you consider that I need have no scruples about the Spaniard's fifteen thousand francs, and that I have a right to them?'

'Certainly; but you haven't tried to question Rosalie?' I said.

'Oh, yes, indeed, sir; but to no purpose! the girl's like a wall. She knows something, but it is impossible to get her to talk.'

After exchanging a few more words with me, my landlady left me a prey to vague and gloomy thoughts, to a romantic curiosity and a religious terror not unlike the profound impression produced on us when by night, on entering a dark church, we perceive a faint light under high arches; a vague figure glides by – the rustle of a robe or cassock is heard, and we shudder.

Suddenly the Grande Bretêche and its tall weeds, its barred windows, its rusty ironwork, its closed doors, its deserted apartments, appeared like a fantastic apparition before me. I essayed to penetrate the mysterious dwelling, and to find the knot of its dark story – the drama that had killed three persons. In my eyes Rosalie became the most interesting person in Vendôme. As I studied her, I discovered the traces of secret care, despite the radiant health that shone in her plump countenance. There was in her the germ of remorse or hope; her attitude revealed a secret, like the attitude of a bigot who prays to excess, or of the infanticide who ever hears the last cry of her child. Yet her manners were rough and ingenuous – her silly smile was not that of a criminal, and could you but have seen the great kerchief that encompassed her portly bust, framed and laced in by a lilac and blue cotton gown, you would have dubbed her innocent. No, I thought, I will not leave Vendôme without learning the history of the Grande Bretêche. To gain my ends I will strike up a friendship with Rosalie, if needs be.

'Rosalie,' said I, one evening.

'Sir?'

'You are not married?'

She started slightly.

'Oh, I can find plenty of men, when the fancy takes me to be made miserable,' she said, laughing.

She soon recovered from the effects of her emotion, for all women, from the great lady to the maid of the inn, possess a composure that is peculiar to them.

'You are too good-looking and well favoured to be short of lovers. But tell me, Rosalie, why did you take service in an inn after leaving Madame de Merret? Did she leave you nothing to live on?'

'Oh, yes! But, sir, my place is the best in all Vendôme.'

The reply was one of those that judges and lawyers would call evasive. Rosalie appeared to me to be situated in this romantic history like the square in the midst of a chessboard. She was at the heart of the truth and chief interest; she seemed to me to be bound in the very knot of it. The conquest of Rosalie was no longer to be an ordinary siege – in this girl was centred the last chapter of a novel, therefore from this moment Rosalie became the object of my preference.

One morning I said to Rosalie: 'Tell me all you know about Madame de Merret.'

'Oh!' she replied in terror, 'do not ask that of me, Monsieur Horace.'

Her pretty face fell – her clear, bright colour faded – and her eyes lost their innocent brightness.

'Well, then,' she said, 'if you must have it so, I will tell you about it; but promise to keep my secret!'

'Done! my dear girl. I must keep your secret with the honour of a thief, which is the most loyal in the world.'

Were I to transcribe Rosalie's diffuse eloquence faithfully, an entire volume would scarcely contain it; so I shall abridge.

The room occupied by Madame de Merret at the Bretêche was on the ground floor. A little closet about four feet deep, built in the thickness of the wall, served as her wardrobe.

Three months before the eventful evening of which I am about to speak,

Madame de Merret had been so seriously indisposed that her husband had left her to herself in her own apartment while he occupied another on the first floor. By one of those chances that it is impossible to foresee, he returned home from the club (where he was accustomed to read the papers and discuss politics with the inhabitants of the place) two hours later than usual. His wife supposed him to be at home, in bed and asleep. But the invasion of France had been the subject of a most animated discussion; the billiard-match had been exciting and he had lost forty francs, an enormous sum for Vendôme, where everyone hoards and where manners are restricted within the limits of a praiseworthy modesty, which perhaps is the source of the true happiness that no Parisian covets. For some time past Monsieur de Merret had been satisfied to ask Rosalie if his wife had gone to bed; and on her reply, which was always in the affirmative, had immediately gained his own room with the good temper engendered by habit and confidence. On entering his house, he took it into his head to go and tell his wife of his misadventure, perhaps by way of consolation. At dinner he had found Madame de Merret most coquettishly attired. On his way to the club it had occurred to him that his wife was restored to health, and that her convalescence had added to her beauty. He was, as husbands are wont to be, somewhat slow in making this discovery. Instead of calling Rosalie, who was occupied just then in watching the cook and coachman play a difficult hand at brisque, Monsieur de Merret went to his wife's room by the light of a lantern that he deposited on the first step of the staircase. His unmistakable step resounded under the vaulted corridor. At the moment that the count turned the handle of his wife's door, he fancied he could hear the door of the closet I spoke of close; but when he entered Madame de Merret was alone before the fireplace. The husband thought ingenuously that Rosalie was in the closet yet a suspicion that jangled in his ear put him on his guard. He looked at his wife and saw in her eyes I know not what wild and hunted expression.

'You are very late,' she said. Her habitually pure, sweet voice seemed changed to him.

Monsieur de Merret did not reply, for at that moment Rosalie entered. It was a thunderbolt for him. He strode about the room, passing from one window to the other, with mechanical motion and folded arms.

'Have you heard bad news, or are you unwell?' enquired his wife timidly, while Rosalie undressed her.

He kept silent.

'You can leave me,' said Madame de Merret to her maid; 'I will put my hair in curl papers myself.'

From the expression of her husband's face she foresaw trouble, and wished to be alone with him. When Rosalie had gone, or was supposed to have gone (for she lingered in the corridor for a few minutes), Monsieur de Merret came and stood in front of his wife, and said coldly to her: 'Madame, there is someone in your closet!'

She looked calmly at her husband, and replied simply: 'No, sir.'

This answer was heartrending to Monsieur de Merret because he did not believe it. Yet his wife had never appeared to him purer or more saintly than at that moment. He rose to open the closet door.

Madame de Merret took his hand, looked at him with an expression of melancholy, and said in a voice that betrayed singular emotion: 'If you find no one there, remember this, all will be over between us!'

The extraordinary dignity of his wife's manner restored the count's profound esteem for her, and inspired him with one of those resolutions that only lack a vaster stage to become immortal.

'No,' said he. 'Josephine, I will not go in there. In either case it would separate us for ever. Hear me. I know how pure you are at heart, and that your life is a holy one. You would not commit a mortal sin to save your life.'

At these words Madamce de Merret turned a haggard gaze upon her husband.

'Here, take your crucifix,' he went on. 'Swear to me before God that there is no one in there; I will believe you. I will never open that door.'

Madame de Merret took the crucifix and said: 'I swear.'

'Louder,' said the husband, 'and repeat, "I swear before God that there is no one in that closet." '

She repeated the sentence calmly.

'That will do,' said of Monsieur de Merret, coldly.

After a moment of silence: 'I never saw this pretty toy before,' he said, examining the ebony crucifix inlaid with silver and most artistically chiselled.

'I found it at Duvivier's, who bought it of a Spanish monk when the prisoners passed through Vendôme last year.'

'Ah!' said Monsieur de Merret, as he replaced the crucifix on the nail, and he rang. Rosalie did not keep him waiting. Monsieur de Merret went quickly to meet her, led her to the bay window that opened on to the garden and whispered to her: 'Listen! I know that Gorenflot wishes to marry you; poverty is the only drawback, and you told him that you would be his wife if he found the means to establish himself as a master mason. Well! go and fetch him, tell him to come here with his trowel and tools. Manage not to awaken anyone in his house but himself; his fortune will be more than your desires. Above all, leave this room without babbling, otherwise – ' He frowned. Rosalie went away, he recalled her. 'Here, take my latchkey,' he said.

'Jean!' then cried Monsieur de Merret, in tones of thunder in the corridor. Jean, who was at the same time his coachman and his confidential servant, left his game of cards and came.

'Go to bed, all of you,' said his master, then, signing to him to approach, added under his breath: 'When they are all asleep – asleep, d'ye hear? – you will come down and tell me.'

Monsieur de Merret, who had not lost sight of his wife all the time he was giving his orders, returned quietly to her at the fireside and began to tell her of the game of billiards and the talk of the club. When Rosalie returned she found Monsieur and Madame de Merret conversing very amicably.

The count had lately had all the ceilings of his reception rooms on the ground floor repaired. Plaster of Paris is difficult to obtain in Vendôme; the carriage raises its price. The count had therefore bought a good deal, being well aware that he could find plenty of purchasers for whatever might remain over. This circumstance inspired him with the design he was about to execute.

'Sir, Gorenflot has arrived,' said Rosalie in low tones.

'Show him in,' replied the count in loud tones.

Madame de Merret turned rather pale when she saw the mason.

'Gorenflot,' said her husband, 'go and fetch bricks from the coachhouse, and bring sufficient to wall up the door of this closet; you will use the plaster I have over to coat the wall with.'

Then calling Rosalie and the workman aside: 'Listen, Gorenflot,' he said in an undertone, 'you will sleep here tonight. But tomorrow you will have a passport to a foreign country, to a town to which I will direct you. I shall give you six thousand francs for your journey. You will stay ten years in that town; if you do not like it, you may establish yourself in another, provided it be in the same country. You will pass through Paris, where you will await me. There I will ensure you an additional six thousand francs by contract, which will be paid to you on your return, provided you have fulfilled the conditions of our bargain. This is the price for your absolute silence as to what you are about to do tonight. As to you, Rosalie, I will give you ten thousand francs on the day of your wedding, on condition of your marrying Gorenflot; but if you wish to marry, you must hold your tongues; or – no dowry.'

'Rosalie,' said Madame de Merret, 'do my hair.'

The husband walked calmly up and down, watching the door, the mason, and his wife, but without betraying any insulting doubts. Madame de Merret chose a moment when the workman was unloading bricks and her husband was at the other end of the room to say to Rosalie: 'A thousand francs a year for you, my child, if you can tell Gorenflot to leave a chink at the bottom.' Then out loud, she added coolly: 'Go and help him!'

Monsieur and Madame de Merret were silent all the time that Gorenflot took to brick up the door. This silence on the part of the husband, who did not choose to furnish his wife with a pretext for saying things of a double meaning, had its purpose; on the part of Madame de Merret it was either pride or prudence. When the wall was about halfway up, the sly workman took advantage of a moment when the count's back was turned to strike a blow with his trowel in one of the glass panes of the closet-door. This act informed Madame de Merret that Rosalie had spoken to Gorenflot.

All three then saw a man's face; it was dark and gloomy with black hair and eyes of flame. Before her husband turned, the poor woman had time to make a sign to the stranger that signified hope.

At four o'clock, towards dawn, for it was the month of September, the construction was finished. The mason was handed over to the care of Jean, and Monsieur de Merret went to bed in his wife's room.

On rising the following morning, he said carelessly: 'The deuce! I must go to the mairie for the passport.' He put his hat on his head, advanced three steps towards the door, altered his mind and took the crucifix.

His wife trembled for joy. 'He is going to Duvivier,' she thought. As soon as the count had left, Madame de Merret rang for Rosalie; then in a terrible voice: 'The trowel, the trowel!' she cried, 'and quick to work! I saw how Gorenflot did it; we shall have time to make a hole and to mend it again.'

In the twinkling of an eye, Rosalie brought a sort of mattock to her mistress, who with unparalleled ardour set about demolishing the wall. She had already knocked out several bricks and was preparing to strike a more decisive blow when she perceived Monsieur de Merret behind her. She fainted.

'Lay Madame on her bed,' said the count coldly. He had foreseen what would happen in his absence and had set a trap for his wife; he had simply written to the mayor, and had sent for Duvivier. The jeweller arrived just as the room had been put in order.

'Duvivier,' inquired the count, 'did you buy crucifixes of the Spaniards who passed through here?'

'No, sir.'

'That will do, thank you,' he said, looking at his wife like a tiger. 'Jean,' he added, 'you will see that my meals are served in the countess's room; she is ill, and I shall not leave her until she has recovered.'

The cruel gentleman stayed with his wife for twenty days. In the beginning, when there were sounds in the walled closet, and Josephine attempted to implore his pity for the dying stranger, he replied, without permitting her to say a word: 'You have sworn on the cross that there is no one there.'

The Haunted and the Haunters

LORD LYTTON

A FRIEND OF MINE, who is a man of letters and a philosopher, said to me one day, as if between jest and earnest – 'Fancy! Since we last met, I have discovered a haunted house in the midst of London.'

'Really haunted? – and by what? – ghosts?'

'Well, I can't answer these questions – all I know is this – six weeks ago I and my wife were in search of a furnished apartment. Passing a quiet street, we saw on the window of one of the houses a bill, "Apartments Furnished". The situation suited us: we entered the house – liked the rooms – engaged them by the week – and left them the third day. No power on earth could have reconciled my wife to stay longer, and I don't wonder at it.'

'What did you see?'

'Excuse me – I have no desire to be ridiculed as a superstitious dreamer – nor, on the other hand, could I ask you to accept on my affirmation what you would hold to be incredible without the evidence of your own senses. Let me only say this, it was not so much what we saw or heard (in which you might fairly suppose that we were the dupes of our own excited fancy, or the victims of imposture in others) that drove us away, as it was an undefinable terror which seized both of us whenever we passed by the door of a certain unfurnished room, in which we neither saw nor heard anything. And the strangest marvel of all was that for once in my life I agreed with my wife – silly woman though she be – and allowed, after the third night, that it was impossible to stay a fourth in that house. Accordingly, on the fourth morning, I summoned the woman who kept the house and attended on us, and told her that the rooms did not quite suit us, and we would not stay out our week. She said, dryly: "I know why; you have stayed longer than any other lodger; few ever stayed a second night; none before you, a third. But I take it they have been very kind to you."

' "They – who?" I asked, affecting a smile.

' "Why, they who haunt the house, whoever they are. I don't mind them; I remember them many years ago, when I lived in this house, not as a servant; but I know they will be the death of me someday. I don't care – I'm old, and must die soon, anyhow; and then I shall be with them, and in this house still." The woman spoke with so dreary a calmness, that really it was a sort of awe that prevented my conversing with her further. I paid for my week, and too happy were I and my wife to get off so cheaply.'

'You excite my curiosity,' said I; 'nothing should I like better than to sleep in a haunted house. Pray give me the address of the one which you left so ignominiously.'

My friend gave me the address; and when we parted, I walked straight towards the house thus indicated.

It is situated on the north side of Oxford Street, in a dull but respectable thoroughfare. I found the house shut up – no bill at the window, and no response to my knock. As I was turning away, a beer-boy, collecting pewter pots at the neighbouring areas, said to me, 'Do you want anyone in that house, sir?'

'Yes, I heard it was to let.'

'Let! – why, the woman who kept it is dead – has been dead these three weeks, and no one can be found to stay there, though Mr J— offered ever so much. He offered mother, who chars for him, a pound a week just to open and shut the windows, and she would not.'

'Would not! – and why?'

'The house is haunted; and the old woman who kept it was found dead in her bed, with her eyes wide open. They say the devil strangled her.'

'Pooh! – you speak of Mr J—. Is he the owner of the house?'

'Yes.'

'Where does he live?'

'In G— Street. No. —.'

'What is he? – in any business?'

'No, sir – nothing particular; a single gentleman.'

I gave the pot-boy the gratuity earned by his liberal information, and proceeded to Mr J—, in G— Street, which was close by the street that boasted the haunted house. I was lucky enough to find Mr J— at home, an elderly man, with intelligent countenance and prepossessing manners.

I communicated my name and my business frankly. I said I heard the house was considered to be haunted – that I had a strong desire to examine a house with so equivocal a reputation – that I should be greatly obliged if he would allow me to hire it, though only for a night. I was willing to pay for that privilege whatever he might be inclined to ask. 'Sir,' said Mr J—, with great courtesy, 'the house is at your service, for as short or as long a time as you please. Rent is out of the question – the obligation will be on my side should you be able to discover the cause of the strange phenomena which at present deprive it of all value. I cannot let it, for I cannot even get a servant to keep it in order or answer the door. Unluckily the house is haunted, if I may use that expression, not only by night, but by day; though at night the disturbances are of a more unpleasant and sometimes of a more alarming character.

'The poor old woman who died in it three weeks ago was a pauper whom I took out of a workhouse, for in her childhood she had been known to some of my family, and had once been in such good circumstances that she had rented that house of my uncle. She was a woman of superior education and strong mind, and was the only person I could ever induce to remain in the house. Indeed, since her death, which was sudden, and the coroner's inquest, which gave it a notoriety in the neighbourhood, I have so despaired of finding any person to take charge of it, much more a tenant, that I would willingly let it rent-free for a year to anyone who would pay its rates and taxes.'

'How long is it since the house acquired this sinister character?'

'That I can scarcely tell you, but very many years since. The old woman I spoke of said it was haunted when she rented it between thirty and forty years ago. The fact is that my life has been spent in the East Indies and in the civil service of the Company. I returned to England last year on inheriting the fortune of an uncle, amongst whose possessions was the house in question. I found it shut up and uninhabited. I was told that it was haunted: that no one would inhabit it. I smiled at what seemed to me so idle a story. I spent some money in repainting and roofing it – added to its old-fashioned furniture a few modern articles – advertised it, and obtained a lodger for a year. He was a colonel retired on half-pay. He came in with his family, a son and a daughter, and four or five servants: they all left the house the next day, and although they deponed that they had all seen something different, that something was equally terrible to all. I really could not in conscience sue, or even blame, the colonel for breach of agreement.

'Then I put in the old woman I have spoken of, and she was empowered to let the house in apartments. I never had one lodger who stayed more than three days. I do not tell you their stories – to no two lodgers have there been exactly the same phenomena repeated. It is better that you should judge for yourself than enter the house with an imagination influenced by previous narratives; only be prepared to see and to hear something or other, and take whatever precautions you yourself please.'

'Have you never had a curiosity yourself to pass a night in that house?'

'Yes. I passed not a night, but three hours in broad daylight alone in that house. My curiosity is not satisfied, but it is quenched. I have no desire to renew the experiment. You cannot complain, you see, sir, that I am not sufficiently candid; and unless your interest be exceedingly eager and your nerves unusually strong, I honestly add that I advise you *not* to pass a night in that house.'

'My interest *is* exceedingly keen,' said I, 'and though only a coward will boast of his nerves in situations wholly unfamiliar to him, yet my nerves have been seasoned in such variety of danger that I have the right to rely on them – even in a haunted house.'

Mr J— said very little more; he took the keys of the house out of his bureau and gave them to me – and thanking him cordially for his frankness, and his urbane concession to my wish, I carried off my prize.

Impatient for the experiment, as soon as I reached home I summoned my confidential servant – a young man of gay spirits, fearless temper, and as free from superstitious prejudice as anyone I could think of.

'F—,' said I, 'you remember in Germany how disappointed we were at not finding a ghost in that old castle, which was said to be haunted by a headless apparition? Well, I have heard of a house in London which, I have reason to hope, is decidedly haunted. I mean to sleep there tonight. From what I hear, there is no doubt that something will allow itself to be seen or to be heard – something, perhaps, excessively horrible. Do you think, if I take you with me, I may rely on your presence of mind, whatever may happen?'

'Oh, sir! pray trust me,' answered F—, grinning with delight.

'Very well – then here are the keys of the house – this is the address. Go now – select for me any bedroom you please; and since the house has not been inhabited for weeks, make up a good fire – air the bed well – see, of course, that there are candles as well as fuel. Take with you my revolver and my dagger – so much for my weapons – arm yourself equally well; and if we are not a match for a dozen ghosts, we shall be but a sorry couple of Englishmen.'

I was engaged for the rest of the day on business so urgent that I had not leisure to think much on the nocturnal adventure to which I had plighted my honour. I dined alone, and very late, and while dining, read, as is my habit. The volume I selected was one of Macaulay's essays. I thought to myself that I would take the book with me; there was so much of healthfulness in the style, and practical life in the subjects, that it would serve as an antidote against the influences of superstitious fancy.

Accordingly, about half-past nine, I put the book into my pocket and strolled leisurely towards the haunted house. I took with me a favourite dog – an exceedingly sharp, bold and vigilant bull-terrier – a dog fond of prowling about strange ghostly corners and passages at night in search of rats – a dog of dogs for a ghost.

It was a summer night, but chilly, the sky somewhat gloomy and overcast. Still, there was a moon – faint and sickly, but still a moon, and if the clouds permitted, after midnight it would be brighter.

I reached the house, knocked, and my servant opened with a cheerful smile.

'All right, sir, and very comfortable.'

'Oh!' said I, rather disappointed; 'have you not seen nor heard anything remarkable?'

'Well, sir, I must own I have heard something queer.'

'What? – what?'

'The sound of feet pattering behind me; and once or twice small noises like whispers close at my ear – nothing more.'

'You are not at all frightened?'

'I! not a bit of it, sir,' and the man's bold look reassured me on one point – viz. that happen what might, he would not desert me.

We were in the hall, the street-door closed, and my attention was now drawn to my dog. He had at first run in eagerly enough, but had sneaked back to the door, and was scratching and whining to get out. After being patted on the head and encouraged gently, the dog seemed to reconcile himself to the situation and followed me and F— through the house, but keeping close at my heels instead of hurrying inquisitively in advance, which was his usual and normal habit in all strange places. We first visited the subterranean apartments, the kitchen and other offices, and especially the cellars, in which last there were two or three bottles of wine still left in a bin, covered with cobwebs, and evidently, by their appearance, undisturbed for many years. It was clear that the ghosts were not winebibbers.

For the rest we discovered nothing of interest. There was a gloomy little backyard, with very high walls. The stones of this yard were very damp – and what with the damp, and what with the dust and smoke-grime on the pavement, our feet left a slight impression where we passed. And now appeared the first strange phenomenon witnessed by myself in this strange abode. I saw, just before me, the print of a foot suddenly form itself, as it were. I stopped, caught hold of my servant, and pointed to it. In advance of that footprint as suddenly dropped another. We both saw it. I advanced quickly to the place; the footprint kept advancing before me, a small footprint – the foot of a child: the impression was too faint thoroughly to distinguish the shape, but it seemed to us both that it was the print of a naked foot. This phenomenon ceased when we arrived at the opposite wall, nor did it repeat itself on returning.

We remounted the stairs, and entered the rooms on the ground floor: a dining parlour, a small back-parlour and a still smaller third room, that had been probably appropriated to a footman – all as still as death. We then visited the drawing-rooms, which seemed fresh and new. In the front room I seated myself in an armchair. F— placed on the table the candlestick with which he had lighted us. I told him to shut the door. As he turned to do so, a chair opposite to me moved from the wall quickly and noiselessly, and dropped itself about a yard from my own chair, immediately fronting it.

'Why, this is better than the turning-tables,' said I, with a half-laugh – and as I laughed, my dog put back his head and howled.

F—, coming back, had not observed the movement of the chair. He employed himself now in stilling the dog. I continued to gaze on the chair, and fancied I saw on it a pale blue misty outline of a human figure, but an outline so indistinct that I could only distrust my own vision. The dog now was quiet. 'Put back that chair opposite to me,' said I to F—; 'put it back to the wall.'

F— obeyed. 'Was that you, sir?' said he, turning abruptly.

'I – what?'

'Why, something struck me. I felt it sharply on the shoulder – just here.'

'No,' said I. 'But we have jugglers present, and though we may not discover their tricks, we shall catch *them* before they frighten *us*.'

We did not stay long in the drawing-rooms – in fact, they felt so damp and so chilly that I was glad to get to the fire upstairs. We locked the doors of the drawing-rooms – a precaution which, I should observe, we had taken with all the rooms we had searched below. The bedroom my servant had selected for me was the best on the floor – a large one, with two windows fronting the street. The four-posted bed, which took up no inconsiderable space, was opposite to the fire, which burned clear and bright; a door in the wall to the left, between the bed and the window, communicated with the room which my servant appropriated to himself.

This last was a small room with a sofa-bed, and had no communication with the landing-place – no other door but that which conducted to the bedroom I was to occupy. On either side of my fireplace was a cupboard, without locks, flush with the wall, and covered with the same dull-brown paper. We examined these cupboards – they contained only hooks to suspend female dresses, nothing else; we sounded the walls – evidently solid – the outer walls of the building. Having finished the survey of these apartments, warmed myself a few moments and lighted my cigar, I then, still accompanied by F—, went forth to complete my reconnoitre. In the landing-place there was another door; it was closed firmly. 'Sir,' said my servant in surprise, 'I unlocked this door with all the others when I first came; it cannot have got locked from the inside, for it is a – '

Before he had finished his sentence the door, which neither of us then was touching, opened quietly of itself. We looked at each other a single instant. The same thought seized both – some human agency might be detected here. I rushed in first, my servant followed. A small blank dreary room without furniture – a few empty boxes and hampers in a corner – a small window – the shutters closed – not even a fireplace – no other door but that by which we had entered – no carpet on the floor, and the floor seemed very old, uneven, worm-eaten, mended here and there, as was shown by the whiter patches on the wood; but no living being, and no visible place in which a living being could have hidden. As we stood gazing around, the door by which we had entered closed as quietly as it had before opened: we were imprisoned.

For the first time I felt a creep of undefinable horror. Not so my servant. 'Why, they don't think to trap us, sir; I could break that trumpery door with a kick of my boot.'

'Try first if it will open to your hand,' said I, shaking off the vague apprehension that had seized me, 'while I open the shutters and see what is without.'

I unbarred the shutters – the window looked on the little backyard I have before described; there was no ledge without – nothing but sheer descent. No man getting out of that window would have found any footing till he had fallen on the stones below.

F—, meanwhile, was vainly attempting to open the door. He now turned round to me, and asked my permission to use force. And I should here state, in justice to the servant, that, far from evincing any superstitious terrors, his nerve, composure and even gaiety amidst circumstances so extraordinary compelled my admiration, and made me congratulate myself on having secured a companion in every way fitted to the occasion. I willingly gave him the permission he required. But though he was a remarkably strong man, his force was as idle as his milder efforts; the door did not even shake to his stoutest kick. Breathless and panting he desisted. I then tried the door myself, equally in vain.

As I ceased from the effort, again that creep of horror came over me; but this time it was more cold and stubborn. I felt as if some strange and ghastly exhalation were rising up from the chinks of that rugged floor, and filling the atmosphere with a venomous influence hostile to human life. The door now very slowly and quietly opened as of its own accord. We precipitated ourselves into the landing-place. We both saw a large pale light – as large as the human figure, but shapeless and unsubstantial – move before us, and ascend the stairs that led from the landing into the attics. I followed the light, and my servant followed me. It entered, to the right of the landing, a small garret, of which the door stood open. I entered in the same instant. The light then collapsed into a small globule, exceedingly brilliant and vivid; rested a moment on a bed in the corner, quivered and vanished. We approached the bed and examined it – a half-tester, such as is commonly found in attics devoted to servants. On the drawers that stood near it we perceived an old faded silk kerchief, with the needle still left in a rent half repaired. The kerchief was covered with dust; probably it had belonged to the old woman who had last died in that house, and this might have been her sleeping-room.

I had sufficient curiosity to open the drawers; there were a few odds and ends of female dress, and two letters tied round with a narrow ribbon of faded yellow. I took the liberty to possess myself of the letters. We found nothing else in the room worth noticing – nor did the light reappear; but we distinctly heard, as we turned to go, a pattering footfall on the floor – just before us. We went through the other attics (in all, four), the footfall still preceding us. Nothing to be seen – nothing but the footfall heard. I had the letters in my hand; just as I was descending the stairs I distinctly felt my wrist seized, and a faint, soft effort made to draw the letters from my clasp. I only held them the more tightly, and the effort ceased.

We regained the bedchamber appropriated to myself, and I then re-marked that my dog had not followed us when we had left it. He was thrusting himself close to the fire, and trembling. I was impatient to examine the letters; and while I read them, my servant opened a little box in which he had deposited the weapons I had ordered him to bring, took them out, placed them on a table close at my bed-head, and then occupied himself in soothing the dog, who, however, seemed to heed him very little.

The letters were short – they were dated; the dates exactly thirty-five years ago. They were evidently from a lover to his mistress, or a husband to some young wife. Not only the terms of expression, but a distinct reference to a former voyage indicated the writer to have been a seafarer. The spelling and handwriting were those of a man imperfectly educated, but still the language itself was forcible. In the expressions of endearment there was a kind of rough wild love; but here and there were dark unintelligible hints at some secret not of love – some secret that seemed of crime. 'We ought to love each other,' was one of the sentences I remember, 'for how everyone else would execrate us if all was known.' Again: 'Don't let anyone be in the same room with you at night – you talk in your sleep.' And again: 'What's done can't be undone; and I tell you there's nothing against us unless the dead could come to life.' Here there was underlined in a better handwriting (a female's), 'They do!' At the end of the letter later in date the same female hand had written these words: 'Lost at sea the 4th of June, the same day as — .'

I put down the letters, and began to muse over their contents.

Fearing, however, that the train of thought into which I fell might unsteady my nerves, I fully determined to keep my mind in a fit state to cope with whatever marvels the advancing night might bring forth. I roused myself – laid the letters on the table – stirred up the fire, which was still bright and cheering – and opened my volume of Macaulay. I read quietly enough till about half-past eleven. I then threw myself dressed upon the bed, and told my servant he might retire to his own room, but must keep himself awake. I bade him leave open the door between the two rooms. Thus alone, I kept two candles burning on the table by my bed-head. I placed my watch beside the weapons, and calmly resumed my Macaulay.

Opposite to me the fire burned clear; and on the hearth-rug, seemingly asleep, lay the dog. In about twenty minutes I felt an exceedingly cold air pass by my cheek, like a sudden draught. I fancied the door to my right, communicating with the landing-place, must have got open; but no – it was closed. I then turned my glance to my left, and saw the flame of the candles violently swayed as by a wind. At the same moment the watch beside the revolver softly slid from the table – softly, softly – no visible hand – it was gone. I sprang up, seizing the revolver with the one hand, the dagger with the other; I was not willing that my weapons should share the fate of the watch. Thus armed, I looked round the floor – no sign of the watch. Three slow, loud, distinct knocks were now heard at the bed-head; my servant called out, 'Is that you, sir?'

'No; be on your guard.'

The dog now roused himself and sat on his haunches, his ears moving quickly backwards and forwards. He kept his eyes fixed on me with a look so strange that he concentrated all my attention on himself. Slowly he rose up, all his hair bristling, and stood perfectly rigid, and with the same wild stare. I had no time, however, to examine the dog. Presently my servant emerged from his room; and if ever I saw horror in the human face, it was then. I should not have recognised him had we met in the street, so altered was every lineament. He passed by me quickly, saying in a whisper that seemed scarcely to come from his lips, 'Run – run! it is after me!' He gained the door to the landing, pulled it open, and rushed forth. I followed him on to the landing involuntarily, calling him to stop; but, without heeding me, he bounded down the stairs, clinging to the balusters and taking several steps at a time. I heard, where I stood, the street-door open – heard it again clap to. I was left alone in the haunted house.

It was but for a moment that I remained undecided whether or not to follow my servant; pride and curiosity alike forbade so dastardly a flight. I re-entered my room, closing the door after me, and proceeded cautiously into the interior chamber. I encountered nothing to justify my servant's terror. I again carefully examined the walls, to see if there were any concealed door. I could find no trace of one – not even a seam in the dull-brown paper with which the room was hung. How, then, had the Thing, whatever it was, which had so scared him, obtained ingress except through my own chamber?

I returned to my room, shut and locked the door that opened upon the interior one, and stood on the hearth, expectant and prepared. I now perceived that the dog had slunk into an angle of the wall, and was pressing himself close against it as if literally trying to force his way into it. I approached the animal and spoke to him; the poor brute was evidently beside himself with terror. He showed all his teeth, the slaver dropping from his jaws, and would certainly have bitten me if I had touched him. He did not seem to recognise me. Whoever has seen at the zoological gardens a rabbit, fascinated by a serpent, cowering in a corner, may form some idea of the anguish which the dog exhibited. Finding all efforts to soothe the animal in vain, and fearing that his bite might be as venomous in that state as if in the madness of hydrophobia, I left him alone, placed my weapons on the table beside the fire, seated myself and recommenced my Macaulay.

Perhaps in order not to appear seeking credit for a courage, or rather a coolness, which the reader may conceive I exaggerate, I may be pardoned if I pause to indulge in one or two egotistical remarks.

As I hold presence of mind, or what is called courage, to be precisely proportioned to familiarity with the circumstances that lead to it, so I should say that I had been long sufficiently familiar with all experiments that appertain to the marvellous. I had witnessed many very extraordinary phenomena in various parts of the world – phenomena that would be either totally disbelieved if I stated them, or ascribed to supernatural agencies. Now, my theory is that the supernatural is the impossible, and that what is called supernatural is only a something in the laws of nature of which we have been hitherto ignorant. Therefore, if a ghost rise before me, I have not the right to say, 'So, then, the supernatural is possible,' but rather, 'So, then, the apparition of a ghost is, contrary to received opinion, within the laws of nature – i.e. not supernatural.'

Now, in all that I had hitherto witnessed, and indeed in all the wonders which the amateurs of mystery in our age record as facts, a material living agency is always required. On the continent you will find still magicians who assert that they can raise spirits. Assume for the moment that they assert truly, still the living material form of the magician is present; and he is the material agency by which from some constitutional peculiarities, certain strange phenomena are represented to your natural senses.

Accept again, as truthful, the tales of spirit manifestation in America – musical or other sounds – writings on paper, produced by no discernible hand – articles of furniture moved about without apparent human agency – or the actual sight and touch of hands, to which no bodies seem to belong – still there must be found the *medium*, or living being, with constitutional peculiarities capable of obtaining these signs. In fine, in all such marvels, supposing even that there is no imposture, there must be a human being like ourselves, by whom, or through whom, the effects presented to human beings are produced. It is so with the now familiar phenomena of mesmerism or electro-biology; the mind of the person operated on is affected through a material living agent. Nor, supposing it true that a mesmerised patient can respond to the will or passes of a mesmeriser a hundred miles distant, is the response less occasioned by a material being; it may be through a material fluid – call it electric, call it odic, call it what you will – which has the power of traversing space and passing obstacles, that the material effect is communicated from one to the other.

Hence all that I had hitherto witnessed, or expected to witness, in this strange house, I believed to be occasioned through some agency or medium as mortal as myself; and this idea necessarily prevented the awe with which those who regard as supernatural things that are not within the ordinary operations of nature, might have been impressed by the adventures of that memorable night.

As, then, it was my conjecture that all that was presented, or would be presented, to my senses, must originate in some human being gifted by constitution with the power so to present them, and having some motive so to do, I felt an interest in my theory which, in its way, was rather philosophical than superstitious. And I can sincerely say that I was in as tranquil a temper for observation as any practical experimentalist could be in awaiting the effects of some rare though perhaps perilous chemical combination. Of course, the more I kept my mind detached from fancy, the more the temper fitted for observation would be obtained; and I therefore riveted eye and thought on the strong daylight sense in the page of my Macaulay.

I now became aware that something interposed between the page and the light – the page was over-shadowed; I looked up, and I saw what I shall find it very difficult, perhaps impossible, to describe.

It was a darkness shaping itself out of the air in very undefined outline. I cannot say it was of a human form, and yet it had more resemblance to a human form, or rather shadow, than anything else. As it stood, wholly apart and distinct from the air and the light around it, its dimensions seemed gigantic, the summit nearly touching the ceiling. While I gazed, a feeling of intense cold seized me. An iceberg before me could not more have chilled me; nor could the cold of an iceberg have been more purely physical. I feel convinced that it was not the cold caused by fear. As I continued to gaze, I thought – but this I cannot say with precision – that I distinguished two eyes looking down on me from the height. One moment I seemed to distinguish them clearly, the next they seemed gone; but still two rays of a pale-blue light frequently shot through the darkness, as from the height on which I half-believed half-doubted that I had encountered the eyes.

I strove to speak – my voice utterly failed me; I could only think to myself, 'Is this fear? it is not fear!' I strove to rise – in vain; I felt as if weighed down by an irresistible force. Indeed, my impression was that of an immense and overwhelming power opposed to my volition; that sense of utter inadequacy to cope with a force beyond men's, which one may feel *physically* in a storm at sea, in a conflagration, or when confronting some terrible wild beast, or rather, perhaps, the shark of the ocean, I felt *morally*. Opposed to my will was another will, as far superior to its strength as storm, fire and shark are superior in material force to the force of men.

And now, as this impression grew on me, now came, at last, horror – horror to a degree that no words can convey. Still I retained pride, if not courage; and in my own mind I said, 'This is horror, but it is not fear; unless I fear, I cannot be harmed; my reason rejects this thing; it is an illusion – I do not fear.' With a violent effort I succeeded at last in stretching out my hand towards the weapon on the table; as I did so, on the arm and shoulder I received a strange shock, and my arm fell to my side powerless. And now, to add to my horror, the light began slowly to wane from the candles – they were not, as it were, extinguished, but their flame seemed very gradually withdrawn; it was the same with the fire – the light was extracted from the fuel; in a few minutes the room was in utter darkness.

The dread that came over me, to be thus in the dark with that dark Thing, whose power was so intensely felt, brought a reaction of nerve. In fact, my terror had reached that climax that either my senses must have deserted me or I must have burst through the spell. I did burst through it. I found voice, though the voice was a shriek. I remember that I broke forth with words like these – 'I do not fear, my soul does not fear'; and at the same time I found the strength to rise. Still in that profound gloom I rushed to one of the windows – tore aside the curtain – flung open the shutters; my first thought was – LIGHT. And when I saw the moon high, clear and calm, I felt a joy that almost compensated for the previous terror. There was the moon, there was also the light from the gas-lamps in the deserted slumberous street. I turned to look back into the room; the moon penetrated its shadow very palely and partially – but still there was light. The dark Thing, whatever it might be, was gone – except that I could yet see a dim shadow which seemed the shadow of that shade, against the opposite wall.

My eye now rested on the table, and from under the table (which was without cloth or cover – an old mahogany round table) there rose a hand, visible as far as the wrist. It was a hand, seemingly, as much of flesh and blood as my own, but the hand of an aged person – lean, wrinkled, small too – a woman's hand.

That hand very softly closed on the two letters that lay on the table: hand and letters both vanished. There then came the same three loud measured knocks I had heard at the bed-head before this extraordinary drama had commenced.

As those sounds slowly ceased, I felt the whole room vibrate sensibly; and at the far end there arose, as from the floor, sparks or globules like bubbles of light, many-coloured – green, yellow, fire-red, azure. Up and down, to and fro, hither, thither, as tiny will-o'-the-wisps, the sparks moved, slow or swift, each at its own caprice. A chair (as in the drawing-room below) was now advanced from the wall without apparent agency, and placed at the opposite side of the table. Suddenly, as forth from the chair, there grew a shape – a woman's shape. It was distinct as a shape of life – ghastly as a shape of death. The face was that of youth, with a strange mournful beauty; the throat and shoulders were bare, the rest of the form in a loose robe of cloudy white. It began sleeking its long yellow hair, which fell over its shoulders; its eyes were not turned towards me, but to the door; it seemed listening, watching, waiting. The shadow of the shade in the background grew darker; and again I thought I beheld the eyes gleaming out from the summit of the shadow – eyes fixed upon that shape.

As if from the door, though it did not open, there grew out another shape equally distinct, equally ghastly – a man's shape – a young man's. It was in the dress of the last century, or rather in a likeness of such dress; for both the male shape and the female, though defined, were evidently unsubstantial, impalpable – simulacra – phantasms; and there was something incongruous, grotesque, yet fearful, in the contrast between the elaborate finery, the courtly precision of that old-fashioned garb, with its ruffles and lace and buckles, and the corpse-like aspect and ghost-like stillness of the flitting wearer. Just as the male shape approached the female, the dark shadow started from the wall, all three for a moment wrapped in darkness. When the pale light returned, the two phantoms were as if in the grasp of the shadow that towered between them; and there was a bloodstain on the breast of the female; and the phantom-male was leaning on its phantom-sword, and blood seemed trickling fast from the ruffles, from the lace; and the darkness of the intermediate shadow swallowed them up – they were gone. And again the bubbles of light shot, and sailed, and undulated, growing thicker and thicker and more wildly confused in their movements.

The closet-door to the right of the fireplace now opened, and from the aperture there came the form of a woman, aged. In her hand she held letters – the very letters over which I had seen *the* hand close; and behind her I heard a footstep. She turned round as if to listen, then she opened the letters and seemed to read; and over her shoulder I saw a livid face, the face as of a man long drowned – bloated, bleached – seaweed tangled in its dripping hair; and at her feet lay a form as of a corpse and beside the corpse there cowered a child, a miserable, squalid child, with famine in its cheeks and fear in its eyes. And as I looked in the old woman's face, the wrinkles and lines vanished, and it became a face of youth – hard-eyed, stony, but still youth; and the shadow darted forth and darkened over these phantoms as it had darkened over the last.

Nothing now was left but the shadow, and on that my eyes were intently fixed, till again eyes grew out of the shadow – malignant, serpent eyes. And the bubbles of light again rose and fell, and in their disordered, irregular, turbulent maze, mingled with the wan moonlight. And now from these globules themselves, as from the shell of an egg, monstrous things burst out; the air grew filled with them; larvae so bloodless and so hideous that I can in no way describe them except to remind the reader of the swarming life which the solar microscope brings before his eyes in a drop of water – things transparent, supple, agile, chasing each other, devouring each other – forms like nought ever beheld by the naked eye. As the shapes were without symmetry, so their movements were without order. In their very vagrancies there was no sport; they came round me and round, thicker and faster and swifter, swarming over my head, crawling over my right arm, which was outstretched in involuntary command against all evil beings.

Sometimes I felt myself touched, but not by them; invisible hands touched me. Once I felt the clutch as of cold soft fingers at my throat. I was still equally conscious that if I gave way to fear I should be in bodily peril; and I concentrated all my faculties in the single focus of resisting, stubborn will. And I turned my sight from the shadow – above all, from those strange serpent eyes – eyes that had now become distinctly visible. For there, though in nought else around me, I was aware that there was a *will*, and a will of intense, creative, working evil, which might crush down my own.

The pale atmosphere in the room began now to redden as if in the air of some near conflagration. The larvae grew lurid as things that live in fire. Again the room vibrated; again were heard the three measured knocks; and again all things were swallowed up in the darkness of the dark shadow, as if out of that darkness all had come, into that darkness all returned.

As the gloom receded, the shadow was wholly gone. Slowly as it had been withdrawn, the flame grew again into the candle on the table, again into the fuel in the grate. The whole room came once more calmly, healthfully into sight.

The two doors were still closed, the door communicating with the servant's room still locked. In the corner of the wall, into which he had so convulsively niched himself, lay the dog. I called to him – no movement; I approached – the animal was dead; his eyes protruded; his tongue out of his mouth; the froth gathered round his jaws. I took him in my arms; I brought him to the fire; I felt acute grief for the loss of my poor favourite – acute self-reproach; I accused myself of his death; I imagined he had died of fright. But what was my surprise on finding that his neck was actually broken – actually twisted out of the vertebrae. Had this been done in the dark? – must it not have been by a hand human as mine? – must there not have been a human agency all the while in that room? Good cause to suspect it. I cannot tell. I cannot do more than state the fact fairly; the reader may draw his own inference.

Another surprising circumstance – my watch was restored to the table from which it had been so mysteriously withdrawn; but it had stopped at the very moment it was so withdrawn; nor, despite all the skill of the watch-maker, has it ever gone since – that is, it will go in a strange erratic way for a few hours, and then comes to a dead stop – it is worthless.

Nothing more chanced for the rest of the night. Nor, indeed, had I long to wait before the dawn broke. Not till it was broad daylight did I quit the haunted house. Before I did so, I revisited the little blind room in which my servant and myself had been for a time imprisoned. I had a strong impression – for which I could not account – that from that room had originated the mechanism of the phenomena – if I may use the term – which had been experienced in my chamber. And though I entered it now in the clear day, with the sun peering through the filmy window, I still felt, as I stood on its floor, the creep of the horror which I had first there experienced the night before, and which had been so aggravated by what had passed in my own chamber. I could not, indeed, bear to stay more than half a minute within those walls. I descended the stairs, and again I heard the footfall before me; and when I opened the street door, I thought I could distinguish a very low laugh. I gained my own home, expecting to find my runaway servant there. But he had not presented himself; nor did I hear more of him for three days, when I received a letter from him, dated from Liverpool, to this effect:

HONOURED SIR – I humbly entreat your pardon, though I can scarcely hope that you will think I deserve it, unless – which heaven forbid! – you saw what I did. I feel that it will be years before I can recover myself; and as to being fit for service, it is out of the question. I am therefore going to my brother-in-law at Melbourne. The ship sails tomorrow. Perhaps the long voyage may set me up. I do nothing but start and tremble, and fancy It is behind me. I humbly beg you, honoured sir, to order my clothes, and whatever wages are due to me, to be sent to my mother's, at Walworth – John knows her address.

The letter ended with additional apologies, somewhat incoherent, and explanatory details as to effects that had been under the writer's charge.

This flight may perhaps warrant a suspicion that the man wished to go to Australia, and had been somehow or other fraudulently mixed up with the events of the night. I say nothing in refutation of that conjecture; rather, I suggest it as one that would seem to many persons the most probable solution of improbable occurrences. My own theory remained unshaken. I returned in the evening to the house, to bring away in a hack-cab the things I had left there, with my poor dog's body. In this task I was not disturbed, nor did any incident worth note befall me, except that still, on ascending and descending the stairs I heard the same footfall in advance. On leaving the house, I went to Mr J—'s. He was at home. I returned him the keys, told him that my curiosity was sufficiently gratified, and was about to relate quickly what had passed, when he stopped me, and said, though with much politeness, that he had no longer any interest in a mystery which none had ever solved.

I determined at least to tell him of the two letters I had read, as well as of the extraordinary manner in which they had disappeared, and I then enquired if he thought they had been addressed to the woman who had died in the house, and if there were anything in her early history which could possibly confirm the dark suspicions to which the letters gave rise. Mr J— seemed startled, and, after musing a few moments, answered, 'I know but little of the woman's earlier history, except, as I before told you, that her family were known to mine. But you revive some vague reminiscence to her prejudice. I will make enquiries, and inform you of their result. Still, even if we could admit the popular superstition that a person who had been either the perpetrator or the victim of dark crimes in life could revisit, as a restless spirit, the scene in which those crimes had been committed, I should observe that the house was infested by strange sights and sounds before the old woman died. You smile – what would you say?'

'I would say this, that I am convinced, if we could get to the bottom of these mysteries, we should find a living human agency.'

'What! you believe it is all an imposture? For what object?'

'Not an imposture in the ordinary sense of the word. If suddenly I were to sink into a deep sleep, from which you could not awake me, but in that sleep could answer questions with an accuracy which I could not pretend to when awake – tell you what money you had in your pocket – nay, describe your very thoughts – it is not necessarily an imposture, any more than it is necessarily supernatural. I should be, unconsciously to myself, under a mesmeric influence, conveyed to me from a distance by a human being who had acquired power over me by previous rapport.'

'Granting mesmerism, so far carried, to be a fact, you are right. And you would infer from this that a mesmeriser might produce the extraordinary effects you and others have witnessed over inanimate objects – fill the air with sights and sounds?'

'Or impress our senses with the belief in them – we never having been *en rapport* with the person acting on us? No. What is commonly called mesmerism could not do this; but there may be a power akin to mesmerism, and superior to it – the power that in the old days was called magic. That such a power may extend to all inanimate objects of matter, I do not say; but if so, it would not be against nature, only a rare power in nature which might be given to constitutions with certain peculiarities, and cultivated by practice to an extraordinary degree. That such a power might extend over the dead – that is, over certain thoughts and memories that the dead may still retain – and compel, not that which ought properly to be called the *soul*, and which is far beyond human reach, but rather a phantom of what has been most earth-stained on earth, to make itself apparent to our senses – is a very ancient though obsolete theory, upon which I will hazard no opinion. But I do not conceive the power would be supernatural.

'Let me illustrate what I mean from an experiment which Paracelsus describes as not difficult, and which the author of the *Curiosities of Literature* cites as credible: A flower perishes; you burn it. Whatever were the elements of that flower while it lived are gone, dispersed, you know not whither; you can never discover nor recollect them. But you can, by chemistry, out of the burnt dust of that flower, raise a spectrum of the flower, just as it seemed in life. It may be the same with the human being. The soul has so much escaped you as the essence or elements of the flower. Still you may make a spectrum of it. And this phantom, though in the popular superstition it is held to be the soul of the departed, must not be confounded with the true soul; it is but the eidolon of the dead form.

'Hence, like the best-attested stories of ghosts or spirits, the thing that most strikes us is the absence of what we hold to be soul – that is, of superior emancipated intelligence. They come for little or no object – they seldom speak, if they do come; they utter no ideas above that of an ordinary person on earth. These American spirit-seers have published volumes of communications in prose and verse, which they assert to be given in the names of the most illustrious dead – Shakespeare, Bacon – heaven knows whom. Those communications, taking the best, are certainly not a whit of higher order than would be communications from living persons of fair talent and education; they are wondrously inferior to what Bacon, Shakespeare and Plato said and wrote when on earth.

'Nor, what is more notable, do they ever contain an idea that was not on the earth before. Wonderful, therefore, as such phenomena may be (granting them to be truthful), I see much that philosophy may question, nothing that it is incumbent on philosophy to deny – viz. nothing supernatural. They are but ideas conveyed somehow or other (we have not yet discovered the means) from one mortal brain to another. Whether, in so doing, tables walk of their own accord, or fiend-like shapes appear in a magic circle, or bodiless hands rise and remove material objects, or a Thing of darkness, such as presented itself to me, freeze our blood – still am I persuaded that these are but agencies conveyed, as by electric wires, to my own brain from the brain of another. In some constitutions there is a natural chemistry, and those may produce chemic wonders – in others a natural fluid, call it electricity, and these produce electric wonders. But they differ in this from normal science – they are alike objectless, purposeless, puerile, frivolous. They lead on to no grand results; and therefore the world does not heed, and true sages have not cultivated them. But sure I am that, of all I saw or heard, a man, human as myself, was the remote originator; and I believe unconsciously to himself as to the exact effects produced, for this reason: no two persons, you say, have ever told you that they experienced exactly the same thing. Well, observe, no two persons ever experience exactly the same dream. If this were an ordinary imposture, the machinery would be arranged for results that would but little vary; if it were a supernatural agency, permitted by the Almighty, it would surely be for some definite end.

'These phenomena belong to neither class; my persuasion is that they originate in some brain now far distant; that that brain had no distinct volition in anything that occurred; that what does occur reflects but its devious, motley, ever-shifting, half-formed thoughts; in short, that it has been but the dreams of such a brain put into action and invested with a semi-substance. That this brain is of immense power, that it can set matter into movement, that it is malignant and destructive, I believe: some material force must have killed my dog; it might, for aught I know, have sufficed to kill me, had I been as subjugated by terror as the dog – had my intellect or my spirit given me no countervailing resistance in my will.'

'It killed your dog! that is fearful! indeed, it is strange that no animal can be induced to stay in that house; not even a cat. Rats and mice are never found in it.'

'The instincts of the brute creation detect influences deadly to their existence. Man's reason has a sense less subtle, because it has a resisting power more supreme. But enough; do you comprehend my theory?'

'Yes, though imperfectly – and I accept any crotchet (pardon the word), however odd, rather than embrace at once the notion of ghosts and hobgoblins we imbibed in our nurseries. Still, to my unfortunate house the evil is the same. What on earth can I do with the house?'

'I will tell you what I would do. I am convinced from my own internal feelings that the small unfurnished room at right angles to the door of the bedroom which I occupied forms a starting-point or receptacle for the influences which haunt the house; and I strongly advise you to have the walls opened, the floor removed – nay, the whole room pulled down. I observe that it is detached from the body of the house, built over the small backyard, and could be removed without injury to the rest of the building.'

'And you think, if I did that – '

'You would cut off the telegraph wires. Try it. I am so persuaded that I am right that I will pay half the expense if you will allow me to direct the operations.'

'Nay, I am well able to afford the cost; for the rest, allow me to write to you.'

About ten days afterwards I received a letter from Mr J—, telling me that he had visited the house since I had seen him; that he had found the two letters I had described, replaced in the drawer from which I had taken them; that he had read them with misgivings like my own; that he had instituted a cautious enquiry about the woman to whom I rightly conjectured they had been written. It seemed that thirty-six years ago (a year before the date of the letters), she had married, against the wish of her relatives, an American of very suspicious character; in fact, he was generally believed to have been a pirate. She herself was the daughter of very respectable tradespeople, and had served in the capacity of a nursery governess before her marriage. She had a brother, a widower, who was considered wealthy, and who had one child of about six years old. A month after the marriage, the body of this brother was found in the Thames, near London Bridge; there seemed some marks of violence about his throat, but they were not deemed sufficient to warrant the inquest in any verdict other than that of 'found drowned'.

The American and his wife took charge of the little boy, the deceased brother having by his will left his sister the guardian of his only child – and in the event of the child's death, the sister inherited. The child died about six months afterwards – it was supposed to have been neglected and ill-treated. The neighbours deposed to have heard it shriek at night. The surgeon who had examined it after death, said that it was emaciated as if from want of nourishment, and the body was covered with livid bruises. It seemed that one winter night the child had sought to escape – crept out into the backyard – tried to scale the wall – fallen back exhausted, and been found at morning on the stones in a dying state. But though there was some evidence of cruelty, there was none of murder; and the aunt and her husband had sought to palliate cruelty by alleging the exceeding stubbornness and perversity of the child, who was declared to be half-witted. Be that as it may, at the orphan's death the aunt inherited her brother's fortune.

Before the first wedded year was out, the American quitted England abruptly, and never returned to it. He obtained a cruising vessel, which was lost in the Atlantic two years afterwards. The widow was left in affluence; but reverses of various kinds had befallen her: a bank broke – an investment failed – she went into a small business and became insolvent – then she entered into service, sinking lower and lower, from housekeeper down to maid-of-all-work – never long retaining a place, though nothing peculiar against her character was ever alleged. She was considered sober, honest, and peculiarly quiet in her ways; still nothing prospered with her. And so she had dropped into the workhouse, from which Mr J— had taken her, to be placed in charge of the very house which she had rented as mistress in the first year of her wedded life.

Mr J— added that he had passed an hour alone in the unfurnished room which I had urged him to destroy, and that his impressions of dread while there were so great, though he had neither heard nor seen anything, that he was eager to have the walls bared and the floors removed as I had suggested. He had engaged persons for the work, and would commence any day I would name.

The day was accordingly fixed. I repaired to the haunted house – we went into the blind dreary room, took up the skirting, and then the floor. Under the rafters, covered with rubbish, was found a trap-door, quite large enough to admit a man. It was closely nailed down, with clamps and rivets of iron. On removing these we descended into a room below, the existence of which had never been suspected. In this room there had been a window and a flue, but they had been bricked over, evidently for many years. By the help of candles we examined this place; it still retained some mouldering furniture – three chairs, an oak settee, a table – all of the fashion of about eighty years ago. There was a chest-of-drawers against the wall, in which we found, half-rotted away, old-fashioned articles of a man's dress, such as might have been worn eighty or a hundred years ago by a gentleman of some rank – costly steel buckles and buttons, like those yet worn on court dresses – a handsome court sword; in a waistcoat which had once been rich with gold lace, but which was now blackened and foul with damp, we found five guineas, a few silver coins, and an ivory ticket, probably for some place of entertainment long since passed away. But our main discovery was in a kind of iron safe fixed to the wall, the lock of which it cost us much trouble to get picked.

In this safe were three shelves and two small drawers. Ranged on the shelves were several small bottles of crystal, hermetically stopped. They contained colourless volatile essences, of what nature I shall say no more than that they were not poisons – phosphor and ammonia entered into some of them. There were also some very curious glass tubes, and a small pointed rod of iron, with a large lump of rock-crystal and another of amber – also a loadstone of great power.

In one of the drawers we found a miniature portrait set in gold, and retaining the freshness of its colours most remarkably, considering the length of time it had probably been there. The portrait was that of a man who might be somewhat advanced in middle life, perhaps forty-seven or forty-eight.

It was a most peculiar face – a most impressive face. If you could fancy some mighty serpent transformed into man, preserving in the human lineaments the old serpent type, you would have a better idea of that countenance than long descriptions can convey: the width and flatness of forehead – the tapering elegance of contour, disguising the strength of the deadly jaw – the long, large, terrible eye, glittering and green as the emerald – and withal a certain ruthless calm, as if from the consciousness of an immense power. The strange thing was this – the instant I saw the miniature I recognised a startling likeness to one of the rarest portraits in the world, the portrait of a man of a rank only below that of royalty, who in his own day had made a considerable noise. History says little or nothing of him; but search the correspondence of his contemporaries, and you find reference to his wild daring, his bold profligacy, his restless spirit, his taste for the occult sciences. While still in the meridian of life he died and was buried, so say the chronicles, in a foreign land. He died in time to escape the grasp of the law, for he was accused of crimes which would have given him to the headsman.

After his death, the portraits of him, which had been numerous, for he had been a munificent encourager of art, were bought up and destroyed – it was supposed by his heirs, who might have been glad could they have razed his very name from their splendid line. He had enjoyed a vast wealth; a large portion of this was believed to have been embezzled by a favourite astrologer or soothsayer – at all events, it had unaccountably vanished at the time of his death. One portrait alone of him was supposed to have escaped the general destruction; I had seen it in the house of a collector some months before. It had made on me a wonderful impression, as it does on all who behold it – a face never to be forgotten; and there was that face in the miniature that lay within my hand. True, that in the miniature the man was a few years older than in the portrait I had seen, or than the original was even at the time of his death. But a few years! – why, between the date in which flourished that direful noble, and the date in which the miniature was evidently painted, there was an interval of more than two centuries.

While I was thus gazing, silent and wondering, Mr J— said: 'But is it possible? I have known this man.'

'How – where?' I cried.

'In India. He was high in the confidence of the Rajah of — and well-nigh drew him into a revolt which would have lost the rajah his dominions. The man was a Frenchman – his name de V—, clever, bold, lawless. We insisted on his dismissal and banishment: it must be the same man – no two faces like his – yet this miniature seems nearly a hundred years old.'

Mechanically I turned round the miniature to examine the back of it, and on the back was engraved a pentacle; in the middle of the pentacle a ladder, and the third step of the ladder was formed by the date 1765. Examining still more minutely, I detected a spring; this, on being pressed, opened the back of the miniature as a lid. Withinside the lid was engraved *Mariana to thee – be faithful in life and in death to —*. Here followed a name that I will not mention, but it was not unfamiliar to me. I had heard it spoken of by old men in my childhood as the name borne by a dazzling charlatan, who had made a great sensation in London for a year or so, and had fled the country on the charge of a double murder within his own house – that of his mistress and his rival. I said nothing of this to Mr J—, to whom reluctantly I resigned the miniature.

We had found no difficulty in opening the first drawer within the iron safe; we found great difficulty in opening the second: it was not locked, but it resisted all efforts till we inserted in the chinks the edge of a chisel. When we had thus drawn it forth, we found a very singular apparatus in the nicest order. Upon a small thin book, or rather tablet, was placed a saucer of crystal; this saucer was filled with a clear liquid – on that liquid floated a kind of compass, with a needle shifting rapidly round, but instead of the usual points of a compass were seven strange characters, not very unlike those used by astrologers to denote the planets. A very peculiar, but not strong nor displeasing odour came from this drawer, which was lined with a wood that we afterwards discovered to be hazel. Whatever the cause of this odour, it produced a material effect on the nerves. We all felt it, even the two workmen who were in the room – a creeping, tingling sensation from the tips of the fingers to the roots of the hair. Impatient to examine the tablet, I removed the saucer. As I did so the needle of the compass went round and round with exceeding swiftness, and I felt a shock that ran through my whole frame, so that I dropped the saucer on the floor. The liquid was spilt – the saucer was broken – the compass rolled to the end of the room – and at that instant the walls shook to and fro, as if a giant had swayed and rocked them.

The two workmen were so frightened that they ran up the ladder by which we had descended from the trap-door; but seeing that nothing more happened, they were easily induced to return.

Meanwhile I had opened the tablet: it was bound in a plain red leather, with a silver clasp; it contained but one sheet of thick vellum, and on that sheet were inscribed, within a double pentacle, words in old monkish Latin, which are literally to be translated thus: 'On all that it can reach within these walls – sentient or inanimate, living or dead – as moves the needle, so work my will! Accursed be the house, and restless be the dwellers therein.'

We found no more. Mr J— burnt the tablet and its anathema. He razed to the foundations the part of the building containing the secret room with the chamber over it. He had then the courage to inhabit the house himself for a month, and a quieter, better conditioned house could not be found in all London. Subsequently he let it to advantage, and his tenant has made no complaints. But my story is not yet done. A few days after Mr J— had removed into the house, I paid him a visit. We were standing by the open window and conversing. A van containing some articles of furniture which he was moving from his former house was at the door. I had just urged on him my theory that all those phenomena regarded as supermundane had emanated from a human brain; adducing the charm, or rather curse, we had found and destroyed in support of my philosophy. Mr J— was observing in reply, 'That even if mesmerism, or whatever analogous power it might be called, could really thus work in the absence of the operator, and produce effects so extraordinary, still could those effects continue when the operator himself was dead? and if the spell had been wrought, and, indeed, the room walled up, more than seventy years ago, the probability was that the operator had long since departed this life.' Mr J—, I say, was thus answering, when I caught hold of his arm and pointed to the street below.

A well-dressed man had crossed from the opposite side, and was accosting the carrier in charge of the van. His face, as he stood, was exactly fronting our window. It was the face of the miniature we had discovered; it was the face of the portrait of the noble three centuries ago.

'Good heavens!' cried Mr J—, 'that is the face of de V—, and scarcely a day older than when I saw it in the rajah's court in my youth!'

Seized by the same thought, we both hastened downstairs. I was first in the street; but the man had already gone. I caught sight of him, however, not many yards in advance, and in another moment I was by his side.

I had resolved to speak to him, but when I looked into his face I felt as if it were impossible to do so. That eye – the eye of the serpent – fixed and held me spellbound. And withal, about the man's whole person there was a dignity, an air of pride and station and superiority, that would have made anyone, habituated to the usages of the world, hesitate long before venturing upon a liberty or impertinence. And what could I say? what was it I would ask? Thus ashamed of my first impulse, I fell a few paces back, still, however, following the stranger, undecided what else to do. Meanwhile he turned the corner of the street; a plain carriage was in waiting, with a servant out of livery, dressed like a *valet-de-place*, at the carriage door. In another moment he had stepped into the carriage, and it drove off. I returned to the house. Mr J— was still at the street door. He had asked the carrier what the stranger had said to him.

'Merely asked whom that house now belonged to.'

The same evening I happened to go with a friend to a place in town called the Cosmopolitan Club, a place open to men of all countries, all opinions, all degrees. One orders one's coffee, smokes one's cigar. One is always sure to meet agreeable, sometimes remarkable persons.

I had not been two minutes in the room before I beheld at a table, convening with an acquaintance of mine, whom I will designate by the initial G, the man – the original of the miniature. He was now without his hat, and the likeness was yet more startling, only I observed that while he was conversing there was less severity in the countenance; there was even a smile, though a very quiet and very cold one. The dignity of mien I had acknowledged in the street was also more striking, a dignity akin to that which invests some prince of the East – conveying the idea of supreme indifference and habitual, indisputable, indolent, but resistless, power.

G— soon after left the stranger, who then took up a scientific journal, which seemed to absorb his attention.

I drew G— aside. 'Who and what is that gentleman?'

'That? Oh, a very remarkable man indeed. I met him last year amidst the caves of Petra – the scriptural Edom. He is the best Oriental scholar I know. We joined company, had an adventure with robbers, in which he showed a coolness that saved our lives; afterwards he invited me to spend a day with him in a house he had bought at Damascus – a house buried amongst almond blossoms and roses – the most beautiful thing! He had lived there for some years, quite as an Oriental, in grand style. I half suspect he is a renegade, immensely rich, very odd; by the by, a great mesmeriser. I have seen him with my own eyes produce an effect on inanimate things. If you take a letter from your pocket and throw it to the other end of the room, he will order it to come to his feet, and you will see the letter wriggle itself along the floor till it has obeyed his command. 'Pon my honour, 'tis true; I have seen him affect even the weather, disperse or collect clouds, by means of a glass tube or wand. But he does not like talking of these matters to strangers. He has only just arrived in England; says he has not been for a great many years; let me introduce him to you.'

'Certainly! He is English, then? What is his name?'

'Oh! – a very homely one – Richards.'

'And what is his birth – his family?'

'How do I know? What does it signify! – no doubt some parvenu, but rich – so infernally rich!'

G— drew me up to the stranger, and the introduction was effected. The manners of Mr Richards were not those of an adventurous traveller. Travellers are in general constitutionally gifted with high animal spirits: they are talkative, eager, imperious. Mr Richards was calm and subdued in tone, with manners which were made distant by the loftiness of punctilious courtesy – the manners of a former age. I observed that the English he spoke was not exactly of our day. I should even have said that the accent was slightly foreign. But then Mr Richards remarked that he had been little in the habit for many years of speaking in his native tongue. The conversation fell upon the changes in the aspect of London since he had last visited our metropolis. G— then glanced off to the moral changes – literary, social, political – the great men who were removed from the stage within the last twenty years – the new great men who were coming on. In all this Mr Richards evinced no interest. He had evidently read none of our living authors, and seemed scarcely acquainted by name with our younger states- men. Once and only once he laughed; it was when G— asked him whether he had any thought of getting into Parliament. And the laugh was inward – sarcastic – sinister – a sneer raised into a laugh.

After a few minutes G— left us to talk to some other acquaintances who had just lounged into the room, and I then said quietly: 'I have seen a miniature of you, Mr Richards, in the house you once inhabited, and perhaps built, if not wholly, at least in part, in — Street. You passed by that house this morning.'

Not till I had finished did I raise my eyes to his, and then he fixed my gaze so steadfastly that I could not withdraw it – those fascinating serpent eyes. But involuntarily, and as if the words that translated my thought were dragged from me, I added in a low whisper, 'I have been a student in the mysteries of life and nature; of those mysteries I have known the occult professors. I have the right to speak to you thus.' And I uttered a certain password.

'Well,' said he, dryly, 'I concede the right – what would you ask?'

'To what extent human will in certain temperaments can extend?'

'To what extent can thought extend? Think, and before you draw breath you are in China.'

'True. But my thought has no power in China.'

'Give it expression, and it may have: you may write down a thought which, sooner or later, may alter the whole condition of China. What is a law but a thought? Therefore thought is infinite – therefore thought has power; not in proportion to its value – a bad thought may make a bad law as potent as a good thought can make a good one.'

'Yes; what you say confirms my own theory. Through invisible currents one human brain may transmit its ideas to other human brains with the same rapidity as a thought promulgated by visible means. And as thought is imperishable – as it leaves its stamp behind it in the natural world even when the thinker has passed out of this world – so the thought of the living may have power to rouse up and revive the thoughts of the dead – such as those thoughts *were in life* – though the thought of the living cannot reach the thoughts which the dead *now* may entertain. Is it not so?'

'I decline to answer if, in my judgement, thought has the limit you would fix to it; but proceed. You have a special question you wish to put.'

'Intense malignity in an intense will, engendered in a peculiar temperament, and aided by natural means within the reach of science, may produce effects like those ascribed of old to evil magic. It might thus haunt the walls of a human habitation with spectral revivals of all guilty thoughts and guilty deeds once conceived and done within those walls; all, in short, with which the evil will claims rapport and affinity – imperfect, incoherent, fragmentary snatches at the old dramas acted therein years ago. Thoughts thus crossing each other haphazard, as in the nightmare of a vision, growing up into phantom sights and sounds, and all serving to create horror, not because those sights and sounds are really visitations from a world without, but that they are ghastly monstrous renewals of what have been in this world itself, set into malignant play by a malignant mortal.

'And it is through the material agency of that human brain that these things would acquire even a human power – would strike as with the shock of electricity, and might kill, if the thought of the person assailed did not rise superior to the dignity of the original assailer – might kill the most powerful animal if unnerved by fear, but not injure the feeblest man, if, while his flesh crept, his mind stood out fearless. Thus, when in old stories we read of a magician rent to pieces by the fiends he has evoked – or still more, in Eastern legends, that one magician succeeds by arts in destroying another – there may be so far truth, that a material being has clothed, from its own evil propensities, certain elements and fluids, usually quiescent or harmless, with awful shape and terrific force – just as the lightning that has lain hidden and innocent in the cloud becomes by natural law suddenly visible, takes a distinct shape to the eye, and can strike destruction on the object to which it is attracted.'

'You are not without glimpses of a very mighty secret,' said Mr Richards, composedly. 'According to your view, could a mortal obtain the power you speak of, he would necessarily be a malignant and evil being.'

'If the power were exercised as I have said, most malignant and most evil – though I believe in the ancient traditions that he could not injure the good. His will could only injure those with whom it has established an affinity, or over whom it forces unresisted sway. I will now imagine an example that may be within the laws of nature, yet seem wild as the fables of a bewildered monk.

'You will remember that Albertus Magnus, after describing minutely the process by which spirits may be invoked and commanded, adds emphatically that the process will instruct and avail only the few – that *a man must be born a magician!* – that is, born with a peculiar physical temperament, as a man is born a poet. Rarely are men in whose constitution lurks this occult power of the highest order of intellect; usually in the intellect there is some twist, perversity or disease. But, on the other hand, they must possess, to an astonishing degree, the faculty to concentrate thought on a single object – the energic faculty that we call *will*. Therefore, though their intellect be not sound, it is exceedingly forcible for the attainment of what it desires. I will imagine such a person, pre-eminently gifted with this constitution and its concomitant forces. I will place him in the loftier grades of society. I will suppose his desires emphatically those of the sensualist – he has, therefore, a strong love of life. He is an absolute egotist – his will is concentrated in himself – he has fierce passions – he knows no enduring, no holy affections, but he can covet eagerly what for the moment he desires – he can hate implacably what opposes itself to his objects – he can commit fearful crimes, yet feel small remorse – he resorts rather to curses upon others, than to penitence for his misdeeds. Circumstances, to which his constitution guides him, lead him to a rare knowledge of the natural secrets which may serve his egotism. He is a close observer where his passions encourage observation, he is a minute calculator, not from love of truth, but where love of self sharpens his faculties – therefore he can be a man of science.

'I suppose such a being, having by experience learned the power of his arts over others, trying what may be the power of will over his own frame, and studying all that in natural philosophy may increase that power. He loves life, he dreads death; he *wills to live on.* He cannot restore himself to youth, he cannot entirely stay the progress of death, he cannot make himself immortal in the flesh and blood; but he may arrest for a time so prolonged as to appear incredible, if I said it, that hardening of the parts which constitutes old age. A year may age him no more than an hour ages another. His intense will, scientifically trained into system, operates, in short, over the wear and tear of his own frame. He lives on. That he may not seem a portent and a miracle, he *dies* from time to time, seemingly, to certain persons. Having schemed the transfer of a wealth that suffices to his wants, he disappears from one corner of the world, and contrives that his obsequies shall be celebrated. He reappears at another corner of the world, where he resides undetected, and does not revisit the scenes of his former career till all who could remember his features are no more. He would be profoundly miserable if he had affections – he has none but for himself. No good man would accept his longevity, and to no men, good or bad, would he or could he communicate its true secret. Such a man might exist; such a man as I have described I see now before me! – Duke of —, in the court of —, dividing time between lust and brawl, alchemists and wizards; again, in the last century, charlatan and criminal, with name less noble, domiciled in the house at which you gazed today, and flying from the law you had outraged, none knew whither; traveller once more revisiting London, with the same earthly passions which filled your heart when races now no more walked through yonder streets; outlaw from the school of all the nobler and diviner mystics; execrable Image of Life in Death and Death in Life, I warn you back from the cities and homes of healthful men; back to the ruins of departed empires; back to the desert of nature unredeemed!'

There answered me a whisper so musical, so potently musical, that it seemed to enter into my whole being, and subdue me despite myself. Thus it said: 'I have sought one like you for the last hundred years. Now I have found you, we part not till I know what I desire. The vision that sees through the past, and cleaves through the veil of the future, is in you at this hour; never before, never to come again. The vision of no puling fantastic girl, of no sick-bed somnambule, but of a strong man with a vigorous brain. Soar and look forth!'

As he spoke I felt as if I rose out of myself upon eagle wings. All the weight seemed gone from air – roofless the room, roofless the dome of space. I was not in the body – where I knew not – but aloft over time, over earth.

Again I heard the melodious whisper. 'You say right. I have mastered great secrets by the power of will; true, by will and by science I can retard the process of years: but death comes not by age alone. Can I frustrate the accidents which bring death upon the young?'

'No; every accident is a providence. Before a providence snaps every human will.'

'Shall I die at last, ages and ages hence, by the slow, though inevitable, growth of time, or by the cause that I call accident?'

'By a cause you call accident.'

'Is not the end still remote?' asked the whisper with a slight tremor.

'Regarded as my life regards time, it is still remote.'

'And shall I, before then, mix with the world of men as I did ere I learned these secrets, resume eager interest in their strife and their trouble – battle with ambition, and use the power of the sage to win the power that belongs to kings?'

'You will yet play a part on the earth that will fill earth with commotion and amaze. For wondrous designs have you, a wonder yourself, been permitted to live on through the centuries. All the secrets you have stored will then have their uses – all that now makes you a stranger amidst the generations will contribute then to make you their lord. As the trees and the straws are drawn into a whirlpool – as they spin round, are sucked to the deep, and again tossed aloft by the eddies, so shall races and thrones be plucked into the charm of your vortex. Awful Destroyer – but in destroying, made, against your own will, a Constructor!'

'And that date, too, is far off?'

'Far off; when it comes, think your end in this world is at hand!'

'How and what is the end? Look east, west, south and north.'

'In the north, where you never yet trod, towards the point whence your instincts have warned you, there a spectre will seize you. 'Tis Death! I see a ship – it is haunted – 'tis chased – it sails on. Baffled navies sail after that ship. It enters the regions of ice. It passes a sky red with meteors. Two moons stand on high, over ice-reefs. I see the ship locked between white defiles – they are ice-rocks. I see the dead strew the decks – stark and livid, green mould on their limbs. All are dead, but one man – it is you! But years, though so slowly they come, have then scathed you. There is the coming of age on your brow, and the will is relaxed in the cells of the brain. Still that will, though enfeebled, exceeds all that man knew before you, through the will you live on, gnawed with famine; and nature no longer obeys you in that death-spreading region; the sky is a sky of iron, and the air has iron clamps, and the ice-rocks wedge in the ship. Hark how it cracks and groans. Ice will imbed it as amber imbeds a straw. And a man has gone forth, living yet, from the ship and its dead; and he has clambered up the spikes of an iceberg, and the two moons gaze down on his form. That man is yourself; and terror is on you – terror; and terror has swallowed your will. And I see swarming up the steep ice-rock, grey grisly things. The bears of the north have scented their quarry – they come near you and nearer, shambling and rolling their bulk. And in that day every moment shall seem to you longer than the centuries through which you have passed. And heed this – after life, moments continued make the bliss or the hell of eternity.'

'Hush,' said the whisper; 'but the day, you assure me, is far off – very far! I go back to the almond and rose of Damascus! – sleep!'

The room swam before my eyes. I became insensible. When I recovered, I found G— holding my hand and smiling. He said, 'You who have always declared yourself proof against mesmerism have succumbed at last to my friend Richards.'

'Where is Mr Richards?'

'Gone, when you passed into a trance – saying quietly to me. "Your friend will not wake for an hour." '

I asked, as collectedly as I could, where Mr Richards lodged.

'At the Trafalgar Hotel.'

'Give me your arm,' said I to G—; 'let us call on him; I have something to say.'

When we arrived at the hotel, we were told that Mr Richards had returned twenty minutes before, paid his bill, left directions with his servant (a Greek) to pack his effects and proceed to Malta by the steamer that should leave Southampton the next day. Mr Richards had merely said of his own movements that he had visits to pay in the neighbourhood of London, and it was uncertain whether he should be able to reach Southampton in time for that steamer; if not, he should follow on the next one.

The waiter asked me my name. On my informing him, he gave me a note that Mr Richards had left for me, in case I called.

The note was as follows:

I wished you to utter what was in your mind. You obeyed. I have therefore established power over you. For three months from this day you can communicate to no living man what has passed between us – you cannot even show this note to the friend by your side. During three months, silence complete as to me and mine. Do you doubt my power to lay on you this command? – try to disobey me. At the end of the third month, the spell is raised. For the rest I spare you. I shall visit your grave a year and a day after it has received you.

So ends this strange story, which I ask no one to believe. I write it down exactly three months after I received the above note. I could not write it before, nor could I show to G—, in spite of his urgent request, the note which I read under the gas-lamp by his side.

Young Goodman Brown

NATHANIEL HAWTHORNE

YOUNG GOODMAN BROWN came forth, at sunset, into the street of Salem village, but put his head back, after crossing the threshold, to exchange a parting kiss with his young wife. And Faith, as the wife was aptly named, thrust own pretty head into the street, letting the wind play with the pink ribbons of her cap, while she called to Goodman Brown.

'Dearest heart,' whispered she, softly and rather sadly, when her lips were close to his ear, 'pr'y thee, put off your journey until sunrise, and sleep in your own bed tonight. A lone woman is troubled with such dreams and such thoughts that she's afeard of herself, sometimes. Pray, tarry with me this night, dear husband, of all nights in the year.'

'My love and my Faith,' replied young Goodman Brown, 'of all nights in the year, this one night must I tarry away from thee. My journey, as thou callest it, forth and back again, must needs be done 'twixt now and sunrise. What, my sweet pretty wife, dost thou doubt me already, and we but three months married!'

'Then, God bless you!' said Faith with the pink ribbons, 'and may you find all well, when you come back.'

'Amen!' cried Goodman Brown. 'Say thy prayers, dear Faith, and go to bed at dusk, and no harm will come to thee.'

So they parted: and the young man pursued his way, until, being about to turn the corner by the meeting-house, he looked back, and saw the head of Faith still peeping after him, with a melancholy air, in spite of her pink ribbons.

'Poor little Faith!' thought he, for his heart smote him. 'What a wretch am I, to leave her on such an errand! She talks of dreams, too. Methought, as she spoke, there was trouble in her face, as if a dream had warned her what work is to be done tonight. But, no, no! 'twould kill her to think it. Well; she's a blessed angel on earth; and after this one night, I'll cling to her skirts and follow her to heaven.'

With this excellent resolve for the future, Goodman Brown felt himself justified in making more haste on his present evil purpose. He had taken a dreary road, darkened by all the gloomiest trees of the forest, which barely stood aside to let the narrow path creep through, and closed immediately behind. It was all as lonely as could be, and there is this peculiarity in such a solitude, that the traveller knows not who may be concealed by the innumerable trunks and the thick boughs overhead; so that, with lonely footsteps, he may yet be passing through an unseen multitude.

'There may be a devilish Indian behind every tree,' said Goodman Brown, to himself; and he glanced fearfully behind him, as he added, 'What if the devil himself should be at my very elbow?'

His head being turned back, he passed a crook of the road, and looking forward again, beheld the figure of a man, in grave and decent attire, seated at the foot of an old tree. He arose at Goodman Brown's approach, and walked onward, side by side with him.

'You are late, Goodman Brown,' said he. 'The clock of the Old South was striking as I came through Boston, and that is full fifteen minutes agone.'

'Faith kept me back awhile,' replied the young man, with a tremor in his voice, caused by the sudden appearance of his companion, though not wholly unexpected.

It was now deep dusk in the forest, and deepest in that part of it where these two were journeying. As nearly as could be discerned, the second traveller was about fifty years old, apparently in the same rank of life as Goodman Brown, and bearing a considerable resemblance to him, though perhaps more in expression than features. Still, they might have been taken for father and son. And yet, though the elder person was as simply clad as the younger, and as simple in manner too, he had an indescribable air of one who knew the world, and would not have felt abashed at the governor's dinner table, or in King William's court, were it possible that his affairs should call him thither. But the only thing about him, that could be fixed upon as remarkable, was his staff, which bore the likeness of a great black snake, so curiously wrought that it might almost be seen to twist and wriggle itself, like a living serpent. This, of course, must have been an ocular deception, assisted by the uncertain light.

Come, Goodman Brown!' cried his fellow traveller, 'this is a dull pace for the beginning of a journey. Take my staff, if you are so soon weary.'

Friend,' said the other, exchanging his slow pace for a full stop; 'having kept covenant by meeting thee here, it is my purpose now to return whence I came. I have scruples, touching the matter thou wot'st of.'

'Sayest thou so?' replied he of the serpent, smiling apart. 'Let us walk on, nevertheless, reasoning as we go, and if I convince thee not, thou shalt turn back. We are but a little way in the forest yet.'

'Too far, too far!' exclaimed the goodman, unconsciously resuming his walk. 'My father never went into the woods on such an errand, nor his father before him. We have been a race of honest men and good Christians, since the days of the martyrs. And shall I be the first of the name of Brown that ever took this path, and kept – '

'Such company, thou wouldst say,' observed the elder person, interpreting his pause. 'Good, Goodman Brown! I have been as well acquainted with your family as with ever; one among the Puritans; and that's no trifle to say. I helped your grandfather, the constable, when he lashed the Quaker woman so smartly through the streets of Salem. And it was I that brought your father a pitch-pine knot, kindled at my own hearth, to set fire to an Indian village in King Philip's war. They were my good friends, both; and many a pleasant walk have we had along this path, and returned merrily after midnight. I would fain be friends with you, for their sake.'

'If it be as thou sayest,' replied Goodman Brown, 'I marvel they never spoke of these matters. Or, verily, I marvel not, seeing that the least rumour of the sort would have driven them from New England. We are a people of prayer, and good works, to boot, and abide no such wickedness.'

'Wickedness or not,' said the traveller with the twisted staff, 'I have a very general acquaintance here in New England. The deacons of many a church have drunk the communion wine with me; the selectmen, of divers towns, make me their chairman; and a majority of the Great and General Court are firm supporters of my interest. The governor and I, too – but these are state secrets.'

'Can this be so!' cried Goodman Brown, with a stare of amazement at his undisturbed companion. 'Howbeit, I have nothing to do with the governor and council; they have their own ways, and are no rule for a simple husbandman, like me. But, were I to go on with thee, how should I meet the eye of that good old man, our minister, at Salem village? Oh, his voice would make me tremble, both Sabbath day and lecture day!'

Thus far the elder traveller had listened with due gravity, but now burst into a fit of irrepressible mirth, shaking himself so violently that his snake-like staff actually seemed to wriggle in sympathy.

'Ha! ha! ha!' shouted he, again and again; then, composing himself, 'Well, go on, Goodman Brown, go on; but pr'y thee, don't kill me with laughing!'

'Well, then, to end the matter at once,' said Goodman Brown, considerably nettled, 'there is my wife, Faith. It would break her dear little heart; and I'd rather break my own!'

'Nay, if that be the case,' answered the other, 'e'en go thy ways, Goodman Brown. I would not, for twenty old women like the one hobbling before us, that Faith should come to any harm.'

As he spoke, he pointed his staff at a female figure on the path, in whom Goodman Brown recognised a very pious exemplary dame, who had taught him his catechism, in youth, and was still his moral and spiritual adviser, jointly with the minister and Deacon Gookin.

'A marvel, truly, that Goody Cloyse should be so far in the wilderness, at nightfall!' said he. 'But, with your leave, friend, I shall take a cut through the woods, until we have left this Christian woman behind. Being a stranger to you, she might ask whom I was consorting with, and whither I was going.'

'Be it so,' said his fellow traveller. 'Betake you to the woods, and let me keep the path.'

Accordingly, the young man turned aside, but took care to watch his companion, who advanced softly along the road, until he had come within a staff's length of the old dame. She, meanwhile, was making the best of her way, with singular speed for so aged a woman, and mumbling some indistinct words, a prayer, doubtless, as she went. The traveller put forth his staff, and touched her withered neck with what seemed the serpent's tail.

'The devil!' screamed the pious old lady.

'Then Goody Cloyse knows her old friend?' observed the traveller, confronting her, and leaning on his writhing stick.

'Ah, forsooth, and is it your worship, indeed?' cried the good dame. 'Yea, truly is it, and in the very image of my old gossip, Goodman Brown, the grandfather of the silly fellow that now is. But, would your worship believe it? My broomstick hath strangely disappeared, stolen, as I suspect, by that unhanged witch, Goody Cory, and that, too, when I was all anointed with the juice of smallage and cinquefoil and wolfsbane' –

'Mingled with fine wheat and the fat of a newborn babe,' said the shape of old Goodman Brown.

'Ah, your worship knows the receipt,' cried the old lady, cackling aloud. 'So, as I was saying, being all ready for the meeting, and no horse to ride on, I made up my mind to foot it; for they tell me, there is a nice young man to be taken into communion tonight. But now your good worship will lend me your arm, and we shall be there in a twinkling.'

'That can hardly be,' answered her friend. 'I may not spare you my arm, Goody Cloyse, but here is my staff, if you will.'

So saying, he threw it down at her feet, where, perhaps, it assumed life, being one of the rods which its owner had formerly lent to the Egyptian Magi. Of this fact, however, Goodman Brown could not take cognisance. He had cast up his eyes in astonishment, and looking down again, beheld neither Goody Cloyse nor the serpentine staff, but his fellow traveller alone, who waited for him as calmly as if nothing had happened.

'That old woman taught me my catechism!' said the young man; and there was a world of meaning in this simple comment.

They continued to walk onward, while the elder traveller exhorted his companion to make good speed and persevere in the path, discoursing so aptly that his arguments seemed rather to spring up in the bosom of his auditor than to be suggested by himself. As they went, he plucked a branch of maple, to serve for a walking stick, and began to strip it of the twigs and little boughs, which were wet with evening dew. The moment his fingers touched them, they became strangely withered and dried up, as with a week's sunshine. Thus the pair proceeded, at a good free pace, until suddenly, in a gloomy hollow of the road, Goodman Brown sat himself down on the stump of a tree, and refused to go any farther.

'Friend,' said he, stubbornly, 'my mind is made up. Not another step will I budge on this errand. What if a wretched old woman do choose to go to the devil, when I thought she was going to heaven! Is that any reason why I should quit my dear Faith, and go after her?'

'You will think better of this, by and by,' said his acquaintance, composedly. 'Sit here and rest yourself awhile; and when you feel like moving again, there is my staff to help you along.'

Without more words, he threw his companion the maple stick, and was as speedily out of sight as if he had vanished into the deepening gloom. The young man sat a few moments, by the roadside, applauding himself greatly, and thinking with how clear a conscience he should meet the minister, in his morning walk, nor shrink from the eye of good old Deacon Gookin. And what calm sleep would be his, that very night, which was to have been spent so wickedly, but purely and sweetly now, in the arms of Faith! Amidst these pleasant and praiseworthy meditations, Goodman Brown heard the tramp of horses along the road, and deemed it advisable to conceal himself within the verge of the forest, conscious of the guilty purpose that had brought him thither, though now so happily turned from it.

On came the hoof tramps and the voices of the riders, two grave old voices, conversing soberly as they drew near. These mingled sounds appeared to pass along the road, within a few yards of the young man's hiding place; but owing, doubtless, to the depth of the gloom at that particular spot, neither the travellers nor their steeds were visible. Though their figures brushed the small boughs by the wayside, it could not be seen that they intercepted, even for a moment, the faint gleam from the strip of bright sky, athwart which they must have passed. Goodman Brown alternately crouched and stood on tiptoe, pulling aside the branches and thrusting forth his head as far as he durst, without discerning so much as a shadow. It vexed him the more because he could have sworn, were such a thing possible, that he recognised the voices of the minister and Deacon Gookin, jogging along quietly, as they were wont to do when bound to some ordination or ecclesiastical council. While yet within hearing, one of the riders stopped to pluck a switch.

'Of the two, reverend sir,' said the voice like the deacon's, 'I had rather miss an ordination dinner than tonight's meeting. They tell me that some of our community are to be here from Falmouth and beyond, and others from Connecticut and Rhode Island; besides several of the Indian powows, who, after their fashion, know almost as much deviltry as the best of us. Moreover, there is a goodly young woman to be taken into communion.'

'Mighty well, Deacon Gookin!' replied the solemn old tones of the minister. 'Spur up, or we shall be late. Nothing can be done, you know, until I get on the ground.'

The hoofs clattered again, and the voices, talking so strangely in the empty air, passed on through the forest, where no church had ever been gathered, nor solitary Christian prayed. Whither, then, could these holy men be journeying, so deep into the heathen wilderness? Young Goodman Brown caught hold of a tree for support, being ready to sink down on the ground, faint and overburdened with the heavy sickness of his heart. He looked up to the sky, doubting whether there really was a heaven above him. Yet there was the blue arch and the stars brightening in it.

'With heaven above, and Faith below, I will yet stand firm against the devil!' cried Goodman Brown.

While he still gazed upward, into the deep arch of the firmament, and had lifted his hands to pray, a cloud, though no wind was stirring, hurried across the zenith, and hid the brightening stars. The blue sky was still visible, except directly overhead, where this black mass of cloud was sweeping swiftly northward. Aloft in the air, as if from the depths of the cloud, came a confused and doubtful sound of voices. Once, the listener fancied that he could distinguish the accents of townspeople of his own, men and women, both pious and ungodly, many of whom he had met at the communion table, and others he had seen rioting at the tavern. The next moment, so indistinct were the sounds, he doubted whether he had heard aught but the murmur of the old forest, whispering without a wind. Then came a stronger swell of those familiar tones, heard daily in the sunshine, at Salem village, but never, until now, from a cloud of night. There was one voice, of a young woman, uttering lamentations, yet with an uncertain sorrow, and entreating for some favour, which, perhaps, it would grieve her to obtain. And all the unseen multitude, both saints and sinners, seemed to encourage her onward.

'Faith!' shouted Goodman Brown, in a voice of agony and desperation; and the echoes of the forest mocked him, crying – 'Faith! Faith!' as if bewildered wretches were seeking her, all through the wilderness.

The cry of grief, rage and terror was yet piercing the night when the unhappy husband held his breath for a response. There was a scream, drowned immediately in a louder murmur of voices, fading into far-off laughter, as the dark cloud swept away, leaving the clear and silent sky above Goodman Brown. But something fluttered lightly down through the air, and caught on the branch of a tree. The young man seized it, and beheld a pink ribbon.

'My Faith is gone!' cried he, after one stupefied moment. 'There is no good on earth; and sin is but a name. Come, devil! for to thee is this world given.'

And maddened with despair, so that he laughed loud and long, did Goodman Brown grasp his staff and set forth again, at such a rate that he seemed to fly along the forest path rather than to walk or run. The road grew wilder and drearier and more faintly traced, and vanished at length, leaving him in the heart of the dark wilderness, still rushing onward, with the instinct that guides mortal man to evil. The whole forest was peopled with frightful sounds; the creaking of the trees, the howling of wild beasts and the yell of Indians; while sometimes the wind tolled like a distant church bell, and sometimes gave a broad roar around the traveller, as if all nature were laughing him to scorn. But he was himself the chief horror of the scene, and shrank not from its other horrors.

'Ha! ha! ha!'roared Goodman Brown, when the wind laughed at him. 'Let us hear which will laugh loudest! Think not to frighten me with your deviltry! Come witch, come wizard, come Indian powow, come devil himself! and here comes Goodman Brown. You may as well fear him as he fear you!'

In truth, all through the haunted forest, there could be nothing more frightful than the figure of Goodman Brown. On he flew, among the black pines, brandishing his staff with frenzied gestures, now giving vent to an inspiration of horrid blasphemy, and now shouting forth such laughter as set all the echoes of the forest laughing like demons around him. The fiend in his own shape is less hideous than when he rages in the breast of man. Thus sped the demoniac on his course, until, quivering among the trees, he saw a red light before him, as when the felled trunks and branches of a clearing have been set on fire and throw up their lurid blaze against the sky at the hour of midnight. He paused, in a lull of the tempest that had driven him onward, and heard the swell of what seemed a hymn, rolling solemnly from a distance, with the weight of many voices. He knew the tune; it was a familiar one in the choir of the village meeting-house. The verse died heavily away, and was lengthened by a chorus, not of human voices, but of all the sounds of the benighted wilderness, pealing in awful harmony together. Goodman Brown cried out, and his cry was lost to his own ear by its unison with the cry of the desert,

In the interval of silence, he stole forward, until the light glared full upon his eyes. At one extremity of an open space, hemmed in by the dark wall of the forest, arose a rock, bearing some rude, natural resemblance either to an altar or a pulpit, and surrounded by four blazing pines, their tops aflame, their stems untouched, like candles at an evening meeting. The mass of foliage that had overgrown the summit of the rock was all on fire, blazing high into the night, and fitfully illuminating the whole field. Each pendent twig and leafy festoon was in a blaze. As the red light arose and fell, a numerous congregation alternately shone forth, then disappeared in shadow, and again grew, as it were, out of the darkness, peopling the heart of the solitary woods at once.

'A grave and dark-clad company!' quoth Goodman Brown.

In truth, they were such. Among them, quivering to and fro between gloom and splendour, appeared faces that would be seen, next day, at the council board of the province, and others which, Sabbath after Sabbath, looked devoutly heavenward, and benignantly over the crowded pews, from the holiest pulpits in the land. Some affirm that the lady of the governor was there. At least, there were high dames well known to her, and wives of honoured husbands, and widows, a great multitude, and ancient maidens, all of excellent repute, and fair young girls, who trembled lest their mothers should espy them. Either the sudden gleams of light, flashing over the obscure field, bedazzled Goodman Brown, or he recognised a score of the church members of Salem village, famous for their especial sanctity. Good old Deacon Gookin had arrived, and waited at the skirts of that venerable saint, his revered pastor. But, irreverently consorting with these grave, reputable and pious people, these elders of the church, these chaste dames and dewy virgins, there were men of dissolute lives and women of spotted fame, wretches given over to all mean and filthy vice, and suspected even of horrid crimes. It was strange to see that the good shrank not from the wicked, nor were the sinners abashed by the saints. Scattered, also, among their pale-faced enemies, were the Indian priests, or powows, who had often scared their native forest with more hideous incantations than any known to English witchcraft.

'But, where is Faith?' thought Goodman Brown; and, as hope came into his heart, he trembled.

Another verse of the hymn arose, a slow and solemn strain, such as the pious love, but joined to words which expressed all that our nature can conceive of sin, and darkly hinted at far more. Unfathomable to mere mortals is the lore of fiends. Verse after verse was sung, and still the chorus of the desert swelled between, like the deepest tone of a mighty organ. And, with the final peal of that dreadful anthem, there came a sound, as if the roaring wind, the rushing streams, the howling beasts and every other voice of the unconverted wilderness were mingling and according with the voice of guilty man, in homage to the prince of all. The four blazing pines threw up a loftier flame and obscurely discovered shapes and visages of horror on the smoke wreaths above the impious assembly. At the same moment, the fire on the rock shot redly forth, and formed a glowing arch above its base, where now appeared a figure. With reverence be it spoken, the apparition bore no slight similitude, both in garb and manner, to some grave divine of the New England churches.

'Bring forth the converts!' cried a voice that echoed through the field and rolled into the forest.

At the word, Goodman Brown stepped forth from the shadow of the trees, and approached the congregation, with whom he felt a loathful brother-hood, by the sympathy of all that was wicked in his heart. He could have well nigh sworn that the shape of his own dead father beckoned him to advance, looking downward from a smoke wreath, while a woman, with dim features of despair, threw out her hand to warn him back. Was it his mother? But he had no power to retreat one step, nor to resist, even in thought, when the minister and good old Deacon Gookin seized his arms and led him to the blazing rock. Thither came also the slender form of a veiled female, led between Goody Cloyse, that pious teacher of the catechism, and Martha Carrier, who had received the devil's promise to be queen of hell. A rampant hag was she! And there stood the proselytes, beneath the canopy of fire.

'Welcome, my children,' said the dark figure, 'to the communion of your grave! Ye have found, thus young, your nature and your destiny. My children, look behind you!'

They turned; and flashing forth, as it were, in a sheet of flame, the fiend worshippers were seen; the smile of welcome gleamed darkly on every visage.

'There,' resumed the sable form, 'are all whom ye have reverenced from youth. Ye deemed them holier than yourselves, and shrank from your own sin, contrasting it with their lives of righteousness and prayerful aspirations heavenward. Yet here are they all in my worshipping assembly! This night it shall be granted you to know their secret deeds: how hoary bearded elders of the church have whispered wanton words to the young maids of their households; how many a woman, eager for widow's weeds, has given her husband a drink at bedtime, and let him sleep his last sleep in her bosom; how beardless youths have made haste to inherit their fathers' wealth; and how fair damsels – blush not, sweet ones! – have dug little graves in the garden, and bidden me, the sole guest, to an infant's funeral. By the sympathy of your human hearts for sin, ye shall scent out all the places – whether in church, bedchamber, street, field or forest – where crime has been committed, and shall exult to behold the whole earth one stain of guilt, one mighty bloodspot. Far more than this! It shall be yours to penetrate, in every bosom, the deep mystery of sin, the fountain of all wicked arts, which inexhaustibly supplies more evil impulses than human power – than my power, at its utmost! – can make manifest in deeds. And now, my children, look upon each other.'

They did so; and, by the blaze of the hell-kindled torches, the wretched man beheld his Faith, and the wife her husband, trembling before that unhallowed altar.

'Lo! there ye stand, my children,' said the figure, in deep and solemn tone, almost sad, with its despairing awfulness, as if his once angelic nature could yet mourn for our miserable race. 'Depending upon one another's hearts, ye had still hoped that virtue were not all a dream. Now are ye undeceived! Evil is the nature of mankind. Evil must be your only happiness. Welcome, again, my children, to the communion of your race!'

'Welcome!' repeated the fiend worshippers, in one cry of despair and triumph.

And there they stood, the only pair, as it seemed, who were yet hesitating on the verge of wickedness, in this dark world. A basin was hollowed, naturally, in the rock. Did it contain water, reddened by the lurid light? or was it blood? or, perchance, a liquid flame? Herein did the Shape of Evil dip his hand and prepare to lay the mark of baptism upon their foreheads, that they might be partakers of the mystery of sin, more conscious of the secret guilt of others, both in deed and thought, than they could now be of their own. The husband cast one look at his pale wife, and Faith at him. What polluted wretches would the next glance show them to each other, shuddering alike at what they disclosed and what they saw?

'Faith! Faith!' cried the husband. 'Look up to heaven, and resist the Wicked One!'

Whether Faith obeyed, he knew not. Hardly had he spoken than he found himself amid calm night and solitude, listening to a roar of the wind, which died heavily away through the forest. He staggered against the rock and felt it chill and damp, while a hanging twig, that had been all on fire, besprinkled his cheek with the coldest dew.

The next morning, young Goodman Brown came slowly into the street of Salem village, staring around him like a bewildered man. The good old minister was taking a walk along the graveyard, to get an appetite for breakfast and meditate his sermon, and bestowed a blessing, as he passed, on Goodman Brown. He shrank from the venerable saint, as if to avoid an anathema. Old Deacon Gookin was at domestic worship, and the holy words of his prayer were heard through the open window. 'What god doth the wizard pray to?' quoth Goodman Brown. Goody Cloyse, that excellent old Christian, stood in the early sunshine, at her own lattice, catechising a little girl, who had brought her a pint of morning's milk. Goodman Brown snatched away the child, as from the grasp of the fiend himself. Turning the corner by the meeting house, he spied the head of Faith, with the pink ribbons, gazing anxiously forth, and bursting into such joy at sight of him that she skipped along the street, and almost kissed her husband before the whole village. But Goodman Brown looked sternly and sadly into her face and passed on without a greeting.

Had Goodman Brown fallen asleep in the forest, and only dreamed a wild dream of a witch meeting?

Be it so, if you will. But, alas! it was a dream of evil omen for young Goodman Brown. A stern, a sad, a darkly meditative, a distrustful, if not a desperate man, did he become from the night of that fearful dream. On the Sabbath day, when the congregation were singing a holy psalm, he could not listen, because an anthem of sin rushed loudly upon his ear and drowned all the blessed strain. When the minister spoke from the pulpit, with power and fervid eloquence and with his hand on the open Bible, of the sacred truths of our religion, and of saintlike lives and triumphant deaths, and of future bliss or misery unutterable, then did Goodman Brown turn pale, dreading lest the roof should thunder down upon the grey blasphemer and his hearers. Often, awaking suddenly at midnight, he shrank from the bosom of Faith, and at morning or eventide, when the family knelt down at prayer, he scowled, and muttered to himself, and gazed sternly at his wife, and turned away. And when he had lived long, and was borne to his grave, a hoary corpse, followed by Faith, an aged woman, and children and grandchildren, a goodly procession – besides neighbours, not a few – they carved no hopeful verse upon his tombstone; for his dying hour was gloom.

The Black Cat

EDGAR ALLAN POE

FOR THE MOST WILD yet most homely narrative which I am about to pen, I neither expect nor solicit belief. Mad indeed would I be to expect it, in a case where my very senses reject their own evidence. Yet, mad am I not – and very surely do I not dream. But tomorrow I die, and today I would unburden my soul. My immediate purpose is to place before the world, plainly, succinctly, and without comment, a series of mere household events. In their consequences, these events have terrified – have tortured – have destroyed me. Yet I will not attempt to expound them. To me, they have presented little but horror – to many they will seem less terrible than *baroques*. Hereafter, perhaps, some intellect may be found which will reduce my phantasm to the commonplace – some intellect more calm, more logical, and far less excitable than my own, which will perceive, in the circumstances I detail with awe, nothing more than an ordinary succession of very natural causes and effects.

From my infancy I was noted for the docility and humanity of my disposition. My tenderness of heart was even so conspicuous as to make me the jest of my companions. I was especially fond of animals, and was indulged by my parents with a great variety of pets. With these I spent most of my time, and never was so happy as when feeding and caressing them. This peculiarity of character grew with my growth, and, in my manhood, I derived from it one of my principal sources of pleasure. To those who have cherished an affection for a faithful and sagacious dog, I need hardly be at the trouble of explaining the nature or the intensity of the gratification thus derivable. There is something in the unselfish and self-sacrificing love of a brute which goes directly to the heart of him who has had frequent occasion to test the paltry friendship and gossamer fidelity of mere *man*.

I married early, and was happy to find in my wife a disposition not uncongenial with my own. Observing my partiality for domestic pets, she lost no opportunity of procuring those of the most agreeable kind. We had birds, goldfish, a fine dog, rabbits, a small monkey and *a cat*.

This latter was a remarkably large and beautiful animal, entirely black, and sagacious to an astonishing degree. In speaking of his intelligence, my wife, who at heart was not a little tinctured with superstition, made frequent allusion to the ancient popular notion which regarded all black cats as witches in disguise. Not that she was ever *serious* upon this point – and I mention the matter at all for no better reason than that it happens, just now, to be remembered.

Pluto – this was the cat's name – was my favourite pet and playmate. I alone fed him, and he attended me wherever I went about the house. It was even with difficulty that I could prevent him from following me through the streets.

Our friendship lasted, in this manner, for several years, during which my general temperament and character – through the instrumentality of the fiend Intemperance – had (I blush to confess it) experienced a radical alteration for the worse. I grew, day by day, more moody, more irritable, more regardless of the feelings of others. I suffered myself to use intemperate language to my wife. At length, I even offered her personal violence. My pets, of course, were made to feel the change in my disposition. I not only neglected, but ill-used them. For Pluto, however, I still retained sufficient regard to restrain me from maltreating him, as I made no scruple of maltreating the rabbits, the monkey, or even the dog, when by accident, or through affection, they came in my way. But my disease grew upon me – for what disease is like alcohol? – and at length even Pluto, who was now becoming old, and consequently somewhat peevish – even Pluto began to experience the effects of my ill temper.

One night, returning home, much intoxicated, from one of my haunts about town, I fancied that the cat avoided my presence. I seized him; when, in his fright at my violence, he inflicted a slight wound upon my hand with his teeth. The fury of a demon instantly possessed me. I knew myself no longer. My original soul seemed, at once, to take its flight from my body; and a more than fiendish malevolence, gin-nurtured, thrilled every fibre of my frame. I took from my waistcoat pocket a penknife, opened it, grasped the poor beast by the throat, and deliberately cut one of its eyes from the socket! I blush, I burn, I shudder, while I pen the damnable atrocity.

When reason returned with the morning – when I had slept off the fumes of the night's debauch – I experienced a sentiment half of horror, half of remorse, for the crime of which I had been guilty; but it was, at best, a feeble and equivocal feeling, and the soul remained untouched. I again plunged into excess, and soon drowned in wine all memory of the deed.

In the meantime the cat slowly recovered. The socket of the lost eye presented, it is true, a frightful appearance, but he no longer appeared to suffer any pain. He went about the house as usual, but, as might be expected, fled in extreme terror at my approach. I had so much of my old heart left, as to be at first grieved by this evident dislike on the part of a creature which had once so loved me. But this feeling soon gave place to irritation. And then came, as if to my final and irrevocable overthrow, the spirit of PERVERSENESS. Of this spirit philosophy takes no account. Yet I am not more sure that my soul lives, than I am that perverseness is one of the primitive impulses of the human heart – one of the indivisible primary faculties, or sentiments, which give direction to the character of man. Who has not, a hundred times, found himself committing a vile or a silly action, for no other reason than because he knows he should *not*? Have we not a perpetual inclination, in the teeth of our best judgement, to violate that which is *law*, merely because we understand it to be such? This spirit of perverseness, I say, came to my final overthrow. It was this unfathomable longing of the soul to *vex itself* – to offer violence to its own nature – to do wrong for the wrong's sake only – that urged me to continue and finally to consummate the injury I had inflicted upon the unoffending brute. One morning, in cool blood, I slipped a noose about its neck and hung it to the limb of a tree – hung it with the tears streaming from my eyes, and with the bitterest remorse at my heart – hung it *because* I knew that it had loved me, and *because* I felt it had given me no reason of offence – hung it *because* I knew that in so doing I was committing a sin – a deadly sin that would so jeopardise my immortal soul as to place it – if such a thing were possible – even beyond the reach of the infinite mercy of the Most Merciful and Most Terrible God.

On the night of the day on which this cruel deed was done, I was aroused from sleep by the cry of 'Fire!' The curtains of my bed were in flames. The whole house was blazing. It was with great difficulty that my wife, a servant, and myself, made our escape from the conflagration. The destruction was complete. My entire worldly wealth was swallowed up, and I resigned myself thenceforward to despair.

I am above the weakness of seeking to establish a sequence of cause and effect between the disaster and the atrocity. But I am detailing a chain of facts, and wish not to leave even a possible link imperfect. On the day succeeding the fire, I visited the ruins. The walls, with one exception, had fallen in. This exception was found in a compartment wall, not very thick, which stood about the middle of the house, and against which had rested the head of my bed. The plastering had here, in great measure, resisted the action of the fire – a fact which I attributed to its having been recently spread. About this wall a dense crowd were collected, and many persons seemed to be examining a particular portion of it with very minute and eager attention. The words 'strange!' 'singular!' and other similar expressions excited my curiosity. I approached and saw, as if graven in bas-relief upon the white surface, the figure of a gigantic *cat*. The impression was given with an accuracy truly marvellous. There was a rope about the animal's neck.

When I first beheld this apparition – for I could scarcely regard it as less – my wonder and my terror were extreme. But at length reflection came to my aid. The cat, I remembered, had been hung in a garden adjacent to the house. Upon the alarm of fire, this garden had been immediately filled by the crowd – by some one of whom the animal must have been cut from the tree and thrown, through an open window, into my chamber. This had probably been done with the view of arousing me from sleep. The falling of other walls had compressed the victim of my cruelty into the substance of the freshly-spread plaster; the lime of which, with the flames and the ammonia from the carcass, had then accomplished the portraiture as I saw it.

Although I thus readily accounted to my reason, if not altogether to my conscience, for the startling fact just detailed, it did not the less fail to make a deep impression upon my fancy. For months I could not rid myself of the phantasm of the cat; and, during this period, there came back into my spirit a half-sentiment that seemed, but was not, remorse. I went so far as to regret the loss of the animal, and to look about me, among the vile haunts which I now habitually frequented, for another pet of the same species, and of somewhat similar appearance, with which to supply its place.

One night as I sat, half stupefied, in a den of more than infamy, my attention was suddenly drawn to some black object, reposing upon the head of one of the immense hogsheads of gin, or of rum, which constituted the chief furniture of the apartment. I had been looking steadily at the top of this hogshead for some minutes, and what now caused me surprise was the fact that I had not sooner perceived the object thereupon. I approached it, and touched it with my hand. It was a black cat – a very large one – fully as large as Pluto, and closely resembling him in every respect but one. Pluto had not a white hair upon any portion of his body; but this cat had a large, although indefinite, splotch of white, covering nearly the whole region of the breast.

Upon my touching him, he immediately arose, purred loudly, rubbed against my hand, and appeared delighted with my notice. This, then, was the very creature of which I was in search. I at once offered to purchase it of the landlord; but this person made no claim to it – knew nothing of it – had never seen it before.

I continued my caresses, and when I prepared to go home, the animal evinced a disposition to accompany me. I permitted it to do so; occasionally stooping and patting it as I proceeded. When it reached the house it domesticated itself at once, and became immediately a great favourite with my wife.

For my own part, I soon found a dislike to it arising within me. This was just the reverse of what I had anticipated; but – I know not how or why it was – its evident fondness for myself rather disgusted and annoyed me. By slow degrees, these feelings of disgust and annoyance rose into the bitter-ness of hatred. I avoided the creature; a certain sense of shame, and the remembrance of my former deed of cruelty, preventing me from physically abusing it. I did not, for some weeks, strike or otherwise violently ill-use it; but gradually – very gradually – I came to look upon it with unutterable loathing, and to flee silently from its odious presence, as from the breath of a pestilence.

What added, no doubt, to my hatred of the beast, was the discovery, on the morning after I brought it home, that, like Pluto, it also had been deprived of one of its eyes. This circumstance, however, only endeared it to my wife, who, as I have already said, possessed, in a high degree, that humanity of feeling which had once been my distinguishing trait, and the source of many of my simplest and purest pleasures.

With my aversion to this cat, however, its partiality for myself seemed to increase. It followed my footsteps with a pertinacity which it would be difficult to make the reader comprehend. Whenever I sat, it would crouch beneath my chair, or spring upon my knees, covering me with its loathsome caresses. If I arose to walk, it would get between my feet, and thus nearly throw me down, or, fastening its long and sharp claws in my dress, clamber, in this manner, to my breast. At such times, although I longed to destroy it with a blow, I was yet withheld from so doing, partly by a memory of my former crime, but chiefly – let me confess it at once – by absolute *dread* of the beast.

This dread was not exactly a dread of physical evil – and yet I should be at a loss how otherwise to define it. I am almost ashamed to own – yes, even in this felon's cell, I am almost ashamed to own – that the terror and horror with which the animal inspired me had been heightened by one of the merest chimeras it would be possible to conceive. My wife had called my attention, more than once, to the character of the mark of white hair of which I have spoken, and which constituted the sole visible difference between the strange beast and the one I had destroyed. The reader will remember that this mark, although large, had been originally very indefinite; but, by slow degrees – degrees nearly imperceptible, and which for a long time my reason struggled to reject as fanciful – it had, at length, assumed a rigorous distinctness of outline. It was now the representation of an object that I shudder to name – and for this, above all, I loathed and dreaded and would have rid myself of the monster *had I dared* – it was now, I say, the image of a hideous – of a ghastly thing – of the GALLOWS! – oh, mournful and terrible engine of horror and of crime – of agony and of death!

And now was I indeed wretched beyond the wretchedness of mere humanity. And *a brute beast* – whose fellow I had contemptuously destroyed – *a brute beast* to work out for *me* – for me, a man, fashioned in the image of the High God – so much of insufferable woe! Alas! neither by day nor by night knew I the blessing of rest any more! During the former the creature left me no moment alone; and, in the latter, I started, hourly, from dreams of unutterable fear, to find the hot breath of *the thing* upon my face, and its vast weight – an incarnate nightmare that I had no power to shake off – incumbent eternally upon my *heart*!

Beneath the pressure of torments such as these, the feeble remnant of the good within me succumbed. Evil thoughts became my sole intimates – the darkest and most evil of thoughts. The moodiness of my usual temper increased to hatred of all things and of all mankind; while, from the sudden, frequent and ungovernable outbursts of a fury to which I now blindly abandoned myself, my uncomplaining wife, alas! was the most usual and the most patient of sufferers.

One day she accompanied me, upon some household errand, into the cellar of the old building which our poverty compelled us to inhabit. The cat followed me down the steep stairs, and, nearly throwing me headlong, exasperated me to madness. Uplifting an axe, and forgetting, in my wrath, the childish dread which had hitherto stayed my hand, I aimed a blow at the animal which, of course, would have proved instantly fatal had it descended as I wished. But this blow was arrested by the hand of my wife. Goaded, by the interference, into a rage more than demoniacal, I withdrew my arm from her grasp and buried the axe in her brain. She fell dead upon the spot, without a groan.

This hideous murder accomplished, I set myself forthwith, and with entire deliberation, to the task of concealing the body. I knew that I could not remove it from the house, either by day or by night, without the risk of being observed by the neighbours. Many projects entered my mind. At one period I thought of cutting the corpse into minute fragments and destroying them by fire. At another, I resolved to dig a grave for it in the floor of the cellar. Again, I deliberated about casting it into the well in the yard – about packing it in a box, as if merchandise, with the usual arrangements, and so getting a porter to take it from the house. Finally I hit upon what I considered a far better expedient than either of these. I determined to wall it up in the cellar – as the monks of the Middle Ages are recorded to have walled up their victims.

For a purpose such as this the cellar was well adapted. Its walls were loosely constructed, and had lately been plastered throughout with a rough plaster, which the dampness of the atmosphere had prevented from hardening. Moreover, in one of the walls was a projection, caused by a false chimney, or fireplace, that had been filled up, and made to resemble the rest of the cellar. I made no doubt that I could readily displace the bricks at this point, insert the corpse, and wall the whole up as before, so that no eye could detect anything suspicious.

And in this calculation I was not deceived. By means of a crowbar I easily dislodged the bricks, and, having carefully deposited the body against the inner wall, I propped it in that position, while, with little trouble, I relaid the whole structure as it originally stood. Having procured mortar, sand and hair, with every possible precaution, I prepared a plaster which could not be distinguished from the old, and with this I very carefully went over the new brickwork. When I had finished, I felt satisfied that all was right. The wall did not present the slightest appearance of having been disturbed. The rubbish on the floor was picked up with the minutest care. I looked around triumphantly, and said to myself, 'Here at least, then, my labour has not been in vain.'

My next step was to look for the beast which had been the cause of so much wretchedness; for I had, at length, firmly resolved to put it to death. Had I been able to meet with it, at the moment, there could have been no doubt of its fate; but it appeared that the crafty animal had been alarmed at the violence of my previous anger, and forebore to present itself in my present mood. It is impossible to describe, or to imagine, the deep, the blissful sense of relief which the absence of the detested creature occasioned in my bosom. It did not make its appearance during the night – and thus for one night at least, since its introduction into the house, I soundly and tranquilly slept; aye, *slept* even with the burden of murder upon my soul!

The second and the third day passed, and still my tormentor came not. Once again I breathed as a free man. The monster, in terror, had fled the premises for ever! I should behold it no more! My happiness was supreme! The guilt of my dark deed disturbed me but little. Some few enquiries had been made, but these had been readily answered. Even a search had been instituted – but of course nothing was to be discovered. I looked upon my future felicity as secured.

Upon the fourth day of the assassination, a party of the police came, very unexpectedly, into the house, and proceeded again to make rigorous investigation of the premises. Secure, however, in the inscrutability of my place of concealment, I felt no embarrassment whatever. The officers bade me accompany them in their search. They left no nook or corner unexplored. At length, for the third or fourth time, they descended into the cellar. I quivered not in a muscle. My heart beat calmly, as that of one who slumbers in innocence. I walked the cellar from end to end. I folded my arms upon my bosom, and roamed easily to and fro. The police were thoroughly satisfied and prepared to depart. The glee at my heart was too strong to be restrained. I burned to say if but one word, by way of triumph, and to render doubly sure their assurance of my guiltlessness.

'Gentlemen,' I said at last, as the party ascended the steps, 'I delight to have allayed your suspicions. I wish you all health and a little more courtesy. By the by, gentlemen, this – this is a very well-constructed house.' (In the rabid desire to say something easily, I scarcely knew what I uttered at all.) 'I may say an *excellently* well-constructed house. These walls – are you going, gentlemen? – these walls are solidly put together' – and here, through the mere frenzy of bravado, I rapped heavily, with a cane which I held in my hand, upon that very portion of the brickwork behind which stood the corpse of the wife of my bosom.

But may God shield and deliver me from the fangs of the Arch-Fiend! No sooner had the reverberation of my blows sunk into silence, than I was answered by a voice from within the tomb! – by a cry, at first muffled and broken, like the sobbing of a child, and then quickly swelling into one long, loud and continuous scream, utterly anomalous and inhuman – a howl – a wailing shriek, half of horror and half of triumph, such as might have arisen only out of hell, conjointly from the throats of the damned in their agony and of the demons that exult in the damnation.

Of my own thoughts it is folly to speak. Swooning, I staggered to the opposite wall. For one instant the party upon the stairs remained motionless, through extremity of terror and of awe. In the next, a dozen stout arms were toiling at the wall. It fell bodily. The corpse, already greatly decayed and clotted with gore, stood erect before the eyes of the spectators. Upon its head, with red extended mouth and solitary eye of fire, sat the hideous beast whose craft had seduced me into murder, and whose informing voice had consigned me to the hangman. I had walled the monster up within the tomb!

The Signalman

CHARLES DICKENS

'Halloa! Below there!'

When he heard a voice thus calling to him, he was standing at the door of his box, with a flag in his hand, furled round its short pole. One would have thought, considering the nature of the ground, that he could not have doubted from what quarter the voice came; but instead of looking up to where I stood on the top of the steep cutting nearly over his head, he turned himself about, and looked down the line. There was something remarkable in his manner of doing so, though I could not have said for my life what. But I know it was remarkable enough to attract my notice, even though his figure was foreshortened and shadowed, down in the deep trench, and mine was high above him, so steeped in the glow of an angry sunset that I had shaded my eyes with my hand before I saw him at all.

'Halloa! Below!'

From looking down the line, he turned himself about again, and raising his eyes, saw my figure high above him.

'Is there any path by which I can come down and speak to you?'

He looked up at me without replying, and I looked down at him without pressing him too soon with a repetition of my idle question. Just then there came a vague vibration in the earth and air, quickly changing into a violent pulsation, and an oncoming rush that caused me to start back, as though it had force to draw me down. When such vapour as rose to my height from this rapid train had passed me, and was skimming away over the landscape, I looked down again, and saw him refurling the flag he had shown while the train went by.

I repeated my enquiry. After a pause, during which he seemed to regard me with fixed attention, he motioned with his rolled-up flag towards a point on my level, some two or three hundred yards distant. I called down to him, 'All right!' and made for that point. There, by dint of looking closely about me, I found a rough zigzag descending path notched out, which I followed.

The cutting was extremely deep, and unusually precipitate. It was made through a clammy stone, that became oozier and wetter as I went down. For these reasons, I found the way long enough to give me time to recall the singular air of reluctance or compulsion with which he had pointed out the path.

When I came down low enough upon the zigzag descent to see him again, I saw that he was standing between the rails on the way by which the train had lately passed, in an attitude as if he were waiting for me to appear. He had his left hand at his chin, and that left elbow rested on his right hand, crossed over his breast. His attitude was one of such expectation and watchfulness that I stopped a moment, wondering at it.

I resumed my downward way, and stepping out upon the level of the railroad, and drawing nearer to him, saw that he was a dark sallow man, with a dark beard and rather heavy eyebrows. His post was in as solitary and dismal a place as ever I saw. On either side, a dripping-wet wall of jagged stone, excluding all view but a strip of sky; the perspective one way only a crooked prolongation of this great dungeon; the shorter perspective in the other direction terminating in a gloomy red light, and the gloomier entrance to a black tunnel, in whose massive architecture there was a barbarous, depressing and forbidding air. So little sunlight ever found its way to this spot that it had an earthy, deadly smell; and so much cold wind rushed through it that it struck chill to me, as if I had left the natural world.

Before he stirred, I was near enough to him to have touched him. Not even then removing his eyes from mine, he stepped back one step, and lifted his hand.

This was a lonesome post to occupy (I said), and it had riveted my attention when I looked down from up yonder. A visitor was a rarity, I should suppose; not an unwelcome rarity, I hoped? In me, he merely saw a man who had been shut up within narrow limits all his life, and who, being at last set free, had a newly awakened interest in these great works. To such purpose I spoke to him; but I am far from sure of the terms I used; for, besides that I am not happy in opening any conversation, there was something in the man that daunted me.

He directed a most curious look towards the red light near the tunnel's mouth, and looked all about it, as if something were missing from it, and then looked at me.

That light was part of his charge? Was it not?

He answered in a low voice, 'Don't you know it is?'

The monstrous thought came into my mind, as I perused the fixed eyes and the saturnine face, that this was a spirit, not a man. I have speculated since, whether there may have been infection in his mind.

In my turn, I stepped back. But in making the action, I detected in his eyes some latent fear of me. This put the monstrous thought to flight.

'You look at me,' I said, forcing a smile, 'as if you had a dread of me.'

'I was doubtful,' he returned, 'whether I had seen you before.'

'Where?'

He pointed to the red light he had looked at.

'There?' I said.

Intently watchful of me, he replied (but without sound), 'Yes.'

'My good fellow, what should I do there? However, be that as it may, I never was there, you may swear.'

'I think I may,' he rejoined. 'Yes; I am sure I may.'

His manner cleared, like my own. He replied to my remarks with readiness, and in well-chosen words. Had he much to do there? Yes; that was to say, he had enough responsibility to bear; but exactness and watchfulness were what was required of him, and of actual work – manual labour – he had next to none. To change that signal, to trim those lights, and to turn this iron handle now and then, was all he had to do under that head. Regarding those many long and lonely hours of which I seemed to make so much, he could only say that the routine of his life had shaped itself into that form, and he had grown used to it. He had taught himself a language down here, if only to know it by sight, and to have formed his own crude ideas of its pronunciation, could be called learning it. He had also worked at fractions and decimals, and tried a little algebra; but he was, and had been as a boy, a poor hand at figures. Was it necessary for him when on duty always to remain in that channel of damp air, and could he never rise into the sunshine between those high stone walls? Why, that depended upon times and circumstances. Under some conditions there would be less upon the line than under others, and the same held good as to certain hours of the day and night. In bright weather, he did choose occasions for getting a little above these lower shadows; but, being at all times liable to be called by his electric bell, and at such times listening for it with redoubled anxiety, the relief was less than I would suppose.

He took me into his box, where there was a fire, a desk for an official book in which he had to make certain entries, a telegraphic instrument with its dial, face and needles, and the little bell of which he had spoken. On my trusting that he would excuse the remark that he had been well educated, and (I hoped I might say without offence) perhaps educated above that station, he observed that instances of slight incongruity in such wise would rarely be found wanting among large bodies of men; that he had heard it was so in workhouses, in the police force, even in that last desperate resource, the army; and that he knew it was so, more or less, in any great railway staff. He had been, when young (if I could believe it, sitting in that hut – he scarcely could), a student of natural philosophy, and had attended lectures; but he had run wild, misused his opportunities, gone down and never risen again. He had no complaint to offer about that. He had made his bed, and he lay upon it. It was far too late to make another.

All that I have here condensed he said in a quiet manner, with his grave dark regards divided between me and the fire. He threw in the word 'sir' from time to time, and especially when he referred to his youth, as though to request me to understand that he claimed to be nothing but what I found him. He was several times interrupted by the little bell, and had to read off messages, and send replies. Once he had to stand without the door, and display a flag as a train passed, and make some verbal communication to the driver. In the discharge of his duties, I observed him to be remarkably exact and vigilant, breaking off his discourse at a syllable, and remaining silent until what he had to do was done.

In a word, I should have set this man down as one of the safest of men to be employed in that capacity, but for the circumstance that while he was speaking to me he twice broke off with a fallen colour, turned his face towards the little bell when it did not ring, opened the door of the hut (which was kept shut to exclude the unhealthy damp), and looked out towards the red light near the mouth of the tunnel. On both of those occasions, he came back to the fire with the inexplicable air upon him which I had remarked, without being able to define, when we were so far asunder.

Said I, when I rose to leave him, 'You almost make me think that I have met with a contented man.'

(I am afraid I must acknowledge that I said it to lead him on.)

'I believe I used to be so,' he rejoined, in the low voice in which he had first spoken; 'but I am troubled, sir, I am troubled.'

He would have recalled the words if he could. He had said them, however, and I took them up quickly.

'With what? What is your trouble?'

'It is very difficult to impart, sir. It is very, very difficult to speak of. If ever you make me another visit, I will try to tell you.'

'But I expressly intend to make you another visit. Say, when shall it be?'

'I go off early in the morning, and I shall be on again at ten tomorrow night, sir.'

'I will come at eleven.'

He thanked me, and went out at the door with me. 'I'll show my white light, sir,' he said, in his peculiar low voice, ''till you have found the way up. When you have found it, don't call out! And when you are at the top, don't call out!'

His manner seemed to make the place strike colder to me, but I said no more than, 'Very well.'

'And when you come down tomorrow night, don't call out! Let me ask you a parting question. What made you cry, "Halloa! Below there!" tonight?'

'Heaven knows,' said I. 'I cried something to that effect – '

'Not to that effect, sir. Those were the very words. I know them well.'

'I admit those were the very words. I said them, no doubt, because I saw you below.'

'For no other reason?'

'What other reason could I possibly have?'

'You had no feeling that they were conveyed to you in any supernatural way?'

'No.'

He wished me good-night, and held up his light. I walked by the side of the down line of rails (with a very disagreeable sensation of a train coming behind me) until I found the path. It was easier to mount than to descend, and I got back to my inn without any adventure.

Punctual to my appointment, I placed my foot on the first notch of the zigzag next night as the distant clocks were striking eleven. He was waiting for me at the bottom, with his white light on. 'I have not called out,' I said, when we came close together; 'may I speak now?' 'By all means, sir.' 'Good-night, then, and here's my hand.' 'Good-night, sir, and here's mine.' With that we walked side by side to his box, entered it, closed the door and sat down by the fire.

'I have made up my mind, sir,' he began, bending forward as soon as we were seated, and speaking in a tone but a little above a whisper, 'that you shall not have to ask me twice what troubles me. I took you for someone else yesterday evening. That troubles me.'

'That mistake?'

'No. That someone else.'

'Who is it?'

'I don't know.'

'Like me?'

'I don't know. I never saw the face. The left arm is across the face, and the right arm is waved – violently waved. This way.'

I followed his action with my eyes, and it was the action of an arm gesticulating, with the utmost passion and vehemence, 'For God's sake, clear the way!'

'One moonlight night,' said the man, 'I was sitting here, when I heard a voice cry, "Halloa! Below there!" I started up, looked from that door, and saw this someone else standing by the red light near the tunnel, waving as I just now showed you. The voice seemed hoarse with shouting, and it cried, "Look out! Look out!" And then again, "Halloa! Below there! Look out!" I caught up my lamp, turned it on red, and ran towards the figure, calling, "What's wrong? What has happened? Where?" It stood just outside the blackness of the tunnel. I advanced so close upon it that I wondered at its keeping the sleeve across its eyes. I ran right up at it, and had my hand stretched out to pull the sleeve away, when it was gone.'

'Into the tunnel?' said I.

'No. I ran on into the tunnel, five hundred yards. I stopped, and held my lamp above my head, and saw the figures of the measured distance, and saw the wet stains stealing down the walls and trickling through the arch. I ran out again faster than I had run in (for I had a mortal abhorrence of the place upon me), and I looked all round the red light with my own red light, and I went up the iron ladder to the gallery atop of it, and I came down again, and ran back here. I telegraphed both ways, "An alarm has been give". Is anything wrong?" The answer came back, both ways, "All's well." '

Resisting the slow touch of a frozen finger tracing out my spine, I showed him how this figure must be a deception of his sense of sight; and how figures, originating in disease of the delicate nerves that minister to the functions of the eye, were known to have often troubled patients, some of whom had become conscious of the nature of their affliction, and had even proved it by experiments upon themselves. 'As to an imaginary cry,' said I, 'do but listen for a moment to the wind in this unnatural valley while we speak so low, and to the wild harp it makes of the telegraph wires.'

That was all very well, he returned, after we had sat listening for a while, and he ought to know something of the wind and the wires – he who so often passed long winter nights there, alone and watching. But he would beg to remark that he had not finished.

I asked his pardon, and he slowly added these words, touching my arm, 'Within six hours after the appearance, the memorable accident on this line happened, and within ten hours the dead and wounded were brought along through the tunnel over the spot where the figure had stood.'

A disagreeable shudder crept over me, but I did my best against it. It was not to be denied, I rejoined, that this was a remarkable coincidence, calculated deeply to impress his mind. But it was unquestionable that remarkable coincidences did continually occur, and they must be taken into account in dealing with such a subject. Though to be sure I must admit, I added (for I thought I saw that he was going to bring the objection to bear upon me), men of common sense did not allow much for coincidences in making the ordinary calculations of life.

He again begged to remark that he had not finished.

I again begged his pardon for being betrayed into interruptions.

'This,' he said, again laying his hand upon my arm, and glancing over his shoulder with hollow eyes, 'was just a year ago. Six or seven months passed, and I had recovered from the surprise and shock, when one morning, as the day was breaking, I, standing at the door, looked towards the red light and saw the spectre again.' He stopped, with a fixed look at me.

'Did it cry out?'

'No. It was silent.'

'Did it wave its arm?'

'No. It leaned against the shaft of the light, with both hands before the face. Like this.'

Once more I followed his action with my eyes. It was an action of mourning. I have seen such an attitude in stone figures on tombs.

'Did you go up to it?'

'I came in and sat down, partly to collect my thoughts, partly because it had turned me faint. When I went to the door again, daylight was above, and the ghost was gone.'

'But nothing followed? Nothing came of this?'

He touched me on the arm with his forefinger twice or thrice, giving a ghastly nod each time: 'That very day, as a train came out of the tunnel, I noticed, at a carriage window on my side, what looked like a confusion of hands and heads, and something waved. I saw it just in time to signal the driver, Stop! He shut off, and put his brake on, but the train drifted past here a hundred and fifty yards or more. I ran after it, and, as I went along, heard terrible screams and cries. A beautiful young lady had died instantaneously in one of the compartments, and was brought in here, and laid down on this floor between us.'

Involuntarily I pushed my chair back, as I looked from the boards at which he pointed to himself.

'True, sir, True. Precisely as it happened, so I tell it you.'

I could think of nothing to say to any purpose, and my mouth was very dry. The wind and the wires took up the story with a long lamenting wail.

He resumed. 'Now, sir, mark this, and judge how my mind is troubled. The spectre came back a week ago. Ever since, it has been there, now and again, by fits and starts.'

'At the light?'

'At the danger-light.'

'What does it seem to do?'

He repeated, if possible with increased passion and vehemence, that former gesticulation of, 'For God's sake, clear the way!'

Then he went on. 'I have no peace or rest from it. It calls to me, for many minutes together, in an agonised manner, "Below there! Look out! Look out!" It stands waving to me. It rings my little bell – '

I caught at that. 'Did it ring your bell yesterday evening when I was here, and you went to the door?'

'Twice.'

'Why, see,' said I, 'how your imagination misleads you. My eyes were on the bell, and my ears were open to the bell, and if I am a living man, it did *not* ring at those times. No, nor at any other time, except when it was rung in the natural course of physical things by the station communicating with you.'

He shook his head. 'I have never made a mistake as to that yet, sir. I have never confused the spectre's ring with the man's. The ghost's ring is a strange vibration in the bell that it derives from nothing else, and I have not asserted that the bell stirs to the eye. I don't wonder that you failed to hear it. But *I* heard it.'

'And did the spectre seem to be there, when you looked out?'

'It *was* there.'

'Both times?'

He repeated firmly, 'Both times.'

'Will you come to the door with me, and look for it now?'

He bit his underlip as though he were somewhat unwilling, but arose. I opened the door, and stood on the step, while he stood in the doorway. There was the danger-light. There was the dismal mouth of the tunnel. There were the high, wet stone walls of the cutting. There were the stars above them.

'Do you see it?' I asked him, taking particular note of his face. His eyes were prominent and strained, but not very much more so, perhaps, than my own had been when I had directed them earnestly towards the same spot.

'No,' he answered, 'it is not there.'

'Agreed,' said I.

We went in again, shut the door, and resumed our seats. I was thinking how best to improve this advantage, if it might be called one, when he took up the conversation in such a matter-of-course way, so assuming that there could be no serious question of fact between us, that I felt myself placed in the weakest of positions.

'By this time you will fully understand, sir,' he said, 'that what troubles me so dreadfully is the question, What does the spectre mean?'

I was not sure, I told him, that I did fully understand.

'What is its warning against?' he said, ruminating, with his eyes on the fire, and only at times turning them on me. 'What is the danger? Where is the danger? There is danger overhanging somewhere on the line. Some dreadful calamity will happen. It is not to be doubted this third time, after what has gone before. But surely this is a cruel haunting of *me*. What can *I* do?'

He pulled out his handkerchief, and wiped the drops from his heated forehead.

'If I telegraphed danger on either side of me, or on both, I can give no reason for it,' he went on, wiping the palms of his hands. 'I should get into trouble, and do no good. They would think I was mad. This is the way it would work: Message – "Danger! Take care!" Answer – "What Danger? Where?" Message – "Don't know. But, for God's sake, take care!" They would displace me. What else could they do?'

His pain of mind was most pitiable to see. It was the mental torture of a conscientious man, oppressed beyond endurance by an unintelligible responsibility involving life.

'When it first stood under the danger-light,' he went on, putting his dark hair back from his head, and drawing his hands outward across and across his temples in an extremity of feverish distress, 'why not tell me where that accident was to happen – if it must happen? Why not tell me how it could be averted – if it could have been averted? When on its second coming it hid its face, why not tell me, instead, "She is going to die. Let them keep her at home"? If it came, on those two occasions, only to show me that its warnings were true, and so to prepare me for the third, why not warn me plainly now? And I, Lord help me! a mere poor signalman on this solitary station! Why not go to somebody with credit to be believed, and power to act?'

When I saw him in this state, I saw that for the poor man's sake, as well as for the public safety, what I had to do for the time was to compose his mind. Therefore, setting aside all question of reality or unreality between us, I represented to him that whoever thoroughly discharged his duty must do well, and that at least it was his comfort that he understood his duty, though he did not understand these confounding appearances. In this effort I succeeded far better than in the attempt to reason him out of his conviction. He became calm; the occupations incidental to his post as the night advanced began to make larger demands on his attention, and I left him at two in the morning. I had offered to stay through the night, but he would not hear of it.

That I more than once looked back at the red light as I ascended the pathway, that I did not like the red light, and that I should have slept but poorly if my bed had been under it, I see no reason to conceal. Nor did I like the two sequences of the accident and the dead girl. I see no reason to conceal that either.

But what ran most in my thoughts was the consideration how ought I to act, having become the recipient of this disclosure? I had proved the man to be intelligent, vigilant, painstaking and exact; but how long might he remain so, in his state of mind? Though in a subordinate position, still he held a most important trust, and would I (for instance) like to stake my own life on the chances of his continuing to execute it with precision?

Unable to overcome a feeling that there would be something treacherous in my communicating what he had told me to his superiors in the company, without first being plain with himself and proposing a middle course to him, I ultimately resolved to offer to accompany him (otherwise keeping his secret for the present) to the wisest medical practitioner we could hear of in those parts, and to take his opinion. A change in his time of duty would come round next night, he had apprised me, and he would be off an hour or two after sunrise, and on again soon after sunset. I had appointed to return accordingly.

Next evening was a lovely evening, and I walked out early to enjoy it. The sun was not yet quite down when I traversed the field path near the top of the deep cutting. I would extend my walk for an hour, I said to myself, half an hour on and half an hour back, and it would then be time to go to my signalman's box.

Before pursuing my stroll, I stepped to the brink and mechanically looked down, from the point from which I had first seen him. I cannot describe the thrill that seized upon me when, close at the mouth of the tunnel, I saw the appearance of a man, with his left sleeve across his eyes, passionately waving his right arm.

The nameless horror that oppressed me passed in a moment, for in a moment I saw that this appearance of a man was a man indeed, and that there was a little group of other men, standing at a short distance, to whom he seemed to be rehearsing the gesture he made. The danger-light was not yet lighted. Against its shaft, a little low hut, entirely new to me, had been made of some wooden supports and tarpaulin. It looked no bigger than a bed.

With an irresistible sense that something was wrong, with a flashing self-reproachful fear that fatal mischief had come of my leaving the man there, and causing no one to be sent to overlook or correct what he did, I descended the notched path with all the speed I could make.

'What is the matter?' I asked the men.

'Signalman killed this morning, sir. '

'Not the man belonging to that box?'

'Yes, sir.'

'Not the man I know?'

'You will recognise him, sir, if you knew him,' said the man who spoke for the others, solemnly uncovering his own head and raising the end of the tarpaulin, 'for his face is quite composed.'

'Oh, how did this happen, how did this happen?' I asked, turning from one to another as the hut closed in again.

'He was cut down by an engine, sir. No man in England knew his work better. But somehow he was not clear of the outer rail. It was just at broad day. He had struck the light, and had the lamp in his hand. As the engine came out of the tunnel, his back was towards her, and she cut him down. That man drove her, and was showing how it happened. Show the gentleman, Tom.'

The man, who wore rough dark dress, stepped back to his former place at the mouth of the tunnel.

'Coming round the curve in the tunnel, sir,' he said, 'I saw him at the end, like as if I saw him down a perspective-glass. There was no time to check speed, and I knew him to be very careful. As he didn't seem to take heed of the whistle, I shut it off when we were running down upon him, and called to him as loud as I could call.'

'What did you say?'

'I said, "Below there! Look out! Look out! For God's sake, clear the way!"'

I started.

'Ah! it was a dreadful time, sir. I never left off calling to him. I put this arm before my eyes not to see, and I waved this arm to the last; but it was no use.'

Without prolonging the narrative to dwell on any one of its curious circumstances more than on any other, I may, in closing it, point out the coincidence that the warning of the engine-driver included, not only the words which the unfortunate signalman had repeated to me as haunting him, but also the words which I myself – not he – had attached, and that only in my own mind, to the gesticulation he had imitated.

Green Tea

SHERIDAN LE FANU

PROLOGUE

Martin Hesselius, the German Physician

THOUGH CAREFULLY EDUCATED in medicine and surgery, I have never practised either. The study of each continues, nevertheless, to interest me profoundly. Neither idleness nor caprice caused my secession from the honourable calling which I had just entered. The cause was a very trifling scratch inflicted by a dissecting knife. This trifle cost me the loss of two fingers, amputated promptly, and the more painful loss of my health, for I have never been quite well since, and have seldom been twelve months together in the same place.

In my wanderings I became acquainted with Dr Martin Hesselius, a wanderer like myself, like me a physician, and like me an enthusiast in his profession. Unlike me in this, that his wanderings were voluntary, and he a man, if not of fortune, as we estimate fortune in England, at least in what our forefathers used to term 'easy circumstances'. He was an old man when I first saw him; nearly five-and-thirty years my senior.

In Dr Martin Hesselius, I found my master. His knowledge was immense, his grasp of a case was an intuition. He was the very man to inspire a young enthusiast, like me, with awe and delight. My admiration has stood the test of time and survived the separation of death. I am sure it was well-founded.

For nearly twenty years I acted as his medical secretary. His immense collection of papers he has left in my care, to be arranged, indexed and bound. His treatment of some of these cases is curious. He writes in two distinct characters. He describes what he saw and heard as an intelligent layman might, and when, in this style of narrative, he had seen the patient either through his own hall-door, to the light of day, or through the gates of darkness, to the caverns of the dead, he returns upon the narrative, and in the terms of his art, and with all the force and originality of genius, proceeds to the work of analysis, diagnosis and illustration.

Here and there a case strikes me as of a kind to amuse or horrify a lay reader with an interest quite different from the peculiar one which it may possess for an expert. With slight modifications, chiefly of language, and of course a change of names, I copy the following. The narrator is Dr Martin Hesselius. I find it among the voluminous notes of cases which he made during a tour in England about sixty-four years ago.

It is related in a series of letters to his friend Professor Van Loo of Leyden. The professor was not a physician, but a chemist, and a man who read history and metaphysics and medicine, and had, in his day, written a play.

The narrative is therefore, if somewhat less valuable as a medical record, necessarily written in a manner more likely to interest an unlearned reader.

These letters, from a memorandum attached, appear to have been returned on the death of the professor, in 1819, to Dr Hesselius. They are written, some in English, some in French, but the greater part in German. I am a faithful though, I am conscious, by no means a graceful translator, and although here and there I omit some passages, and shorten others, and disguise names, I have interpolated nothing.

I

Dr Hesselius Relates How He Met the Reverend Mr Jennings

The Reverend Mr Jennings is tall and thin. He is middle-aged, and dresses with a natty, old-fashioned, high-church precision. He is naturally a little stately, but not at all stiff. His features, without being handsome, are well formed, and their expression extremely kind, but also shy.

I met him one evening at Lady Mary Heyduke's. The modesty and benevolence of his countenance are extremely prepossessing.

We were but a small party, and he joined agreeably enough in the conversation. He seems to enjoy listening very much more than contributing to the talk; but what he says is always to the purpose and well said. He is a great favourite of Lady Mary's, who, it seems, consults him upon many things and thinks him the most happy and blessed person on earth. Little knows she about him.

The Reverend Mr Jennings is a bachelor, and has, they say, sixty thousand pounds in the funds. He is a charitable man. He is most anxious to be actively employed in his sacred profession, and yet, though always tolerably well elsewhere, when he goes down to his vicarage in Warwickshire to engage in the actual duties of his sacred calling, his health soon fails him, and in a very strange way. So says Lady Mary.

There is no doubt that Mr Jennings' health does break down, in generally a sudden and mysterious way, sometimes in the very act of officiating in his old and pretty church at Kenlis. It may be his heart, it may be his brain. But so it has happened three or four times, or oftener, that, after proceeding a certain way in the service, he has on a sudden stopped short, and after a silence, apparently quite unable to resume, he has fallen into solitary, inaudible prayer, his hands and his eyes uplifted, and then, pale as death and in the agitation of a strange shame and horror, descended trembling and got into the vestry-room, leaving his congregation, without explanation, to themselves. This occurred when his curate was absent. When he goes down to Kenlis now, he always takes care to provide a clergyman to share his duty, and to supply his place on the instant should he become thus suddenly incapacitated.

When Mr Jennings breaks down quite, and beats a retreat from the vicarage and returns to London, where, in a dark street off Piccadilly, he inhabits a very narrow house, Lady Mary says that he is always perfectly well. I have my own opinion about that. There are degrees, of course. We shall see.

Mr Jennings is a perfectly gentlemanlike man. People, however, remark something odd. There is an impression a little ambiguous. One thing which certainly contributes to it, people I think don't remember; or, perhaps, distinctly remark. But I did, almost immediately. Mr Jennings has a way of looking sidelong upon the carpet, as if his eye followed the movements of something there. This, of course, is not always. It occurs only now and then. But often enough to give a certain oddity, as I have said, to his manner, and in this glance travelling along the floor there is something both shy and anxious.

A medical philosopher, as you are good enough to call me, elaborating theories by the aid of cases sought out by himself and by him watched and scrutinised with more time at command and consequently infinitely more minuteness than the ordinary practitioner can afford, falls insensibly into habits of observation which accompany him everywhere and are exercised, as some people would say, impertinently, upon every subject that presents itself with the least likelihood of rewarding enquiry.

There was a promise of this kind in the slight, timid, kindly, but reserved gentleman whom I met for the first time at this agreeable little evening gathering. I observed, of course, more than I here set down; but I reserve all that borders on the technical for a strictly scientific paper.

I may remark that when I here speak of medical science, I do so, as I hope some day to see it more generally understood, in a much more comprehensive sense than its generally material treatment would warrant. I believe the entire natural world is but the ultimate expression of that spiritual world from which, and in which alone, it has its life. I believe that the essential man is a spirit, that the spirit is an organised substance, but as different in point of material from what we ordinarily understand by matter as light or electricity is; that the material body is, in the most literal sense, a vesture, and death consequently no interruption of the living man's existence, but simply his extrication from the natural body – a process which commences at the moment of what we term death, and the completion of which, at furthest a few days later, is the resurrection 'in power'.

The person who weighs the consequences of these positions will probably see their practical bearing upon medical science. This is, however, by no means the proper place for displaying the proofs and discussing the consequences of this too generally unrecognised state of facts.

In pursuance of my habit, I was covertly observing Mr Jennings, with all my caution – I think he perceived it – and I saw plainly that he was as cautiously observing me. Lady Mary happening to address me by my name, as Dr Hesselius, I saw that he glanced at me more sharply, and then became thoughtful for a few minutes.

After this, as I conversed with a gentleman at the other end of the room, I saw him look at me more steadily, and with an interest which I thought I understood. I then saw him take an opportunity of chatting with Lady Mary, and was, as one always is, perfectly aware of being the subject of a distant enquiry and answer.

This tall clergyman approached me by and by, and in a little time we had got into conversation. When two people who like reading and know books and places, having travelled, wish to discourse, it is very strange if they can't find topics. It was not accident that brought him near me and led him into conversation. He knew German, and had read my *Essays on Metaphysical Medicine*, which suggest more than they actually say.

This courteous man, gentle, shy, plainly a man of thought and reading, who, moving and talking among us, was not altogether of us, and whom I already suspected of leading a life whose transactions and alarms were carefully concealed, with an impenetrable reserve, from not only the world, but his best beloved friends – was cautiously weighing in his own mind the idea of taking a certain step with regard to me.

I penetrated his thoughts without his being aware of it, and was careful to say nothing which could betray to his sensitive vigilance my suspicions respecting his position, or my surmises about his plans respecting myself.

We chatted upon indifferent subjects for a time but at last he said: 'I was very much interested by some papers of yours, Dr Hesselius, upon what you term metaphysical medicine – I read them in German, ten or twelve years ago – have they been translated?'

'No, I'm sure they have not – I should have heard. They would have asked my leave, I think.'

'I asked the publishers here, a few months ago, to get the book for me in the original German; but they tell me it is out of print.'

'So it is, and has been for some years; but it flatters me as an author to find that you have not forgotten my little book, although,' I added, laughing, 'ten or twelve years is a considerable time to have managed without it, but I suppose you have been turning the subject over again in your mind, or something has happened lately to revive your interest in it.'

At this remark, accompanied by a glance of enquiry, a sudden embarrassment disturbed Mr Jennings, analogous to that which makes a young lady blush and look foolish. He dropped his eyes, and folded his hands together uneasily, and looked oddly and, you would have said, guiltily, for a moment.

I helped him out of his awkwardness in the best way, by appearing not to observe it, and, going straight on, I said: 'Those revivals of interest in a subject happen to me often; one book suggests another, and often sends me back a wild-goose chase over an interval of twenty years. But if you still care to possess a copy, I shall be only too happy to provide you; I have still got two or three by me – and if you allow me to present one to you I shall be very much honoured.'

'You are very good indeed,' he said, quite at his ease again in a moment: 'I almost despaired – I don't know how to thank you.'

'Pray don't say a word; the thing is really so little worth that I am only ashamed of having offered it, and if you thank me any more I shall throw it into the fire in a fit of modesty.'

Mr Jennings laughed. He enquired where I was staying in London, and after a little more conversation on a variety of subjects, he took his departure.

II

The Doctor Questions Lady Mary, and She Answers

'I like your vicar so much, Lady Mary,' said I, as soon as he was gone. 'He has read, travelled and thought, and having also suffered, he ought to be an accomplished companion.'

'So he is, and, better still, he is a really good man,' said she. 'His advice is invaluable about my schools, and all my little undertakings at Dawlbridge, and he's so painstaking, he takes so much trouble – you have no idea – wherever he thinks he can be of use; he's so good-natured and so sensible.'

'It is pleasant to hear so good an account of his neighbourly virtues. I can only testify to his being an agreeable and gentle companion, and, in addition to what you have told me, I think I can tell you two or three things about him,' said I.

'Really!'

'Yes, to begin with, he's unmarried.'

'Yes, that's right – go on.'

'He has been writing, that is he *was* writing, but for two or three years perhaps he has not gone on with his work, and the book was upon some rather abstract subject – perhaps theology.'

'Well, he was writing a book, as you say; I'm not quite sure what it was about, but only that it was nothing that I cared for; very likely you are right, and he certainly did stop – yes.'

'And although he only drank a little coffee here tonight, he likes tea, at least, did like it, extravagantly.'

'Yes, that's *quite* true.'

'He drank green tea, a good deal, didn't he?' I pursued.

'Well, that's very odd! Green tea was a subject on which we used almost to quarrel.'

'But he has quite given that up,' said I.

'So he has.'

'And, now, one more fact. His mother or his father – did you know them?'

'Yes, both; his father is only ten years dead, and their place is near Dawlbridge. We knew them very well,' she answered.

'Well, either his mother or his father – I should rather think his father, saw a ghost,' said I.

'Well, you really are a conjurer, Dr Hesselius.'

'Conjurer or no, haven't I said right?' I answered merrily.

'You certainly have, and it was his father: he was a silent, whimsical man, and he used to bore my father about his dreams, and at last he told him a story about a ghost he had seen and talked with, and a very odd story it was. I remember it particularly because I was so afraid of him. This story was long before he died – when I was quite a child – and his ways were so silent and moping, and he used to drop in sometimes, in the dusk, when I was alone in the drawing-room, and I used to fancy there were ghosts about him.'

I smiled and nodded.

'And now, having established my character as a conjurer, I think I must say good-night,' said I.

'But how did you find it out?'

'By the planets, of course, as the gypsies do,' I answered, and so, gaily, we said good-night.

Next morning I sent the little book he had been enquiring after and a note to Mr Jennings, and, on returning late that evening, I found that he had called at my lodgings and left his card. He asked whether I was at home, and asked at what hour he would be most likely to find me.

Does he intend opening his case and consulting me 'professionally', as they say. I hope so. I have already conceived a theory about him. It is supported by Lady Mary's answers to my parting questions. I should like much to ascertain the truth from his own lips. But what can I do, consistent with good breeding, to invite a confession? Nothing. I rather think he meditates one. At all events, my dear Van Loo, I shan't make myself difficult of access; I mean to return his visit tomorrow. It will be only civil in return for his politeness, to ask to see him. Perhaps something may come of it. Whether much, little or nothing, my dear Van Loo, you shall hear.

III

Dr Hesselius Picks Up Something in Latin Books

Well, I have called at Blank Street.

On my enquiring at the door, the servant told me that Mr Jennings was engaged very particularly with a gentleman, a clergyman from Kenlis, his parish in the country. Intending to reserve my privilege, and to call again, I merely intimated that I should try another time, and had turned to go, when the servant begged my pardon, and asked me, looking at me a little more attentively than well-bred persons of his order usually do, whether I was Dr Hesselius; and, on learning that I was, he said, 'Perhaps then, sir, you would allow me to mention it to Mr Jennings, for I am sure he wishes to see you.'

The servant returned in a moment, with a message from Mr Jennings asking me to go into his study, which was in effect his back drawing-room, and promising to be with me in a very few minutes.

This really was a study – almost a library. The room was lofty, with two tall slender windows, and rich dark curtains. It was much larger than I had expected, and stored with books on every side from the floor to the ceiling. The upper carpet – for to my tread it felt that there were two or three – was a Turkey carpet. My steps fell noiselessly. The bookcases, standing out, placed the windows, particularly narrow ones, in deep recesses. The effect of the room was, although extremely comfortable and even luxurious, decidedly gloomy, and aided by the silence, almost oppressive. Perhaps, however, I ought to have allowed something for association. My mind had connected peculiar ideas with Mr Jennings. I stepped into this perfectly silent room, of a very silent house, with a peculiar foreboding; and its darkness and solemn clothing of books – for except where two narrow looking-glasses were set in the wall, they were everywhere – helped this sombre feeling.

While awaiting Mr Jennings' arrival, I amused myself by looking into some of the books with which his shelves were laden. Not among these, but immediately under them, with their backs upward, on the floor, I lighted upon a complete set of Swedenborg's *Arcana Caelestia*, in the original Latin, a very fine folio set, bound in the natty livery which theology affects, pure vellum, namely, with gold letters and carmine edges. There were paper markers in several of these volumes. I raised and placed them, one after the other, upon the table, and opening where these papers were placed, I read in the solemn Latin phraseology a series of sentences indicated by a pencilled line at the margin. Of these I copy here a few, translating them into English.

When man's interior sight is opened, which is that of his spirit, then there appear the things of another life, which cannot possibly be made visible to the bodily sight . . .

By the internal sight it has been granted me to see the things that are in the other life more clearly than I see those that are in the world. From these considerations, it is evident that external vision exists from interior vision, and this from a vision still more interior, and so on . . .

There are with every man at least two evil spirits . . .

With wicked genii there is also a fluent speech, but harsh and grating. There is also among them a speech which is not fluent, wherein the dissent of the thoughts is perceived as something secretly creeping along within it . . .

The evil spirits associated with man are indeed from the hells, but when with man they are not then in hell, but are taken out thence. The place where they then are is in the midst between heaven and hell, and is called the world of spirits – when the evil spirits who are with man are in that world, they are not in any infernal torment but in every thought and affection of the man, and so in all that the man himself enjoys. But when they are remitted into their hell, they return to their former state . . .

If evil spirits could perceive that they were associated with man and yet that they were spirits separate from him, and if they could flow into the things of his body, they would attempt by a thousand means to destroy him; for they hate man with a deadly hatred . . .

Knowing, therefore, that I was a man in the body, they were continually striving to destroy me, not as to the body only, but especially as to the soul; for to destroy any man or spirit is the very delight of the life of all who are in hell; but I have been continually protected by the Lord. Hence it appears how dangerous it is for man to be in a living consort with spirits, unless he be in the good of faith . . .

Nothing is more carefully guarded from the knowledge of associate spirits than their being thus conjoint with a man, for if they knew it they would speak to him, with the intention to destroy him . . .

The delight of hell is to do evil to man, and to hasten his eternal ruin.

A long note, written with a very sharp and fine pencil, in Mr Jennings' neat hand, at the foot of the page, caught my eye. Expecting his criticism upon the text, I read a word or two, and stopped, for it was something quite different, and began with these words, *Deus misereatur mei* – 'May God compassionate me.' Thus warned of its private nature, I averted my eyes and shut the book, replacing all the volumes as I had found them, except one which interested me, and in which, as men studious and solitary in their habits will do, I grew so absorbed as to take no cognisance of the outer world, nor to remember where I was.

I was reading some pages which refer to 'representatives' and 'correspondents', in the technical language of Swedenborg, and had arrived at a passage the substance of which is that evil spirits, when seen by other eyes than those of their infernal associates, present themselves, by 'correspondence', in the shape of the beast *(fera)* which represents their particular lust and life, in aspect direful and atrocious. This is a long passage and particularises a number of those bestial forms.

IV

Four Eyes Were Reading the Passage

I was running the head of my pencil-case along the line as I read it, and something caused me to raise my eyes.

Directly before me was one of the mirrors I have mentioned, in which I saw reflected the tall shape of my friend, Mr Jennings, leaning over my shoulder and reading the page at which I was busy, and with a face so dark and wild that I should hardly have known him.

I turned and rose. He stood erect also, and with an effort laughed a little, saying: 'I came in and asked you how you did, but without succeeding in awaking you from your book; so I could not restrain my curiosity, and very impertinently, I'm afraid, peeped over your shoulder. This is not your first time of looking into those pages. You have looked into Swedenborg, no doubt, long ago?'

'Oh dear, yes! I owe Swedenborg a great deal; you will discover traces of him in the little book on metaphysical medicine, which you were so good as to remember.'

Although my friend affected a gaiety of manner, there was a slight flush in his face, and I could perceive that he was inwardly much perturbed.

'I'm scarcely yet qualified, I know so little of Swedenborg. I've only had them a fortnight,' he answered, 'and I think they are rather likely to make a solitary man nervous – that is, judging from the very little I have read. I don't say that they have made me so,' he laughed; 'and I'm so very much obliged for the book. I hope you got my note?'

I made all proper acknowledgments and modest disclaimers.

'I never read a book that I go with, so entirely, as that of yours,' he continued. 'I saw at once there is more in it than is quite unfolded. Do you know Dr Harley?' he asked, rather abruptly.

[In passing, the editor remarks that the physician here named was one of the most eminent who had ever practised in England.]

I did, having exchanged letters with him, and had experienced from him great courtesy and considerable assistance during my visit to England,

'I think that man one of the very greatest fools I ever met in my life,' said Mr Jennings.

This was the first time I had ever heard him say a sharp thing of anybody, and such a term applied to so high a name a little startled me.

'Really! and in what way?' I asked.

'In his profession,' he answered.

I smiled.

'I mean this,' he said: 'he seems to me, one half blind – I mean one half of all he looks at is dark – preternaturally bright and vivid all the rest; and the worst of it is, it seems *wilful*. I can't get him – I mean he won't – I've had some experience of him as a physician, but I look on him as, in that sense, no better than a paralytic mind, an intellect half dead. I'll tell you – I know I shall some time – all about it,' he said, with a little agitation. 'You stay some months longer in England. If I should be out of town during your stay for a little time, would you allow me to trouble you with a letter?'

'I should be only too happy,' I assured him.

'Very good of you. I am so utterly dissatisfied with Harley.'

'A little leaning to the materialistic school,' I said.

'A *mere* materialist,' he corrected me; 'you can't think how that sort of thing worries one who knows better. You won't tell anyone – any of my friends you know – that I am hippish; now, for instance, no one knows – not even Lady Mary – that I have seen Dr Harley, or any other doctor. So pray don't mention it; and, if I should have any threatening of an attack, you'll kindly let me write, or, should I be in town, have a little talk with you.'

I was full of conjecture and unconsciously I found I had fixed my eyes gravely on him, for he lowered his for a moment, and he said: 'I see you think I might as well tell you now, or else you are forming a conjecture; but you may as well give it up. If you were guessing all the rest of your life, you will never hit on it.'

He shook his head smiling, and over that wintry sunshine a black cloud suddenly came down, and he drew his breath in, through his teeth, as men do in pain.

'Sorry, of course, to learn that you apprehend occasion to consult any of us; but, command me when and how you like, and I need not assure you that your confidence is sacred.'

He then talked of quite other things, and in a comparatively cheerful way, and after a little time, I took my leave.

V

Dr Hesselius is Summoned to Richmond

We parted cheerfully, but he was not cheerful, nor was I. There are certain expressions of that powerful organ of spirit – the human face – which, although I have seen them often, and possess a doctor's nerve, yet disturb me profoundly. One look of Mr Jennings haunted me. It had seized my imagination with so dismal a power that I changed my plans for the evening and went to the opera, feeling that I wanted a change of ideas.

I heard nothing of or from him for two or three days, when a note in his hand reached me. It was cheerful, and full of hope. He said that he had been for some little time so much better – quite well, in fact – that he was going to make a little experiment, and run down for a month or so to his parish, to try whether a little work might not quite set him up. There was in it a fervent religious expression of gratitude for his restoration, as he now almost hoped he might call it.

A day or two later I saw Lady Mary, who repeated what his note had announced, and told me that he was actually in Warwickshire, having resumed his clerical duties at Kenlis; and she added, 'I begin to think that he is really perfectly well, and that there never was anything the matter more than nerves and fancy; we are all nervous, but I fancy there is nothing like a little hard work for that kind of weakness, and he has made up his mind to try it. I should not be surprised if he did not come back for a year.'

Notwithstanding all this confidence, only two days later I had this note, dated from his house off Piccadilly:

DEAR SIR – I have returned disappointed. If I should feel at all able to see you, I shall write to ask you kindly to call. At present, I am too low, and, in fact, simply unable to say all I wish to say. Pray don't mention my name to my friends. I can see no one. By and by, please God, you shall hear from me. I mean to take a run into Shropshire, where some of my people are. God bless you! May we, on my return, meet more happily than I can now write.

About a week after this I saw Lady Mary at her own house, the last person, she said, left in town, and just on the wing for Brighton, for the London season was quite over. She told me that she had heard from Mr Jennings' niece, Martha, in Shropshire. There was nothing to be gathered from her letter, more than that he was low and nervous. In those words, of which healthy people think so lightly, what a world of suffering is sometimes hidden!

Nearly five weeks had passed without any further news of Mr Jennings. At the end of that time I received a note from him. He wrote:

I have been in the country, and have had change of air, change of scene, change of faces, change of everything and in everything – but *myself*. I have made up my mind, so far as the most irresolute creature on earth can do it, to tell my case fully to you. If your engagements will permit, pray come to me today, tomorrow or the next day; but, pray defer as little as possible. You know not how much I need help. I have a quiet house at Richmond, where I now am. Perhaps you can manage to come to dinner, or to luncheon, or even to tea. You shall have no trouble in finding me out. The servant at Blank Street, who takes this note, will have a carriage at your door at any hour you please; and I am always to be found. You will say that I ought not to be alone. I have tried everything. Come and see.

I called up the servant, and decided on going out the same evening, which accordingly I did.

He would have been much better in a lodging-house, or hotel, I thought, as I drove up through a short double row of sombre elms to a very old-fashioned brick house, darkened by the foliage of these trees, which overtopped and nearly surrounded it. It was a perverse choice, for nothing could be imagined more triste and silent. The house, I found, belonged to him. He had stayed for a day or two in town, and, finding it for some cause insupportable, had come out here, probably because, its being furnished and his own, he was relieved of the thought and delay of selection by coming here.

The sun had already set, and the red reflected light of the western sky illuminated the scene with the peculiar effect with which we are all familiar. The hall seemed very dark, but, getting to the back drawing-room, whose windows commanded the west, I was again in the same dusky light.

I sat down, looking out upon the richly-wooded landscape that glowed in the grand and melancholy light which was every moment fading. The corners of the room were already dark; all was growing dim, and the gloom was insensibly toning my mind, already prepared for what was sinister. I was waiting alone for his arrival, which soon took place. The door communicating with the front room opened, and the tall figure of Mr Jennings, faintly seen in the ruddy twilight, came with quiet stealthy steps into the room.

We shook hands, and, taking a chair to the window, where there was still light enough to enable us to see each other's faces, he sat down beside me, and, placing his hand upon my arm, with scarcely a word of preface began his narrative.

VI

How Mr Jennings Met His Companion

The faint glow of the west, the pomp of the then lonely woods of Richmond, were before us, behind and about us the darkening room, and on the stony face of the sufferer – for the character of his face, though still gentle and sweet, was changed – rested that dim, odd glow which seems to descend and produce, where it touches, lights, sudden though faint, which are lost, almost without gradation, in darkness. The silence, too, was utter: not a distant wheel, or bark, or whistle from without; and within the depressing stillness of an invalid bachelor's house.

I guessed well the nature, though not even vaguely the particulars, of the revelations I was about to receive from that fixed face of suffering, that so oddly flushed stood out, like a portrait of Schalken's, before its background of darkness.

'It began,' he said, 'on the 15th of October, three years and eleven weeks ago, and two days – I keep very accurate count, for every day is torment. If I leave anywhere a chasm in my narrative tell me.

'About four years ago I began a work, which had cost me very much thought and reading. It was upon the religious metaphysics of the ancients.'

'I know,' said I; 'the actual religion of educated and thinking paganism, quite apart from symbolic worship? A wide and very interesting field.'

'Yes; but not good for the mind – the Christian mind, I mean. Paganism is all bound together in essential unity, and, with evil sympathy, their religion involves their art, and both their manners, and the subject is a degrading fascination and the Nemesis sure. God forgive me!

'I wrote a great deal; I wrote late at night. I was always thinking on the subject, walking about, wherever I was, everywhere. It thoroughly infected me. You are to remember that all the material ideas connected with it were more or less of the beautiful, the subject itself delightfully interesting, and I, then, without a care.'

He sighed heavily.

'I believe that everyone who sets about writing in earnest does his work, as a friend of mine phrased it, *on* something – tea, or coffee, or tobacco. I suppose there is a material waste that must be hourly supplied in such occupations, or we should grow too abstracted, and the mind, as it were, pass out of the body, unless it were reminded often of the connection by actual sensation. At all events, I felt the want, and I supplied it. Tea was my companion – at first the ordinary black tea, made in the usual way, not too strong; but I drank a good deal, and increased its strength as I went on. I never experienced an uncomfortable symptom from it. I began to take a little green tea. I found the effect pleasanter, it cleared and intensified the power of thought so. I had come to take it frequently, but not stronger than one might take it for pleasure. I wrote a great deal out here, it was so quiet, and in this room. I used to sit up very late, and it became a habit with me to sip my tea – green tea – every now and then as my work proceeded. I had a little kettle on my table, that swung over a lamp, and made tea two or three times between eleven o'clock and two or three in the morning, my hours of going to bed. I used to go into town every day. I was not a monk, and, although I spent an hour or two in a library, hunting up authorities and looking out lights upon my theme, I was in no morbid state as far as I can judge. I met my friends pretty much as usual and enjoyed their society, and, on the whole, existence had never been, I think, so pleasant before.

'I had met with a man who had some odd old books, German editions in medieval Latin, and I was only too happy to be permitted access to them. This obliging person's books were in the City, a very out-of-the-way part of it. I had rather out-stayed my intended hour, and, on coming out, seeing no cab near, I was tempted to get into the omnibus which used to drive past this house. It was darker than this by the time the bus had reached an old house you may have remarked, with four poplars at each side of the door, and there the last passenger but myself got out. We drove along rather faster. It was twilight now. I leaned back in my corner next the door ruminating pleasantly.

'The interior of the omnibus was nearly dark. I had observed in the corner opposite to me at the other side, and at the end next the horses, two small circular reflections, as it seemed to me of a reddish light. They were about two inches apart, and about the size of those small brass buttons that yachting men used to put upon their jackets. I began to speculate, as listless men will, upon this trifle, as it seemed. From what centre did that faint but deep red light come, and from what – glass beads, buttons, toy decorations – was it reflected? We were lumbering along gently, having nearly a mile still to go. I had not solved the puzzle, and it became in another minute more odd, for these two luminous points, with a sudden jerk, descended nearer the floor, keeping still their relative distance and horizontal position, and then, as suddenly, they rose to the level of the seat on which I was sitting and I saw them no more.

'My curiosity was now really excited, and, before I had time to think, I saw again these two dull lamps, again together near the floor; again they disappeared, and again in their old corner I saw them.

'So, keeping my eyes upon them, I edged quietly up my own side, towards the end at which I still saw these tiny discs of red.

'There was very little light in the bus. It was nearly dark. I leaned forward to aid my endeavour to discover what these little circles really were. They shifted their position a little as I did so. I began now to perceive an outline of something black, and I soon saw, with tolerable distinctness, the outline of a small black monkey, pushing its face forward in mimicry to meet mine; those were its eyes, and I now dimly saw its teeth grinning at me.

'I drew back, not knowing whether it might not meditate a spring. I fancied that one of the passengers had forgot this ugly pet, and wishing to ascertain something of its temper, though not caring to trust my fingers to it, I poked my umbrella softly towards it – it remained immovable – up to it, *through* it. For through it, and back and forward it passed, without the slightest resistance.

'I can't, in the least, convey to you the kind of horror that I felt. When I had ascertained that the thing was an illusion, as I then supposed, there came a misgiving about myself and a terror that fascinated me in impotence to remove my gaze from the eyes of the brute for some moments. As I looked, it made a little skip back, quite into the corner, and I, in a panic, found myself at the door, having put my head out, drawing deep breaths of the outer air, and staring at the lights and trees we were passing, too glad to reassure myself of reality.

'I stopped the bus and got out. I perceived the man look oddly at me as I paid him. I dare say there was something unusual in my looks and manner, for I had never felt so strangely before.'

VII

The Journey: First Stage

'When the omnibus drove on, and I was alone upon the road, I looked carefully round to ascertain whether the monkey had followed me. To my indescribable relief I saw it nowhere. I can't describe easily what a shock I had received, and my sense of genuine gratitude on finding myself, as I supposed, quite rid of it.

'I had got out a little before we reached this house, two or three hundred steps. A brick wall runs along the footpath, and inside the wall is a hedge of yew, or some dark evergreen of that kind, and within that again the row of fine trees which you may have remarked as you came.

'This brick wall is about as high as my shoulder, and happening to raise my eyes I saw the monkey, with that stooping gait, on all fours, walking – or creeping – close beside me on top of the wall. I stopped, looking at it with a feeling of loathing and horror. As I stopped so did it. It sat up on the wall with its long hands on its knees looking at me. There was not light enough to see it much more than in outline, nor was it dark enough to bring the peculiar light of its eyes into strong relief. I still saw, however, that red foggy light plainly enough. It did not show its teeth, nor exhibit any sign of irritation, but seemed jaded and sulky, and was observing me steadily.

'I drew back into the middle of the road. It was an unconscious recoil, and there I stood, still looking at it. It did not move.

'With an instinctive determination to try something – anything, I turned about and walked briskly towards town with askance look, all the time watching the movements of the beast. It crept swiftly along the wall, at exactly my pace.

'Where the wall ends, near the turn of the road, it came down, and with a wiry spring or two brought itself close to my feet, and continued to keep up with me as I quickened my pace. It was at my left side, so close to my leg that I felt every moment as if I should tread upon it.

'The road was quite deserted and silent, and it was darker every moment. I stopped, dismayed and bewildered, turning as I did so the other way – I mean, towards this house away from which I had been walking. When I stood still, the monkey drew back to a distance of, I suppose, about five or six yards, and remained stationary, watching me.

I had been more agitated than I have said. I had read, of course, as everyone has, something about 'spectral illusions', as you physicians term the phenomena of such cases. I considered my situation and looked my misfortune in the face.

'These affections, I had read, are sometimes transitory and sometimes obstinate. I had read of cases in which the appearance, at first harmless, had, step by step, degenerated into something direful and insupportable, and ended by wearing its victim out. Still as I stood there, but for my bestial companion quite alone, I tried to comfort myself by repeating again and again the assurance, "the thing is purely disease, a well-known physical affection as distinctly as smallpox or neuralgia. Doctors are all agreed on that, philosophy demonstrates it. I must not be a fool. I've been sitting up too late, and I dare say my digestion is quite wrong, and, with God's help, I shall be all right, and this is but a symptom of nervous dyspepsia." Did I believe all this? Not one word of it, no more than any other miserable being ever did who is once seized and riveted in this satanic captivity. Against my convictions, I might say my knowledge, I was simply bullying myself into a false courage.

'I now walked homeward. I had only a few hundred yards to go. I had forced myself into a sort of resignation, but I had not got over the sickening shock and the flurry of the first certainty of my misfortune.

'I made up my mind to pass the night at home. The brute moved close beside me, and I fancied there was the sort of anxious drawing towards the house which one sees in tired horses or dogs, sometimes, as they come towards home.

'I was afraid to go into town, I was afraid of anyone's seeing and recognising me. I was conscious of an irrepressible agitation in my manner. Also, I was afraid of any violent change in my habits, such as going to a place of amusement or walking from home in order to fatigue myself. At the hall door it waited till I mounted the steps, and when the door was opened entered with me.

'I drank no tea that night. I got cigars and some brandy and water. My idea was that I should act upon my material system, and by living for a while in sensation apart from thought, send myself forcibly, as it were, into a new groove. I came up here to this drawing-room. I sat just here. The monkey then got upon a small table that then stood there. It looked dazed and languid. An irrepressible uneasiness as to its movements kept my eyes always upon it. Its eyes were half closed, but I could see them glow. It was looking steadily at me. In all situations, at all hours, it is awake and looking at me. That never changes.

'I shall not continue in detail my narrative of this particular night. I shall describe, rather, the phenomena of the first year, which never varied, essentially. I shall describe the monkey as it appeared in daylight. In the dark, as you shall presently hear, there are peculiarities. It is a small monkey, perfectly black. It has only one peculiarity – a character of malignity – unfathomable malignity. During the first year it looked sullen and sick. But this character of intense malice and vigilance was always underlying that surly languor. During all that time it acted as if on a plan of giving me as little trouble as was consistent with watching me. Its eyes were never off me. I have never lost sight of it, except in my sleep, light or dark, day or night, since it came here, excepting when it withdraws for some weeks at a time, unaccountably.

'In total dark it is visible as in daylight. I do not mean merely its eyes. It is as visible distinctly in a halo that resembles a glow of red embers, and which accompanies it in all its movements.

'When it leaves me for a time, it is always at night, in the dark, and in the same way. It grows at first uneasy, and then furious, and then advances towards me, grinning and shaking, its paws clenched, and, at the same time, there comes the appearance of fire in the grate. I never have any fire – I can't sleep in the room where there is any – and it draws nearer and nearer to the chimney, quivering, it seems, with rage, and when its fury rises to the highest pitch, it springs into the grate, and up the chimney, and I see it no more.

'When first this happened, I thought I was released. I was now a new man. A day passed – a night – and no return, and a blessed week – a week – another week. I was always on my knees, Dr Hesselius, always, thanking God and praying. A whole month passed of liberty, but on a sudden, it was with me again.'

VIII

The Second Stage

'It was with me, and the malice which before was torpid under a sullen exterior, was now active. It was perfectly unchanged in every other respect. This new energy was apparent in its activity and its looks, and soon in other ways.

'For a time, you will understand, the change was shown only in an increased vivacity, and an air of menace, as if it was always brooding over some atrocious plan. Its eyes, as before, were never off me.'

'Is it here now?' I asked.

'No,' he replied, 'it has been absent exactly a fortnight and a day – fifteen days. It has sometimes been away so long as nearly two months, once for three. Its absence always exceeds a fortnight, although it may be but by a single day. Fifteen days having past since I saw it last, it may return now at any moment.'

'Is its return,' I asked, 'accompanied by any peculiar manifestation?'

'Nothing – no,' he said. 'It is simply with me again. On lifting my eyes from a book, or turning my head, I see it, as usual, looking at me, and then it remains, as before, for its appointed time. I have never told so much and so minutely before to any one.'

I perceived that he was agitated, and looking like death, and he repeatedly applied his handkerchief to his forehead; I suggested that he might be tired, and told him that I would call, with pleasure, in the morning, but he said: 'No, if you don't mind hearing it all now. I have got so far, and I should prefer making one effort of it. When I spoke to Dr Harley, I had nothing like so much to tell. You are a philosophic physician. You give spirit its proper rank. If this thing is real – '

He paused, looking at me with agitated inquiry.

'We can discuss it by and by, and very fully. I will give you all I think,' I answered, after an interval.

'Well – very well. If it is anything real. I say, it is prevailing, little by little, and drawing me more interiorly into hell. Optic nerves, he talked of. Ah! well – there are other nerves of communication. May God Almighty help me! You shall hear.

'Its power of action, I tell you, had increased. Its malice became, in a way aggressive. About two years ago, some questions that were pending between me and the bishop having been settled, I went down to my parish in Warwickshire, anxious to find occupation in my profession. I was not prepared for what happened, although I have since thought I might have apprehended something like it. The reason of my saying so is this – '

He was beginning to speak with a great deal more effort and reluctance, and sighed often, and seemed at times nearly overcome. But at this time his manner was not agitated. It was more like that of a sinking patient, who has given himself up.

'Yes, but I will first tell you about Kenlis, my parish.

'It was with me when I left this place for Dawlbridge. It was my silent travelling companion, and it remained with me at the vicarage. When I entered on the discharge of my duties, another change took place. The thing exhibited an atrocious determination to thwart me. It was with me in the church – in the reading-desk – in the pulpit – within the communion rails. At last, it reached this extremity, that while I was reading to the congregation, it would spring upon the open book and squat there, so that I was unable to see the page. This happened more than once.

'I left Dawlbridge for a time. I placed myself in Dr Harley's hands. I did everything he told me. He gave my case a great deal of thought. It interested him, I think. He seemed successful. For nearly three months I was perfectly free from a return. I began to think I was safe. With his full assent I returned to Dawlbridge.

'I travelled in a chaise. I was in good spirits. I was more – I was happy and grateful. I was returning, as I thought, delivered from a dreadful hallucination, to the scene of duties which I longed to enter upon. It was a beautiful sunny evening, everything looked serene and cheerful, and I was delighted, I remember, looking out of the window, to see the spire of my church at Kenlis among the trees, at the point where one has the earliest view of it. It is exactly where the little stream that bounds the parish passes under the road by a culvert, and where it emerges at the roadside, a stone with an old inscription is placed. As we passed this point, I drew my head in and sat down, and in the corner of the chaise was the monkey.

'For a moment I felt faint, and then quite wild with despair and horror. I called to the driver, and got out, and sat down at the roadside, and prayed to God silently for mercy. A despairing resignation supervened. My companion was with me as I re-entered the vicarage. The same persecution followed. After a short struggle I submitted, and soon I left the place.

'I told you,' he said, 'that the beast has before this become in certain ways aggressive. I will explain a little. It seemed to be actuated by intense and increasing fury whenever I said my prayers, or even meditated prayer. It amounted at last to a dreadful interruption. You will ask, how could a silent immaterial phantom effect that? It was thus, whenever I meditated praying; it was always before me, and nearer and nearer.

'It used to spring on a table, on the back of a chair, on the chimney-piece, and slowly to swing itself from side to side, looking at me all the time. There is in its motion an indefinable power to dissipate thought, and to contract one's attention to that monotony, till the ideas shrink, as it were, to a point, and at last to nothing – and unless I had started up and shaken off the catalepsy I have felt as if my mind were on the point of losing itself. There are other ways,' he sighed heavily; 'thus, for instance, while I pray with my eyes closed, it comes closer and closer, and I see it. I know it is not to be accounted for physically, but I do actually see it, though my lids are closed, and so it rocks my mind, as it were, and overpowers me, and I am obliged to rise from my knees. If you had ever yourself known this, you would be acquainted with desperation.'

IX

The Third Stage

'I see, Dr Hesselius, that you don't lose one word of my statement. I need not ask you to listen specially to what I am now going to tell you. They talk of the optic nerves, and of spectral illusions, as if the organ of sight was the only point assailable by the influences that have fastened upon me – I know better. For two years in my direful case that limitation prevailed. But as food is taken in softly at the lips, and then brought under the teeth, as the tip of the little finger caught in a mill crank will draw in the hand, and the arm, and the whole body, so the miserable mortal who has been once caught firmly by the end of the finest fibre of his nerve, is drawn in and in, by the enormous machinery of hell, until he is as I am. Yes, doctor, as I am, for while I talk to you, and implore relief, I feel that my prayer is for the impossible, and my pleading with the inexorable.'

I endeavoured to calm his visibly increasing agitation, and told him that he must not despair.

While we talked the night had overtaken us. The filmy moonlight was wide over the scene which the window commanded, and I said: 'Perhaps you would prefer having candles. This light, you know, is odd. I should wish you, as much as possible, under your usual conditions while I make my diagnosis, shall I call it – otherwise I don't care.'

'All lights are the same to me,' he said; 'except when I read or write, I care not if night were perpetual. I am going to tell you what happened about a year ago. The thing began to speak to me.'

'Speak! How do you mean – speak as a man does, do you mean?'

'Yes; speak in words and consecutive sentences, with perfect coherence and articulation; but there is a peculiarity. It is not like the tone of a human voice. It is not by my ears it reaches me – it comes like a singing through my head.

'This faculty, the power of speaking to me, will be my undoing. It won't let me pray, it interrupts me with dreadful blasphemies. I dare not go on, I could not. Oh! doctor, can the skill, and thought, and prayers of man avail me nothing!'

'You must promise me, my dear sir, not to trouble yourself with unnecessarily exciting thoughts; confine yourself strictly to the narrative of *facts*; and recollect, above all, that even if the thing that infests you be, as you seem to suppose, a reality with an actual independent life and will, yet it can have no power to hurt you unless it be given from above: its access to your senses depends mainly upon your physical condition – this is, under God, your comfort and reliance; we are all alike environed. It is only that in your case, the '*paries*', the veil of the flesh, the screen, is a little out of repair, and sights and sounds are transmitted. We must enter on a new course, sir – be encouraged. I'll give tonight to the careful consideration of the whole case.'

'You are very good, sir; you think it worth trying, you don't give me quite up; but, sir, you don't know, it is gaining such an influence over me: it orders me about, it is such a tyrant, and I'm growing so helpless. May God deliver me!'

'It orders you about – of course you mean by speech?'

'Yes, yes; it is always urging me to crimes, to injure others, or myself. You see, doctor, the situation is urgent, it is indeed. When I was in Shropshire, a few weeks ago' (Mr Jennings was speaking rapidly and trembling now, holding my arm with one hand and looking in my face), 'I went out one day with a party of friends for a walk: my persecutor, I tell you, was with me at the time. I lagged behind the rest; the country near the Dee, you know, is beautiful. Our path happened to lie near a coal mine, and at the verge of the wood is a perpendicular shaft, they say, a hundred and fifty feet deep. My niece had remained behind with me – she knows, of course, nothing of the nature of my sufferings. She knew, however, that I had been ill, and was low, and she remained to prevent my being quite alone. As we loitered slowly on together, the brute that accompanied me was urging me to throw myself down the shaft. I tell you now – oh, sir, think of it! – the one consideration that saved me from that hideous death was the fear lest the shock of witnessing the occurrence should be too much for the poor girl. I asked her to go on and take her walk with her friends, saying that I could go no farther. She made excuses, and the more I urged her the firmer she became. She looked doubtful and frightened. I suppose there was something in my looks or manner that alarmed her; but she would not go, and that literally saved me. You had no idea, sir, that a living man could be made so abject a slave of Satan,' he said, with a ghastly groan and a shudder.

There was a pause here, and I said, 'You *were* preserved nevertheless. It was the act of God. You are in His hands and in the power of no other being: be therefore confident for the future.'

X

Home

I made him have candles lighted, and saw the room looking cheery and inhabited before I left him. I told him that he must regard his illness strictly as one dependent on physical, though *subtle* physical causes. I told him that he had evidence of God's care and love in the deliverance which he had just described, and that I had perceived with pain that he seemed to regard its peculiar features as indicating that he had been delivered over to spiritual reprobation. Than such a conclusion nothing could be, I insisted, less warranted; and not only so, but more contrary to facts, as disclosed in his mysterious deliverance from that murderous influence during his Shropshire excursion. First, his niece had been retained by his side without his intending to keep her near him; and, secondly, there had been infused into his mind an irresistible repugnance to execute the dreadful suggestion in her presence.

As I reasoned this point with him, Mr Jennings wept. He seemed comforted. One promise I exacted, which was that should the monkey at any time return, I should be sent for immediately; and, repeating my assurance that I would give neither time nor thought to any other subject until I had thoroughly investigated his case, and that tomorrow he should hear the result, I took my leave.

Before getting into the carriage I told the servant that his master was far from well, and that he should make a point of frequently looking into his room.

My own arrangements I made with a view to being quite secure from interruption. I merely called at my lodgings, and, with a travelling-desk and carpet-bag, set off in a hackney carriage for an inn about two miles out of town called the Horns, a very quiet and comfortable house, with good thick walls. And there I resolved, without the possibility of intrusion or distraction, to devote some hours of the night, in my comfortable sitting-room, to Mr Jennings' case, and so much of the morning as it might require.

[There occurs here a careful note of Dr Hesselius's opinion upon the case, and of the habits, dietary, and medicines which he prescribed. It is curious – some persons would say mystical. But, on the whole, I doubt whether it would sufficiently interest a reader, of the kind I am likely to meet with, to warrant its being here reprinted. The whole letter was plainly written at the inn where he had hid himself for the occasion. The next letter is dated from his town lodgings.]

I left town for the inn where I slept last night at half-past nine, and did not arrive at my room in town until one o'clock this afternoon. I found a letter in Mr Jennings' hand upon my table. It had not come by post, and, on enquiry, I learned that Mr Jennings' servant had brought it, and on learning that I was not to return until today, and that no one could tell him my address, he seemed very uncomfortable, and said that his orders from his master were that he was not to return without an answer.

I opened the letter and read:

> DEAR DR HESSELIUS – It is here. You had not been an hour gone when it returned. It is speaking. It knows all that has happened. It knows everything – it knows you, and is frantic and atrocious. It reviles. I send you this. It knows every word I have written – I write. This I promised, and I therefore write, but I fear very confused, very incoherently. I am so interrupted, disturbed.
>
> Ever yours, sincerely yours,
>
> ROBERT LYNDER JENNINGS

'When did this come?' I asked.

'About eleven last night; the man was here again, and has been here three times today. The last time was about an hour since.'

Thus answered, and with the notes I had made upon his case in my pocket, I was in a few minutes driving towards Richmond, to see Mr Jennings.

I by no means, as you perceive, despaired of Mr Jennings' case. He had himself remembered and applied, though quite in a mistaken way, the principle which I lay down in my *Metaphysical Medicine*, and which governs all such cases. I was about to apply it in earnest. I was profoundly interested, and very anxious to see and examine him while the 'enemy' was actually present.

I drove up to the sombre house, and ran up the steps and knocked. The door, in a little time, was opened by a tall woman in black silk. She looked ill, and as if she had been crying. She curtsied, and heard my question, but she did not answer. She turned her face away, extending her hand towards two men who were: coming downstairs; and thus having, as it were, tacitly made me over to them, she passed through a side-door hastily and shut it.

The man who was nearest the hall, I at once accosted, but being now close to him, I was shocked to see that both his hands were covered with blood.

I drew back a little, and the man, passing downstairs, merely said in a low tone, 'Here's the servant, sir.'

The servant had stopped on the stairs, confounded and dumb at seeing me. He was rubbing his hands in a handkerchief, and it was steeped in blood.

'Jones, what is it? what has happened?' I asked, while a sickening suspicion overpowered me.

The man asked me to come up to the lobby. I was beside him in a moment, and, frowning and pallid, with contracted eyes, he told me the horror which I already half guessed.

His master had made away with himself.

I went upstairs with him to the room – what I saw there I won't tell you. He had cut his throat with his razor. It was a frightful gash. The two men had laid him on the bed, and composed his limbs. It had happened, as the immense pool of blood on the floor declared, at some distance between the bed and the window. There was carpet round his bed, and a carpet under his dressing-table, but none on the rest of the floor, for the man said he did not like a carpet in his bedroom. In this sombre and now terrible room, one of the great elms that darkened the house was slowly moving the shadow of one of its great boughs upon this dreadful floor.

I beckoned to the servant, and we went downstairs together. I turned off the hall into an old-fashioned panelled room, and there standing, I heard all the servant had to tell. It was not a great deal.

'I concluded, sir, from your words and looks, sir, as you left last night, that you thought my master seriously ill. I thought it might be that you were afraid of a fit, or something. So I attended very close to your directions. He sat up late, till past three o'clock. He was not writing or reading. He was talking a great deal to himself, but that was nothing unusual. At about that hour I assisted him to undress, and left him in his slippers and dressing-gown. I went back softly in about half an hour. He was in his bed, quite undressed, and a pair of candles lighted on the table beside his bed. He was leaning on his elbow, and looking out at the other side of the bed when I came in. I asked him if he wanted anything, and he said no.

'I don't know whether it was what you said to me, sir, or something a little unusual about him, but I was uneasy, uncommon uneasy about him last night.

'In another half-hour, or it might have been a little more, I went up again. I did not hear him talking as before. I opened the door a little. The candles were both out, which was not usual. I had a bedroom candle, and I let the light in a little bit, looking softly round. I saw him sitting in that chair beside the dressing-table with his clothes on again. He turned round and looked at me. I thought it strange he should get up and dress, and put out the candles to sit in the dark, that way. But I only asked him again if I could do anything for him. He said, 'No,' rather sharp, I thought. I asked if I might light the candles, and he said, 'Do as you like, Jones.' So I lighted them, and I lingered about the room, and he said, 'Tell me the truth, Jones; why did you come again – you did not hear anyone cursing?' 'No, sir,' I said, wondering what he could mean.

'No,' said he, after me, 'of course, no;' and I said to him, 'Wouldn't it be well, sir, if you went to bed? It's just five o'clock;' and he said nothing but, 'Very likely; good-night, Jones.' So I went, sir, but in less than an hour I came again. The door was fast, and he heard me, and called as I thought from the bed to know what I wanted, and he desired me not to disturb him again. I lay down and slept for a little. It must have been between six and seven when I went up again. The door was still fast, and he made no answer, so I did not like to disturb him and, thinking he was asleep, I left him till nine. It was his custom to ring when he wished me to come, and I had no particular hour for calling him. I tapped very gently, and getting no answer, I stayed away a good while, supposing he was getting some rest then. It was not till eleven o'clock I grew really uncomfortable about him – for at the latest he was never, that I could remember, later than half-past ten. I got no answer. I knocked and called, and still no answer. So not being able to force the door, I called Thomas from the stables, and together we forced it, and found him in the shocking way you saw.'

Jones had no more to tell. Poor Mr Jennings was very gentle, and very kind. All his people were fond of him. I could see that the servant was very much moved.

So, dejected and agitated, I passed from that terrible house, and its dark canopy of elms, and I hope I shall never see it more. While I write to you I feel like a man who has but half waked from a frightful and monotonous dream. My memory rejects the picture with incredulity and horror. Yet I know it is true. It is the story of the process of a poison, a poison which excites the reciprocal action of spirit and nerve, and paralyses the tissue that separates those cognate functions of the senses, the external and the interior. Thus we find strange bedfellows, and the mortal and immortal prematurely make acquaintance.

CONCLUSION

A Word for Those Who Suffer

My dear Van Loo, you have suffered from an affection similar to that which I have just described. You twice complained of a return of it.

Who, under God, cured you? Your humble servant, Martin Hesselius? Let me rather adopt the more emphasised piety of a certain good old French surgeon of three hundred years ago: 'I treated, and God cured you.'

Come, my friend, you are not to be hippish. Let me tell you a fact.

I have met with, and treated, as my book shows, fifty-seven cases of this kind of vision, which I term indifferently 'sublimated', 'precocious' and 'interior'.

There is another class of affections which are truly termed – though commonly confounded with those which I describe – spectral illusions. These latter I look upon as being no less simply curable than a cold in the head or a trifling dyspepsia.

It is those which rank in the first category that test our promptitude of thought. Fifty-seven such cases have I encountered, neither more nor less. And in how many of these have I failed? In no one single instance.

There is no one affliction of mortality more easily and certainly reducible, with a little patience and a rational confidence in the physician. With these simple conditions, I look upon the cure as absolutely certain.

You are to remember that I had not even commenced to treat Mr Jennings' case. I have not any doubt that I should have cured him perfectly in eighteen months, or possibly it might have extended to two years. Some cases are very rapidly curable, others extremely tedious. Every intelligent physician who will give thought and diligence to the task, will effect a cure.

You know my tract on 'The Cardinal Functions of the Brain'. I there, by the evidence of innumerable facts, prove, as I think, the high probability of a circulation, arterial and venous in its mechanism, through the nerves. Of this system, thus considered, the brain is the heart. The fluid, which is propagated hence through one class of nerves, returns in an altered state through another, and the nature of that fluid is spiritual, though not immaterial, any more than, as I before remarked, light or electricity are so.

By various abuses, among which the habitual use of such agents as green tea is one, this fluid may be affected as to its quality, but it is more frequently disturbed as to equilibrium. This fluid being that which we have in common with spirits, a congestion found upon the masses of brain or nerve, connected with the interior sense, forms a surface unduly exposed, on which disembodied spirits may operate; communication is thus more or less effectually established. Between this brain circulation and the heart circulation there is an intimate sympathy. The seat, or rather the instrument, of exterior vision, is the eye. The seat of interior vision is the nervous tissue and brain, immediately about and above the eyebrow. You remember how effectually I dissipated your pictures by the simple application of iced eau-de-cologne. Few cases, however, can be treated exactly alike with anything like rapid success. Cold acts powerfully as a repellent of the nervous fluid. Long enough continued it will even produce that permanent insensibility which we call numbness, and a little longer, muscular as well as sensational paralysis.

I have not, I repeat, the slightest doubt that I should have first dimmed and ultimately sealed that inner eye which Mr Jennings had inadvertently opened. The same senses are opened in delirium tremens, and entirely shut up again when the over-action of the cerebral heart, and the prodigious nervous congestions that attend it, are terminated by a decided change in the state of the body. It is by acting steadily upon the body, by a simple process, that this result is produced – and inevitably produced. I have never yet failed.

Poor Mr Jennings made away with himself. But that catastrophe was the result of a totally different malady, which, as it were, projected itself upon that disease which was established. His case was in the distinctive manner a complication, and the complaint under which he really succumbed was hereditary suicidal mania. Poor Mr Jennings I cannot call a patient of mine, for I had not even begun to treat his case, and he had not yet given me, I am convinced, his full and unreserved confidence. If the patient does not array himself on the side of the disease, his cure is certain.

A Terribly Strange Bed

WILKIE COLLINS

SHORTLY AFTER MY EDUCATION at college was finished, I happened to be staying at Paris with an English friend. We were both young men then, and lived, I am afraid, rather a wild life, in the delightful city of our sojourn. One night we were idling about the neighbourhood of the Palais Royal, doubtful to what amusement we should next betake ourselves. My friend proposed a visit to Frascati's, but his suggestion was not to my taste. I knew Frascati's, as the French saying is, by heart; had lost and won plenty of five-franc pieces there, merely for amusement's sake, until it was amusement no longer; and was thoroughly tired, in fact, of all the ghastly respectabilities of such a social anomaly as a respectable gambling-house. 'For heaven's sake,' said I to my friend, 'let us go somewhere where we can see a little genuine, blackguard, poverty-stricken gaming, with no false gingerbread glitter thrown over it at all. Let us get away from fashionable Frascati's to a house where they don't mind letting in a man with a ragged coat, or a man with no coat, ragged or otherwise.' 'Very well,' said my friend, 'we needn't go out of the Palais Royal to find the sort of company you want. Here's the place just before us, as blackguard a place, by all report, as you could possibly wish to see.' In another minute we arrived at the door, and entered the house.

When we got upstairs, and had left our hats and sticks with the doorkeeper, we were admitted into the chief gambling-room. We did not find many people assembled there. But, few as the men were who looked up at us on our entrance, they were all types – lamentably true types – of their respective classes.

We had come to see blackguards, but these men were something worse. There is a comic side, more or less appreciable, in all blackguardism – here there was nothing but tragedy – mute, weird tragedy. The quiet in the room was horrible. The thin, haggard, long-haired young man, whose sunken eyes fiercely watched the turning of the cards, never spoke; the flabby, fat-faced, pimply player, who pricked his piece of pasteboard perseveringly, to register how often black won, and how often red – never spoke; the dirty wrinkled old man, with the vulture eyes and the darned greatcoat, who had lost his last sou, and still looked on desperately, after he could play no longer – never spoke. Even the voice of the croupier sounded as if it were strangely dulled and thickened in the atmosphere of the room. I had entered the place to laugh, but the spectacle before me was something to weep over. I soon found it necessary to take refuge in excitement from the depression of spirits which was fast stealing on me. Unfortunately I sought the nearest excitement, by going to the table and beginning to play. Still more unfortunately, as the event will show, I won – won prodigiously, won incredibly, won at such a rate, that the regular players at the table crowded round me and, staring at my stakes with hungry, superstitious eyes, whispered to one another that the English stranger was going to break the bank.

The game was Rouge et Noir. I had played at it in every city in Europe, without, however, the care or the wish to study the Theory of Chances – that philosopher's stone of all gamblers! And a gambler, in the strict sense of the word, I had never been. I was heart-whole from the corroding passion for play. My gaming was a mere idle amusement. I never resorted to it by necessity, because I never knew what it was to want money. I never practised it so incessantly as to lose more than I could afford, or to gain more than I could coolly pocket without being thrown off my balance by good luck. In short, I had hitherto frequented gambling-tables – just as I frequented ballrooms and opera-houses – because they amused me, and because I had nothing better to do with my leisure hours.

But on this occasion it was very different – now, for the first time in my life, I felt what the passion for play really was. My success first bewildered, and then, in the most literal meaning of the word, intoxicated me. Incredible as it may appear, it is nevertheless true, that I only lost when I attempted to estimate chances, and played according to previous calculation. If I left everything to luck, and staked without any care or consideration, I was sure to win – to win in the face of every recognised probability in favour of the bank. At first, some of the men present ventured their money safely enough on my colour, but I speedily increased my stakes to sums which they dared not risk. One after another they left off playing, and breathlessly looked on at my game.

Still, time after time, I staked higher and higher, and still won. The excitement in the room rose to fever pitch. The silence was interrupted by a deep-muttered chorus of oaths and exclamations, in different languages, every time the gold was shovelled across to my side of the table – even the imperturbable croupier dashed his rake on the floor in a (French) fury of astonishment at my success. But one man present preserved his self-possession, and that man was my friend. He came to my side, and whispering in English, begged me to leave the place, satisfied with what I had already gained. I must do to him the justice to say that he repeated his warnings and entreaties several times, and only left me and went away after I had rejected his advice (I was to all intents and purposes gambling drunk) in terms which rendered it impossible for him to address me again that night.

Shortly after he had gone, a hoarse voice behind me cried: 'Permit me, my dear sir! – permit me to restore to their proper place two Napoleons which you have dropped. Wonderful luck, sir! I pledge you my word of honour, as an old soldier, in the course of my long experience in this sort of thing, I never saw such luck as yours! – never! Go on, sir – *Sacré mille bombes!* Go on boldly, and break the bank!'

I turned round and saw, nodding and smiling at me with inveterate civility, a tall man, dressed in a frogged and braided surtout.

If I had been in my senses, I should have considered him, personally, as being rather a suspicious specimen of an old soldier. He had goggling bloodshot eyes, mangy mustachios and a broken nose. His voice betrayed a barrack-room intonation of the worst order, and he had the dirtiest pair of hands I ever saw – even in France. These little personal peculiarities exercised, however, no repelling influence on me. In the mad excitement, the reckless triumph of that moment, I was ready to 'fraternise' with anybody who encouraged me in my game. I accepted the old soldier's offered pinch of snuff, clapped him on the back and swore he was the honestest fellow in the world – the most glorious relic of the Grand Army that I had ever met with. 'Go on!' cried my military friend, snapping his fingers in ecstasy, – 'Go on, and win! Break the bank – *Mille tonnerres!* my gallant English comrade, break the bank!'

And I *did* go on – went on at such a rate that in another quarter of an hour the croupier called out: 'Gentlemen! the bank has discontinued for tonight.' All the notes and all the gold in that 'bank' now lay in a heap under my hands, the whole floating capital of the gambling-house was waiting to pour into my pockets!

'Tie up the money in your pocket-handkerchief, my worthy sir,' said the old soldier, as I wildly plunged my hands into my heap of gold. 'Tie it up, as we used to tie up a bit of dinner in the Grand Army, your winnings are too heavy for any breeches pockets that ever were sewed. There! that's it! – shovel them in, notes and all! *Credie!* what luck! – Stop! another Napoleon on the floor! Ah! *sacré petit polisson de Napoléon!* have I found thee at last? Now then, sir – two tight double knots each way with your honourable permission, and the money's safe. Feel it! feel it, fortunate sire! hard and round as a cannon ball – Ah, bah! if they had only fired such cannon balls at us at Austerlitz – *nom d'une pipe!* if they only had! And now, as an ancient grenadier, as an ex-brave of the French army, what remains for me to do? I ask what? Simply this, to entreat my valued English friend to drink a bottle of champagne with me, and toast the goddess Fortune in foaming goblets before we part!'

Excellent ex-brave! Convivial ancient gambler! Champagne by all means! An English cheer for an old soldier! Hurrah! hurrah! Another English cheer for the goddess Fortune! Hurrah! hurrah! hurrah!

'Bravo! the Englishman, the amiable, gracious Englishman, in whose veins circulates the vivacious blood of France! Another glass? Ah, bah! – the bottle is empty! Never mind! *Vive le vin!* I, the old soldier, order another bottle, and half a pound of *bonbons* with it!'

'No, no, ex-brave, never – ancient grenadier! *Your* bottle last time, *my* bottle this. Behold it! Toast away! The French Army! – the great Napoleon! – the present company! the croupier! the honest croupier's wife and daughters – if he has any! the ladies generally! Everybody in the world!'

By the time the second bottle of champagne was emptied, I felt as if I had been drinking liquid fire – my brain seemed all aflame. No excess in wine had ever had this effect on me before in my life. Was it the result of a stimulant acting upon my system when I was in a highly excited state? Was my stomach in a particularly disordered condition? Or was the champagne amazingly strong?

'Ex-brave of the French Army!' cried I, in a mad state of exhilaration, '*I* am on fire! how are *you*? You have set me on fire! Do you hear, my hero of Austerlitz? Let us have a third bottle of champagne to put the flame out!'

The old soldier wagged his head, rolled his goggle eyes, until I expected to see them slip out of their sockets, placed his dirty forefinger by the side of his dirty broken nose, solemnly ejaculated 'Coffee!' and immediately ran off into an inner room.

The word pronounced by the eccentric veteran seemed to have a magical effect on the rest of the company present. With one accord they all rose to depart. Probably they had expected to profit by my intoxication, but, finding that my new friend was benevolently bent on preventing me from getting dead drunk, had now abandoned all hope of thriving pleasantly on my winnings. Whatever their motive might be, at any rate they went away in a body. When the old soldier returned and sat down again opposite me at the table, we had the room to ourselves. I could see the croupier, in a sort of vestibule which opened out of it, eating his supper in solitude. The silence was now deeper than ever.

A sudden change, too, had come over the 'ex-brave'. He assumed a portentously solemn look and when he spoke to me again his speech was ornamented by no oaths, enforced by no finger-snapping, enlivened by no apostrophes or exclamations.

'Listen, my dear sir,' said he, in mysteriously confidential tones, 'listen to an old soldier's advice. I have been to the mistress of the house (a very charming woman, with a genius for cookery!) to impress on her the necessity of making us some particularly strong and good coffee. You must drink this coffee in order to get rid of your little amiable exaltation of spirits before you think of going home – you *must*, my good and gracious friend! With all that money to take home tonight, it is a sacred duty to yourself to have your wits about you. You are known to be a winner to an enormous extent by several gentlemen present tonight, who, in a certain point of view, are very worthy and excellent fellows, but they are mortal men, my dear sir, and they have their amiable weaknesses! Need I say more? Ah, no, no! you understand me!

Now, this is what you must do – send for a cabriolet when you feel quite well again – draw up all the windows when you get into it – and tell the driver to take you home only through the large well-lighted thoroughfares. Do this, and you and your money will be safe. Do this, and tomorrow you will thank an old soldier for giving you a word of honest advice.'

Just as the ex-brave ended his oration in very lachrymose tones, the coffee came in, ready poured out in two cups. My attentive friend handed me one of the cups with a bow. I was parched with thirst, and drank it off at a draught. Almost instantly afterwards, I was seized with a fit of giddiness, and felt more completely intoxicated than ever. The room whirled round and round furiously, the old soldier seemed to be regularly bobbing up and down before me like the piston of a steam-engine. I was half deafened by a violent singing in my ears; a feeling of utter bewilderment, helplessness, idiocy, overcame me. I rose from my chair, holding on by the table to keep my balance, and stammered out that I felt dreadfully unwell – so unwell that I did not know how I was to get home.

'My dear friend,' answered the old soldier – and even his voice seemed to be bobbing up and down as he spoke – 'my dear friend, it would be madness to go home in *your* state, you would be sure to lose your money; you might be robbed and murdered with the greatest ease. *I* am going to sleep here, do *you* sleep here, too – they make up capital beds in this house – take one, sleep off the effects of the wine, and go home safely with your winnings tomorrow – tomorrow, in broad daylight.'

I had but two ideas left – one, that I must never let go hold of my handkerchief full of money, the other, that I must lie down somewhere immediately, and fall off into a comfortable sleep. So I agreed to the proposal about the bed, and took the offered arm of the old soldier, carrying my money with my disengaged hand. Preceded by the croupier, we passed along some passages and up a flight of stairs into the bedroom which I was to occupy. The ex-brave shook me warmly by the hand, proposed that we should breakfast together, and then, followed by the croupier, left me for the night.

I ran to the wash-hand stand; drank some of the water in my jug; poured the rest out, and plunged my face into it; then sat down in a chair and tried to compose myself. I soon felt better. The change for my lungs from the fetid atmosphere of the gambling-room to the cool air of the apartment I now occupied, the almost equally refreshing change for my eyes from the glaring lights of the 'salon' to the dim, quiet flicker of one bedroom candle, both aided wonderfully the restorative effects of cold water. The giddiness left me, and I began to feel a little like a reasonable being again. My first thought was of the risk of sleeping all night in a gambling-house; my second, of the still greater risk of trying to get out after the house was closed, and of going home alone at night, through the streets of Paris, with a large sum of money about me. I had slept in worse places than this on my travels; so I determined to lock, bolt and barricade my door and take my chance till the next morning.

Accordingly, I secured myself against all intrusion; looked under the bed, and into the cupboard; tried the fastening of the window; and then, satisfied that I had taken every proper precaution, pulled off my upper clothing, put my light, which was a dim one, on the hearth among a feathery litter of wood ashes, and got into bed, with the handkerchief full of money under my pillow.

I soon felt that I could not go to sleep – that I could not even close my eyes. I was wide awake, and in a high fever. Every nerve in my body trembled – every one of my senses seemed to be preternaturally sharpened. I tossed and rolled, and tried every kind of position, and perseveringly sought out the cold corners of the bed, and all to no purpose. Now, I thrust my arms over the clothes; now, I violently shot my legs straight out down to the bottom of the bed; now, I convulsively coiled them up as near my chin as they would go; now, I shook out my crumpled pillow, changed it to the cool side, patted it flat, and lay down quietly on my back: now, I fiercely doubled it in two, set it up on end, thrust it against the board of the bed, and tried a sitting posture. Every effort was in vain; I groaned in vexation, as I felt that I was in for a sleepless night.

What could I do. I had no book to read. And yet, unless I found out some method of diverting my mind, I felt certain that I was in the condition to imagine all sorts of horrors; to rack my brain with forebodings of every possible and impossible danger; in short, to pass the night in suffering all conceivable varieties of nervous terror.

I raised myself on my elbow, and looked about the room – which was brightened by a lovely moonlight pouring straight through the window – to see if it contained any pictures or ornaments that I could at all clearly distinguish. While my eyes wandered from wall to wall, a remembrance of Le Maistre's delightful little book, *Voyage autour de ma chambre*, occurred to me. I resolved to imitate the French author, and find occupation and amusement enough to relieve the tedium of my wakefulness by making a mental inventory of every article of furniture I could see, and by following up to their sources the multitude associations which even a chair, a table or a wash-hand stand may be made to call forth.

In the nervous unsettled state of my mind at that moment, I found it much easier to make my inventory than to make my reflections, and thereupon soon gave up all hope of thinking in Le Maistre's fanciful track – or, indeed, of thinking at all. I looked about the room at different articles of furniture; and did nothing more.

There was, first, the bed I was lying in; a four-post bed, of all things in the world to meet with in Paris! – yes, a thorough clumsy British four-poster, with the regular top lined with chintz – the regular fringed valance all round – the regular stifling unwholesome curtains, which I remembered having mechanically drawn back against the posts without particularly noticing the bed when I first got into the room. Then there was the marble-topped wash-hand stand, from which the water I had spilt, in my hurry to pour it out, was still dripping, slowly and more slowly, on to the brick floor. Then two small chairs, with my coat, waistcoat and trousers flung on them. Then a large elbow-chair, covered with dirty-white dimity, with my cravat and shirt collar thrown over the back. Then a chest of drawers with two of the brass handles off, and a tawdry, broken china inkstand placed on it by way of ornament for the top. Then the dressing table, adorned by a very small looking-glass and a very large pin-cushion. Then the window – an unusually large window. Then a dark old picture, which the feeble candle dimly showed me. It was the picture of a fellow in a high Spanish hat, crowned with a plume of towering feathers. A swarthy sinister ruffian, looking upward, shading his eyes with his hand and looking intently upward – it might be at some tall gallows on which he was going to be hanged. At any rate, he had the appearance of thoroughly deserving it.

This picture put a kind of constraint upon me to look upward too – at the top of the bed. It was a gloomy and not an interesting object, and I looked back at the picture. I counted the feathers in the man's hat – they stood out in relief – three white, two green. I observed the crown of his hat, which was of a conical shape, according to the fashion supposed to have been favoured by Guido Fawkes. I wondered what he was looking up at. It couldn't be at the stars; such a desperado was neither astrologer nor astronomer. It must be the high gallows, and he was going to be hanged presently. Would the executioner come into possession of his conical-crowned hat and plume of feathers? I counted the feathers again – three white, two green.

While I still lingered over this very improving and intellectual employment, my thoughts insensibly began to wander. The moonlight shining into the room reminded me of a certain moonlight night in England – the night after a picnic party in a Welsh valley. Every incident of the drive homeward, through lovely scenery, which the moonlight made lovelier than ever, came back to my remembrance, though I had never given the picnic a thought for years – though, if I had *tried* to recollect it, I could certainly have recalled little or nothing of that scene long past. Of all the wonderful faculties that help to tell us we are immortal, which speaks the sublime truth more eloquently than memory? Here was I, in a strange house of the most suspicious character, in a situation of uncertainty and even of peril, which might seem to make the cool exercise of my recollection almost out of the question, nevertheless, remembering, quite involuntarily, places, people, conversations, minute circumstances of every kind, which I had thought forgotten forever; which I could not possibly have recalled at will, even under the most favourable auspices. And what cause had produced in a moment the whole of this strange, complicated, mysterious effect? Nothing but some rays of moonlight shining in at my bedroom window.

I was still thinking of that picnic – of our merriment on the drive home –

of the sentimental young lady who *would* quote *Childe Harold* because it was moonlight. I was absorbed by these past scenes and past amusements, when, in an instant, the thread on which my memories hung snapped asunder, my attention immediately came back to present things more vividly than ever and I found myself, I neither knew why nor wherefore, looking hard at the picture again.

Looking for what?

Good God! the man had pulled his hat down on his brows! – No! the hat itself was gone! Where was the conical crown? Where were the feathers – three white, two green? Not there? In place of the hat and feathers, what dusky object was it that now hid his forehead, his eyes, his shading hand?

Was the bed moving?

I turned on my back and looked up. Was I mad? – drunk? – dreaming? – giddy again? – or was the top of the bed really moving down – sinking slowly, regularly, silently, horribly, right down throughout the whole of its length and breadth – right down upon me, as I lay underneath?

My blood seemed to stand still. A deadly paralysing coldness stole all over me as I turned my head round on the pillow, and determined to test whether the bed-top was really moving or not by keeping my eye on the man in the picture.

The next look in that direction was enough. The dull, black, frowsy outline of the valance above me was within an inch of being parallel with his waist. I still looked breathlessly. And steadily, and slowly – very slowly – I saw the figure, and the line of frame below the figure, vanish, as the valance moved down before it.

I am, constitutionally, anything but timid. I have been on more than one occasion in peril of my life, and have not lost my self-possession for an instant, but when the conviction first settled on my mind that the bed top was really moving, was steadily and continuously sinking down upon me, I looked up shuddering, helpless, panic-stricken, beneath the hideous machinery for murder which was advancing closer and closer to suffocate me where I lay.

I looked up, motionless, speechless, breathless. The candle fully spent, went out, but the moonlight still brightened the room. Down and down, without pausing and without sounding, came the bed-top, and still my panic-terror seemed to bind me faster and faster to the mattress on which I lay – down and down it sank, till the dusty odour from the lining of the canopy came stealing into my nostrils.

At that final moment the instinct of self-preservation startled me out of my trance, and I moved at last. There was just room for me to roll myself sideways off the bed. As I dropped noiselessly to the floor, the edge of the murderous canopy touched me on the shoulder.

Without stopping to draw my breath, without wiping the cold sweat from my face, I rose instantly on my knees to watch the bed-top. I was literally spellbound by it. If I had heard footsteps behind me, I could not have turned round; if a means of escape had been miraculously provided for me, I could not have moved to take advantage of it. The whole life in me was, at that moment, concentrated in my eyes.

It descended – the whole canopy, with the fringe round it, came down – down – close down, so close that there was not room now to squeeze my finger between the bed-top and the bed. I felt at the sides, and discovered that what had appeared to me from beneath to be the ordinary light canopy of a four-poster bed, was in reality a thick, broad mattress, the substance of which was concealed by the valance and its fringe. I looked up and saw the four posts rising hideously bare. In the middle of the bed-top was a huge wooden screw that had evidently worked it down through a hole in the ceiling, just as ordinary presses are worked down on the substance selected for compression. The frightful apparatus moved without making the faintest noise. There had been no creaking as it came down; there was not the faintest sound from the room above. Amid a dead and awful silence I beheld before me – in the nineteenth century, and in the civilised capital of France – such a machine for secret murder by suffocation as might have existed in the worst days of the Inquisition, in the lonely inns among the Hartz Mountains, in the mysterious tribunals of Westphalia! Still, as I looked on it, I could not move, I could hardly breathe, but I began to recover the power of thinking, and in a moment I discovered the murderous conspiracy framed against me in all its horror.

My cup of coffee had been drugged, and drugged too strongly. I had been saved from being smothered by having taken an overdose of some narcotic. How I had chafed and fretted at the fever-fit which had preserved my life by keeping me awake! How recklessly I had confided myself to the two wretches who had led me into this room, determined, for the sake of my winnings, to kill me in my sleep by the surest and most horrible contrivance for secretly accomplishing my destruction! How many men, winners like me, had slept, as I had proposed to sleep, in that bed, and had never been seen or heard of more? I shuddered at the bare idea of it.

But, ere long, all thought was again suspended by the sight of the murderous canopy moving once more. After it had remained on the bed – as nearly as I could guess – about ten minutes, it began to move up again. The villains who worked it from above evidently believed that their purpose was now accomplished. Slowly and silently, as it descended, that horrible bed-top rose towards its former place. When it reached the upper extremities of the four posts, it reached the ceiling too. Neither hole nor screw could be seen, the bed became in appearance an ordinary bed again – the canopy an ordinary canopy – even to the most suspicious eyes.

Now, for the first time, I was able to move – to rise from my knees – to dress myself in my upper clothing – and to consider of how I should escape. If I betrayed, by the smallest noise, that the attempt to suffocate me had failed, I was certain to be murdered. Had I made any noise already? I listened intently, looking towards the door.

No! no footsteps in the passage outside – no sound of a tread, light or heavy, in the room above – absolute silence everywhere. Besides locking and bolting my door, I had moved an old wooden chest against it, which I had found under the bed. To remove this chest (my blood ran cold as I thought of what its contents *might* be!) without making some disturbance was impossible, and, moreover, to think of escaping through the house, now barred up for the night, was sheer insanity. Only one chance was left me – the window. I stole to it on tiptoe.

My bedroom was on the first floor, above an *entresol*, and looked into a back street. I raised my hand to open the window, knowing that on that action hung, by the merest hair's breadth, my chance of safety. They keep vigilant watch in a House of Murder. If any part of the frame cracked, if the hinge creaked, I was a lost man! It must have occupied me at least five minutes, reckoning by time – five *hours*, reckoning by suspense – to open that window. I succeeded in doing it silently – in doing it with all the dexterity of a housebreaker – and then looked down into the street. To leap the distance beneath me would be almost certain destruction! Next, I looked round at the sides of the house. Down the left side ran a thick waterpipe – it passed close by the outer edge of the window. The moment I saw the pipe, I knew I must be saved. My breath came and went freely for the first time since I had seen the canopy of the bed moving down upon me!

To some men the means of escape which I had discovered might have seemed difficult and dangerous enough – to *me* the prospect of slipping down the pipe into the street did not suggest even a thought of peril. I had always been accustomed, by the practice of gymnastics, to keep up my schoolboy powers as a daring and expert climber, and knew that my head, hands and feet would serve me faithfully in any hazards of ascent or descent. I had already got one leg over the window-sill when I remembered the handkerchief filled with money under my pillow. I could have well afforded to leave it behind me, but I was revengefully determined that the miscreants of the gambling-house should miss their plunder as well as their victim. So I went back to the bed and tied the heavy handkerchief at my back by my cravat.

Just as I had made it tight and fixed it in a comfortable place, I thought I heard a sound of breathing outside the door. The chill feeling of horror ran through me again as I listened. No! dead silence still in the passage – I had only heard the night air blowing softly into the room. The next moment I was on the window-sill – and the next I had a firm grip on the waterpipe with my hands and knees.

I slid down into the street easily and quietly, as I thought I should, and immediately set off at the top of my speed to a branch prefecture of police, which I knew was situated in the immediate neighbourhood. A sub-prefect, and several picked men among his subordinates, happened to be up, maturing, I believe, some scheme for discovering the perpetrator of a mysterious murder which all Paris was talking of just then. When I began my story, in a breathless hurry and in very bad French, I could see that the sub-prefect suspected me of being a drunken Englishman who had robbed somebody, but he soon altered his opinion as I went on, and before I had anything like concluded, he shoved all the papers before him into a drawer, put on his hat, supplied me with another (for I was bare-headed), ordered a file of soldiers, desired his expert followers to get ready all sorts of tools for breaking open doors and ripping up brick-flooring, and took my arm, in the most friendly and familiar manner possible, to lead me with him out of the house. I will venture to say that when the sub-prefect was a little boy, and was taken for the first time to the play, he was not half as much pleased as he was now at the job in prospect for him at the gambling-house!

Away we went through the streets, the sub-prefect cross-examining and congratulating me in the same breath as we marched at the head of our formidable *posse comitatus*. Sentinels were placed at the back and front of the house the moment we got to it and a tremendous battery of knocks was directed against the door; a light appeared at a window; I was told to conceal myself behind the police; then came more knocks, and a cry of, 'Open in the name of the law !' At that terrible summons bolts and locks gave way before an invisible hand, and the moment after the sub-prefect was in the passage, confronting a waiter half dressed and ghastly pale. This was the short dialogue which immediately took place:

'We want to see the Englishman who is sleeping in this house.'

'He went away hours ago.'

'He did no such thing. His friend went away, *he* remained. Show us to his bedroom!'

'I swear to you, Monsieur le Sous-prefect, he is not here! He – '

'I swear to you, Monsieur le garçon, he is. He slept here – he didn't find your bed comfortable – he came to us to complain of it – here he is among my men – and here am I ready to look for a flea or two in his bedstead. Renaudin!' (calling to one of the subordinates, and pointing to the waiter) 'collar that man, and tie his hands behind him. Now then, gentlemen, let us walk upstairs.'

Every man and woman in the house was secured – the 'old soldier' the first. Then I identified the bed in which I had slept, and then we went into the room above.

No object that was at all extraordinary appeared in any part of it. The sub-prefect looked round the place, commanded everybody to be silent, stamped twice on the floor, called for a candle, looked attentively at the spot he had stamped on, and ordered the flooring there to be carefully taken up. This was done in no time. Lights were produced, and we saw a deep raftered cavity between the floor of this room and the ceiling of the room beneath. Through this cavity there ran perpendicularly a sort of case of iron thickly greased, and inside the case appeared the screw, which communicated with the bed-top below. Extra lengths of screws, freshly oiled, levers covered with felt, all the complete upper works of a heavy press – constructed with infernal ingenuity so as to join the fixtures below, and when taken to pieces again to go into the smallest possible compass – were next discovered and pulled out on the floor. After some little difficulty, the sub-prefect succeeded in putting the machinery together and, leaving his men to work it, descended with me to the bedroom. The smothering canopy was then lowered, but not so noiselessly as I had seen it lowered. When I mentioned this to the sub-prefect, his answer, simple as it was, had a terrible significance. 'My men,' said he, 'are working down the bed-top for the first time – the men whose money you won were in better practice.'

We left the house in the sole possession of two police agents – every one of the inmates being removed to prison on the spot. The sub-prefect, after taking down my *procès verbal* in his office, returned with me to my hotel to get my passport. 'Do you think,' I asked, as I gave it to him, 'that any men have really been smothered in that bed, as they tried to smother me?'

'I have seen dozens of drowned men laid out at the morgue,' answered the sub-prefect, 'in whose pocket-books were found letters stating that they had committed suicide in the Seine, because they had lost everything at the gaming-table. Do I know how many of those men entered the same gambling-house that you entered? – won as *you* won? – took that bed as you took it? – slept in it? – were smothered in it? – and were privately thrown into the river, with a letter of explanation written by the murderers and placed in their pocket-books? No man can say how many or how few have suffered the fate from which you have escaped. The people of the gambling-house kept their bedstead machinery a secret from *us* – even from the police! The dead keet the rest of the secret for them. Good-night, or rather good-morning, Monsieur Faulkner! Be at my office again at nine o'clock – in the meantine, *au revoir*!'

The rest of my story is soon told. I was examined and re-examined, the gambling-house was strictly searched all through from top to bottom, the prisoners were separately interrogated and two of the less guilty among them made a confession. I discovered that the old soldier was the master of the gambling-house – justice discovered that he had been drummed out of the army as a vagabond years ago, that he had been guilty of all sorts of villainies since, that he was in possession of stolen property, which the owners identified, and that he, the croupier, another accomplice, and the woman who had made my cup of coffee, were all in the secret of the bedstead. There appeared some reason to doubt whether the inferior persons attached to the house knew anything of the suffocating machinery, and they received the benefit of that doubt by being treated simply as thieves and vagabonds. As for the old soldier and his two head-myrmidons, they went to the galleys; the woman who had drugged my coffee was imprisoned for I forget how many years, the regular attendants at the gambling-house were considered 'suspicious', and placed under 'surveillance', and I became, for one whole week (which is a long time), the head 'lion' in Parisian society. My adventure was dramatised by three illustrious play-makers, but never saw theatrical daylight, for the censorship forbade the introduction on the stage of a correct copy of the gambling-house bedstead.

One good result was produced by my adventure, which any censorship must have approved – it cured me of ever again trying Rouge et Noir as an amusement. The sight of a green cloth with packs of cards and heaps of money on it will henceforth be forever associated in my mind with the sight of a bed-canopy descending to suffocate me in the silence and darkness of the night.

The Damned Thing

AMBROSE BIERCE

I

One Does Not Always Eat What Is on the Table

BY THE LIGHT OF A TALLOW CANDLE which had been placed on one end of a rough table a man was reading something written in a book. It was an old account book, greatly worn; and the writing was not, apparently, very legible, for the man sometimes held the page close to the flame of the candle to get a stronger light on it. The shadow of the book would then throw into obscurity a half of the room, darkening a number of faces and figures; for besides the reader, eight other men were present. Seven of them sat against the rough log walls, silent, motionless, and the room being small, not very far from the table. By extending an arm any one of them could have touched the eighth man, who lay on the table, face upward, partly covered by a sheet, his arms at his sides. He was dead.

The man with the book was not reading aloud, and no one spoke; all seemed to be waiting for something to occur; the dead man only was without expectation. From the blank darkness outside came in, through the aperture that served for a window, all the ever unfamiliar noises of night in the wilderness – the long nameless note of a distant coyote; the stilly pulsing thrill of tireless insects in trees; strange cries of night birds, so different from those of the birds of day; the drone of great blundering beetles, and all that mysterious chorus of small sounds that seem always to have been but half heard when they have suddenly ceased, as if conscious of an indiscretion. But nothing of all this was noted in that company; its members were not overmuch addicted to idle interest in matters of no practical importance; that was obvious in every line of their rugged faces – obvious even in the dim light of the single candle. They were evidently men of the vicinity – farmers and woodsmen.

The person reading was a trifle different; one would have said of him that he was of the world, worldly, albeit there was that in his attire which attested a certain fellowship with the organisms of his environment. His coat would hardly have passed muster in San Francisco; his footgear was not of urban origin, and the hat that lay by him on the floor (he was the only one uncovered) was such that if one had considered it as an article of mere personal adornment one would have missed its meaning. In countenance the man was rather prepossessing, with just a hint of sternness; though that he may have assumed or cultivated, as appropriate to one in authority. For he was a coroner. It was by virtue of his office that he had possession of the book in which he was reading; it had been found among the dead man's effects – in his cabin, where the inquest was now taking place.

When the coroner had finished reading he put the book into his breast pocket. At that moment the door was pushed open and a young man entered. He, clearly, was not of mountain birth and breeding: he was clad as those who dwell in cities. His clothing was dusty, however, as from travel. He had, in fact, been riding hard to attend the inquest.

The coroner nodded; no one else greeted him.

'We have waited for you,' said the coroner. 'It is necessary to have done with this business tonight.'

The young man smiled. 'I am sorry to have kept you,' he said. 'I went away, not to evade your summons, but to post to my newspaper an account of what I suppose I am called back to relate.'

The coroner smiled.

'The account that you posted to your newspaper,' he said, 'differs, probably, from that which you will give here under oath.'

'That,' replied the other, rather hotly and with a visible flush, 'is as you please. I used manifold paper and have a copy of what I sent. It was not written as news, for it is incredible, but as fiction. It may go as a part of my testimony under oath.'

'But you say it is incredible.'

'That is nothing to you, sir, if I also swear that it is true.'

The coroner was silent for a time, his eyes upon the floor. The men about the sides of the cabin talked in whispers, but seldom withdrew their gaze from the face of the corpse. Presently the coroner lifted his eyes and said: 'We will resume the inquest.'

The men removed their hats. The witness was sworn.

'What is your name?' the coroner asked.

'William Harker.'

'Age?'

'Twenty-seven.'

'You knew the deceased, Hugh Morgan?'

'Yes.'

'You were with him when he died?'

'Near him.'

'How did that happen – your presence, I mean?'

'I was visiting him at this place to shoot and fish. A part of my purpose, however, was to study him and his odd, solitary way of life. He seemed a good model for a character in fiction. I sometimes write stories.'

'I sometimes read them.'

'Thank you.'

'Stories in general – not yours.'

Some of the jurors laughed. Against a sombre background humour shows high lights. Soldiers in the intervals of battle laugh easily, and a jest in the death chamber conquers by surprise.

'Relate the circumstances of this man's death,' said the coroner. 'You may use any notes or memoranda that you please.'

The witness understood. Pulling a manuscript from his breast pocket he held it near the candle and turning the leaves until he found the passage that he wanted began to read.

II

What May Happen in a Field of Wild Oats

'. . . The sun had hardly risen when we left the house. We were looking for quail, each with a shotgun, but we had only one dog. Morgan said that our best ground was beyond a certain ridge that he pointed out, and we crossed it by a trail through the *chaparral*. On the other side was comparatively level ground, thickly covered with wild oats. As we emerged from the *chaparral* Morgan was but a few yards in advance. Suddenly we heard, at a little distance to our right and partly in front, a noise as of some animal thrashing about in the bushes, which we could see were violently agitated.

' "We've started a deer," I said. " I wish we had brought a rifle."

'Morgan, who had stopped and was intently watching the agitated *chaparral*, said nothing, but had cocked both barrels of his gun and was holding it in readiness to aim. I thought him a trifle excited, which surprised me, for he had a reputation for exceptional coolness, even in moments of sudden and imminent peril.

' "Oh, come," I said. "You are not going to fill up a deer with quail-shot, are you?"

'Still he did not reply; but catching a sight of his face as he turned it slightly toward me I was struck by the intensity of his look. Then I understood that we had serious business in hand, and my first conjecture was that we had "jumped" a grizzly. I advanced to Morgan's side, cocking my piece as I moved.

'The bushes were now quiet and the sounds had ceased, but Morgan was as attentive to the place as before.

' "What is it? What the devil is it?" I asked.

' "That Damned Thing!" he replied, without turning his head. His voice was husky and unnatural. He trembled visibly.

'I was about to speak further, when I observed the wild oats near the place of the disturbance moving – in the most inexplicable way. I can hardly describe it. They seemed as if stirred by a streak of wind, which not only bent them, but pressed them down – crushed them so that they did not rise; and this movement was slowly prolonging itself directly towards us.

'Nothing that I had ever seen had affected me so strangely as this unfamiliar and unaccountable phenomenon, yet I am unable to recall any sense of fear. I remember – and tell it here because, singularly enough, I recollected it then – that once in looking carelessly out of an open window I momentarily mistook a small tree close at hand for one of a group of larger trees at a little distance away. It looked the same size as the others, but being more distinctly and sharply defined in mass and detail seemed out of harmony with them. It was a mere falsification of the law of aerial perspective, but it startled, almost terrified me. We so rely upon the orderly operation of familiar natural laws that any seeming suspension of them is noted as a menace to our safety, a warning of unthinkable calamity. So now the apparently causeless movement of the herbage and the slow, undeviating approach of the line of disturbance were distinctly disquieting. My companion appeared actually frightened, and I could hardly credit my senses when I saw him suddenly throw his gun to his shoulder and fire both barrels at the agitated grain! Before the smoke of the discharge had cleared away I heard a loud savage cry – a scream like that of a wild animal – and flinging his gun upon the ground Morgan sprang away and ran swiftly from the spot. At the same instant I was thrown violently to the ground by the impact of something unseen in the smoke – some soft, heavy substance that seemed thrown against me with great force.

'Before I could get upon my feet and recover my gun, which seemed to have been struck from my hands, I heard Morgan crying out as if in mortal agony, and mingling with his cries were such hoarse, savage sounds as one hears from fighting dogs. Inexpressibly terrified, I struggled to my feet and looked in the direction of Morgan's retreat; and may heaven in mercy spare me from another sight like that! At a distance of less than thirty yards was my friend, down upon one knee, his head thrown back at a frightful angle, hatless, his long hair in disorder and his whole body in violent movement from side to side, backwards and forwards. His right arm was lifted and seemed to lack the hand – at least, I could see none. The other arm was invisible. At times, as my memory now reports this extraordinary scene, I could discern but a part of his body; it was as if he had been partly blotted out – I cannot otherwise express it – then a shifting of his position would bring it all into view again.

'All this must have occurred within a few seconds, yet in that time Morgan assumed all the postures of a determined wrestler vanquished by superior weight and strength. I saw nothing but him, and him not always distinctly. During the entire incident his shouts and curses were heard, as if through an enveloping uproar of such sounds of rage and fury as I had never heard from the throat of man or brute!

'For a moment only I stood irresolute, then throwing down my gun I ran forward to my friend's assistance. I had a vague belief that he was suffering from a fit, or some form of convulsion. Before I could reach his side he was down and quiet. All sounds had ceased, but with a feeling of such terror as even these awful events had not inspired I now saw again the mysterious movement of the wild oats, prolonging itself from the trampled area about the prostrate man towards the edge of a wood. It was only when it had reached the wood that I was able to withdraw my eyes and look at my companion. He was dead.'

III

A Man Though Naked May Be in Rags

The coroner rose from his seat and stood beside the dead man. Lifting an edge of the sheet he pulled it away, exposing the entire body, altogether naked and showing in the candlelight a clay-like yellow. It had, however, broad maculations of bluish black, obviously caused by extravasated blood from contusions. The chest and sides looked as if they had been beaten with a bludgeon. There were dreadful lacerations; the skin was torn in strips and shreds.

The coroner moved round to the end of the table and undid a silk handkerchief which had been passed under the chin and knotted on the top of the head. When the handkerchief was drawn away it exposed what had been the throat. Some of the jurors who had risen to get a better view repented their curiosity and turned away their faces. Witness Harker went to the open window and leaned out across the sill, faint and sick. Dropping the handkerchief upon the dead man's neck the coroner stepped to an angle of the room and from a pile of clothing produced one garment after another, each of which he held up a moment for inspection. All were torn, and stiff with blood. The jurors did not make a closer inspection. They seemed rather uninterested. They had, in truth, seen all this before, the only thing that was new to them being Harker's testimony.

'Gentlemen,' the coroner said, 'we have no more evidence, I think. Your duty has been already explained to you; if there is nothing you wish to ask you may go outside and consider your verdict.'

The foreman rose – a tall, bearded man of sixty, coarsely clad.

'I should like to ask one question, Mr Coroner,' he said. 'What asylum did this yer last witness escape from?'

'Mr Harker,' said the coroner gravely and tranquilly, 'from what asylum did you last escape?'

Harker flushed crimson again, but said nothing, and the seven jurors rose and solemnly filed out of the cabin.

'If you have done insulting me, sir,' said Harker, as soon as he and the officer were left alone with the dead man, 'I suppose I am at liberty to go?'

'Yes.'

Harker started to leave, but paused, with his hand on the door latch. The habit of his profession was strong in him – stronger than his sense of personal dignity. He turned about and said: 'The book that you have there – I recognise it as Morgan's diary. You seemed greatly interested in it; you read in it while I was testifying. May I see it? The public would like – '

'The book will cut no figure in this matter,' replied the official, slipping it into his coat pocket; 'all the entries in it were made before the writer's death.'

As Harker passed out of the house the jury re-entered and stood about the table, on which the now covered corpse showed under the sheet with sharp definition. The foreman seated himself near the candle, produced from his breast pocket a pencil and scrap of paper and wrote rather laboriously the following verdict, which with various degrees of effort all signed: 'We, the jury, do find that the remains come to their death at the hands of a mountain lion, but some of us thinks, all the same, they had fits.'

IV

An Explanation from the Tomb

In the diary of the late Hugh Morgan are certain interesting entries having, possibly, a scientific value as suggestions. At the inquest upon his body the book was not put in evidence; possibly the coroner thought it not worth-while to confuse the jury. The date of the first of the entries mentioned cannot be ascertained; the upper part of the leaf is torn away; the part of the entry remaining follows:

> . . . would run in a half-circle, keeping his head turned always towards the centre, and again he would stand still, barking furiously. At last he ran away into the brush as fast as he could go. I thought at first that he had gone mad, but on returning to the house found no other alteration in his manner than what was obviously due to fear of punishment.
>
> Can a dog see with his nose? Do odours impress some cerebral centre with images of the thing that emitted them? . . .

September 2 – Looking at the stars last night as they rose above the crest of the ridge east of the house, I observed them successively disappear – from left to right. Each was eclipsed but an instant, and only a few at the same time, but along the entire length of the ridge all that were within a degree or two of the crest were blotted out. It was as if something had passed along between me and them; but I could not see it, and the stars were not thick enough to define its outline. Ugh! don't like this . . .

Several weeks' entries are missing, three leaves being torn from the book.

September 27 – It has been about here again – I find evidences of its presence every day. I watched again all last night in the same cover, gun in hand, double-charged with buckshot. In the morning the fresh footprints were there, as before. Yet I would have sworn that I did not sleep – indeed, I hardly sleep at all. It is terrible, insupportable! If these amazing experiences are real I shall go mad; if they are fanciful I am mad already.

October 3 – I shall not go – it shall not drive me away. No, this is *my* house, *my* land. God hates a coward . . .

October 5 – I can stand it no longer; I have invited Harker to pass a few weeks with me – he has a level head. I can judge from his manner if he thinks me mad.

October 7 – I have the solution of the mystery; it came to me last night – suddenly, as by revelation. How simple – how terribly simple!

There are sounds that we cannot hear. At either end of the scale are notes that stir no chord of that imperfect instrument, the human ear. They are too high or too grave. I have observed a flock of blackbirds occupying an entire tree-top – the tops of several trees – and all in full song. Suddenly – in a moment – at absolutely the same instant – all sprang into the air and flew away. How? They could not all see one another – whole tree-tops intervened. At no point could a leader have been visible to all. There must have been a signal of warning or command, high and shrill above the din, but by me unheard. I have observed, too, the same simultaneous flight when all were silent, among not only blackbirds, but other birds – quail, for example, widely separated by bushes – even on opposite sides of a hill.

It is known to seamen that a school of whales basking or sporting on the surface of the ocean, miles apart, with the convexity of the earth between, will sometimes dive at the same instant – all gone out of sight in a moment. The signal has been sounded – too grave for the ear of the sailor at the masthead and his comrades on the deck – who nevertheless feel its vibrations in the ship as the stones of a cathedral are stirred by the bass of the organ.

As with sounds, so with colours. At each end of the solar spectrum the chemist can detect the presence of what are known as 'actinic' rays. They represent colours – integral colours in the composition of light – which we are unable to discern. The human eye is an imperfect instrument; its range is but a few octaves of the real 'chromatic scale'. I am not mad; there are colours that we cannot see.

And, God help me! the Damned Thing is of such a colour!

The Jolly Corner

HENRY JAMES

I

'EVERYONE ASKS me what I "think" of everything,' said Spencer Brydon; 'and I make answer as I can – begging or dodging the question, putting them off with any nonsense. It wouldn't matter to any of them really,' he went on, 'for, even were it possible to meet in that stand-and-deliver way so silly a demand on so big a subject, my "thoughts" would still be almost altogether about something that concerns only myself.' He was talking to Miss Staverton, with whom for a couple of months now he had availed himself of every possible occasion to talk; this disposition and this resource, this comfort and support, as the situation in fact presented itself, having promptly enough taken the first place in the considerable array of rather unattenuated surprises attending his so strangely belated return to America. Everything was somehow a surprise; and that might be natural when one had so long and so consistently neglected everything, taken pains to give surprises so much margin for play. He had given them more than thirty years – thirty-three, to be exact; and they now seemed to him to have organised their performance quite on the scale of that licence. He had been twenty-three on leaving New York – he was fifty-six today: unless indeed he were to reckon as he had sometimes, since his repatriation, found himself feeling; in which case he would have lived longer than is often allotted to man. It would have taken a century, he repeatedly said to himself, and said also to Alice Staverton, it would have taken a longer absence and a more averted mind than those even of which he had been guilty, to pile up the differences, the newnesses, the queernesses, above all the bignesses, for the better or the worse, that at present assaulted his vision wherever he looked.

The great fact all the while however had been the incalculability; since he *had* supposed himself, from decade to decade, to be allowing, and in the most liberal and intelligent manner, for brilliancy of change. He actually saw that he had allowed for nothing; he missed what he would have been sure of finding, he found what he would never have imagined. Proportions and values were upside-down; the ugly things he had expected, the ugly things of his far-away youth, when he had too promptly waked up to a sense of the ugly – these uncanny phenomena placed him rather, as it happened, under the charm; whereas the 'swagger' things, the modern, the monstrous, the famous things, those he had more particularly, like thousands of ingenuous enquirers every year, come over to see, were exactly his sources of dismay. They were as so many set traps for displeasure, above all for reaction, of which his restless tread was constantly pressing the spring. It was interesting, doubtless, the whole show, but it would have been too disconcerting hadn't a certain finer truth saved the situation. He had distinctly not, in this steadier light, come over *all* for the monstrosities; he had come, not only in the last analysis but quite on the face of the act, under an impulse with which they had nothing to do. He had come – putting the thing pompously – to look at his 'property', which he had thus for a third of a century not been within four thousand miles of; or, expressing it less sordidly, he had yielded to the humour of seeing again his house on the jolly corner, as he usually, and quite fondly, described it – the one in which he had first seen the light, in which various members of his family had lived and had died, in which the holidays of his overschooled boyhood had been passed and the few social flowers of his chilled adolescence gathered, and which, alienated then for so long a period, had, through the successive deaths of his two brothers and the termination of old arrangements, come wholly into his hands. He was the owner of another, not quite so 'good' – the jolly corner having been, from far back, superlatively extended and consecrated; and the value of the pair represented his main capital, with an income consisting, in these later years, of their respective rents which (thanks precisely to their original excellent type) had never been depressingly low. He could live in 'Europe', as he had been in the habit of living, on the product of these flourishing New York leases, and all the better since that of the second structure, the mere number in its long row, having within a twelvemonth fallen in, renovation at a high advance had proved beautifully possible.

These were items of property indeed, but he had found himself since his arrival distinguishing more than ever between them. The house within the street, two bristling blocks westward, was already in course of reconstruction as a tall mass of flats; he had acceded, some time before, to overtures for this conversion – in which, now that it was going forward, it had been not the least of his astonishments to find himself able, on the spot, and though without a previous ounce of such experience, to participate with a certain intelligence, almost with a certain authority. He had lived his life with his back so turned to such concerns and his face addressed to those of so different an order that he scarce knew what to make of this lively stir, in a compartment of his mind never yet penetrated, of a capacity for business and a sense for construction. These virtues, so common all round him now, had been dormant in his own organism – where it might be said of them perhaps that they had slept the sleep of the just. At present, in the splendid autumn weather – the autumn at least was a pure boon in the terrible place –

he loafed about his 'work' undeterred, secretly agitated; not in the least 'minding' that the whole proposition, as they said, was vulgar and sordid, and ready to climb ladders, to walk the plank, to handle materials and look wise about them, to ask questions, in fine, and challenge explanations and really 'go into' figures.

It amused, it verily quite charmed him; and, by the same stroke, it amused, and even more, Alice Staverton, though perhaps charming her perceptibly less. She wasn't however going to be better-off for it, as *he* was – and so astonishingly much; nothing was now likely, he knew, ever to make her better-off than she found herself, in the afternoon of life, as the delicately frugal possessor and tenant of the small house in Irving Place to which she had subtly managed to cling through her almost unbroken New York career. If he knew the way to it now better than to any other address among the dreadful multiplied numberings which seemed to him to reduce the whole place to some vast ledger-page, overgrown, fantastic, of ruled and criss-crossed lines and figures – if he had formed, for his consolation, that habit, it was really not a little because of the charm of his having encountered and recognised, in the vast wilderness of the wholesale, breaking through the mere gross generalisation of wealth and force and success, a small still scene where items and shades, all delicate things, kept the sharpness of the notes of a high voice perfectly trained, and where economy hung about like the scent of a garden. His old friend lived with one maid and herself dusted her relics and trimmed her lamps and polished her silver; she stood off, in the awful modern crush, when she could, but she sallied forth and did battle when the challenge was really to 'spirit', the spirit she after all confessed to, proudly and a little shyly, as to that of the better time, that of *their* common, their quite far-away and antediluvian social period and order. She made use of the street-cars when need be, the terrible things that people scrambled for as the panic-stricken at sea scramble for the boats; she affronted, inscrutably, under stress, all the public concussions and ordeals; and yet, with that slim mystifying grace of her appearance, which defied you to say if she were a fair young woman who looked older through trouble, or a fine smooth older one who looked young through successful indifference; with her precious refer-ence, above all, to memories and histories into which he could enter, she was as exquisite for him as some pale pressed flower (a rarity to begin with), and, failing other sweetnesses, she was a sufficient reward of his effort. They had communities of knowledge, 'their' knowledge (this discriminating possessive was always on her lips) of presences of the other age, presences all overlaid, in his case, by the experience of a man and the freedom of a wanderer, overlaid by pleasure, by infidelity, by passages of life that were strange and dim to her, just by 'Europe' in short, but still unobscured, still exposed and cherished, under that pious visitation of the spirit from which she had never been diverted.

She had come with him one day to see how his 'apartment-house' was rising; he had helped her over gaps and explained to her plans, and while they were there had happened to have, before her, a brief but lively discussion with the man in charge, the representative of the building-firm that had undertaken his work. He had found himself quite 'standing-up' to this personage over a failure on the latter's part to observe some detail of one of their noted conditions, and had so lucidly argued his case that, besides ever so prettily flushing, at the time, for sympathy in his triumph, she had afterwards said to him (though to a slightly greater effect of irony) that he had clearly for too many years neglected a real gift. If he had but stayed at home he would have anticipated the inventor of the skyscraper. If he had but stayed at home he would have discovered his genius in time really to start some new variety of awful architectural hare and run it till it burrowed in a goldmine. He was to remember these words, while the weeks elapsed, for the small silver ring they had sounded over the queerest and deepest of his own lately most disguised and most muffled vibrations.

It had begun to be present to him after the first fortnight, it had broken out with the oddest abruptness, this particular wanton wonderment; it met him there – and this was the image under which he himself judged the matter, or at least, not a little, thrilled and flushed with it – very much as he might have been met by some strange figure, some unexpected occupant, at a turn of one of the dim passages of an empty house. The quaint analogy quite hauntingly remained with him, when he didn't indeed rather improve it by a still intenser form: that of his opening a door behind which he would have made sure of finding nothing, a door into a room shuttered and void, and yet so coming, with a great suppressed start, on some quite erect confronting presence, something planted in the middle of the place and facing him through the dusk. After that visit to the house in construction he walked with his companion to see the other and always so much the better one, which in the eastward direction formed one of the corners, the 'jolly' one precisely, of the street now so generally dishonoured and disfigured in its westward reaches, and of the comparatively conservative avenue. The avenue still had pretensions, as Miss Staverton said, to decency; the old people had mostly gone, the old names were unknown, and here and there an old association seemed to stray, all vaguely, like some very aged person, out too late, whom you might meet and feel the impulse to watch or follow, in kindness, for safe restoration to shelter.

They went in together, our friends; he admitted himself with his key, as he kept no one there, he explained, preferring, for his reasons, to leave the place empty, under a simple arrangement with a good woman living in the neighbourhood who came for a daily hour to open windows and dust and sweep. Spencer Brydon had his reasons and was growingly aware of them; they seemed to him better each time he was there, though he didn't name them all to his companion, any more than he told her as yet how often, how quite absurdly often, he himself came. He only let her see for the present, while they walked through the great blank rooms, that absolute vacancy reigned and that, from top to bottom, there was nothing but Mrs Muldoon's broomstick, in a corner, to tempt the burglar. Mrs Muldoon was then on the premises, and she loquaciously attended the visitors, preceding them from room to room and pushing back shutters and throwing up sashes – all to show them, as she remarked, how little there was to see. There was little indeed to see in the great gaunt shell where the main dispositions and the general apportionment of space, the style of an age of ampler allowances, had nevertheless for its master their honest pleading message, affecting him as some good old servant's, some lifelong retainer's appeal for a character, or even for a retiring-pension; yet it was also a remark of Mrs Muldoon's that, glad as she was to oblige him by her noonday round, there was a request she greatly hoped he would never make of her. If he should wish her for any reason to come in after dark she would just tell him, if he 'plased', that he must ask it of somebody else.

The fact that there was nothing to see didn't militate for the worthy woman against what one *might* see, and she put it frankly to Miss Staverton that no lady could be expected to like, could she? 'craping up to thim top storeys in the ayvil hours'. The gas and the electric light were off in the house, and she fairly evoked a gruesome vision of her march through the great grey rooms – so many of them as there were too! – with her glimmering taper. Miss Staverton met her honest glare with a smile and the profession that she herself certainly would recoil from such an adventure. Spencer Brydon meanwhile held his peace – for the moment; the question of the 'evil' hours in his old home had already become too grave for him. He had begun some time since to 'crape', and he knew just why a packet of candles addressed to that pursuit had been stowed by his own hand, three weeks before, at the back of a drawer of the fine old sideboard that occupied, as a 'fixture', the deep recess in the dining-room. Just now he laughed at his companions – quickly however changing the subject; for the reason that, in the first place, his laugh struck him even at that moment as starting the odd echo, the conscious human resonance (he scarce knew how to qualify it) that sounds made while he was there alone sent back to his ear or his fancy; and that, in the second, he imagined Alice Staverton for the instant on the point of asking him, with a divination, if he ever so prowled. There were divinations he was unprepared for, and he had at all events averted enquiry by the time Mrs Muldoon had left them, passing on to other parts.

There was happily enough to say, on so consecrated a spot, that could be said freely and fairly; so that a whole train of declarations was precipitated by his friend's having herself broken out, after a yearning look round: 'But I hope you don't mean they want you to pull *this* to pieces!' His answer came, promptly, with his reawakened wrath: it was of course exactly what they wanted, and what they were 'at' him for daily, with the iteration of people who couldn't for their life understand a man's liability to decent feelings. He had found the place, just as it stood and beyond what he could express, an interest and a joy. There were values other than the beastly rent-values, and in short, in short – ! But it was thus Miss Staverton took him up. 'In short, you're to make so good a thing of your skyscraper that, living in luxury on *those* illgotten gains, you can afford for a while to be sentimental here!' Her smile had for him, with the words, the particular mild irony with which he found half her talk suffused; an irony without bitterness and that came, exactly, from her having so much imagination – not, like the cheap sarcasms with which one heard most people, about the world of 'society', bid for the reputation of cleverness, from nobody's really having any. It was agreeable to him at this very moment to be sure that when he had answered, after a brief demur, 'Well yes: so, precisely, you may put it!' her imagination would still do him justice. He explained that even if never a dollar were to come to him from the other house he would nevertheless cherish this one; and he dwelt, further, while they lingered and wandered, on the fact of the stupefaction he was already exciting, the positive mystification he felt himself create.

He spoke of the value of all he read into it, into the mere sight of the walls, mere shapes of the rooms, mere sound of the floors, mere feel, in his hand, of the old silver-plated knobs of the several mahogany doors, which suggested the pressure of the palms of the dead; the seventy years of the past in fine that these things represented, the annals of nearly three generations, counting his grandfather's, the one that had ended there, and the impalpable ashes of his long-extinct youth, afloat in the very air like microscopic motes. She listened to everything; she was a woman who answered intimately but who utterly didn't chatter. She scattered abroad therefore no cloud of words; she could assent, she could agree, above all she could encourage, without doing that. Only at the last she went a little further than he had done himself. 'And then how do you know? You may still, after all, want to live here.'

It rather indeed pulled him up, for it wasn't what he had been thinking, at least in her sense of the words. 'You mean I may decide to stay on for the sake of it?'

'Well, with *such* a home – !' But, quite beautifully, she had too much tact to dot so monstrous an i, and it was precisely an illustration of the way she didn't rattle. How could anyone – of any wit – insist on anyone else's 'wanting' to live in New York?

'Oh,' he said, 'I *might* have lived here (since I had my opportunity early in life); I might have put in here all these years. Then everything would have been different enough – and, I dare say, "funny" enough. But that's another matter. And then the beauty of it – I mean of my perversity, of my refusal to agree to a "deal" – is just in the total absence of a reason. Don't you see that if I had a reason about the matter at all it would *have* to be the other way, and would then be inevitably a reason of dollars? There are no reasons here *but* of dollars. Let us therefore have none whatever – not the ghost of one.'

They were back in the hall then for departure, but from where they stood the vista was large, through an open door, into the great square main saloon, with its almost antique felicity of brave spaces between windows. Her eyes came back from that reach and met his own a moment. 'Are you very sure the "ghost" of one doesn't, much rather, serve – ?'

He had a positive sense of turning pale. But it was as near as they were then to come. For he made answer, he believed, between a glare and a grin: 'Oh, ghosts – of course the place must swarm with them! I should be ashamed of it if it didn't. Poor Mrs Muldoon's right, and it's why I haven't asked her to do more than look in.'

Miss Staverton's gaze again lost itself, and things she didn't utter, it was clear, came and went in her mind. She might even for the minute, off there in the fine room, have imagined some element dimly gathering. Simplified like the death-mask of a handsome face, it perhaps produced for her just then an effect akin to the stir of an expression in the 'set' commemorative plaster. Yet whatever her impression may have been she produced instead a vague platitude. 'Well, if it were only furnished and lived in – !'

She appeared to imply that in case of its being still furnished he might have been a little less opposed to the idea of a return. But she passed straight into the vestibule, as if to leave her words behind her, and the next moment he had opened the house-door and was standing with her on the steps. He closed the door and, while he repocketed his key, looking up and down, they took in the comparatively harsh actuality of the avenue, which reminded him of the assault of the outer light of the desert on the traveller emerging from an Egyptian tomb. But he risked before they stepped into the street his gathered answer to her speech. 'For me it *is* lived in. For me it *is* furnished.' At which it was easy for her to sigh, 'Ah yes – !' all vaguely and discreetly; since his parents and his favourite sister, to say nothing of other kin, in numbers, had run their course and met their end there. That represented, within the walls, ineffaceable life.

It was a few days after this that, during an hour passed with her again, he had expressed his impatience of the too flattering curiosity – among the people he met – about his appreciation of New York. He had arrived at none at all that was socially producible, and as for that matter of his 'thinking' (thinking the better or the worse of anything there) he was wholly taken up with one subject of thought. It was mere vain egoism, and it was moreover, if she liked, a morbid obsession. He found all things came back to the question of what he personally might have been, how he might have led his life and 'turned out', if he had not so, at the outset, given it up. And confessing for the first time to the intensity within him of this absurd speculation – which but proved also, no doubt, the habit of too selfishly thinking – he affirmed the impotence there of any other source of interest, any other native appeal. 'What would it have made of me, what would it have made of me? I keep for ever wondering, all idiotically; as if I could possibly know! I see what it has made of dozens of others, those I meet, and it positively aches within me, to the point of exasperation, that it would have made something of me as well. Only I can't make out *what*, and the worry of it, the small rage of curiosity never to be satisfied, brings back what I remember to have felt, once or twice, after judging best, for reasons, to burn some important letter unopened. I've been sorry, I've hated it – I've never known what was in the letter. You may of course say it's a trifle – !'

'I don't say it's a trifle,' Miss Staverton gravely interrupted.

She was seated by her fire, and before her, on his feet and restless, he turned to and fro between this intensity of his idea and a fitful and unseeing inspection, through his single eye-glass, of the dear little old objects on her chimney-piece. Her interruption made him for an instant look at her harder. 'I shouldn't care if you did!' he laughed, however; 'and it's only a figure, at any rate, for the way I now feel. *Not* to have followed my perverse young course – and almost in the teeth of my father's curse, as I may say; not to have kept it up, so, "over there", from that day to this, without a doubt or a pang; not, above all, to have liked it, to have loved it, so much, loved it, no doubt, with such an abysmal conceit of my own preference: some variation from *that*, I say, must have produced some different effect for my life and for my "form". I should have stuck here – if it had been possible; and I was too young, at twenty-three, to judge, *pour deux sous*, whether it *were* possible. If I had waited I might have seen it was, and then I might have been, by staying here, something nearer to one of these types who have been hammered so hard and made so keen by their conditions. It isn't that I admire them so much – the question of any charm in them, or of any charm, beyond that of the rank money-passion, exerted by their conditions for them, has nothing to do with the matter; it's only a question of what fantastic, yet perfectly possible, development of my own nature I mayn't have missed. It comes over me that I had then a strange *alter ego* deep down somewhere within me, as the full-blown flower is in the small tight bud, and that I just took the course, I just transferred him to the climate, that blighted him for once and for ever.'

'And you wonder about the flower,' Miss Staverton said. 'So do I, if you want to know; and so I've been wondering these several weeks. I believe in the flower,' she continued, 'I feel it would have been quite splendid, quite huge and monstrous.'

'Monstrous above all!' her visitor echoed; 'and I imagine, by the same stroke, quite hideous and offensive.'

'You don't believe that,' she returned; 'if you did you wouldn't wonder. You'd know, and that would be enough for you. What you feel – and what I feel for you – is that you'd have had power.'

'You'd have liked me that way?' he asked.

She barely hung fire. 'How should I not have liked you?'

'I see. You'd have liked me, have preferred me, a billionaire!'

'How should I not have liked you?' she simply again asked.

He stood before her still – her question kept him motionless. He took it in, so much there was of it; and indeed his not otherwise meeting it testified to that. 'I know at least what I am,' he simply went on; 'the other side of the medal's clear enough. I've not been edifying – I believe I'm thought in a hundred quarters to have been barely decent. I've followed strange paths and worshipped strange gods; it must have come to you again and again – in fact, you've admitted to me as much – that I was leading, at any time these thirty years, a selfish frivolous scandalous life. And you see what it has made of me.'

She just waited, smiling at him. 'You see what it has made of *me*.'

'Oh, you're a person whom nothing can have altered. You were born to be what you are, anywhere, anyway: you've the perfection nothing else could have blighted. And don't you see how, without my exile, I shouldn't have been waiting till now – ?' But he pulled up for the strange pang.

'The great thing to see,' she presently said, 'seems to me to be that it has spoiled nothing. It hasn't spoiled your being here at last. It hasn't spoiled this. It hasn't spoiled you speaking – ' She also however faltered.

He wondered at everything her controlled emotion might mean. 'Do you believe then – too dreadfully! – that I *am* as good as I might ever have been?'

'Oh no! Far from it!' With which she got up from her chair and was nearer to him. 'But I don't care,' she smiled.

'You mean I'm good enough?'

She considered a little. 'Will you believe it if I say so? I mean will you let that settle your question for you?' And then as if making out in his face that he drew back from this, that he had some idea which, however absurd, he couldn't yet bargain away: 'Oh you don't care either – but very differently: you don't care for anything but yourself.'

Spencer Brydon recognised it – it was in fact what he had absolutely professed. Yet he importantly qualified. '*He* isn't myself. He's the just so totally other person. But I do want to see him,' he added. 'And I can. And I shall.'

Their eyes met for a minute while he guessed from something in hers that she divined his strange sense. But neither of them otherwise expressed it, and her apparent understanding, with no protesting shock, no easy derision, touched him more deeply than anything yet, constituting for his stifled perversity, on the spot, an element that was like breathable air. What she said however was unexpected. 'Well, *I've* seen him.'

'You – ?'

'I've seen him in a dream.'

'Oh a "dream" – !' It let him down.

'But twice over,' she continued. 'I saw him as I see you now.'

'You've dreamed the same dream?'

'Twice over,' she repeated. 'The very same.'

This did somehow a little speak to him, as it also gratified him. 'You dream about me at that rate?'

'Ah, about *him*!' she smiled.

His eyes again sounded her. 'Then you know all about him.' And as she said nothing more: 'What's the wretch like?'

She hesitated, and it was as if he were pressing her so hard that, resisting for reasons of her own, she had to turn away. 'I'll tell you some other time!'

II

It was after this that there was most of a virtue for him, most of a cultivated charm, most of a preposterous secret thrill, in the particular form of surrender to his obsession and of address to what he more and more believed to be his privilege. It was what in these weeks he was living for – since he really felt life to begin but after Mrs Muldoon had retired from the scene and, visiting the ample house from attic to cellar, making sure he was alone, he knew himself in safe possession and, as he tacitly expressed it, let himself go. He sometimes came twice in the twenty-four hours; the moments he liked best were those of gathering dusk, of the short autumn twilight; this was the time of which, again and again, he found himself hoping most. Then he could, as seemed to him, most intimately wander and wait, linger and listen, feel his fine attention, never in his life before so fine, on the pulse of the great vague place; he preferred the lampless hour and only wished he might have prolonged each day the deep crepuscular spell. Later – rarely much before midnight, but then for a considerable vigil – he watched with his glimmering light; moving slowly, holding it high, playing it far, rejoicing above all, as much as he might, in open vistas, reaches of communication between rooms and by passages; the long straight chance or show, as he would have called it, for the revelation he pretended to invite. It was a practice he found he could perfectly 'work' without exciting remark; no one was in the least the wiser for it; even Alice Staverton, who was moreover a well of discretion, didn't quite fully imagine.

He let himself in and let himself out with the assurance of calm proprietorship; and accident so far favoured him that, if a fat avenue 'officer' had happened on occasion to see him entering at eleven-thirty, he had never yet, to the best of his belief, been noticed as emerging at two. He walked there on the crisp November nights, arrived regularly at the evening's end; it was as easy to do this after dining out as to take his way to a club or to his hotel. When he left his club, if he hadn't been dining out, it was ostensibly to go to his hotel; and when he left his hotel, if he had spent a part of the evening there, it was ostensibly to go to his club. Everything was easy in fine; everything conspired and promoted: there was truly even in the strain of his experience something that glossed over, something that salved and simplified, all the rest of consciousness. He circulated, talked, renewed, loosely and pleasantly, old relations – met indeed, so far as he could, new expectations and seemed to make out on the whole that in spite of the career, of such different contacts, which he had spoken of to Miss Staverton as ministering so little, for those who might have watched it, to edification, he was positively rather liked than not. He was a dim secondary social success – and all with people who had truly not an idea of him. It was all mere surface sound, this murmur of their welcome, this popping of their corks – just as his gestures of response were the extravagant shadows, emphatic in proportion as they meant little, of some game of *ombres chinoises*. He projected himself all day, in thought, straight over the bristling line of hard unconscious heads and into the other, the real, the waiting life; the life that, as soon as he had heard behind him the click of his great house-door, began for him, on the jolly corner, as beguilingly as the slow opening bars of some rich music follow the tap of the conductor's wand.

He always caught the first effect of the steel point of his stick on the old marble of the hall pavement, large black-and-white squares that he remembered as the admiration of his childhood and that had then made in him, as he now saw, for the growth of an early conception of style. This effect was the dim reverberating tinkle as of some far-off bell hung who should say where? – in the depths of the house, of the past, of that mystical other world that might have flourished for him had he not, for weal or woe, abandoned it. On this impression he did ever the same thing; he put his stick noiselessly away in a corner – feeling the place once more in the likeness of some great glass bowl, all precious concave crystal, set delicately humming by the play of a moist finger round its edge. The concave crystal held, as it were, this mystical other world, and the indescribably fine murmur of its rim was the sigh there, the scarce audible pathetic wail to his strained ear, of all the old baffled forsworn possibilities. What he did therefore by this appeal of his hushed presence was to wake them into such measure of ghostly life as they might still enjoy. They were shy, all but unappeasably shy, but they weren't really sinister; at least they weren't as he had hitherto felt them – before they had taken the Form he so yearned to make them take, the Form he at moments saw himself in the light of fairly hunting on tiptoe, the points of his evening-shoes, from room to room and from storey to storey.

That was the essence of his vision – which was all rank folly, if one would, while he was out of the house and otherwise occupied, but which took on the last verisimilitude as soon as he was placed and posted. He knew what he meant and what he wanted; it was as clear as the figure on a cheque presented in demand for cash. His *alter ego* 'walked' – that was the note of his image of him, while his image of his motive for his own odd pastime was the desire to waylay him and meet him. He roamed, slowly, warily, but all restlessly, he himself did – Mrs Muldoon had been right, absolutely, with her figure of their 'craping'; and the presence he watched for would roam restlessly too. But it would be as cautious and as shifty; the conviction of its probable, in fact its already quite sensible, quite audible evasion of pursuit grew for him from night to night, laying on him finally a rigour to which nothing in his life had been comparable. It had been the theory of many superficially-judging persons, he knew, that he was wasting that life in a surrender to sensations, but he had tasted of no pleasure so fine as this actual tension, had been introduced to no sport that demanded at once the patience and the nerve of this stalking of a creature more subtle, yet at bay perhaps more formidable, than any beast of the forest. The terms, the comparisons, the very practices of the chase positively came again into play; there were even moments when passages of his occasional experience as a sportsman stirred memories, from his younger time, of moor and mountain and desert, revived for him – and to the increase of his keenness – by the tremendous force of analogy. He found himself at moments – once he had placed his single light on some mantelshelf or in some recess – stepping back into shelter or shade, effacing himself behind a door or in an embrasure, as he had sought of old the vantage of rock and tree; he found himself holding his breath and living in the joy of the instant, the supreme suspense created by big game alone.

He wasn't afraid (though putting himself the question as he believed gentlemen on Bengal tiger-shoots or in close quarters with the great bear of the Rockies had been known to confess to having put it); and this indeed – since here at least he might be frank! – because of the impression, so intimate and so strange, that he himself produced as yet a dread, produced certainly a strain, beyond the liveliest he was likely to feel. They fell for him into categories, they fairly became familiar, the signs, for his own perception, of the alarm his presence and his vigilance created; though leaving him always to remark, portentously, on his probably having formed a relation, his probably enjoying a consciousness, unique in the experience of man. People enough, first and last, had been in terror of apparitions, but who had ever before so turned the tables and become himself, in the apparitional world, an incalculable terror? He might have found this sublime had he quite dared to think of it; but he didn't too much insist, truly, on that side of his privilege. With habit and repetition he gained to an extraordinary degree the power to penetrate the dusk of distances and the darkness of corners, to resolve back into their innocence the treacheries of uncertain light, the evil-looking forms taken in the gloom by mere shadows, by accidents of the air, by shifting effects of perspective; putting down his dim luminary he could still wander on without it, pass into other rooms and, only knowing it was there behind him in case of need, see his way about, visually project for his purpose a comparative clearness. It made him feel, this acquired faculty, like some monstrous stealthy cat; he wondered if he would have glared at these moments with large shining yellow eyes, and what it mightn't verily be, for the poor hard-pressed *alter ego*, to be confronted with such a type.

He liked however the open shutters; he opened everywhere those Mrs Muldoon had closed, closing them as carefully afterwards, so that she shouldn't notice: he liked – oh, this he did like, and above all in the upper rooms! – the sense of the hard silver of the autumn stars through the window-panes, and scarcely less the flare of the street-lamps below, the white electric lustre which it would have taken curtains to keep out. This was human, actual, social; this was of the world he had lived in, and he was more at his ease certainly for the countenance, coldly general and impersonal, that all the while and in spite of his detachment it seemed to give him. He had support of course mostly in the rooms at the wide front and the prolonged side; it failed him considerably in the central shades and the parts at the back. But if he sometimes, on his rounds, was glad of his optical reach, so none the less often the rear of the house affected him as the very jungle of his prey. The place was there more subdivided; a large 'extension' in particular, where small rooms for servants had been multiplied, abounded in nooks and corners, in closets and passages, in the ramifications especially of an ample back staircase over which he leaned, many a time, to look far down – not deterred from his gravity even while aware that he might, for a spectator, have figured some solemn simpleton playing at hide-and-seek. Outside in fact he might himself make that ironic *rapprochement*; but within the walls, and in spite of the clear windows, his consistency was proof against the cynical light of New York.

It had belonged to that idea of the exasperated consciousness of his victim to become a real test for him; since he had quite put it to himself from the first that, oh distinctly! he could 'cultivate' his whole perception. He had felt it as above all open to cultivation – which indeed was but another name for his manner of spending his time. He was bringing it on, bringing it to perfection, by practice; in consequence of which it had grown so fine that he was now aware of impressions, attestations of his general postulate, that couldn't have broken upon him at once. This was the case more specifically with a phenomenon at last quite frequent for him in the upper rooms, the recognition – absolutely unmistakeable, and by a turn dating from a particular hour, his resumption of his campaign after a diplomatic drop, a calculated absence of three nights – of his being definitely followed, tracked at a distance carefully taken and to the express end that he should the less confidently, less arrogantly, appear to himself merely to pursue. It worried, it finally quite broke him up, for it proved, of all the conceivable impressions, the one least suited to his book. He was kept in sight while remaining himself – as regards the essence of his position – sightless, and his only recourse then was in abrupt turns, rapid recoveries of ground.

He wheeled about, retracing his steps, as if he might so catch in his face at least the stirred air of some other quick revolution. It was indeed true that his fully dislocalised thought of these manoeuvres recalled to him Pantaloon, at the Christmas farce, buffeted and tricked from behind by ubiquitous Harlequin; but it left intact the influence of the conditions themselves each time he was re-exposed to them, so that in fact this association had he suffered it to become constant, would on a certain side have but ministered to his intenser gravity. He had made, as I have said, to create on the premises the baseless sense of a reprieve, his three absences; and the result of the third was to confirm the after-effect of the second.

On his return, that night – the night succeeding his last intermission – he stood in the hall and looked up the staircase with a certainty more intimate than any he had yet known. 'He's *there*, at the top, and waiting – not, as in general, falling back for disappearance. He's holding his ground, and it's the first time – which is a proof, isn't it? that something has happened for him.' So Brydon argued with his hand on the banister and his foot on the lowest stair; in which position he felt as never before the air chilled by his logic. He himself turned cold in it, for he seemed of a sudden to know what now was involved. 'Harder pressed? – yes, he takes it in, with its thus making clear to him that I've come, as they say, "to stay". He finally doesn't like and can't bear it, in the sense, I mean, that his wrath, his menaced interest, now balances with his dread. I've hunted him till he has "turned": that, up there, is what has happened – he's the fanged or the antlered animal brought at last to bay.' There came to him, as I say – but determined by an influence beyond my notation! – the acuteness of this certainty; under which however the next moment he had broken into a sweat that he would as little have consented to attribute to fear as he would have dared immediately to act upon it for enterprise. It marked none the less a prodigious thrill, a thrill that represented sudden dismay, no doubt, but also represented, and with the selfsame throb, the strangest, the most joyous, possibly the next minute almost the proudest, duplication of consciousness.

'He has been dodging, retreating, hiding, but now, worked up to anger, he'll fight!' – this intense impression made a single mouthful, as it were, of terror and applause. But what was wondrous was that the applause, for the felt fact, was so eager, since, if it was his other self he was running to earth, this ineffable identity was thus in the last resort not unworthy of him. It bristled there – somewhere near at hand, however unseen still – as the hunted thing, even as the trodden worm of the adage *must* at last bristle; and Brydon at this instant tasted probably of a sensation more complex than had ever before found itself consistent with sanity. It was as if it would have shamed him that a character so associated with his own should triumphantly succeed in just skulking, should to the end not risk the open; so that the drop of this danger was, on the spot, a great lift of the whole situation. Yet with another rare shift of the same subtlety he was already trying to measure by how much more he himself might now be in peril of fear; so rejoicing that he could, in another form, actively inspire that fear, and simultaneously quaking for the form in which he might passively know it.

The apprehension of knowing it must after a little have grown in him, and the strangest moment of his adventure perhaps, the most memorable or really most interesting, afterwards, of his crisis, was the lapse of certain instants of concentrated conscious *combat*, the sense of a need to hold on to something, even after the manner of a man slipping and slipping on some awful incline; the vivid impulse, above all, to move, to act, to charge, somehow and upon something – to show himself, in a word, that he wasn't afraid. The state of 'holding-on' was thus the state to which he was momentarily reduced; if there had been anything, in the great vacancy, to seize he would presently have been aware of having clutched it as he might under a shock at home have clutched the nearest chair-back. He had been surprised at any rate – of this he *was* aware – into something unprecedented since his original appropriation of the place; he had closed his eyes, held them tight, for a long minute, as with that instinct of dismay and that terror of vision. When he opened them the room, the other contiguous rooms, extraordinarily, seemed lighter – so light, almost, that at first he took the change for day. He stood firm, however that might be, just where he had paused; his resistance had helped him – it was as if there were something he had tided over. He knew after a little what this was – it had been in the imminent danger of flight. He had stiffened his will against going; without this he would have made for the stairs, and it seemed to him that, still with his eyes closed, he would have descended them, would have known how, straight and swiftly, to the bottom.

Well, as he had held out, here he was – still at the top, among the more intricate upper rooms and with the gauntlet of the others, of all the rest of the house, still to run when it should be his time to go. He would go at his time – only at his time: didn't he go every night very much at the same hour? He took out his watch – there was light for that: it was scarcely a quarter past one, and he had never withdrawn so soon. He reached his lodgings for the most part at two – with his walk of a quarter of an hour. He would wait for the last quarter – he wouldn't stir till then; and he kept his watch there with his eyes on it, reflecting while he held it that this deliberate wait, a wait with an effort, which he recognised, would serve perfectly for the attestation he desired to make. It would prove his courage – unless indeed the latter might most be proved by his budging at last from his place. What he mainly felt now was that, since he hadn't originally scuttled, he had his dignities – which had never in his life seemed so many – all to preserve and to carry aloft. This was before him in truth as a physical image, an image almost worthy of an age of greater romance. That remark indeed glimmered for him only to glow the next instant with a finer light; since what age of romance, after all, could have matched either the state of his mind or, 'objectively', as they said, the wonder of his situation? The only difference would have been that, brandishing his dignities over his head as in a parchment scroll, he might then – that is in the heroic time – have proceeded downstairs with a drawn sword in his other grasp.

At present, really, the light he had set down on the mantel of the next room would have to figure his sword; which utensil, in the course of a minute, he had taken the requisite number of steps to possess himself of. The door between the rooms was open, and from the second another door opened to a third. These rooms, as he remembered, gave all three upon a common corridor as well, but there was a fourth, beyond them, without issue save through the preceding. To have moved, to have heard his step again, was appreciably a help; though even in recognising this he lingered once more a little by the chimney-piece on which his light had rested. When he next moved, just hesitating where to turn, he found himself considering a circumstance that, after his first and comparatively vague apprehension of it, produced in him the start that often attends some pang of recollection, the violent shock of having ceased happily to forget. He had come into sight of the door in which the brief chain of communication ended and which he now surveyed from the nearer threshold, the one not directly facing it. Placed at some distance to the left of this point, it would have admitted him to the last room of the four, the room without other approach or egress, had it not, to his intimate conviction, been closed *since* his former visitation, the matter probably of a quarter of an hour before. He stared with all his eyes at the wonder of the fact, arrested again where he stood and again holding his breath while he sounded its sense. Surely it had been *subsequently* closed – that is it had been on his previous passage indubitably open!

He took it full in the face that something had happened between – that he couldn't not have noticed before (by which he meant on his original tour of all the rooms that evening) that such a barrier had exceptionally presented itself. He had indeed since that moment undergone an agitation so extraordinary that it might have muddled for him any earlier view; and he tried to convince himself that he might perhaps then have gone into the room and, inadvertently, automatically, on coming out, have drawn the door after him. The difficulty was that this exactly was what he never did; it was against his whole policy, as he might have said, the essence of which was to keep vistas clear. He had them from the first, as he was well aware, quite on the brain: the strange apparition, at the far end of one of them, of his baffled 'prey' (which had become by so sharp an irony so little the term now to apply!) was the form of success his imagination had most cherished, projecting into it always a refinement of beauty. He had known fifty times the start of perception that had afterwards dropped; had fifty times gasped to himself, 'There!' under some fond brief hallucination. The house, as the case stood, admirably lent itself; he might wonder at the taste, the native architecture of the particular time, which could rejoice so in the multiplication of doors – the opposite extreme to the modern, the actual almost complete proscription of them; but it had fairly contributed to provoke this obsession of the presence encountered telescopically, as he might say, focused and studied in diminishing perspective and as by a rest for the elbow.

It was with these considerations that his present attention was charged – they perfectly availed to make what he saw portentous. He *couldn't*, by any lapse, have blocked that aperture; and if he hadn't, if it was unthinkable, why! what else was clear but that there had been another agent? Another agent? – he had been catching, as he felt, a moment back, the very breath of him; but when had he been so close as in this simple, this logical, this completely personal act? It was so logical, that is, that one might have *taken* it for personal; yet for what did Brydon take it, he asked himself, while, softly panting, he felt his eyes almost leave their sockets. Ah, this time at last they *were*, the two, the opposed projections of him, in presence; and this time, as much as one would, the question of danger loomed. With it rose, as not before, the question of courage – for what he knew the blank face of the door to say to him was, 'Show us how much you have!' It stared, it glared back at him with that challenge; it put to him the two alternatives: should he just push it open or not? Oh, to have this consciousness was to *think* – and to think, Brydon knew, as he stood there, was, with the lapsing moments, not to have acted! Not to have acted – that was the misery and the pang – was even still not to act; was in fact *all* to feel the thing in another, in a new and terrible way. How long did he pause and how long did he debate? There was presently nothing to measure it; for his vibration had already changed – as just by the effect of its intensity. Shut up there, at bay, defiant, and with the prodigy of the thing palpably proveably *done*, thus giving notice like some stark signboard – under that accession of accent the situation itself had turned; and Brydon at last remarkably made up his mind on what it had turned to.

It had turned altogether to a different admonition; to a supreme hint, for him, of the value of Discretion! This slowly dawned, no doubt – for it could take its time; so perfectly, on his threshold, had he been stayed, so little as yet had he either advanced or retreated. It was the strangest of all things that now when, by his taking ten steps and applying his hand to a latch, or even his shoulder and his knee, if necessary, to a panel, all the hunger of his prime need might have been met, his high curiosity crowned, his unrest assuaged – it was amazing, but it was also exquisite and rare, that insistence should have, at a touch, quite dropped from him. Discretion – he jumped at that; and yet not, verily, at such a pitch, because it saved his nerves or his skin, but because, much more valuably, it saved the situation. When I say he 'jumped' at it I feel the consonance of this term with the fact that – at the end indeed of I know not how long – he did move again, he crossed straight to the door. He wouldn't touch it – it seemed now that he might *if* he would: he would only just wait there a little, to show, to prove, that he wouldn't. He had thus another station, close to the thin partition by which revelation was denied him; but with his eyes bent and his hands held off in a mere intensity of stillness. He listened as if there had been something to hear, but this attitude, while it lasted, was his own communication. 'If you

won't then – good: I spare you and I give up. You affect me as by the appeal
positively for pity; you convince me that for reasons rigid and sublime –
what do I know? – we both of us should have suffered. I respect them then,
and, though moved and privileged as, I believe, it has never been given to
man, I retire, I renounce – never, on my honour, to try again. So rest for
ever – and let *me*!'

That, for Brydon was the deep sense of this last demonstration – solemn,
measured, directed, as he felt it to be. He brought it to a close, he turned
away; and now verily he knew how deeply he had been stirred. He retraced
his steps, taking up his candle, burnt, he observed, well-nigh to the socket,
and marking again, lighten it as he would, the distinctness of his footfall; after
which, in a moment, he knew himself at the other side of the house. He did
here what he had not yet done at these hours – he opened half a casement,
one of those in the front, and let in the air of the night; a thing he would have
taken at any time previous for a sharp rupture of his spell. His spell was
broken now, and it didn't matter – broken by his concession and his
surrender, which made it idle henceforth that he should ever come back. The
empty street – its other life so marked even by the great lamplit vacancy – was
within call, within touch; he stayed there as to be in it again, high above it
though he was still perched; he watched as for some comforting common
fact, some vulgar human note, the passage of a scavenger or a thief, some
night-bird however base. He would have blessed that sign of life; he would
have welcomed positively the slow approach of his friend the policeman,
whom he had hitherto only sought to avoid, and was not sure that if the
patrol had come into sight he mightn't have felt the impulse to get into
relation with it, to hail it, on some pretext, from his fourth floor.

The pretext that wouldn't have been too silly or too compromising, the
explanation that would have saved his dignity and kept his name, in such a
case, out of the papers, was not definite to him: he was so occupied with the
thought of recording his Discretion – as an effect of the vow he had just
uttered to his intimate adversary – that the importance of this loomed large
and something had overtaken all ironically his sense of proportion. If there
had been a ladder applied to the front of the house, even one of the
vertiginous perpendiculars employed by painters and roofers and sometimes
left standing overnight, he would have managed somehow, astride of the
window-sill, to compass by outstretched leg and arm that mode of descent. If
there had been some such uncanny thing as he had found in his room at
hotels, a workable fire-escape in the form of notched cable or a canvas shoot,
he would have availed himself of it as a proof – well, of his present delicacy.
He nursed that sentiment, as the question stood, a little in vain, and even – at
the end of he scarce knew, once more, how long – found it, as by the action
on his mind of the failure of response of the outer world, sinking back to
vague anguish. It seemed to him he had waited an age for some stir of the
great grim hush; the life of the town was itself under a spell – so unnaturally,

up and down the whole prospect of known and rather ugly objects, the blankness and the silence lasted. Had they ever, he asked himself, the hard-faced houses, which had begun to look livid in the dim dawn, had they ever spoken so little to any need of his spirit? Great builded voids, great crowded stillnesses put on, often, in the heart of cities, for the small hours, a sort of sinister mask, and it was of this large collective negation that Brydon presently became conscious – all the more that the break of day was, almost incredibly, now at hand, proving to him what a night he had made of it.

He looked again at his watch, saw what had become of his time-values (he had taken hours for minutes – not, as in other tense situations, minutes for hours) and the strange air of the streets was but the weak, the sullen flush of a dawn in which everything was still locked up. His choked appeal from his own open window had been the sole note of life, and he could but break off at last as for a worse despair. Yet while so deeply demoralised he was capable again of an impulse denoting – at least by his present measure – extraordinary resolution; of retracing his steps to the spot where he had turned cold with the extinction of his last pulse of doubt as to there being in the place another presence than his own. This required an effort strong enough to sicken him; but he had his reason, which overmastered for the moment everything else. There was the whole of the rest of the house to traverse, and how should he screw himself to that if the door he had seen closed were at present open? He could hold to the idea that the closing had practically been for him an act of mercy, a chance offered him to descend, depart, get off the ground and never again profane it. This conception held together, it worked; but what it meant for him depended now clearly on the amount of forbearance his recent action, or rather his recent inaction, had engendered. The image of the 'presence', whatever it was, waiting there for him to go – this image had not yet been so concrete for his nerves as when he stopped short of the point at which certainty would have come to him. For, with all his resolution, or more exactly with all his dread, he did stop short – he hung back from really seeing. The risk was too great and his fear too definite: it took at this moment an awful specific form.

He knew – yes, as he had never known anything – that *should* he see the door open, it would all too abjectly be the end of him. It would mean that the agent of his shame – for his shame was the deep abjection – was once more at large and in general possession; and what glared him thus in the face was the act that this would determine for him. It would send him straight about to the window he had left open, and by that window, be long ladder and dangling rope as absent as they would, he saw himself uncontrollably, insanely, fatally take his way to the street. The hideous chance of this he at least could avert; but he could only avert it by recoiling in time from assurance. He had the whole house to deal with, this fact was still there; only he now knew that uncertainty alone could start him. He stole back from where he had checked himself – merely to do so was suddenly like safety – and, making blindly for the greater staircase, left gaping rooms and sounding passages behind. Here was the top of the stairs, with a fine large dim descent and three spacious landings to mark off. His instinct was all for mildness, but his feet were harsh on the floors, and, strangely, when he had in a couple of minutes become aware of this, it counted somehow for help. He couldn't have spoken, the tone of his voice would have scared him, and the common conceit or resource of 'whistling in the dark' (whether literally or figuratively) have appeared basely vulgar; yet he liked none the less to hear himself go, and when he had reached his first landing – taking it all with no rush, but quite steadily, that stage of success drew from him a gasp of relief.

The house, withal, seemed immense, the scale of space again inordinate; the open rooms, to no one of which his eyes deflected, gloomed in their shuttered state like mouths of caverns; only the high skylight that formed the crown of the deep well created for him a medium in which he could advance, but which might have been, for queerness of colour, some watery under-world. He tried to think of something noble, as that his property was really grand, a splendid possession; but this nobleness took the form too of the clear delight with which he was finally to sacrifice it. They might come in now, the builders, the destroyers – they might come as soon as they would. At the end of two flights he had dropped to another zone, and from the middle of the third, with only one more left, he recognised the influence of the lower windows, of half-drawn blinds, of the occasional gleam of street-lamps, of the glazed spaces of the vestibule. This was the bottom of the sea, which showed an illumination of its own and which he even saw paved – when at a given moment he drew up to sink a long look over the banisters – with the marble squares of his childhood. By that time indubitably he felt, as he might have said in a commoner cause, better; it had allowed him to stop and draw breath, and the ease increased with the sight of the old black-and-white slabs. But what he most felt was that now surely, with the element of impunity pulling him as by hard firm hands, the case was settled for what he might have seen above had he dared that last look. The closed door, blessedly remote now, was still closed – and he had only in short to reach that of the house.

He came down further, he crossed the passage forming the access to the last flight; and if here again he stopped an instant it was almost for the sharpness of the thrill of assured escape. It made him shut his eyes – which opened again to the straight slope of the remainder of the stairs. Here was impunity still, but impunity almost excessive, inasmuch as the sidelights and the high fan-tracery of the entrance were glimmering straight into the hall; an appearance produced, he the next instant saw, by the fact that the vestibule gaped wide, that the hinged halves of the inner door had been thrown far back. Out of that again the *question* sprang at him, making his eyes, as he felt, half-start from his head, as they had done, at the top of the house, before the sign of the other door. If he had left that one open, hadn't he left this one closed, and wasn't he now in *most* immediate presence of some inconceivable occult activity? It was as sharp, the question, as a knife in his side, but the answer hung fire still and seemed to lose itself in the vague darkness to which the thin admitted dawn, glimmering archwise over the whole outer door, made a semicircular margin, a cold silvery nimbus that seemed to play a little as he looked – to shift and expand and contract.

It was as if there had been something within it, protected by indistinctness and corresponding in extent with the opaque surface behind, the painted panels of the last barrier to his escape, of which the key was in his pocket. The indistinctness mocked him even while he stared, affected him as somehow shrouding or challenging certitude, so that after faltering an instant on his step he let himself go with the sense that here *was* at last something to meet, to touch, to take, to know – something all unnatural and dreadful, but to advance upon which was the condition for him either of liberation or of supreme defeat. The penumbra, dense and dark, was the virtual screen of a figure which stood in it as still as some image erect in a niche or as some black-vizored sentinel guarding a treasure. Brydon was to know afterwards, was to recall and make out, the particular thing he had believed during the rest of his descent. He saw, in its great grey glimmering margin, the central vagueness diminish, and he felt it to be taking the very form toward which, for so many days, the passion of his curiosity had yearned. It gloomed, it loomed, it was something, it was somebody, the prodigy of a personal presence.

Rigid and conscious, spectral yet human, a man of his own substance and stature waited there to measure himself with his power to dismay. This only could it be – this only till he recognised, with his advance, that what made the face dim was the pair of raised hands that covered it and in which, so far from being offered in defiance, it was buried as for dark deprecation. So Brydon, before him, took him in; with every fact of him now, in the higher light, hard and acute – his planted stillness, his vivid truth, his grizzled bent head and white masking hands, his queer actuality of evening-dress, of dangling double eye-glass, of gleaming silk lappet and white linen, of pearl button and gold watch-guard and polished shoe. No portrait by a great modern master could have presented him with more intensity, thrust him out of his frame with more art, as if there had been 'treatment', of the consummate sort, in his every shade and salience. The revulsion, for our friend, had become, before he knew it, immense – this drop, in the act of apprehension, to the sense of his adversary's inscrutable manoeuvre. That meaning at least, while he gaped, it offered him; for he could but gape at his other self in this other anguish, gape as a proof that *he*, standing there for the achieved, the enjoyed, the triumphant life, couldn't be faced in his triumph. Wasn't the proof in the splendid covering hands, strong and completely spread? – so spread and so intentional that, in spite of a special verity that surpassed every other, the fact that one of these hands had lost two fingers, which were reduced to stumps, as if accidentally shot away, the face was effectually guarded and saved.

'Saved', though, *would* it be? – Brydon breathed his wonder till the very impunity of his attitude and the very insistence of his eyes produced, as he felt, a sudden stir which showed the next instant as a deeper portent, while the head raised itself, the betrayal of a braver purpose. The hands, as he looked, began to move, to open; then, as if deciding in a flash, dropped from the face and left it uncovered and presented. Horror, with the sight, had leaped into Brydon's throat, gasping there in a sound he couldn't utter; for the bared identity was too hideous as *his*, and his glare was the passion of his protest. The face, *that* face, Spencer Brydon's? he searched it still, but looking away from it in dismay and denial, falling straight from his height of sublimity. It was unknown, inconceivable, awful, disconnected from any possibility – ! He had been 'sold', he inwardly moaned, stalking such game as this: the presence before him was a presence, the horror within him a horror, but the waste of his nights had been only grotesque and the success of his adventure an irony. Such an identity fitted his at *no* point, made its alternative monstrous. A thousand times yes, as it came upon him nearer now – the face was the face of a stranger. It came upon him nearer now, quite as one of those expanding fantastic images projected by the magic lantern of childhood; for the stranger, whoever he might be, evil, odious, blatant, vulgar, had advanced as for aggression, and he knew himself give ground. Then harder pressed still, sick with the force of his shock, and falling back as under the hot breath and the roused passion of a life larger than his own, a rage of personality before which his own collapsed, he felt the whole vision turn to darkness and his very feet give way. His head went round; he was going; he had gone.

III

What had next brought him back, clearly – though after how long? – was Mrs Muldoon's voice, coming to him from quite near, from so near that he seemed presently to see her as kneeling on the ground before him while he lay looking up at her; himself not wholly on the ground, but half-raised and upheld – conscious, yes, of tenderness of support and, more particularly, of a head pillowed in extraordinary softness and fainly refreshing fragrance. He considered, he wondered, his wit but half at his service; then another face intervened, bending more directly over him, and he finally knew that Alice Staverton had made her lap an ample and perfect cushion to him, and that she had to this end seated herself on the lowest degree of the staircase, the rest of his long person remaining stretched on his old black-and-white slabs. They were cold, these marble squares of his youth; but he somehow was not, in this rich return of consciousness – the most wonderful hour, little by little, that he had ever known, leaving him, as it did, so gratefully, so abysmally passive, and yet as with a treasure of intelligence waiting all round him for quiet appropriation; dissolved, he might call it, in the air of the place and producing the golden glow of a late autumn afternoon. He had come back, yes – come back from further away than any man but himself had ever travelled; but it was strange how with this sense what he had come back *to* seemed really the great thing, and as if his prodigious journey had been all for the sake of it. Slowly but surely his consciousness grew, his vision of his state thus completing itself: he had been miraculously *carried* back – lifted and carefully borne as from where he had been picked up, the uttermost end of an interminable grey passage. Even with this he was suffered to rest, and what had now brought him to knowledge was the break in the long mild motion.

It had brought him to knowledge, to knowledge – yes, this was the beauty of his state; which came to resemble more and more that of a man who has gone to sleep on some news of a great inheritance, and then, after dreaming it away, after profaning it with matters strange to it, has waked up again to serenity of certitude and has only to lie and watch it grow. This was the drift of his patience – that he had only to let it shine on him. He must moreover, with intermissions, still have been lifted and borne; since why and how else should he have known himself, later on, with the afternoon glow intenser, no longer at the foot of his stairs – situated as these now seemed at that dark other end of his tunnel – but on a deep window-bench of his high saloon, over which had been spread, couch-fashion, a mantle of soft stuff lined with grey fur that was familiar to his eyes and that one of his hands kept fondly feeling as for its pledge of truth. Mrs Muldoon's face had gone, but the other, the second he had recognised, hung over him in a way that showed how he was still propped and pillowed. He took it all in, and the more he took it the more it seemed to suffice: he was as much at peace as if he had had food and drink. It was the two women who had found him, on Mrs Muldoon's having plied, at her usual hour, her latch-key – and on her having above all arrived while Miss Staverton still lingered near the house. She had been turning away, all anxiety, from worrying the vain bell-handle – her calculation having been of the hour of the good woman's visit; but the latter, blessedly, had come up while she was still there, and they had entered together. He had then lain, beyond the vestibule, very much as he was lying now – quite, that is, as he appeared to have fallen, but all so wondrously without bruise or gash; only in a depth of stupor. What he most took in, however, at present, with the steadier clearance, was that Alice Staverton had for a long unspeakable moment not doubted he was dead.

'It must have been that I *was*.' He made it out as she held him. 'Yes – I can only have died. You brought me literally to life. Only,' he wondered, his eyes rising to her, 'only, in the name of all the benedictions, how?'

It took her but an instant to bend her face and kiss him, and something in the manner of it, and in the way her hands clasped and locked his head while he felt the cool charity and virtue of her lips, something in all this beatitude somehow answered everything. 'And now I keep you,' she said.

'Oh! keep me, keep me!' he pleaded while her face still hung over him: in response to which it dropped again and stayed close, clingingly close. It was the seal of their situation – of which he tasted the impress for a long blissful moment in silence. But he came back. 'Yet how did you know – ?'

'I was uneasy. You were to have come, you remember – and you had sent no word.'

'Yes, I remember – I was to have gone to you at one today.' It caught on to their 'old' life and relation – which were so near and so far. 'I was still out there in my strange darkness – where was it, what was it? I must have stayed there so long.' He could but wonder at the depth and the duration of his swoon.

'Since last night?' she asked with a shade of fear for her possible indiscretion.

'Since this morning – it must have been: the cold dim dawn of today. Where have I been,' he vaguely wailed, 'where have I been?' He felt her hold him close, and it was as if this helped him now to make in all security his mild moan. 'What a long dark day!'

All in her tenderness she had waited a moment. 'In the cold dim dawn?' she quavered.

But he had already gone on piecing together the parts of the whole prodigy. 'As I didn't turn up you came straight – ?'

She barely cast about. 'I went first to your hotel – where they told me of your absence. You had dined out last evening and hadn't been back since. But they appeared to know you had been at your club.'

'So you had the idea of *this* – ?'

'Of what?' she asked in a moment.

'Well – of what has happened.'

'I believed at least you'd have been here. I've known, all along,' she said, 'that you've been coming.'

' "Known" it – ?'

'Well, I've believed it. I said nothing to you after that talk we had a month ago – but I felt sure. I knew you would,' she declared.

'That I'd persist, you mean?'

'That you'd see him.'

'Ah, but I didn't!' cried Brydon with his long wail. 'There's somebody – an awful beast; whom I brought, too horribly, to bay. But it's not me.'

At this she bent over him again, and her eyes were in his eyes. 'No – it's not you.' And it was as if, while her face hovered, he might have made out in it, hadn't it been so near, some particular meaning blurred by a smile. 'No, thank heaven,' she repeated – 'it's not you! Of course it wasn't to have been.'

'Ah, but it *was*,' he gently insisted. And he stared before him now as he had been staring for so many weeks. 'I was to have known myself.'

'You couldn't!' she returned consolingly. And then reverting, and as if to account further for what she had herself done, 'But it wasn't only *that*, that you hadn't been at home,' she went on. 'I waited till the hour at which we had found Mrs Muldoon that day of my going with you; and she arrived, as I've told you, while, failing to bring anyone to the door, I lingered in my despair on the steps. After a little, if she hadn't come, by such a mercy, I should have found means to hunt her up. But it wasn't,' said Alice Staverton, as if once more with her fine intention – 'it wasn't only that.'

His eyes, as he lay, turned back to her. 'What more then?'

She met it, the wonder she had stirred. 'In the cold dim dawn, you say? Well, in the cold dim dawn of this morning I too saw you.'

'Saw *me* – ?'

'Saw him,' said Alice Staverton. 'It must have been at the same moment.'

He lay an instant taking it in – as if he wished to be quite reasonable. 'At the same moment?'

'Yes – in my dream again, the same one I've named to you. He came back to me. Then I knew it for a sign. He had come to you.'

At this Brydon raised himself; he had to see her better. She helped him when she understood his movement, and he sat up, steadying himself beside her there on the window-bench and with his right hand grasping her left. '*He* didn't come to me.'

'You came to yourself,' she beautifully smiled.

'Ah, I've come to myself now – thanks to you, dearest. But this brute, with his awful face – this brute's a black stranger. He's none of *me*, even as I *might* have been,' Brydon sturdily declared.

But she kept the clearness that was like the breath of infallibility. 'Isn't the whole point that you'd have been different?'

He almost scowled for it. 'As different as *that* – ?'

Her look again was more beautiful to him than the things of this world. 'Haven't you exactly wanted to know *how* different? So this morning,' she said, 'you appeared to me.'

'Like *him*?'

'A black stranger!'

'Then how did you know it was I?'

'Because, as I told you weeks ago, my mind, my imagination, had worked so over what you might, what you mighn't have been – to show you, you see, how I've thought of you. In the midst of that you came to me – that my wonder might be answered. So I knew,' she went on; 'and believed that, since the question held you too so fast, as you told me that day, you too would see for yourself. And when this morning I again saw I knew it would be because you had – and also then, from the first moment, because you somehow wanted me. *He* seemed to tell me of that. So why,' she strangely smiled, 'shouldn't I like him?'

It brought Spencer Brydon to his feet. 'You "like" that horror – ?'

'I *could* have liked him. And to me,' she said, 'he was no horror. I had accepted him.'

' "Accepted" – ?' Brydon oddly sounded.

'Before, for the interest of his difference – yes. And as *I* didn't disown him, as *I* knew him – which you at last, confronted with him in his difference, so cruelly didn't, my dear – well, he must have been, you see, less dreadful to me. And it may have pleased him that I pitied him.'

She was beside him on her feet, but still holding his hand – still with her arm supporting him. But though it all brought for him thus a dim light, 'You "pitied" him?' he grudgingly, resentfully asked.

'He has been unhappy, he has been ravaged,' she said.

'And haven't I been unhappy? Am not I – you've only to look at me! – ravaged?'

'Ah, I don't say I like him *better*,' she granted after a thought. 'But he's grim, he's worn – and things have happened to him. He doesn't make shift, for sight, with your charming monocle.'

'No' – it struck Brydon: 'I couldn't have sported mine downtown. They'd have guyed me there.'

'His great convex pince-nez – I saw it, I recognised the kind – is for his poor ruined sight. And his poor right hand – !'

'Ah!' Brydon winced – whether for his proved identity or for his lost fingers. Then, 'He has a million a year,' he lucidly added. 'But he hasn't you.'

'And he isn't – no, he isn't – *you*,' she murmured as he drew her to his breast.

Dracula's Guest

BRAM STOKER

PREFACE

WHEN WE STARTED for our drive the sun was shining brightly on Munich, and the air was full of the joyousness of early summer. Just as we were about to depart, Herr Delbrück (the *maître d'hôtel* of the Quatre Saisons, where I was staying) came down, bareheaded, to the carriage and, after wishing me a pleasant drive, said to the coachman, still holding his hand on the handle of the carriage door: 'Remember to be back by nightfall. The sky looks bright but there is a shiver in the north wind that says there may be a sudden storm. But I am sure you will not be late,' here he smiled, and added, 'for you know what night it is.'

Johann answered with an emphatic, 'Ja, mein Herr,' and, touching his hat, drove off quickly. When we had cleared the town, I said, after signalling to him to stop: 'Tell me, Johann, what is tonight?'

He crossed himself, as he answered laconically: 'Walpurgis nacht.' Then he took out his watch, a great, old-fashioned German silver thing as big as a turnip, and looked at it, with his eyebrows gathered together and a little impatient shrug of his shoulders. I realised that this was his way of respectfully protesting against the unnecessary delay, and sank back in the carriage, merely motioning him to proceed. He started off rapidly, as if to make up for lost time. Every now and then the horses seemed to throw up their heads and sniff the air suspiciously. On such occasions I often looked round in alarm. The road was pretty bleak, for we were traversing a sort of high, wind-swept plateau. As we drove, I saw a road that looked but seldom used, and which seemed to dip through a little, winding valley. It looked so inviting that, even at the risk of offending him, I called Johann to stop – and when he had pulled up, I told him I would like to drive down that road. He made all sorts of excuses, and frequently crossed himself as he spoke. This somewhat piqued my curiosity, so I asked him various questions. He answered fencingly, and repeatedly looked at his watch in protest. Finally I said: 'Well, Johann, I want to go down this road. I shall not ask you to come unless you like; but tell me why you do not like to go, that is all I ask.' For answer he seemed to throw himself off the box, so quickly did he reach the ground. Then he stretched out his hands appealingly to me, and implored me not to go. There was just enough of English mixed with the German for me to understand the drift of his talk. He seemed always just about to tell me something – the very idea of which evidently frightened him; but each time he pulled himself up, saying, as he crossed himself: 'Walpurgis Nacht!'

I tried to argue with him, but it was difficult to argue with a man when I did not know his language. The advantage certainly rested with him, for although he began to speak in English, of a very crude and broken kind, he always got excited and broke into his native tongue – and every time he did so, he looked at his watch. Then the horses became restless and sniffed the air. At this he grew very pale, and, looking around in a frightened way, he suddenly jumped forward, took them by the bridles and led them on some twenty feet. I followed, and asked why he had done this. For answer he crossed himself, pointed to the spot we had left and drew his carriage in the direction of the other road, indicating a cross, and said, first in German, then in English: 'Buried him – him what killed themselves.'

I remembered the old custom of burying suicides at crossroads: 'Ah! I see, a suicide. How interesting!' But for the life of me I could not make out why the horses were frightened.

Whilst we were talking, we heard a sort of sound between a yelp and a bark. It was far away; but the horses got very restless, and it took Johann all his time to quiet them. He was pale, and said, 'It sounds like a wolf – but yet there are no wolves here now.'

'No?' I said, questioning him; 'isn't it long since the wolves were so near the city?'

'Long, long,' he answered, 'in the spring and summer; but with the snow the wolves have been here not so long.'

Whilst he was petting the horses and trying to quiet them, dark clouds drifted rapidly across the sky. The sunshine passed away, and a breath of cold wind seemed to drift past us. It was only a breath, however, and more in the nature of a warning than a fact, for the sun came out brightly again. Johann looked under his lifted hand at the horizon and said: 'The storm of snow, he comes before long time.' Then he looked at his watch again, and, straightway holding his reins firmly – for the horses were still pawing the ground restlessly and shaking their heads – he climbed to his box as though the time had come for proceeding on our journey.

I felt a little obstinate and did not at once get into the carriage.

'Tell me,' I said, 'about this place where the road leads,' and I pointed down.

Again he crossed himself and mumbled a prayer, before he answered, 'It is unholy.'

'What is unholy?' I enquired.

'The village.'

'Then there is a village?'

'No, no. No one lives there hundreds of years.' My curiosity was piqued, 'But you said there was a village.'

'There was.'

'Where is it now?'

Whereupon he burst out into a long story in German and English, so mixed up that I could not quite understand exactly what he said, but roughly I gathered that long ago, hundreds of years, men had died there and been buried in their graves; and sounds were heard under the clay, and when the graves were opened, men and women were found rosy with life, and their mouths red with blood. And so, in haste to save their lives (aye, and their souls! – and here he crossed himself) those who were left fled away to other places, where the living lived, and the dead were dead and not – not something. He was evidently afraid to speak the last words. As he proceeded with his narration, he grew more and more excited. It seemed as if his imagination had got hold of him, and he ended in a perfect paroxysm of fear – white-faced, perspiring, trembling and looking round him, as if expecting that some dreadful presence would manifest itself there in the bright sunshine on the open plain. Finally, in an agony of desperation, he cried: 'Walpurgis nacht!' and pointed to the carriage for me to get in. All my English blood rose at this, and, standing back, I said: 'You are afraid, Johann – you are afraid. Go home; I shall return alone; the walk will do me good.' The carriage door was open. I took from the seat my oak walking-stick – which I always carry on my holiday excursions – and closed the door, pointing back to Munich, and said, 'Go home, Johann – Walpurgis nacht doesn't concern Englishmen.'

The horses were now more restive than ever, and Johann was trying to hold them in while excitedly imploring me not to do anything so foolish. I pitied the poor fellow, he was deeply in earnest; but all the same I could not help laughing. His English was quite gone now. In his anxiety he had forgotten that his only means of making me understand was to talk my language, so he jabbered away in his native German. It began to be a little tedious. After giving the direction, 'Home!' I turned to go down the cross-road into the valley.

With a despairing gesture, Johann turned his horses towards Munich. I leaned on my stick and looked after him. He went slowly along the road for a while; then there came over the crest of the hill a man tall and thin. I could see so much in the distance. When he drew near the horses, they began to jump and kick about, then to scream with terror. Johann could not hold them in; they bolted down the road, running away madly. I watched them out of sight, then looked for the stranger, but I found that he, too, was gone.

With a light heart I turned down the side road through the deepening valley to which Johann had objected. There was not the slightest reason, that

I could see, for his objection; and I dare say I tramped for a couple of hours without thinking of time or distance, and certainly without seeing a person or a house. So far as the place was concerned, it was desolation itself. But I did not notice this particularly till, on turning a bend in the road, I came upon a scattered fringe of wood; then I recognised that I had been impressed unconsciously by the desolation of the region through which I had passed.

I sat down to rest myself, and began to look around. It struck me that it was considerably colder than it had been at the commencement of my walk – a sort of sighing sound seemed to be around me, with, now and then, high overhead, a sort of muffled roar. Looking upwards I noticed that great thick clouds were drifting rapidly across the sky from north to south at a great height. There were signs of coming storm in some lofty stratum of the air. I was a little chilly, and, thinking that it was the sitting still after the exercise of walking, I resumed my journey.

The ground I passed over was now much more picturesque. There were no striking objects that the eye might single out; but in all there was a charm of beauty. I took little heed of time and it was only when the deepening twilight forced itself upon me that I began to think of how I should find my way home. The brightness of the day had gone. The air was cold, and the drifting of clouds high overhead was more marked. They were accompanied by a sort of far-away rushing sound, through which seemed to come at intervals that mysterious cry which the driver had said came from a wolf. For a while I hesitated. I had said I would see the deserted village, so on I went, and presently came on a wide stretch of open country, shut in by hills all around. Their sides were covered with trees which spread down to the plain, dotting, in clumps, the gentler slopes and hollows which showed here and there. I followed with my eye the winding of the road, and saw that it curved close to one of the densest of these clumps and was lost behind it.

As I looked there came a cold shiver in the air, and the snow began to fall. I thought of the miles and miles of bleak country I had passed, and then hurried on to seek the shelter of the wood in front. Darker and darker grew the sky, and faster and heavier fell the snow, till the earth before and around me was a glistening white carpet, the further edge of which was lost in misty vagueness. The road was here but crude, and when on the level its boundaries were not so marked as when it passed through the cuttings; and in a little while I found that I must have strayed from it, for I missed underfoot the hard surface, and my feet sank deeper in the grass and moss. Then the wind grew stronger and blew with ever increasing force, till I was fain to run before it. The air became icy-cold, and in spite of my exercise I began to suffer. The snow was now falling so thickly and whirling around me in such rapid eddies that I could hardly keep my eyes open. Every now and then the heavens were torn asunder by vivid lightning, and in the flashes I could see ahead of me a great mass of trees, chiefly yew and cypress, all heavily coated with snow.

I was soon amongst the shelter of the trees, and there, in comparative silence, I could hear the rush of the wind high overhead. Presently the blackness of the storm had become merged in the darkness of the night. By and by the storm seemed to be passing away: it now only came in fierce bursts or blasts. At such moments the weird sound of the wolf appeared to be echoed by many similar sounds around me.

Now and again, through the black mass of drifting cloud, came a straggling ray of moonlight, which lit up the expanse, and showed me that I was at the edge of a dense mass of cypress and yew trees. As the snow had ceased to fall, I walked out from the shelter and began to investigate more closely. It appeared to me that, amongst so many old foundations as I had passed, there might be still standing a house in which, though in ruins, I could find some sort of shelter for a while. As I skirted the edge of the copse, I found that a low wall encircled it, and following this I presently found an opening. Here the cypresses formed an alley leading up to a square mass of some kind of building. Just as I caught sight of this, however, the drifting clouds obscured the moon, and I passed up the path in darkness The wind must have grown colder, for I felt myself shiver as I walked; but there was hope of shelter, and I groped my way blindly on.

I stopped, for there was a sudden stillness. The storm had passed; and, perhaps in sympathy with nature's silence, my heart seemed to cease to beat. But this was only momentarily; for suddenly the moonlight broke through the clouds, showing me that I was in a graveyard, and that the square object before me was a great massive tomb of marble, as white as the snow that lay on and all around it. With the moonlight there came a fierce sigh of the storm, which appeared to resume its course with a long, low howl, as of many dogs or wolves. I was awed and shocked, and felt the cold perceptibly grow upon me till it seemed to grip me by the heart. Then while the flood of moonlight still fell on the marble tomb, the storm gave further evidence of renewing, as though it was returning on its track. Impelled by some sort of fascination, I approached the sepulchre to see what it was, and why such a thing stood alone in such a place. I walked around it, and read, over the Doric door, in German:

COUNTESS DOLINGEN OF GRATZ
IN STYRIA
SOUGHT AND FOUND DEATH
1801

On the top of the tomb, seemingly driven through the solid marble – for the structure was composed of a few vast blocks of stone – was a great iron spike or stake. On going to the back I saw, graven in great Russian letters:

THE DEAD TRAVEL FAST

There was something so weird and uncanny about the whole thing that it gave me a turn and made me feel quite faint. I began to wish, for the first time, that I had taken Johann's advice. Here a thought struck me, which came under almost mysterious circumstances and with a terrible shock. This was Walpurgis Night!

Walpurgis Night, when, according to the belief of millions of people, the devil was abroad – when the graves were opened and the dead came forth and walked. When all evil things of earth and air and water held revel. This very place the driver had specially shunned. This was the depopulated village of centuries ago. This was where the suicide lay; and this was the place where I was alone – unmanned, shivering with cold in a shroud of snow with a wild storm gathering again upon me! It took all my philosophy, all the religion I had been taught, all my courage, not to collapse in a paroxysm of fright.

And now a perfect tornado burst upon me. The ground shook as though thousands of horses thundered across it; and this time the storm bore on its icy wings, not snow, but great hailstones which drove with such violence that they might have come from the thongs of Balearic slingers – hailstones that beat down leaf and branch and made the shelter of the cypresses of no more avail than if their stems were standing-corn. At the first I had rushed to the nearest tree; but I was soon fain to leave it and seek the only spot that seemed to afford refuge, the deep Doric doorway of the marble tomb. There, crouching against the massive bronze door, I gained a certain amount of protection from the beating of the hailstones, for now they only drove against me as they ricocheted from the ground and the side of the marble.

As I leaned against the door, it moved slightly and opened inwards. The shelter of even a tomb was welcome in that pitiless tempest, and I was about to enter it when there came a flash of forked-lightning that lit up the whole expanse of the heavens. In the instant, as I am a living man, I saw, as my eyes were turned into the darkness of the tomb, a beautiful woman, with rounded cheeks and red lips, seemingly sleeping on a bier. As the thunder broke overhead, I was grasped as by the hand of a giant and hurled out into the storm. The whole thing was so sudden that, before I could realise the shock, moral as well as physical, I found the hailstones beating me down. At the same time I had a strange, dominating feeling that I was not alone. I looked towards the tomb. Just then there came another blinding flash, which seemed to strike the iron stake that surmounted the tomb and to pour through to the earth, blasting and crumbling the marble, as in a burst of flame. The dead woman rose for a moment of agony, while she was lapped in the flame, and her bitter scream of pain was drowned in the thundercrash. The last thing I heard was this mingling of dreadful sound, as again I was seized in the giant-grasp and dragged away, while the hailstones beat on me, and the air around seemed reverberant with the howling of wolves. The last sight that I remembered was a vague, white, moving mass, as if all the graves around me had sent out the phantoms of their sheeted-dead, and that they were closing in on me through the white cloudiness of the driving hail.

Gradually there came a sort of vague beginning of consciousness; then a sense of weariness that was dreadful. For a time I remembered nothing; but slowly my senses returned. My feet seemed positively racked with pain, yet I could not move them. They seemed to be numbed. There was an icy feeling at the back of my neck and all down my spine, and my ears, like my feet, were dead, yet in torment; but there was in my breast a sense of warmth which was, by comparison, delicious. It was as a nightmare – a physical nightmare, if one may use such an expression; for some heavy weight on my chest made it difficult for me to breathe.

This period of semi-lethargy seemed to remain a long time, and as it faded away I must have slept or swooned. Then came a sort of loathing, like the first stage of sea-sickness, and a wild desire to be free from something – I knew not what. A vast stillness enveloped me, as though all the world were asleep or dead – only broken by the low panting as of some animal close to me. I felt a warm rasping at my throat, then came a consciousness of the awful truth, which chilled me to the heart and sent the blood surging up through my brain. Some great animal was lying on me and now licking my throat. I feared to stir, for some instinct of prudence bade me lie still; but the brute seemed to realise that there was now some change in me, for it raised its head. Through my eyelashes I saw above me the two great flaming eyes of a gigantic wolf. Its sharp white teeth gleamed in the gaping red mouth, and I could feel its hot breath fierce and acrid upon me.

For another spell of time I remembered no more. Then I became conscious of a low growl, followed by a yelp, renewed again and again. Then, seemingly very far away, I heard a 'Holloa! holloa!' as of many voices calling in unison. Cautiously I raised my head and looked in the direction whence the sound came; but the cemetery blocked my view. The wolf still continued to yelp in a strange way, and a red glare began to move round the grove of cypresses, as though following the sound. As the voices drew closer, the wolf yelped faster and louder. I feared to make either sound or motion. Nearer came the red glow, over the white pall which stretched into the darkness around me. Then all at once from beyond the trees there came at a trot a troop of horsemen bearing torches. The wolf rose from my breast and made for the cemetery. I saw one of the horsemen (soldiers by their caps and their long military cloaks) raise his carbine and take aim. A companion knocked up his arm, and I heard the ball whizz over my head. He had evidently taken my body for that of the wolf. Another sighted the animal as it slunk away, and a shot followed. Then, at a gallop, the troop rode forward – some towards me, others following the wolf as it disappeared amongst the snow-clad cypresses.

As they drew nearer I tried to move, but was powerless, although I could see and hear all that went on around me. Two or three of the soldiers jumped from their horses and knelt beside me. One of them raised my head, and placed his hand over my heart.

'Good news, comrades!' he cried. 'His heart still beats!'

Then some brandy was poured down my throat; it put vigour into me, and I was able to open my eyes fully and look around. Lights and shadows were moving among the trees, and I heard men call to one another. They drew together, uttering frightened exclamations; and the lights flashed as the others came pouring out of the cemetery pell-mell, like men possessed. When the farther ones came close to us, those who were around me asked them eagerly: 'Well, have you found him?'

The reply rang out hurriedly: 'No! no! Come away quick, quick! This is no place to stay, and on this of all nights!'

'What was it?' was the question, asked in all manner of keys. The answer came variously and all indefinitely as though the men were moved by some common impulse to speak, yet were restrained by some common fear from giving their thoughts.

'It – it – indeed!' gibbered one, whose wits had plainly given out for the moment.

'A wolf – and yet not a wolf!' another put in shudderingly.

'No use trying for him without the sacred bullet,' a third remarked in a more ordinary manner.

'Serve us right for coming out on this night! Truly we have earned our thousand marks!' were the ejaculations of a fourth.

'There was blood on the broken marble,' another said after a pause – 'the lightning never brought that there. And for him – is he safe? Look at his throat! See, comrades, the wolf has been lying on him and keeping his blood warm.'

The officer looked at my throat and replied: 'He is all right; the skin is not pierced. What does it all mean? We should never have found him but for the yelping of the wolf.'

'What became of it?' asked the man who was holding up my head, and who seemed the least panic-stricken of the party, for his hands were steady and without tremor. On his sleeve was the chevron of a petty officer.

'It went to its home,' answered the man, whose long face was pallid, and who actually shook with terror as he glanced around him fearfully. 'There are graves enough there in which it may lie. Come, comrades – come quickly! Let us leave this cursed spot.'

The officer raised me to a sitting posture, as he uttered a word of command; then several men placed me upon a horse. He sprang to the saddle behind me, took me in his arms, gave the word to advance; and, turning our faces away from the cypresses, we rode away in swift, military order.

As yet my tongue refused its office, and I was perforce silent. I must have fallen asleep; for the next thing I remembered was finding myself standing up, supported by a soldier on each side of me. It was almost broad daylight, and to the north a red streak of sunlight was reflected, like a path of blood, over the waste of snow. The officer was telling the men to say nothing of what they had seen, except that they had found an English stranger, guarded by a large dog.

'Dog! that was no dog,' cut in the man who had exhibited such fear. 'I think I know a wolf when I see one.'

The young officer answered calmly: 'I said a dog.'

'Dog!' reiterated the other ironically. It was evident that his courage was rising with the sun; and, pointing to me, he said, 'Look at his throat. Is that the work of a dog, master?'

Instinctively I raised my hand to my throat, and as I touched it I cried out in pain. The men crowded round to look, some stooping down from their saddles; and again there came the calm voice of the young officer: 'A dog, as I said. If aught else were said we should only be laughed at.'

I was then mounted behind a trooper, and we rode on into the suburbs of Munich. Here we came across a stray carriage, into which I was lifted, and it was driven off to the Quatre Saisons – the young officer accompanying me, whilst a trooper followed with his horse, and the others rode off to their barracks.

When we arrived, Herr Delbrück rushed so quickly down the steps to meet me that it was apparent he had been watching within. Taking me by both hands he solicitously led me in. The officer saluted me and was turning to withdraw, when I recognised his purpose, and insisted that he should come to my rooms. Over a glass of wine I warmly thanked him and his brave comrades for saving me. He replied simply that he was more than glad, and that Herr Delbrück had at the first taken steps to make all the searching party pleased; at which ambiguous utterance the *maître d'hôtel* smiled, while the officer pleaded duty and withdrew.

'But Herr Delbrück,' I enquired, 'how and why was it that the soldiers searched for me?'

He shrugged his shoulders, as if in depreciation of his own deed, as he replied: 'I was so fortunate as to obtain leave from the commander of the regiment in which I served, to ask for volunteers.'

'But how did you know I was lost?' I asked.

'The driver came hither with the remains of his carriage, which had been upset when the horses ran away.'

'But surely you would not send a search-party of soldiers merely on this account?'

'Oh, no!' he answered; 'but even before the coachman arrived, I had this telegram from the boyar whose guest you are,' and he took from his pocket a telegram which he handed to me, and I read:

Bistritz

Be careful of my guest – his safety is most precious to me. Should aught happen to him, or if he be missed, spare nothing to find him and ensure his safety. He is English and therefore adventurous. There are often dangers from snow and wolves and night. Lose not a moment if you suspect harm to him. I answer your zeal with my fortune.

DRACULA

As I held the telegram in my hand, the room seemed to whirl around me; and, if the attentive *maître d'hôtel* had not caught me, I think I should have fallen. There was something so strange in all this, something so weird and impossible to imagine, that there grew on me a sense of my being in some way the sport of opposite forces – the mere vague idea of which seemed in a way to paralyse me. I was certainly under some form of mysterious protection. From a distant country had come, in the very nick of time, a message that took me out of the danger of the snow-sleep and the jaws of the wolf.

Vendetta

GUY DE MAUPASSANT

PALO SAVERINI'S WIDOW dwelt alone with her son in a small, mean house on the ramparts of Bonifacio. Built on a spur of the mountain and in places actually overhanging the sea, the town looks across the rock-strewn straits to the low-lying coast of Sardinia. On the other side, girdling it almost completely, there is a fissure in the cliff, like an immense corridor, which serves as a port, and down this long channel, as far as the first houses, sail the small Italian and Sardinian fishing-boats, and once a fortnight the broken-winded old steamer from Ajaccio. Clustered together on the white hillside, the houses form a patch of even more dazzling whiteness. Clinging to the rock, gazing down upon those deadly straits where scarcely a ship ventures, they look like the nests of birds of prey. The sea and the barren coast, stripped of all but a scanty covering of grass, are forever harassed by a restless wind, which sweeps along the narrow funnel, ravaging the banks on either side. In all directions the black points of innumerable rocks jut out from the water, with trails of white foam streaming from them, like torn shreds of cloth, floating and quivering on the surface of the waves.

The widow Saverini's house was planted on the very edge of the cliff and its three windows opened upon this wild and dreary prospect. She lived there with her son Antoine and their dog Sémillante, a great gaunt brute of the sheepdog variety, with a long, rough coat, whom the young man took with him when he went out shooting.

One evening, Antoine Saverini was treacherously stabbed in a quarrel by Nicolas Ravolati, who escaped that same night to Sardinia.

At the sight of the body, which was brought home by passers-by, the old mother shed no tears, but she gazed long and silently at her dead son. Then, laying her wrinkled hand upon the corpse, she promised him the vendetta. She would not allow anyone to remain with her, and shut herself up with the dead body. The dog Sémillante, who remained with her, stood at the foot of the bed and howled, with her head turned towards her master and her tail between her legs. Neither of them stirred, neither the dog nor the old mother, who was now leaning over the body, gazing at it fixedly, and silently shedding great tears. Still wearing his rough jacket, which was pierced and torn at the breast, the boy lay on his back as if asleep, but there was blood all about him – on his shirt, which had been torn open in order to expose the wound, on his waistcoat, trousers, face and hands. His beard and hair were matted with clots of blood.

The old mother began to talk to him, and at the sound of her voice the dog stopped howling.

'Never fear, never fear, you shall be avenged, my son, my little son, my poor child. You may sleep in peace. You shall be avenged, I tell you. You have your mother's word, and you know she never breaks it.'

Slowly she bent down and pressed her cold lips to the dead lips of her son.

Sémillante resumed her howling, uttering a monotonous, long-drawn wail, heart-rending and terrible. And thus the two remained, the woman and the dog, till morning.

The next day Antoine Saverini was buried, and soon his name ceased to be mentioned in Bonifacio.

He had no brother, nor any near male relation. There was no man in the family who could take up the vendetta. Only his mother, his old mother, brooded over it.

From morning till night she could see, just across the straits, a white speck upon the coast. This was the little Sardinian village of Longosardo, where the Corsican bandits took refuge whenever the hunt for them grew too hot. They formed almost the entire population of the hamlet. In full view of their native shores they waited for a chance to return home and regain the bush. She knew that Nicolas Ravolati had sought shelter in that village.

All day long she sat alone at her window gazing at the opposite coast and thinking of her revenge, but what was she to do with no one to help her, and she herself so feeble and near her end? But she had promised, she had sworn by the dead body of her son, she could not forget, and she dared not delay. What was she to do? She could not sleep at night she knew not a moment of rest or peace, but racked her brains unceasingly. Sémillante, asleep at her feet, would now and then raise her head and emit a piercing howl. Since her master had disappeared, this had become a habit; it was as if she were calling him, as if she, too, were inconsolable and preserved in her canine soul an ineffaceable memory of the dead.

One night, when Sémillante began to whine, the old mother had an inspiration of savage, vindictive ferocity. She thought about it till morning. At daybreak she rose and betook herself to church. Prostrate on the stone floor, humbling herself before God, she besought Him to aid and support her, to lend to her poor, worn-out body the strength she needed to avenge her son.

Then she returned home. In the yard stood an old barrel with one end knocked in, in which was caught the rain-water from the eaves. She turned it over, emptied it, and fixed it to the ground with stakes and stones. Then she chained up Sémillante to this kennel and went into the house.

With her eyes fixed on the Sardinian coast, she walked restlessly up and down her room. He was over there, the murderer.

The dog howled all day and all night. The next morning, the old woman brought her a bowl of water, but no food, neither soup not bread. Another day passed. Sémillante was worn out and slept. The next morning her eyes were gleaming, and her coat staring, and she tugged frantically at her chain. And again the old woman gave her nothing to eat. Maddened with hunger Sémillante barked hoarsely. Another night went by.

At daybreak, the widow went to a neighbour and begged for two trusses of straw. She took some old clothes that had belonged to her husband, stuffed them with straw to represent a human figure, and made a head out of a bundle of old rags. Then, in front of Sémillante's kennel, she fixed a stake in the ground and fastened the dummy to it in an upright position.

The dog looked at the straw figure in surprise and, although she was famished, stopped howling.

The old woman went to the pork butcher and bought a long piece of black pudding. When she came home she lighted a wood fire in the yard, close to the kennel, and fried the black pudding. Sémillante bounded up and down in a frenzy, foaming at the mouth, her eyes fixed on the gridiron with its maddening smell of meat.

Her mistress took the steaming pudding and wound it like a tie round the dummy's neck. She fastened it on tightly with string as if to force it inwards. When she had finished she unchained the dog.

With one ferocious leap, Sémillante flew at the dummy's throat and with her paws on its shoulders began to tear it. She fell back with a portion of her prey between her jaws, sprang at it again, slashing at the string with her fangs, tore away some scraps of food, dropped for a moment, and hurled herself at it in renewed fury. She tore away the whole face with savage rendings and reduced the neck to shreds.

Motionless and silent, with burning eyes, the old woman looked on. Presently she chained the dog up again. She starved her another two days, and then put her through the same strange performance. For three months she accustomed her to this method of attack, and to tear her meals away with her fangs. She was no longer kept on the chain. At a sign from her mistress, the dog would fly at the dummy's throat.

She learned to tear it to pieces even when no food was concealed about its throat. Afterwards as a reward she was always given the black pudding her mistress had cooked for her.

As soon as she caught sight of the dummy, Sémillante quivered with excitement and looked at her mistress, who would raise her finger and cry in a shrill voice, 'Tear him.'

One Sunday morning when she thought the time had come, the widow Saverini went to confession and communion, in an ecstasy of devotion.

Then she disguised herself as a tattered old beggar man, and struck a bargain with a Sardinian fisherman, who took her and her dog across to the opposite shore.

She carried a large piece of black pudding wrapped in a cloth bag. Sémillante had been starved for two days and her mistress kept exciting her by letting her smell the savoury food.

The pair entered the village of Longosardo. The old woman hobbled along to a baker and asked for the house of Nicolas Ravolati. He had resumed his former occupation, which was that of a joiner, and he was working alone in the back of his shop.

The old woman threw open the door and called: 'Nicolas! Nicolas!'

He turned round. Slipping the dog's lead, she cried: 'Tear him! Tear him!'

The maddened dog flew at his throat. The man flung out his arms, grappled with the brute and they rolled on the ground together. For some moments he struggled, kicking the floor with his feet. Then he lay still, while Sémillante tore his throat to shreds.

Two neighbours, seated at their doors, remembered having seen an old beggar man emerge from the house and, at his heels, a lean black dog, which was eating, as it went along, some brown substance that its master was giving it.

By the evening the old woman had reached home again.

That night she slept well.

Thrawn Janet

ROBERT LOUIS STEVENSON

THE REVEREND MURDOCH SOULIS was long minister of the moorland parish of Balweary, in the vale of Dule. A severe, bleak-faced old man, dreadful to his hearers, he dwelt in the last years of his life, without relative or servant or any human company, in the small and lonely manse under the Hanging Shaw. In spite of the iron composure of his features, his eye was wild, scared and uncertain; and when he dwelt, in private admonitions, on the future of the impenitent, it seemed as if his eye pierced through the storms of time to the terrors of eternity. Many young persons coming to prepare themselves against the season of the holy communion were dreadfully affected by his talk. He had a sermon on 1 Peter 5: 8, 'the devil, as a roaring lion', on the Sunday after every seventeenth of August, and he was accustomed to surpass himself upon that text both by the appalling nature of the matter and the terror of his bearing in the pulpit. The children were frightened into fits, and the old looked more than usually oracular, and were, all that day, full of those hints that Hamlet deprecated. The manse itself, where it stood by the water of Dule among some thick trees, with the Shaw overhanging it on the one side, and on the other many cold, moorish hill-tops rising towards the sky, had begun, at a very early period of Mr Soulis's ministry, to be avoided in the dusk hours by all who valued themselves upon their prudence; and guidmen sitting at the clachan alehouse shook their heads together at the thought of passing late by that uncanny neighbourhood. There was one spot, to be more particular, which was regarded with especial awe. The manse stood between the high road and the water of Dule, with a gable to each; its back was towards the kirktown of Balweary, nearly half a mile away; in front of it, a bare garden, hedged with thorn, occupied the land between the river and the road. The house was two storeys high, with two large rooms on each. It opened not directly on the garden, but on a causewayed path or passage, giving on the road on the one hand and closed on the other by the tall willows and elders that bordered on the stream. And it was this strip of causeway that enjoyed among the young parishioners of Balweary so infamous a reputation. The minister walked there often after dark, sometimes groaning aloud in the instancy of his unspoken prayers; and when he was from home, and the manse door was locked, the more daring schoolboys ventured, with beating hearts, to 'follow my leader' across that legendary spot.

This atmosphere of terror, surrounding, as it did, a man of God of spotless character and orthodoxy, was a common cause of wonder and subject of enquiry among the few strangers who were led by chance or business into that unknown, outlying country. But many even of the people of the parish were ignorant of the strange events which had marked the first year of Mr Soulis's ministrations; and among those who were better informed, some were naturally reticent, and others shy of that particular topic. Now and again, only, one of the older folk would warm into courage over his third tumbler, and recount the cause of the minister's strange looks and solitary life.

Fifty years syne, when Mr Soulis cam' first into Ba'weary, he was still a young man – a callant, the folk said – fu' o' book learnin' and grand at the exposition, but, as was natural in sae young a man, wi' nae leevin' experience in religion. The younger sort were greatly taken wi' his gifts and his gab; but auld, concerned, serious men and women were moved even to prayer for the young man, whom they took to be a self-deceiver, and the parish that was like to be sae ill-supplied. It was before the days o' the Moderates – weary fa' them; but ill things are like guid – they baith come bit by bit, a pickle at a time; and there were folk even then that said the Lord had left the college professors to their ain devices, an' the lads that went to study wi' them wad hae done mair and better sittin' in a peat-bog, like their forebears of the persecution, wi' a Bible under their oxter and a speerit o' prayer in their heart. There was nae doubt, onyway, but that Mr Soulis had been ower lang at the college. He was careful and troubled for mony things besides the ae thing needful. He had a feck o' books wi' him – mair than had ever been seen before in a' that presbytery; and a sair wark the carrier had wi' them, for they were a' like to have smoored in the Deil's Hag between this and Kilmackerlie. They were books o' divinity, to be sure, or so they ca'd them; but the serious were o' opinion there was little service for sae mony, when the hail o' God's Word would gang in the neuk of a plaid. Then he wad sit half the day and half the nicht forbye, which was scant decent – writin', nae less; and first, they were feared he wad read his sermons; and syne it was proved he was writin' a book himsel', which was surely no fittin' for ane of his years an' sma' experience.

Onyway it behoved him to get an auld, decent wife to keep the manse for him an' see to his bit denners; and he was recommended to an auld limmer – Janet M'Clour, they ca'd her – and sae far left to himsel' as to be ower persuaded. There was mony advised him to the contrar, for Janet was mair than suspeckit by the best folk in Ba'weary. Lang or that, she had had a

---

* To come forrit – to offer oneself as a communicant.

wean to a dragoon; she hadnae come forrit* for maybe thretty year; and bairns had seen her mumblin' to hersel' up on Key's Loan in the gloamin', whilk was an unco time an' place for a God-fearin' woman. Howsoever, it was the laird himsel' that had first tauld the minister o' Janet; and in thae days he wad have gane a far gate to pleesure the laird. When folk tauld him that Janet was sib to the deil, it was a' superstition by his way of it; an' when they cast up the Bible to him an' the witch of Endor, he wad threep it doun their thrapples that thir days were a' gane by, and the deil was mercifully restrained.

Weel, when it got about the clachan that Janet M'Clour was to be servant at the manse, the folk were fair mad wi' her an' him thegether; and some of the guidwives had nae better to dae than get round her door cheeks and chairge her wi' a' that was ken't again her, frae the sodger's bairn to John Tamson's twa kye. She was nae great speaker; folk usually let her gang her ain gate, an' she let them gang theirs, wi' neither Fair-guid-een nor Fair-guid-day; but when she buckled to, she had a tongue to deave the miller. Up she got, an' there wasnae an auld story in Ba'weary but she gart somebody lowp for it that day; they couldnae say ae thing but she could say twa to it; till, at the hinder end, the guidwives up and claucht haud of her, and clawed the coats aff her back, and pu'd her doun the clachan to the water o' Dule, to see if she were a witch or no, soum or droun. The carline skirled till ye could hear her at the Hangin' Shaw, and she focht like ten; there was mony a guidwife bure the mark of her neist day an' mony a lang day after; and just in the hettest o' the collieshangie, wha suld come up (for his sins) but the new minister.

'Women,' said he (and he had a grand voice), 'I charge you in the Lord's name to let her go.'

Janet ran to him – she was fair wud wi' terror – an' clang to him, an' prayed him, for Christ's sake, save her frae the cummers; an' they, for their pairt, tauld him a' that was ken't, and maybe mair.

'Woman,' says he to Janet, 'is this true?'

'As the Lord sees me,' says she, 'as the Lord made me, no a word o't. Forbye the bairn,' says she, 'I've been a decent woman a' my days.'

'Will you,' says Mr Soulis, 'in the name of God, and before me, His unworthy minister, renounce the devil and his works?'

Weel, it wad appear that when he askit that, she gave a girn that fairly frichtit them that saw her, an' they could hear her teeth play dirl thegether in her chafts; but there was naething for it but the ae way or the ither; an' Janet lifted up her hand and renounced the deil before them a'.

'And now,' says Mr Soulis to the guidwives, 'home with ye, one and all, and pray to God for His forgiveness.'

And he gied Janet his arm, though she had little on her but a sark, and took her up the clachan to her ain door like a leddy of the land; an' her screighin' and laughin' as was a scandal to be heard.

There were mony grave folk lang ower their prayers that nicht; but when the morn cam' there was sic a fear fell upon a' Ba'weary that the bairns hid theirsels, and even the menfolk stood and keekit frae their doors. For there was Janet comin' doun the clachan – her or her likeness, nane could tell – wi' her neck thrawn, and her heid on ae side, like a body that has been hangit, and a girn on her face like an unstreakit corp. By an' by they got used wi' it, and even speered at her to ken what was wrang; but frae that day forth she couldnae speak like a Christian woman, but slavered and played click wi' her teeth like a pair o' shears; and frae that day forth the name o' God cam' never on her lips. Whiles she would try to say it, but it michtnae be. Them that kenned best said least; but they never gied that Thing the name o' Janet M'Clour; for the auld Janet, by their way o't, was in muckle hell that day. But the minister was neither to haud nor to bind; he preached about naething but the folk's cruelty that had gi'en her a stroke of the palsy; he skelpt the bairns that meddled her; and he had her up to the manse that same nicht, and dwalled there a' his lane wi' her under the Hangin' Shaw.

Weel, time gaed by; and the idler sort commenced to think mair lichtly o' that black business. The minister was weel thocht o'; he was aye late at the writing, folk wad see his can'le doun by the Dule water after twal' at e'en; and he seemed pleased wi' himsel' and upsitten as at first, though a' body could see that he was dwining. As for Janet she cam' an' she gaed; if she didnae speak muckle afore, it was reason she should speak less then; she meddled naebody; but she was an eldritch thing to see, an' nane wad hae mistrysted wi' her for Ba'weary glebe.

About the end o' July there cam' a spell o' weather, the like o't never was in that countryside; it was lown an' het an' heartless; the herds couldnae win up the Black Hill, the bairns were ower weariet to play; an' yet it was gousty too, wi' claps o' het wund that rumm'led in the glens, and bits o' shouers that slockened naething. We aye thocht it but to thun'er on the morn; but the morn cam', an' the morn's morning, and it was aye the same uncanny weather, sair on folks and bestial. Of a' that were the waur, nane suffered like Mr Soulis; he could neither sleep, nor eat, he tauld his elders; an' when he wasnae writin' at his weary book, he wad be stravaguin' ower a' the countryside like a man possessed, when a' body else was blythe to keep caller ben the house.

Abune Hangin' Shaw, in the bield o' the Black Hill, there's a bit enclosed grund wi' an iron yett; and it seems, in the auld days, that was the kirkyaird o' Ba'weary, and consecrated by the papists before the blessed licht shone upon the kingdom. It was a great howff o' Mr Soulis's onyway; there he would sit an' consider his sermons; and indeed it's a bieldy bit. Weel, as he cam' ower the wast end o' the Black Hill, ae day, he saw first twa, an' syne fower, an' syne seeven corbie craws fleein' round an' round abune the auld kirkyaird. They flew laigh and heavy, an' squawked to ither as they gaed; and it was clear to Mr Soulis that something had put them frae their

ordinar. He wasnae easy fleyed, an' gaed straucht up to the wa's; an' what
suld he find there but a man, or the appearance of a man, sittin' in the inside
upon a grave. He was of a great stature, an' black as hell, and his e'en were
singular to see.* Mr Soulis had heard tell o' black men, mony's the time; but
there was something unco about this black man that daunted him. Het as he
was, he took a kind o' cauld grue in the marrow o' his banes; but up he spak
for a' that; an' says he: 'My friend, are you a stranger in this place?' The
black man answered never a word; he got upon his feet, an' begude to hirsle
to the wa' on the far side; but he aye lookit at the minister; an' the minister
stood an' lookit back; till a' in a meenute the black man was ower the wa' an'
rinnin' for the bield o' the trees. Mr Soulis, he hardly kenned why, ran after
him; but he was sair forjaskit wi' his walk an' the het, unhalesome weather;
and rin as he likit, he got nae mair than a glisk o' the black man amang the
birks, till he won doun to the foot o' the hillside, an' there he saw him ance
mair, gaun, hap, step, an' lowp, ower Dule water to the manse.

Mr Soulis wasnae weel pleased that this fearsome gangrel suld mak' sae
free wi' Ba'weary manse; an' he ran the harder, an', wet shoon, ower the
burn an' up the walk; but the deil a black man was there to see. He stepped
out upon the road, but there was naebody there; he gaed a' ower the
gairden, but na, nae black man. At the hinder end, and a bit feared as was
but natural, he lifted the hasp and into the manse; and there was Janet
M'Clour before his een, wi' her thrawn craig, and nane sae pleased to see
him. And he aye minded sinsyne, when first he set his een upon her, he had
the same cauld and deidly grue.

'Janet,' says he, 'have you seen a black man?'

'A black man?' quo' she. 'Save us a'! Ye're no wise, minister. There's nae
black man in a' Ba'weary.'

But she didnae speak plain, ye maun understand; but yammered, like a
powney wi' the bit in its moo.

'Weel,' says he, 'Janet, if there was nae black man, I have spoken with the
Accuser of the Brethren.'

And he sat down like ane wi' a fever, an' his teeth chittered in his heid.

'Hoots,' says she, 'think shame to yoursel', minister'; an' gied him a drap
brandy that she keept aye by her.

Syne Mr Soulis gaed into his study amang a' his books. It's a lang, laigh,
mirk chalmer, perishin' cauld in winter, an' no very dry even in the tap o'
the simmer, for the manse stands near the burn. Sae doun he sat, and thocht
of a' that had come an' gane since he was in Ba'weary, an' his hame, an' the
days when he was a bairn an' ran daffin' on the braes; and that black man aye
ran in his heid like the owercome of a sang. Aye the mair he thocht, the mair

---

* It was a common belief in Scotland that the devil appeared as a black man. This appears in
several witch trials and I think in Law's *Memorials*, that delightful storehouse of the quaint
and grisly.

he thocht o' the black man. He tried the prayer, an' the words wouldnae come to him; an' he tried, they say, to write at his book, but he could nae mak' nae mair o' that. There was whiles he thocht the black man was at his oxter, an' the swat stood upon him cauld as well-water; and there was other whiles, when he cam' to himsel' like a christened bairn and minded naething.

The upshot was that he gaed to the window an' stood glowrin' at Dule Water. The trees are unco thick, an' the water lies deep an' black under the manse; an' there was Janet washin' the cla'es wi' her coats kilted. She had her back to the minister, an' he, for his pairt, hardly kenned what he was lookin' at. Syne she turned round, an' shawed her face; Mr Soulis had the same cauld grue as twice that day afore, an' it was borne in upon him what folk said, that Janet was deid lang syne, an' this was a bogle in her clay-cauld flesh. He drew back a pickle and he scanned her narrowly. She was tramp-trampin' in the cla'es, croonin' to hersel'; and eh! Gude guide us, but it was a fearsome face. Whiles she sang louder, but there was nae man born o' woman that could tell the words o' her sang; an' whiles she lookit sidelang doun, but there was naething there for her to look at. There gaed a scunner through the flesh upon his banes; and that was heeven's advertisement. But Mr Soulis just blamed himsel', he said, to think sae ill of a puir auld afflicted wife that hadnae a freend forbye himsel'; an' he put up a bit prayer for him and her, an' drank a little caller water – for his heart rose again the meat – an' gaed up to his naked bed in the gloaming.

That was a nicht that has never been forgotten in Ba'weary, the nicht o' the seventeenth of August, seventeen hun'er' an' twal'. It had been het afore, as I hae said, but that nicht it was hetter than ever. The sun gaed doun among unco-lookin' clouds; it fell as mirk as the pit; no a star, no a breath o' wund; ye couldnae see your han' afore your face, and even the auld folk cuist the covers frae their beds and lay pechin' for their breath. Wi' a' that he had upon his mind, it was gey and unlikely Mr Soulis wad get muckle sleep. He lay an' he tummled; the gude, caller bed that he got into brunt his very banes; whiles he slept, and whiles he waukened; whiles he heard the time o' nicht, and whiles a tyke yowlin' up the muir, as if somebody was deid; whiles he thocht he heard bogles claverin' in his lug, an' whiles he saw spunkies in the room. He behoved, he judged, to be sick; an' sick he was – little he jaloosed the sickness.

At the hinder end, he got a clearness in his mind, sat up in his sark on the bedside, and fell thinkin' ance mair o' the black man an' Janet. He couldnae weel tell how – maybe it was the cauld to his feet – but it cam' in upon him wi' a spate that there was some connection between thir twa, an' that either or baith o' them were bogles. And just at that moment, in Janet's room, which was neist to his, there cam' a stramp o' feet as if men were wars'lin', an' then a loud bang; an' then a wund gaed reishling round the fower quarters of the house; an' then a' was aince mair as seelent as the grave.

Mr Soulis was feared for neither man nor deevil. He got his tinderbox, an' lit a can'le, an' made three steps o't ower to Janet's door. It was on the hasp, an' he pushed it open, an' keeked bauldly in. It was a big room, as big as the minister's ain, an' plenished wi' grand, auld solid gear, for he had naething else. There was a fower-posted bed wi' auld tapestry; and a braw cabinet of aik, that was fu' o' the minister's divinity books, an' put there to be out o' the gate; an' a wheen duds o' Janet's lying here and there about the floor. But nae Janet could Mr Soulis see; nor ony sign of a contention. In he gaed (an' there's few that wad ha'e followed him) an' lookit a' round, an' listened. But there was naethin' to be heard, neither inside the manse nor in a' Ba'weary parish, an' naethin' to be seen but the muckle shadows turnin' round the can'le. An' then a' at aince, the minister's heart played dunt an' stood stock-still; an' a cauld wund blew amang the hairs o' his heid. Whaten a weary sicht was that for the puir man's een! For there was Janet hangin' frae a nail beside the auld aik cabinet: her heid aye lay on her shoother, her een were steeked, the tongue projekit frae her mouth, and her heels were twa feet clear abune the floor.

'God forgive us all!' thocht Mr Soulis; 'poor Janet's dead.'

He cam' a step nearer to the corp; an' then his heart fair whammled in his inside. For by what cantrip it wad ill-beseem a man to judge, she was hingin' frae a single nail an' by a single wursted thread for darnin' hose.

It's an awfu' thing to be your lane at nicht wi' siccan prodigies o' darkness; but Mr Soulis was strong in the Lord. He turned an' gaed his ways oot o' that room, and lockit the door ahint him; and step by step, down the stairs, as heavy as leed; and set doon the can'le on the table at the stairfoot. He couldnae pray, he couldnae think, he was dreepin' wi' caul' swat, an' naething could he hear but the dunt-dunt-duntin' o' his ain heart. He micht maybe have stood there an hour, or maybe twa, he minded sae little; when a' o' a sudden, he heard a laigh, uncanny steer upstairs; a foot gaed to an' fro in the cha'mer whaur the corp was hingin'; syne the door was opened, though he minded weel that he had lockit it; an' syne there was a step upon the landin', an' it seemed to him as if the corp was lookin' ower the rail and doun upon him whaur he stood.

He took up the can'le again (for he couldnae want the licht), and as saftly as ever he could, gaed straucht out o' the manse an' to the far end o' the causeway. It was aye pit-mirk; the flame o' the can'le, when he set it on the grund, brunt steedy and clear as in a room; naething moved, but the Dule water seepin' and sabbin' doon the glen, an' yon unhaly footstep that cam' ploddin' doun the stairs inside the manse. He kenned the foot over weel, for it was Janet's; and at ilka step that cam' a wee thing nearer, the cauld got deeper in his vitals. He commended his soul to Him that made an' keepit him; 'and O Lord,' said he, 'give me strength this night to war against the powers of evil.'

By this time the foot was comin' through the passage for the door; he could hear a hand skirt alang the wa', as if the fearsome thing was feelin' for its way. The saughs tossed an' maned thegether, a lang sigh cam' ower the hills, the flame o' the can'le was blawn aboot; an' there stood the corp of Thrawn Janet, wi' her grogram goun an' her black mutch, wi' the heid aye upon the shouther, an' the girn still upon the face o't – leevin', ye wad hae said – deid, as Mr Soulis weel kenned – upon the threshold o' the manse.

It's a strange thing that the saul of man should be that thirled into his perishable body; but the minister saw that, an' his heart didnae break.

She didnae stand there lang; she began to move again an' cam' slowly towards Mr Soulis whaur he stood under the saughs. A' the life o' his body, a' the strength o' his speerit, were glowerin' frae his een. It seemed she was gaun to speak, but wanted words, an' made a sign wi' the left hand. There cam' a clap o' wund, like a cat's fuff; oot gaed the can'le, the saughs skreighed like folk; an' Mr Soulis kenned that, live or die, this was the end o't.

'Witch, beldame, devil!' he cried, 'I charge you, by the power of God, begone – if you be dead, to the grave – if you be damned, to hell.'

An' at that moment the Lord's ain hand out o' the heevens struck the Horror whaur it stood; the auld, deid, desecrated corp o' the witch-wife, sae lang keepit frae the grave and hirsled round by deils, lowed up like a brunstane spunk and fell in ashes to the grund; the thunder followed, peal on dirling peal, the rairing rain upon the back o' that; and Mr Soulis lowped through the garden hedge, and ran, wi' skelloch upon skelloch, for the clachan.

That same mornin', John Christie saw the black man pass the Muckle Cairn as it was chappin' six; before eicht, he gaed by the change-house at Knockdow; an' no lang after, Sandy M'Lellan saw him gaun linkin' doun the braes frae Kilmackerlie. There's little doubt but it was him that dwalled sae lang in Janet's body; but he was awa' at last; and sinsyne the deil has never fashed us in Ba'weary.

But it was a sair dispensation for the minister; lang, lang he lay ravin' in his bed; and frae that hour to this, he was the man ye ken the day.

The Brazilian Cat

SIR ARTHUR CONAN DOYLE

IT IS HARD LUCK on a young fellow to have expensive tastes, great expectations, aristocratic connections, but no actual money in his pocket, and no profession by which he may earn any. The fact was that my father, a good, sanguine, easy-going man, had such confidence in the wealth and benevolence of his bachelor elder brother, Lord Southerton, that he took it for granted that I, his only son, would never be called upon to earn a living for myself. He imagined that if there were not a vacancy for me on the great Southerton Estates, at least there would be found some post in that diplomatic service which still remains the special preserve of our privileged classes. He died too early to realise how false his calculations had been. Neither my uncle nor the state took the slightest notice of me, or showed any interest in my career. An occasional brace of pheasants, or basket of hares, was all that ever reached me to remind me that I was heir to Otwell House and one of the richest estates in the country. In the meantime, I found myself a bachelor and man about town, living in a suite of apartments in Grosvenor Mansions, with no occupation save that of pigeon-shooting and polo-playing at Hurlingham. Month by month I realised that it was more and more difficult to get the brokers to renew my bills, or to cash any further post-obits upon an unentailed property. Ruin lay right across my path, and every day I saw it clearer, nearer and more absolutely unavoidable.

What made me feel my own poverty the more was that, apart from the great wealth of Lord Southerton, all my other relations were fairly well-to-do. The nearest of these was Everard King, my father's nephew and my own first cousin, who had spent an adventurous life in Brazil, and had now returned to this country to settle down on his fortune. We never knew how he made his money, but he appeared to have plenty of it, for he bought the estate of Greylands, near Clipton-on-the-Marsh, in Suffolk. For the first year of his residence in England he took no more notice of me than my miserly uncle; but at last, one summer morning, to my very great relief and joy, I received a letter asking me to come down that very day and spend a short visit at Greylands Court. I was expecting a rather long visit to the bankruptcy court at the time, and this interruption seemed almost providential. If I could only get on terms with this unknown relative of mine, I might pull through yet. For the family credit he could not let me go entirely to the wall. I ordered my valet to pack my valise, and I set off the same evening for Clipton-on-the-Marsh.

After changing at Ipswich, a little local train deposited me at a small, deserted station lying amidst a rolling grassy country, with a sluggish and winding river curving in and out amidst the valleys, between high, silted banks, which showed that we were within reach of the tide. No carriage was awaiting me (I found afterwards that my telegram had been delayed), so I hired a dogcart at the local inn. The driver, an excellent fellow, was full of my relative's praises, and I learned from him that Mr Everard King was already a name to conjure with in that part of the country. He had entertained the schoolchildren, he had thrown his grounds open to visitors, he had subscribed to charities – in short, his benevolence had been so universal that my driver could only account for it on the supposition that he had parliamentary ambitions.

My attention was drawn away from my driver's panegyric by the appearance of a very beautiful bird which settled on a telegraph-post beside the road. At first I thought that it was a jay, but it was larger with a brighter plumage. The driver accounted for its presence at once by saying that it belonged to the very man whom we were about to visit. It seems that the acclimatisation of foreign creatures was one of his hobbies, and that he had brought with him from Brazil a number of birds and beasts which he was endeavouring to rear in England. When once we had passed the gates of Greylands Park we had ample evidence of this taste of his. Some small spotted deer, a curious wild pig known, I believe, as a peccary, a gorgeously feathered oriole, some sort of armadillo and a singular lumbering intoed beast, like a very fat badger, were among the creatures which I observed as we drove along the winding avenue.

Mr Everard King, my unknown cousin, was standing in person upon the steps of his house, for he had seen us in the distance, and guessed that it was I. His appearance was very homely and benevolent, short and stout, forty-five years old perhaps, with a round, good-humoured face, burned brown with the tropical sun and shot with a thousand wrinkles. He wore white linen clothes, in true planter style, with a cigar between his lips and a large panama hat upon the back of his head. It was such a figure as one associates with a veranda-ed bungalow, and it looked curiously out of place in front of this broad, stone English mansion, with its solid wings and its Palladio pillars before the doorway.

'My dear!' he cried, glancing over his shoulder; 'my dear, here is our guest! Welcome, welcome to Greylands! I am delighted to make your acquaintance, Cousin Marshall, and I take it as a great compliment that you should honour this sleepy little country place with your presence.'

Nothing could be more hearty than his manner, and he set me at my ease in an instant. But it needed all his cordiality to atone for the frigidity and even rudeness of his wife, a tall, haggard woman, who came forward at his summons. She was, I believe, of Brazilian extraction, though she spoke excellent English, and I excused her manners on the score of her ignorance of our customs. She did not attempt to conceal, however, either then or afterwards, that I was no very welcome visitor at Greylands Court. Her actual words were, as a rule, courteous, but she was the possessor of a pair of particularly expressive dark eyes, and I read in them very clearly from the first that she heartily wished me back in London once more.

However, my debts were too pressing and my designs upon my wealthy relative were too vital for me to allow them to be upset by the ill-temper of his wife, so I disregarded her coldness and reciprocated the extreme cordiality of his welcome. No pains had been spared by him to make me comfortable. My room was a charming one. He implored me to tell him anything which could add to my happiness. It was on the tip of my tongue to inform him that a blank cheque would materially help towards that end, but I felt that it might be premature in the present state of our acquaintance. The dinner was excellent, and as we sat together afterwards over his Havanas and coffee, which latter he told me was specially prepared upon his own plantation, it seemed to me that all my driver's eulogies were justified, and that I had never met a more large-hearted and hospitable man.

But, in spite of his cheery good nature, he was a man with a strong will and a fiery temper of his own. Of this I had an example upon the following morning. The curious aversion which Mrs Everard King had conceived towards me was so strong that her manner at breakfast was almost offensive. But her meaning became unmistakable when her husband had quitted the room.

'The best train in the day is at twelve fifteen,' said she.

'But I was not thinking of going, today,' I answered, frankly – perhaps even defiantly, for I was determined not to be driven out by this woman.

'Oh, if it rests with you – ' said she, and stopped, with a most insolent expression in her eyes.

'I am sure,' I answered, 'that Mr Everard King would tell me if I were outstaying my welcome.'

'What's this? What's this?' said a voice, and there he was in the room. He had overheard my last words, and a glance at our faces had told him the rest. In an instant his chubby, cheery face set into an expression of absolute ferocity.

'Might I trouble you to walk outside, Marshall,' said he. (I may mention that my own name is Marshall King.)

He closed the door behind me, and then, for an instant, I heard him talking in a low voice of concentrated passion to his wife. This gross breach of hospitality had evidently hit upon his tenderest point. I am no eaves-dropper, so I walked out on to the lawn. Presently I heard a hurried step behind me, and there was the lady, her face pale with excitement, and her eyes red with tears.

'My husband has asked me to apologise to you, Mr Marshall King,' said she, standing with downcast eyes before me.

'Please do not say another word, Mrs King.'

Her dark eyes suddenly blazed out at me.

'You fool!' she hissed, with frantic vehemence, and turning on her heel, swept back to the house.

The insult was so outrageous, so insufferable, that I could only stand staring after her in bewilderment. I was still there when my host joined me. He was his cheery, chubby self once more.

'I hope that my wife has apologised for her foolish remarks,' said he.

'Oh, yes – yes, certainly!'

He put his hand through my arm and walked with me up and down the lawn.

'You must not take it seriously,' said he. 'It would grieve me inexpressibly if you curtailed your visit by one hour. The fact is – there is no reason why there should be any concealment between relatives – that my poor dear wife is incredibly jealous. She hates that anyone – male or female – should for an instant come between us. Her ideal is a desert island and an eternal *tête-à-tête*. That gives you the clue to her actions, which are, I confess, upon this particular point, not very far removed from mania. Tell me that you will think no more of it.'

'No, no; certainly not.'

'Then light this cigar and come round with me and see my little menagerie.'

The whole afternoon was occupied by this inspection, which included all the birds, beasts and even reptiles which he had imported. Some were free, some in cages, a few actually in the house. He spoke with enthusiasm of his successes and his failures, his births and his deaths, and he would cry out in his delight, like a schoolboy, when, as we walked, some gaudy bird would flutter up from the grass or some curious beast slink into the cover. Finally he led me down a corridor which extended from one wing of the house. At the end of this there was a heavy door with a sliding shutter in it, and beside it there projected from the wall an iron handle attached to a wheel and a drum. A line of stout bars extended across the passage.

'I am about to show you the jewel of my collection,' said he. 'There is only one other specimen in Europe, now that the Rotterdam cub is dead. It is a Brazilian cat.'

'But how does that differ from any other cat?'

'You will soon see that,' said he, laughing. 'Will you kindly draw that shutter and look through?'

I did so, and found that I was gazing into a large, empty room, with stone flags, and small, barred windows upon the farther wall.

In the centre of this room, lying in the middle of a golden patch of sunlight, there was stretched a huge creature, as large as a tiger, but as black and sleek as ebony. It was simply a very enormous and very well-kept black cat, and it cuddled up and basked in that yellow pool of light exactly as a cat would do. It was so graceful, so sinewy, and so gently and smoothly diabolical, that I could not take my eyes from the opening.

'Isn't he splendid?' said my host, enthusiastically.

'Glorious! I never saw such a noble creature.'

'Some people call it a black puma, but really it is not a puma at all. That fellow is nearly eleven feet from tail to tip. Four years ago he was a little ball of black fluff, with two yellow eyes staring out of it. He was sold me as a new-born cub up in the wild country at the headwaters of the Rio Negro. They speared his mother to death after she had killed a dozen of them.'

'They are ferocious, then?'

'The most absolutely treacherous and bloodthirsty creatures upon earth. You talk about a Brazilian cat to an upcountry Indian, and see him get the jumps. They prefer humans to game. This fellow has never tasted living blood yet, but when he does he will be a terror. At present he won't stand anyone but me in his den. Even Baldwin, the groom, dare not go near him. As to me, I am his mother and father in one.'

As he spoke he suddenly, to my astonishment, opened the door and slipped in, closing it instantly behind him. At the sound of his voice the huge, lithe creature rose, yawned, and rubbed its round, black head affectionately against his side, while he patted and fondled it.

'Now, Tommy, into your cage!' said he.

The monstrous cat walked over to one side of the room and coiled itself up under a grating. Everard Ring came out, and taking the iron handle which I have mentioned, he began to turn it. As he did so the line of bars in the corridor began to pass through a slot in the wall and closed up the front of this grating, so as to make an effective cage. When it was in position he opened the door once more and invited me into the room, which was heavy with the pungent, musty smell peculiar to the great carnivora.

'That's how we work it,' said he. 'We give him the run of the room for exercise, and then at night we put him in his cage. You can let him out by turning the handle from the passage, or you can, as you have seen, coop him up in the same way. No, no, you should not do that!'

I had put my hand between the bars to pat the glossy, heaving flank. He pulled it back, with a serious face.

'I assure you that he is not safe. Don't imagine that because I can take liberties with him anyone else can. He is very exclusive in his friends – aren't you, Tommy? Ah, he hears his lunch coming to him! Don't you, boy?'

A step sounded in the stone-flagged passage, and the creature had sprung to his feet, and was pacing up and down the narrow cage, his yellow eyes gleaming and his scarlet tongue rippling and quivering over the white line of his jagged teeth. A groom entered with a coarse joint upon a tray, and thrust it through the bars to him. He pounced lightly upon it, carried it off to the corner, and there, holding it between his paws, tore and wrenched at it, raising his bloody muzzle every now and then to look at us. It was a malignant and yet fascinating sight.

'You can't wonder that I am fond of him, can you?' said my host, as we left the room, 'especially when you consider that I have had the rearing of him. It was no joke bringing him over from the centre of South America; but here he is safe and sound – and, as I have said, far the most perfect specimen in Europe. The people at the zoo are dying to have him, but I really can't part with him. Now, I think that I have inflicted my hobby upon you long enough, so we cannot do better than follow Tommy's example, and go to our lunch.'

My South American relative was so engrossed by his grounds and their curious occupants, that I hardly gave him credit at first for having any interests outside them. That he had some, and pressing ones, was soon borne in upon me by the number of telegrams which he received. They arrived at all hours, and were always opened by him with the utmost eagerness and anxiety upon his face. Sometimes I imagined that it must be the turf, and sometimes the Stock Exchange, but certainly he had some very urgent business going forward which was not transacted upon the downs of Suffolk. During the six days of my visit he had never fewer than three or four telegrams a day, and sometimes as many as seven or eight.

I had occupied these six days so well that by the end of them I had succeeded in getting upon the most cordial terms with my cousin. Every night we had sat up late in the billiard-room, he telling me the most extraordinary stories of his adventures in America – stories so desperate and reckless, that I could hardly associate them with the brown little chubby man before me. In return, I ventured upon some of my own reminiscences of London life, which interested him so much that he vowed he would come up to Grosvenor Mansions and stay with me. He was anxious to see the faster side of city life, and certainly, though I say it, he could not have chosen a more competent guide. It was not until the last day of my visit that I ventured to approach that which was on my mind. I told him frankly about my pecuniary difficulties and my impending ruin, and I asked his advice – though I hoped for something more solid. He listened attentively, puffing hard at his cigar.

'But surely,' said he, 'you are the heir of our relative, Lord Southerton?'

'I have every reason to believe so, but he would never make me any allowance.'

'No, no, I have heard of his miserly ways. My poor Marshall, your position has been a very hard one. By the way, have you heard any news of Lord Southerton's health lately?'

'He has always been in a critical condition ever since my childhood.'

'Exactly – a creaking hinge, if ever there was one. Your inheritance may be a long way off. Dear me, how awkwardly situated you are!'

'I had some hopes, sir, that you, knowing all the facts, might be inclined to advance – '

'Don't say another word, my dear boy,' he cried, with the utmost cordiality; 'we shall talk it over tonight, and I give you my word that whatever is in my power shall be done.'

I was not sorry that my visit was drawing to a close, for it is unpleasant to feel that there is one person in the house who eagerly desires your departure. Mrs King's sallow face and forbidding eyes had become more and more hateful to me. She was no longer actively rude – her fear of her husband prevented her – but she pushed her insane jealousy to the extent of ignoring me, never addressing me, and in every way making my stay at Greylands as uncomfortable as she could. So offensive was her manner during that last day that I should certainly have left had it not been for that interview with my host in the evening which would, I hoped, retrieve my broken fortunes.

It was very late when it occurred, for my relative, who had been receiving even more telegrams than usual during the day, went off to his study after dinner, and only emerged when the household had retired to bed. I heard him go round locking the doors, as his custom was of a night, and finally he joined me in the billiard-room. His stout figure was wrapped in a dressing-gown, and he wore a pair of red Turkish slippers without any heels. Settling down into an armchair, he brewed himself a glass of grog, in which I could not help noticing that the whisky considerably predominated over the water.

'My word!' said he, 'what a night!'

It was, indeed. The wind was howling and screaming round the house, and the latticed windows rattled and shook as if they were coming in. The glow of the yellow lamps and the flavour of our cigars seemed the brighter and more fragrant for the contrast.

'Now, my boy,' said my host, 'we have the house and the night to ourselves. Let me have an idea of how your affairs stand, and I will see what can be done to set them in order. I wish to hear every detail.'

Thus encouraged, I entered into a long exposition, in which all my tradesmen and creditors, from my landlord to my valet, figured in turn. I had notes in my pocket-book, and I marshalled my facts, and gave, I flatter myself, a very businesslike statement of my own unbusinesslike ways and lamentable position. I was depressed, however, to notice that my companion's eyes were vacant and his attention elsewhere. When he did occasionally throw out a remark, it was so entirely perfunctory and pointless, that I was sure he had not in the least followed my remarks. Every now and then he roused himself and put on some show of interest, asking me to repeat or to explain more fully, but it was always to sink once more into the same brown study. At last he rose and threw the end of his cigar into the grate.

'I'll tell you what, my boy,' said he. 'I never had a head for figures, so you will excuse me. You must jot it all down upon paper, and let me have a note of the amount. I'll understand it when I see it in black and white.'

The proposal was encouraging. I promised to do so.

'And now it's time we were in bed. By Jove, there's one o'clock striking in the hall.'

The tinging of the chiming clock broke through the deep roar of the gale. The wind was sweeping past with the rush of a great river.

'I must see my cat before I go to bed,' said my host. 'A high wind excites him. Will you come?'

'Certainly,' said I.

'Then tread softly and don't speak, for everyone is asleep.'

We passed quietly down the lamplit Persian-rugged hall, and through the door at the farther end. All was dark in the stone corridor, but a stable lantern hung on a hook, and my host took it down and lit it. There was no grating visible in the passage, so I knew that the beast was in its cage.

'Come in!' said my relative, and opened the door.

A deep growling as we entered showed that the storm had really excited the creature. In the flickering light of the lantern, we saw it, a huge black mass, coiled in the corner of its den and throwing a squat, uncouth shadow upon the whitewashed wall. Its tail switched angrily among the straw.

'Poor Tommy is not in the best of tempers,' said Everard King, holding up the lantern and looking in at him. 'What a black devil he looks, doesn't he? I must give him a little supper to put him in a better humour. Would you mind holding the lantern for a moment?'

I took it from his hand and he stepped to the door.

'His larder is just outside here,' said he. 'You will excuse me for an instant, won't you?' He passed out, and the door shut with a sharp metallic click behind him.

That hard crisp sound made my heart stand still. A sudden wave of terror passed over me. A vague perception of some monstrous treachery turned me cold. I sprang to the door, but there was no handle upon the inner side.

'Here!' I cried. 'Let me out!'

'All right! Don't make a row!' said my host from the passage. 'You've got the light all right.'

'Yes, but I don't care about being locked in alone like this.'

'Don't you?' I heard his hearty, chuckling laugh. 'You won't be alone long.'

'Let me out, sir!' I repeated angrily. 'I tell you I don't allow practical jokes of this sort.'

'Practical is the word,' said he, with another hateful chuckle. And then suddenly I heard, amidst the roar of the storm, the creak and whine of the winch-handle turning, and the rattle of the grating as it passed through the slot. Great God, he was letting loose the Brazilian cat!

In the light of the lantern I saw the bars sliding slowly before me. Already there was an opening a foot wide at the farther end. With a scream I seized the last bar with my hands and pulled with the strength of a madman. I *was* a madman with rage and horror. For a minute or more I held the thing motionless. I knew that he was straining with all his force upon the handle, and that the leverage was sure to overcome me. I gave inch by inch, my feet sliding along the stones, and all the time I begged and prayed this inhuman monster to save me from this horrible death. I conjured him by his kinship. I reminded him that I was his guest; I begged to know what harm I had ever done him. His only answers were the tugs and jerks upon the handle, each of which, in spite of all my struggles, pulled another bar through the opening. Clinging and clutching, I was dragged across the whole front of the cage, until at last, with aching wrists and lacerated fingers, I gave up the hopeless struggle. The grating clanged back as I released it, and an instant later I heard the shuffle of the Turkish slippers in the passage, and the slam of the distant door. Then everything was silent.

The creature had never moved during this time. He lay still in the corner, and his tail had ceased switching. This apparition of a man adhering to his bars and dragged screaming across him had apparently filled him with amazement. I saw his great eyes staring steadily at me. I had dropped the lantern when I seized the bars, but it still burned upon the floor, and I made a movement to grasp it, with some idea that its light might protect me. But the instant I moved, the beast gave a deep and menacing growl. I stopped and stood still, quivering with fear in every limb. The cat (if one may call so fearful a creature by so homely a name) was not more than ten feet from me. The eyes glimmered like two discs of phosphorus in the darkness. They appalled and yet fascinated me. I could not take my own eyes from them. Nature plays strange tricks with us at such moments of intensity, and those glimmering lights waxed and waned with a steady rise and fall. Sometimes they seemed to be tiny points of extreme brilliancy – little electric sparks in the black obscurity – then they would widen and widen until all that corner of the room was filled with their shifting and sinister light. And then suddenly they went out altogether.

The beast had closed its eyes. I do not know whether there may be any truth in the old idea of the dominance of the human gaze, or whether the huge cat was simply drowsy, but the fact remains that, far from showing any symptom of attacking me, it simply rested its sleek, black head upon its huge forepaws and seemed to sleep. I stood, fearing to move lest I should rouse it into malignant life once more. But at least I was able to think clearly now that the baleful eyes were off me. Here I was shut up for the night with the ferocious beast. My own instincts, to say nothing of the words of the plausible villain who laid this trap for me, warned me that the animal was as savage as its master. How could I stave it off until morning? The door was hopeless, and so were the narrow, barred windows. There was no shelter anywhere in the bare, stone-flagged room. To cry for assistance was absurd. I knew that this den was an outhouse, and that the corridor which connected it with the house was at least a hundred feet long. Besides, with that gale thundering outside, my cries were not likely to be heard. I had only my own courage and my own wits to trust to.

And then, with a fresh wave of horror, my eyes fell upon the lantern. The candle had burned low and was already beginning to gutter. In ten minutes it would be out. I had only ten minutes then in which to do something, for I felt that if I were once left in the dark with that fearful beast I should be incapable of action. The very thought of it paralysed me. I cast my despairing eyes round this chamber of death, and they rested upon one spot which seemed to promise I will not say safety, but less immediate and imminent danger than the open floor.

I have said that the cage had a top as well as a front, and this top was left standing when the front was wound through the slot in the wall. It consisted of bars at a few inches' interval, with stout wire netting between, and it rested upon a strong stanchion at each end. It stood now as a great barred canopy over the crouching figure in the corner. The space between this iron shelf and the roof may have been from two to three feet. If I could only get up there, squeezed in between bars and ceiling I should have only one vulnerable side. I should be safe from below, from behind, and from each side. Only on the open face of it could I be attacked. There, it is true, I had no protection whatever; but, at least, I should be out of the brute's path when he began to pace about his den. He would have to come out of his way to reach me. It was now or never, for if once the light were out it would be impossible. With a gulp in my throat I sprang up, seized the iron edge of the top, and swung myself panting on to it. I writhed in face downwards, and found myself looking straight into the terrible eyes and yawning jaws of the cat. Its fetid breath came up into my face like the steam from some foul pot.

It appeared, however, to be rather curious than angry. With a sleek ripple of its long, black back it rose, stretched itself, and then rearing itself on its hind legs, with one forepaw against the wall, it raised the other and drew its claws across the wire meshes beneath me. One sharp, white hook tore through my trousers – for I may mention that I was still in evening dress – and dug a furrow in my knee. It was not meant as an attack, but rather as an experiment, for upon my giving a sharp cry of pain, he dropped down again, and springing lightly into the room, he began walking swiftly round it, looking up every now and again in my direction. For my part I shuffled backwards until I lay with my back against the wall, screwing myself into the smallest space possible. The farther I got the more difficult it was for him to attack me.

He seemed more excited now that he had begun to move about, and he ran swiftly and noiselessly round and round the den, passing continually underneath the iron couch upon which I lay. It was wonderful to see so great a bulk passing like a shadow, with hardly the softest thudding of velvety pads. The candle was burning low – so low that I could hardly see the creature. And then, with a last flare and splutter it went out altogether. I was alone with the cat in the dark!'

It helps one to face a danger when one knows that one has done all that possibly can be done. There is nothing for it then but quietly to await the result. In this case, there was no chance of safety anywhere except the precise spot where I was. I stretched myself out, therefore, and lay silently, almost breathlessly, hoping that the beast might forget my presence if I did nothing to remind him. I reckoned that it must already be two o'clock. At four it would be full dawn. I had not more than two hours to wait for daylight.

Outside, the storm was still raging, and the rain lashed continually against the little windows. Inside the poisonous and fetid air was overpowering. I could neither hear nor see the cat. I tried to think about other things – but only one had power enough to draw my mind from my terrible position. That was the contemplation of my cousin's villainy, his unparalleled hypocrisy, his malignant hatred of me. Beneath that cheerful face there lurked the spirit of a medieval assassin. And as I thought of it I saw more clearly how cunningly the thing had been arranged. He had apparently gone to bed with the others. No doubt he had his witnesses to prove it. Then, unknown to them he had slipped down, had lured me into this den and abandoned me. His story would be so simple. He had left me to finish my cigar in the billiard-room. I had gone down on my own account to have a last look at the cat. I had entered the room without observing that the cage was opened, and I had been caught. How could such a crime be brought home to him? Suspicion, perhaps – but proof, never!

How slowly those dreadful two hours went by! Once I heard a low, rasping sound, which I took to be the creature licking its own fur. Several times those greenish eyes gleamed at me through the darkness, but never in a fixed stare, and my hopes grew stronger that my presence had been forgotten or ignored. At last the least faint glimmer of light came through the windows – I first dimly saw them as two grey squares upon the black wall, then grey turned to white, and I could see my terrible companion once more. And he, alas, could see me!

It was evident to me at once that he was in a much more dangerous and aggressive mood than when I had seen him last. The cold of the morning had irritated him, and he was hungry as well. With a continual growl he paced swiftly up and down the side of the room which was farthest from my refuge, his whiskers bristling angrily, and his tail switching and lashing. As he turned at the corners his savage eyes always looked upwards at me with a dreadful menace. I knew then that he meant to kill me. Yet I found myself even at that moment admiring the sinuous grace of the devilish thing, its long, undulating, rippling movements, the gloss of its beautiful flanks, the vivid, palpitating scarlet of the glistening tongue which hung from the jet-black muzzle. And all the time that deep, threatening growl was rising and rising in an unbroken crescendo. I knew that the crisis was at hand.

It was a miserable hour to meet such a death – so cold, so comfortless, shivering in my light dress-clothes upon this gridiron of torment upon which I was stretched. I tried to brace myself to it, to raise my soul above it, and at the same time, with the lucidity which comes to a perfectly desperate man, I cast round for some possible means of escape. One thing was clear to me. If that front of the cage was only back in its position once more, I could find a sure refuge behind it. Could I possibly pull it back? I hardly dared to move for fear of bringing the creature upon me. Slowly, very slowly, I put my hand forward until it grasped the edge of the front, the final bar which protruded through the wall. To my surprise it came quite easily to my jerk. Of course the difficulty of drawing it out arose from the fact that I was clinging to it. I pulled again, and three inches of it came through. It ran apparently on wheels. I pulled again . . . and then the cat sprang!

It was so quick, so sudden, that I never saw it happen. I simply heard the savage snarl, and in an instant afterwards the blazing yellow eyes, the flattened black head with its red tongue and flashing teeth, were within reach of me. The impact of the creature shook the bars upon which I lay, until I thought (as far as I could think of anything at such a moment) that they were coming down. The cat swayed there for an instant, the head and front paws quite close to me, the hind paws clawing to find a grip upon the edge of the grating. I heard the claws rasping as they clung to the wire netting, and the breath of the beast made me sick. But its bound had been miscalculated. It could not retain its position. Slowly, grinning with rage and scratching madly at the bars, it swung backwards and dropped heavily upon the floor. With a growl it instantly faced round to me and crouched for another spring.

I knew that the next few moments would decide my fate. The creature had learned by experience. It would not miscalculate again. I must act promptly, fearlessly, if I were to have a chance of life. In an instant I had formed my plan. Pulling off my dress-coat, I threw it down over the head of the beast. At the same moment I dropped over the edge, seized the end of the front grating, and pulled it frantically out of the wall.

It came more easily than I could have expected. I rushed across the room, bearing it with me; but, as I rushed, the accident of my position put me upon the outer side. Had it been the other way, I might have come off scathless. As it was, there was a moment's pause as I stopped it and tried to pass in through the opening which I had left. That moment was enough to give time to the creature to toss off the coat with which I had blinded him and to spring upon me. I hurled myself through the gap and pulled the rails to behind me, but he seized my leg before I could entirely withdraw it. One stroke of that huge paw tore off my calf as a shaving of wood curls off before a plane. The next moment, bleeding and fainting, I was lying among the foul straw with a line of friendly bars between me and the creature which ramped so frantically against them.

Too wounded to move, and too faint to be conscious of fear, I could only lie, more dead than alive, and watch it. It pressed its broad, black chest against the bars and angled for me with its crooked paws as I have seen a kitten do before a mousetrap. It ripped my clothes, but, stretch as it would, it could not quite reach me. I have heard of the curious numbing effect produced by wounds from the great carnivora, and now I was destined to experience it, for I had lost all sense of personality, and was as interested in the cat's failure or success as if it were some game which I was watching. And then gradually my mind drifted away into strange, vague dreams, always with that black face and red tongue coming back into them, and so I lost myself in the nirvana of delirium, the blessed relief of those who are too sorely tried.

Tracing the course of events afterwards, I conclude that I must have been insensible for about two hours. What roused me to consciousness once more was that sharp metallic click which had been the precursor of my terrible experience. It was the shooting back of the spring lock. Then, before my senses were clear enough entirely to apprehend what they saw, I was aware of the round, benevolent face of my cousin peering in through the opened door. What he saw evidently amazed him. There was the cat crouching on the floor. I was stretched upon my back in my shirt sleeves within the cage, my trousers torn to ribbons and a great pool of blood all round me. I can see his amazed face now, with the morning sunlight upon it. He peered at me, and peered again. Then he closed the door behind him, and advanced to the cage to see if I were really dead.

I cannot undertake to say what happened. I was not in a fit state to witness or to chronicle such events. I can only say that I was suddenly conscious that his face was away from me – that he was looking towards the animal.

'Good old Tommy!' he cried. 'Good old Tommy!'

Then he came near the bars, with his back still towards me.

'Down, you stupid beast!' he roared. 'Down sir! Don't you know your master?'

Suddenly even in my bemuddled brain a remembrance came of those words of his when he had said that the taste of blood would turn the cat into a fiend. My blood had done it, but he was to pay the price.

'Get away!' he screamed. 'Get away, you devil! Baldwin! Baldwin! Oh, my God!'

And then I heard him fall, and rise, and fall again, with a sound like the ripping of sacking. His screams grew fainter until they were lost in the worrying snarl. And then, after I thought that he was dead, I saw, as in a nightmare, a blinded, tattered, blood-soaked figure running wildly round the room – and that was the last glimpse I had of him before I fainted once again.

I was many months in my recovery – in fact, I cannot say that I have ever recovered, for to the end of my days I shall carry a stick as a sign of my night with the Brazilian cat. Baldwin, the groom, and the other servants could not tell what had occurred when, drawn by the death cries of their master, they found me behind the bars, and his remains – or what they afterwards discovered to be his remains – in the clutch of the creature which he had reared. They stalled him off with hot irons, and afterwards shot him through the loophole of the door before they could finally extricate me. I was carried to my bedroom, and there, under the roof of my would-be murderer, I remained between life and death for several weeks. They had sent for a surgeon from Clipton and a nurse from London, and in a month I was able to be carried to the station, and so conveyed back once more to Grosvenor Mansions.

I have one remembrance of that illness, which might have been part of the ever-changing panorama conjured up by a delirious brain were it not so definitely fixed in my memory. One night, when the nurse was absent, the door of my chamber opened, and a tall woman in blackest mourning slipped into the room. She came across to me, and as she bent her sallow face I saw by the faint gleam of the night-light that it was the Brazilian woman whom my cousin had married. She stared intently into my face, and her expression was more kindly than I had ever seen it.

'Are you conscious?' she asked.

I feebly nodded – for I was still very weak.

'Well, then, I only wished to say to you that you have yourself to blame. Did I not do all I could for you? From the beginning I tried to drive you from the house. By every means, short of betraying my husband, I tried to save you from him. I knew that he had a reason for bringing you here. I knew that he would never let you get away again. No one knew him as I knew him, who had suffered from him so often. I did not dare to tell you all this. He would have killed me. But I did my best for you. As things have turned out, you have been the best friend that I have ever had. You have set me free, and I fancied that nothing but death would do that. I am sorry if you are hurt, but I cannot reproach myself. I told you that you were a fool – and a fool you have been.' She crept out of the room, the bitter, singular woman, and I was never destined to see her again. With what remained from her husband's property she went back to her native land, and I have heard that she afterwards took the veil at Pernambuco.

It was not until I had been back in London for some time that the doctors pronounced me to be well enough to do business. It was not a very welcome permission to me, for I feared that it would be the signal for an inrush of creditors; but it was Summers, my lawyer, who first took advantage of it.

'I am very glad to see that your lordship is so much better,' said he. 'I have been waiting a long time to offer my congratulations.'

'What do you mean, Summers? This is no time for joking.'

'I mean what I say,' he answered. 'You have been Lord Southerton for the last six weeks, but we feared that it would retard your recovery if you were to learn it.'

Lord Southerton! One of the richest peers in England! I could not believe my ears. And then suddenly I thought of the time which had elapsed, and how it coincided with my injuries.

'Then Lord Southerton must have died about the same time that I was hurt?'

'His death occurred upon that very day.' Summers looked hard at me as I spoke, and I am convinced – for he was a very shrewd fellow – that he had guessed the true state of the case. He paused for a moment, as if awaiting a confidence from me, but I could not see what was to be gained by exposing such a family scandal. 'Yes, a very curious coincidence,' he continued, with the same knowing look. 'Of course, you are aware that your cousin Everard King was the next heir to the estates. Now, if it had been you instead of him who had been torn to pieces by this tiger, or whatever it was, then of course he would have been Lord Southerton at the present moment.'

'No doubt,' said I.

'And he took such an interest in it,' said Summers. 'I happen to know that the late Lord Southerton's valet was in his pay, and that he used to have telegrams from him every few hours to tell him how he was getting on. That would be about the time when you were down there. Was it not strange that he should wish to be so well informed, since he knew that he was not the direct heir?'

'Very strange,' said I. 'And now, Summers, if you will bring me my bills and a new chequebook, we will begin to get things into order.'

'Oh, Whistle, and I'll Come to You, My Lad'

M. R. JAMES

'I SUPPOSE you will be getting away pretty soon, now Full term is over, professor,' said a person not in the story to the professor of ontology, soon after they had sat down next to each other at a feast in the hospitable hall of St James's College.

The professor was young, neat, and precise in speech.

'Yes,' he said; 'my friends have been making me take up golf this term, and I mean to go to the East Coast – in point of fact, to Burnstow (I dare say you know it) – for a week or ten days, to improve my game. I hope to get off tomorrow.'

'Oh, Parkins,' said his neighbour on the other side, 'if you are going to Burnstow, I wish you would look at the site of the Templars' preceptory, and let me know if you think it would be any good to have a dig there in the summer.'

It was, as you might suppose, a person of antiquarian pursuits who said this, but, since he merely appears in this prologue, there is no need to give his entitlements.

'Certainly,' said Parkins, the professor: 'if you will describe to me whereabouts the site is, I will do my best to give you an idea of the lie of the land when I get back; or I could write to you about it, if you would tell me where you are likely to be.'

'Don't trouble to do that, thanks. It's only that I'm thinking of taking my family in that direction in the Long, and it occurred to me that, as very few of the English preceptories have ever been properly planned, I might have an opportunity of doing something useful on off-days.'

The professor rather sniffed at the idea that planning out a preceptory could be described as useful.

His neighbour continued: 'The site – I doubt if there is anything showing above ground – must be down quite close to the beach now. The sea has encroached tremendously, as you know, all along that bit of coast. I should think, from the map, that it must be about three-quarters of a mile from the Globe Inn, at the north end of the town. Where are you going to stay?'

'Well, *at* the Globe Inn, as a matter of fact,' said Parkins; 'I have engaged a room there. I couldn't get in anywhere else; most of the lodging-houses are shut up in winter, it seems; and, as it is, they tell me that the only room of any size I can have is really a double-bedded one, and that they haven't a corner in which to store the other bed, and so on. But I must have a fairly large room, for I am taking some books down, and mean to do a bit of work; and though I don't quite fancy having an empty bed – not to speak of two – in what I may call for the time being my study, I suppose I can manage to rough it for the short time I shall be there.'

'Do you call having an extra bed in your room roughing it, Parkins?' said a bluff person opposite. 'Look here, I shall come down and occupy it for a bit; it'll be company for you.'

The professor quivered, but managed to laugh in a courteous manner.

'By all means, Rogers; there's nothing I should like better. But I'm afraid you would find it rather dull; you don't play golf, do you?'

'No, thank heaven!' said rude Mr Rogers.

'Well, you see, when I'm not writing I shall most likely be out on the links, and that, as I say, would be rather dull for you, I'm afraid.'

'Oh, I don't know! There's certain to be somebody I know in the place; but, of course, if you don't want me, speak the word, Parkins; I shan't be offended. Truth, as you always tell us, is never offensive.'

Parkins was, indeed, scrupulously polite and strictly truthful. It is to be feared that Mr Rogers sometimes practised upon his knowledge of these characteristics. In Parkins's breast there was a conflict now raging, which for a moment or two did not allow him to answer. That interval being over, he said: 'Well, if you want the exact truth, Rogers, I was considering whether the room I speak of would really be large enough to accommodate us both comfortably; and also whether (mind, I shouldn't have said this if you hadn't pressed me) you would not constitute something in the nature of a hindrance to my work.'

Rogers laughed loudly.

'Well done, Parkins!' he said. 'It's all right. I promise not to interrupt your work; don't you disturb yourself about that. No, I won't come if you don't want me; but I thought I should do so nicely to keep the ghosts off.' Here he might have been seen to wink and to nudge his next neighbour. Parkins might also have been seen to become pink. 'I beg pardon, Parkins,' Rogers continued; 'I oughtn't to have said that. I forgot you didn't like levity on these topics.'

'Well,' Parkins said, 'as you have mentioned the matter, I freely own that I do *not* like careless talk about what you call ghosts. A man in my position,' he went on, raising his voice a little, 'cannot, I find, be too careful about appearing to sanction the current beliefs on such subjects. As you know, Rogers, or as you ought to know; for I think I have never concealed my views –'

'No, you certainly have not, old man,' put in Rogers *sotto voce*.

' – I hold that any semblance, any appearance of concession to the view that such things might exist is equivalent to a renunciation of all that I hold most sacred. But I'm afraid I have not succeeded in securing your attention.'

'Your *undivided* attention, was what Dr Blimber actually *said*,'* Rogers interrupted, with every appearance of an earnest desire for accuracy. 'But I beg your pardon, Parkins: I'm stopping you.'

'No, not at all,' said Parkins. 'I don't remember Blimber; perhaps he was before my time. But I needn't go on. I'm sure you know what I mean.'

'Yes, yes,' said Rogers, rather hastily – 'just so. We'll go into it fully at Burnstow, or somewhere.'

In repeating the above dialogue I have tried to give the impression which it made on me, that Parkins was something of an old woman – rather hen-like, perhaps, in his little ways; totally destitute, alas! of the sense of humour, but at the same time dauntless and sincere in his convictions, and a man deserving of the greatest respect. Whether or not the reader has gathered so much, that was the character which Parkins had.

On the following day Parkins did, as he had hoped, succeed in getting away from his college, and in arriving at Burnstow. He was made welcome at the Globe Inn, was safely installed in the large double-bedded room of which we have heard, and was able before retiring to rest to arrange his materials for work in apple-pie order upon a commodious table which occupied the outer end of the room, and was surrounded on three sides by windows looking out seaward; that is to say, the central window looked straight out to sea, and those on the left and right commanded prospects along the shore to the north and south respectively. On the south you saw the village of Burnstow. On the north no houses were to be seen, but only the beach and the low cliff backing it. Immediately in front was a strip – not considerable – of rough grass, dotted with old anchors, capstans, and so forth; then a broad path; then the beach. Whatever may have been the original distance between the Globe Inn and the sea, not more than sixty yards now separated them.

The rest of the population of the inn was, of course, a golfing one, and included few elements that call for a special description. The most conspicuous figure was, perhaps, that of an *ancien militaire*, secretary of a London club and possessed of a voice of incredible strength and of views of a pronouncedly Protestant type. These were apt to find utterance after his attendance upon the ministrations of the vicar, an estimable man with inclinations towards a picturesque ritual, which he gallantly kept down as far as he could out of deference to East Anglian tradition.

Professor Parkins, one of whose principal characteristics was pluck, spent the greater part of the day following his arrival at Burnstow in what he had called improving his game, in company with this Colonel Wilson; and during the afternoon – whether the process of improvement were to blame

---

* Mr Rogers was wrong, *vide* Charles Dickens, *Dombey and Son*, chapter xii.

or not, I am not sure – the colonel's demeanour assumed a colouring so lurid that even Parkins jibbed at the thought of walking home with him from the links. He determined, after a short and furtive look at that bristling moustache and those incarnadined features, that it would be wiser to allow the influences of tea and tobacco to do what they could with the colonel before the dinner-hour should render a meeting inevitable.

'I might walk home tonight along the beach,' he reflected – 'yes, and take a look – there will be light enough for that – at the ruins of which Disney was talking. I don't exactly know where they are, by the way; but I expect I can hardly help stumbling on them.'

This he accomplished, I may say, in the most literal sense, for in picking his way from the links to the shingle beach his foot caught, partly in a gorse-root and partly on a biggish stone, and over he went. When he got up and surveyed his surroundings, he found himself in a patch of somewhat broken ground covered with small depressions and mounds. These latter, when he came to examine them, proved to be simply masses of flints embedded in mortar and grown over with turf. He must, he quite rightly concluded, be on the site of the preceptory he had promised to look at. It seemed not unlikely to reward the spade of the explorer; enough of the foundations was probably left at no great depth to throw a good deal of light on the general plan. He remembered vaguely that the Templars, to whom this site had belonged, were in the habit of building round churches, and he thought a particular series of the humps or mounds near him did appear to be arranged in something of a circular form. Few people can resist the temptation to try a little amateur research in a department quite outside their own, if only for the satisfaction of showing how successful they would have been had they only taken it up seriously. Our professor, however, if he felt something of this mean desire, was also only anxious to oblige Mr Disney. So he paced with care the circular area he had noticed, and wrote down its rough dimensions in his pocket-book. Then he proceeded to examine an oblong eminence which lay east of the centre of the circle, and seemed to his thinking likely to be the base of a platform or altar. At one end of it, the northern, a patch of the turf was gone – removed by some boy or other creature *ferae naturae*. It might, he thought, be as well to probe the soil here for evidences of masonry, and he took out his knife and began scraping away the earth. And now followed another little discovery: a portion of soil fell inward as he scraped, and disclosed a small cavity. He lighted one match after another to help him to see of what nature the hole was, but the wind was too strong for them all. By tapping and scratching the sides with his knife, however, he was able to make out that it must be an artificial hole in masonry. It was rectangular, and the sides, top and bottom, if not actually plastered, were smooth and regular. Of course it was empty. No! As he withdrew the knife he heard a metallic clink, and when he introduced his hand it met with a cylindrical object lying on the floor of the hole. Naturally enough, he picked it up, and when he brought it into the light, now fast fading, he could see that it, too, was of man's making – a metal tube about four inches long, and evidently of some considerable age.

By the time Parkins had made sure that there was nothing else in this odd receptacle, it was too late and too dark for him to think of undertaking any further search. What he had done had proved so unexpectedly interesting that he determined to sacrifice a little more of the daylight on the morrow to archaeology. The object which he now had safe in his pocket was bound to be of some slight value at least, he felt sure.

Bleak and solemn was the view on which he took a last look before starting homeward. A faint yellow light in the west showed the links, on which a few figures moving towards the club-house were still visible, the squat martello tower, the lights of Aldsey village, the pale ribbon of sands intersected at intervals by black wooden groynes, the dim and murmuring sea. The wind was bitter from the north, but was at his back when he set out for the Globe. He quickly rattled and clashed through the shingle and gained the sand, upon which, but for the groynes which had to be got over every few yards, the going was both good and quiet. One last look behind, to measure the distance he had made since leaving the ruined Templars' church, showed him a prospect of company on his walk, in the shape of a rather indistinct personage, who seemed to be making great efforts to catch up with him, but made little, if any, progress. I mean that there was an appearance of running about his movements, but that the distance between him and Parkins did not seem materially to lessen. So, at least, Parkins thought, and decided that he almost certainly did not know him, and that it would be absurd to wait until he came up. For all that, company, he began to think, would really be very welcome on that lonely shore, if only you could choose your companion. In his unenlightened days he had read of meetings in such places which even now would hardly bear thinking of. He went on thinking of them, however, until he reached home, and particularly of one which catches most people's fancy at some time of their childhood. 'Now I saw in my dream that Christian had gone but a very little way when he saw a foul fiend coming over the field to meet him.' 'What should I do now,' he thought, 'if I looked back and caught sight of a black figure sharply defined against the yellow sky, and saw that it had horns and wings? I wonder whether I should stand or run for it. Luckily, the gentleman behind is not of that kind, and he seems to be about as far off now as when I saw him first. Well, at this rate he won't get his dinner as soon as I shall; and, dear me! it's within a quarter of an hour of the time now. I must run!'

Parkins had, in fact, very little time for dressing. When he met the colonel at dinner, Peace – or as much of her as that gentleman could manage – reigned once more in the military bosom; nor was she put to flight in the hours of bridge that followed dinner, for Parkins was a more than respectable player. When, therefore, he retired towards twelve o'clock, he felt that he had spent his evening in quite a satisfactory way, and that, even for so long as a fortnight or three weeks, life at the Globe would be supportable under similar conditions – 'especially,' thought he, 'if I go on improving my game.'

As he went along the passages he met the boots of the Globe, who stopped and said, 'Beg your pardon, sir, but as I was a-brushing your coat just now there was something fell out of the pocket. I put it on your chest of drawers, sir, in your room, sir – a piece of a pipe or somethink of that sort, sir. Thank you, sir. You'll find it on your chest of drawers, sir – yes, sir. Good-night, sir.'

The speech served to remind Parkins of his little discovery of that afternoon. It was with some considerable curiosity that he turned it over by the light of his candles. It was of bronze, he now saw, and was shaped very much after the manner of the modern dog-whistle; in fact, it was – yes, certainly it was – actually no more nor less than a whistle. He put it to his lips, but it was quite full of a fine, caked-up sand or earth, which would not yield to knocking but must be loosened with a knife. Tidy as ever in his habits, Parkins cleared out the earth on to a piece of paper and took the latter to the window to empty it out. The night was clear and bright, as he saw when he had opened the casement, and he stopped for an instant to look at the sea and note a belated wanderer stationed on the shore in front of the inn. Then he shut the window, a little surprised at the late hours people kept at Burnstow, and took his whistle to the light again. Why, surely there were marks on it, and not merely marks, but letters! A very little rubbing rendered the deeply-cut inscription quite legible, but the professor had to confess, after some earnest thought, that the meaning of it was as obscure to him as the writing on the wall to Belshazzar. There were legends both on the front and on the back of the whistle. The one read thus:

FLA.

FUR   BIS

FLE

The other:

🕈 QUIS EST ISTE QUI VENIT 🕈

'I ought to be able to make it out,' he thought; 'but I suppose I am a little rusty in my Latin. When I come to think of it, I don't believe I even know the word for a whistle. The long one does seem simple enough. It ought to mean, 'Who is this who is coming?' Well, the best way to find out is evidently to whistle for him.'

He blew tentatively and stopped suddenly, startled and yet pleased at the note he had elicited. It had a quality of infinite distance in it, and, soft as it was, he somehow felt it must be audible for miles round. It was a sound, too, that seemed to have the power (which many scents possess) of forming pictures in the brain. He saw quite clearly for a moment a vision of a wide, dark expanse at night, with a fresh wind blowing, and in the midst a lonely figure – how employed, he could not tell. Perhaps he would have seen more had not the picture been broken by the sudden surge of a gust of wind against his casement, so sudden that it made him look up, just in time to see the white glint of a sea-bird's wing somewhere outside the dark panes.

The sound of the whistle had so fascinated him that he could not help trying it once more, this time more boldly. The note was little, if at all, louder than before, and repetition broke the illusion – no picture followed, as he had half hoped it might. 'But what is this? Goodness! what force the wind can get up in a few minutes! What a tremendous gust! There! I knew that window-fastening was no use! Ah! I thought so – both candles out. It's enough to tear the room to pieces.'

The first thing was to get the window shut. While you might count twenty Parkins was struggling with the small casement, and felt almost as if he were pushing back a sturdy burglar, so strong was the pressure. It slackened all at once, and the window banged to and latched itself. Now to relight the candles and see what damage, if any, had been done. No, nothing seemed amiss; no glass even was broken in the casement. But the noise had evidently roused at least one member of the household: the colonel was to be heard stumping in his stockinged feet on the floor above, and growling.

Quickly as it had risen, the wind did not fall at once. On it went, moaning and rushing past the house, at times rising to a cry so desolate that, as Parkins disinterestedly said, it might have made fanciful people feel quite uncomfortable; even the unimaginative, he thought after a quarter of an hour, might be happier without it.

Whether it was the wind, or the excitement of golf or of the researches in the preceptory, that kept Parkins awake, he was not sure. Awake he remained, in any case, long enough to fancy (as I am afraid I often do myself under such conditions) that he was the victim of all manner of fatal disorders: he would lie counting the beats of his heart, convinced that it was going to stop work every moment, and would entertain grave suspicions of his lungs, brain, liver, etc. – suspicions which he was sure would be dispelled by the return of daylight, but which until then refused to be put aside. He found a little vicarious comfort in the idea that someone else was in the same boat. A near neighbour (in the darkness it was not easy to tell his direction) was tossing and rustling in his bed, too.

The next stage was that Parkins shut his eyes and determined to give sleep every chance. Here again over-excitement asserted itself in another form – that of making pictures. *Experto crede*, pictures do come to the closed eyes of one trying to sleep, and are often so little to his taste that he must open his eyes and disperse them.

Parkins's experience on this occasion was a very distressing one. He found that the picture which presented itself to him was continuous. When he opened his eyes, of course, it went; but when he shut them once more it framed itself afresh, and acted itself out again, neither quicker nor slower than before.

What he saw was this. A long stretch of shore – shingle edged by sand and intersected at short intervals with black groynes running down to the water – a scene, in fact, so like that of his afternoon's walk that, in the absence of any landmark, it could not be distinguished therefrom. The light was obscure, conveying an impression of gathering storm, late winter evening, and slight cold rain. On this bleak stage at first no actor was visible. Then, in the distance, a bobbing black object appeared; a moment more, and it was a man running, jumping, clambering over the groynes, and every few seconds looking eagerly back. The nearer he came the more obvious it was that he was not only anxious, but even terribly frightened, though his face was not to be distinguished. He was, moreover, almost at the end of his strength. On he came; each successive obstacle seemed to cause him more difficulty than the last. 'Will he get over this next one?' thought Parkins; 'it seems a little higher than the others.' Yes; half climbing, half throwing himself, he did get over, and fell all in a heap on the other side (the side nearest to the spectator). There, as if really unable to get up again, he remained crouching under the groyne, looking up in an attitude of painful anxiety.

So far no cause whatever for the fear of the runner had been shown; but now there began to be seen, far up the shore, a little flicker of something light-coloured moving to and fro with great swiftness and irregularity. Rapidly growing larger, it, too, declared itself as a figure, in pale, fluttering draperies, ill-defined. There was something about its motion which made Parkins very unwilling to see it at close quarters. It would stop, raise its arms, bow itself towards the sand, then run stooping across the beach to the water's edge and back again; and then, rising upright, once more continue its course forward at a speed that was startling and terrifying. The moment came when the pursuer was hovering about from left to right only a few yards beyond the groyne where the runner lay in hiding. After two or three ineffectual castings hither and thither it came to a stop, stood upright, with arms raised high, and then started straight forward towards the groyne.

It was at this point that Parkins always failed in his resolution to keep his eyes shut. With many misgivings as to incipient failure of eyesight, overworked brain, excessive smoking, and so on, he finally resigned himself to light his candle, get out a book, and pass the night waking, rather than be tormented by this persistent panorama, which he saw clearly enough could only be a morbid reflection of his walk and his thoughts on that very day.

The scraping of match on box and the glare of light must have startled some creatures of the night – rats or what not – which he heard scurry across the floor from the side of his bed with much rustling. Dear, dear! the match is out! Fool that it is! But the second one burnt better, and a candle and book were duly procured, over which Parkins pored till sleep of a wholesome kind came upon him, and that in no long space. For about the first time in his orderly and prudent life he forgot to blow out the candle, and when he was called next morning at eight there was still a flicker in the socket and a sad mess of guttered grease on the top of the little table.

After breakfast he was in his room, putting the finishing touches to his golfing costume – fortune had again allotted the colonel to him for a partner – when one of the maids came in.

'Oh, if you please,' she said, 'would you like any extra blankets on your bed, sir?'

'Ah! thank you,' said Parkins. 'Yes, I think I should like one. It seems likely to turn rather colder.'

In a very short time the maid was back with the blanket.

'Which bed should I put it on, sir?' she asked.

'What? Why, that one – the one I slept in last night,' he said, pointing to it.

'Oh yes! I beg your pardon, sir, but you seemed to have tried both of 'em; leastways, we had to make 'em both up this morning.'

'Really? How very absurd!' said Parkins. 'I certainly never touched the other, except to lay some things on it. Did it actually seem to have been slept in?'

'Oh yes, sir!' said the maid. 'Why, all the things was crumpled and throwed about all ways, if you'll excuse me, sir – quite as if anyone 'adn't passed but a very poor night, sir.'

'Dear me,' said Parkins. 'Well, I may have disordered it more than I thought when I unpacked my things. I'm very sorry to have given you the extra trouble, I'm sure. I expect a friend of mine soon, by the way – gentleman from Cambridge – to come and occupy it for a night or two. That will be all right, I suppose, won't it?'

'Oh yes, to be sure, sir. Thank you, sir. It's no trouble, I'm sure,' said the maid, and departed to giggle with her colleagues.

Parkins set forth, with a stern determination to improve his game.

I am glad to be able to report that he succeeded so far in this enterprise that the colonel, who had been rather repining at the prospect of a second day's play in his company, became quite chatty as the morning advanced; and his voice boomed out over the flats, as certain also of our own minor poets have said, 'like some great bourdon in a minster tower'.

'Extraordinary wind, that, we had last night,' he said. 'In my old home we should have said someone had been whistling for it.'

'Should you, indeed!' said Parkins. 'Is there a superstition of that kind still current in your part of the country?'

'I don't know about superstition,' said the colonel. 'They believe in it all over Denmark and Norway, as well as on the Yorkshire coast; and my experience is, mind you, that there's generally something at the bottom of what these countryfolk hold to, and have held to for generations. But it's your drive' (or whatever it might have been: the golfing reader will have to imagine appropriate digressions at the proper intervals).

When conversation was resumed, Parkins said, with a slight hesitancy, 'Apropos of what you were saying just now, colonel, I think I ought to tell you that my own views on such subjects are very strong. I am, in fact, a convinced disbeliever in what is called the "supernatural". '

'What!' said the colonel, 'do you mean to tell me you don't believe in second-sight, or ghosts, or anything of that kind?'

'In nothing whatever of that kind,' returned Parkins firmly.

'Well,' said the colonel, 'it appears to me at that rate, sir, that you must be little better than a Sadducee.'

Parkins was on the point of answering that, in his opinion, the Sadducees were the most sensible persons he had ever read of in the Old Testament; but, feeling some doubt as to whether much mention of them was to be found in that work, he preferred to laugh the accusation off.

'Perhaps I am,' he said; 'but – Here, give me my cleek, boy! – Excuse me one moment, colonel.' A short interval. 'Now, as to whistling for the wind, let me give you my theory about it. The laws which govern winds are really not at all perfectly known – to fisherfolk and such, of course, not known at all. A man or woman of eccentric habits, perhaps, or a stranger, is seen repeatedly on the beach at some unusual hour, and is heard whistling. Soon afterwards a violent wind arises; a man who could read the sky perfectly or who possessed a barometer could have foretold that it would. The simple people of a fishing-village have no barometers, and only a few rough rules for prophesying weather. What more natural than that the eccentric personage I postulated should be regarded as having raised the wind, or that he or she should clutch eagerly at the reputation of being able to do so? Now, take last night's wind: as it happens, I myself was whistling. I blew a whistle twice, and the wind seemed to come absolutely in answer to my call. If anyone had seen me – '

The audience had been a little restive under this harangue, and Parkins had, I fear, fallen somewhat into the tone of a lecturer; but at the last sentence the colonel stopped him.

'Whistling, were you?' he said. 'And what sort of whistle did you use? Play this stroke first.' Interval.

'About that whistle you were asking, colonel. It's rather a curious one. I have it in my – No; I see I've left it in my room. As a matter of fact, I found it yesterday.'

And then Parkins narrated the manner of his discovery of the whistle, upon hearing which the colonel grunted, and opined that, in Parkins's place, he should himself be careful about using a thing that had belonged to a set of papists, of whom, speaking generally, it might be affirmed that you never knew what they might not have been up to. From this topic he diverged to the enormities of the vicar, who had given notice on the previous Sunday that Friday would be the Feast of St Thomas the Apostle, and that there would be a service at eleven o'clock in the church. This and other similar proceedings constituted in the colonel's view a strong presumption that the vicar was a concealed papist, if not a Jesuit; and Parkins, who could not very readily follow the colonel in this region, did not disagree with him. In fact, they got on so well together in the morning that there was no talk on either side of their separating after lunch.

Both continued to play well during the afternoon, or, at least, well enough to make them forget everything else until the light began to fail them. Not until then did Parkins remember that he had meant to do some more investigating at the preceptory; but it was of no great importance, he reflected. One day was as good as another; he might as well go home with the colonel.

As they turned the corner of the house, the colonel was almost knocked down by a boy who rushed into him at the very top of his speed, and then, instead of running away, remained hanging on to him and panting. The first words of the warrior were naturally those of reproof and objurgation, but he very quickly discerned that the boy was almost speechless with fright. Enquiries were useless at first. When the boy got his breath he began to howl, and still clung to the colonel's legs. He was at last detached, but continued to howl.

'What in the world *is* the matter with you? What have you been up to? What have you seen?' said the two men.

'Ow, I seen it wive at me out of the winder,' wailed the boy, 'and I don't like it.'

'What window?' said the irritated colonel. 'Come, pull yourself together, my boy.'

'The front winder it was, at the 'otel,' said the boy.

At this point Parkins was in favour of sending the boy home, but the colonel refused; he wanted to get to the bottom of it, he said; it was most dangerous to give a boy such a fright as this one had had, and if it turned out that people had been playing jokes, they should suffer for it in some way. And by a series of questions he made out this story: The boy had been playing about on the grass in front of the Globe with some others; then they had gone home to their teas, and he was just going, when he happened to look up 'at the front winder and see it a-wiving' at him. *It* seemed to be a figure of some sort, in white as far as he knew – couldn't see its face; but it waved at him, and 'it warn't a right thing – not to say not a right person'. Was there a light in the room? No, he didn't think to look if there was a light. Which was the window? Was it the top one or the second one? The 'seckind one it was – the big winder what's got two little uns at the sides'.

'Very well, my boy,' said the colonel, after a few more questions. 'You run away home now. I expect it was some person trying to give you a start. Another time, like a brave English boy, you just throw a stone – well, no, not that exactly, but you go and speak to the waiter, or to Mr Simpson, the landlord, and – yes – and say that I advised you to do so.'

The boy's face expressed some of the doubt he felt as to the likelihood of Mr Simpson's lending a favourable ear to his complaint, but the colonel did not appear to perceive this, and went on, 'And here's a sixpence – no, I see it's a shilling – and you be off home, and don't think any more about it.'

The youth hurried off with agitated thanks, and the colonel and Parkins went round to the front of the Globe and reconnoitred. There was only one window answering to the description they had been hearing.

'Well, that's curious,' said Parkins; 'it's evidently my window the lad was talking about. Will you come up for a moment, Colonel Wilson? We ought to be able to see if anyone has been taking liberties in my room.'

They were soon in the passage, and Parkins made as if to open the door. Then he stopped and felt in his pockets.

'This is more serious than I thought,' was his next remark. 'I remember now that before I started this morning I locked the door. It is locked now, and, what is more, here is the key.' And he held it up. 'Now,' he went on, 'if the servants are in the habit of going into one's room during the day when one is away, I can only say that – well, that I don't approve of it at all.' Conscious of a somewhat weak climax, he busied himself in opening the door (which was indeed locked) and in lighting candles. 'No,' he said, 'nothing seems disturbed.'

'Except your bed,' put in the colonel.

'Excuse me, that isn't my bed,' said Parkins. 'I don't use that one. But it does look as if someone had been playing tricks with it.'

It certainly did: the clothes were bundled up and twisted together in a most tortuous confusion. Parkins pondered.

'That must be it,' he said at last: 'I disordered the clothes last night in unpacking, and they haven't made it since. Perhaps they came in to make it, and that boy saw them through the window; and then they were called away and locked the door after them. Yes, I think that must be it.'

'Well, ring and ask,' said the colonel, and this appealed to Parkins as practical.

The maid appeared, and, to make a long story short, deposed that she had made the bed in the morning when the gentleman was in the room, and hadn't been there since. No, she 'hadn't no other key'. Mr Simpson he 'kep' the keys'; he'd be able to tell the gentleman if anyone had been up.

This was a puzzle. Investigation showed that nothing of value had been taken, and Parkins remembered the disposition of the small objects on tables and so forth well enough to be pretty sure that no pranks had been played with them. Mr and Mrs Simpson furthermore agreed that neither of them had given the duplicate key of the room to any person whatever during the day. Nor could Parkins, fair-minded man as he was, detect anything in the demeanour of master, mistress or maid that indicated guilt.

He was much more inclined to think that the boy had been imposing on the colonel.

The latter was unwontedly silent and pensive at dinner and throughout the evening. When he bade good-night to Parkins, he murmured in a gruff undertone, 'You know where I am if you want me during the night.'

'Why, yes, thank you, Colonel Wilson, I think I do; but there isn't much prospect of my disturbing you, I hope. By the way,' he added, 'did I show you that old whistle I spoke of? I think not. Well, here it is.'

The colonel turned it over gingerly in the light of the candle.

'Can you make anything of the inscription?' asked Parkins, as he took it back.

'No, not in this light. What do you mean to do with it?'

'Oh, well, when I get back to Cambridge I shall submit it to some of the archaeologists there, and see what they think of it; and very likely, if they consider it worth having, I may present it to one of the museums.'

'Mm!' said the colonel. 'Well, you may be right. All I know is that, if it were mine, I should chuck it straight into the sea. It's no use talking, I'm well aware, but I expect that with you it's a case of live and learn. I hope so, I'm sure, and I wish you a good-night.'

He turned away, leaving Parkins at the bottom of the stairs, about to make some reply; soon each was in his own bedroom.

By some unfortunate accident, there were neither blinds nor curtains to the windows of the professor's room. The previous night he had thought little of this, but tonight there seemed every prospect of a bright moon rising to shine directly on his bed, and probably wake him later on. When he noticed this he was a good deal annoyed, but, with an ingenuity which I can only envy, he succeeded in rigging up, with the help of a railway-rug, some safety-pins, a stick and an umbrella, a screen which, if it only held together, would completely keep the moonlight off his bed. And shortly afterwards he was comfortably in that bed. When he had read a somewhat solid work long enough to produce a decided wish for sleep, he cast a drowsy glance round the room, blew out the candle and fell back upon the pillow.

He must have slept soundly for an hour or more, when a sudden clatter shook him up in a most unwelcome manner. In a moment he realised what had happened: his carefully constructed screen had given way, and a very bright frosty moon was shining directly on his face. This was highly annoying. Could he possibly get up and reconstruct the screen? or could he manage to sleep if he did not?

For some minutes he lay and pondered over the possibilities; then he turned over sharply, and with all his eyes open lay breathlessly listening. There had been a movement, he was sure, in the empty bed on the opposite side of the room. Tomorrow he would have it moved, for there must be rats or something playing about in it. It was quiet now. No! the commotion began again. There was a rustling and shaking: surely more than any rat could cause.

I can figure to myself something of the professor's bewilderment and horror, for I have in a dream thirty years back seen the same thing happen; but the reader will hardly, perhaps, imagine how dreadful it was to him to see a figure suddenly sit up in what he had known was an empty bed. He was out of his own bed in one bound, and made a dash towards the window, where lay his only weapon, the stick with which he had propped his screen. This was, as it turned out, the worst thing he could have done, because the personage in the empty bed, with a sudden smooth motion, slipped from the bed and took up a position, with outspread arms, between the two beds, and in front of the door. Parkins watched it in a horrid perplexity. Somehow, the idea of getting past it and escaping through the door was intolerable to him; he could not have borne – he didn't know why – to touch it; and as for its touching him, he would sooner dash himself through the window than have that happen. It stood for the moment in a band of dark shadow and he could not see what its face was like. Now it began to move, in a stooping posture, and all at once the spectator realised, with some horror and some relief, that it must be blind, for it seemed to feel about it with its muffled arms in a groping and random fashion. Turning half away from him, it became suddenly conscious of the bed he had just left, and darted towards it, and bent over and felt the pillows in a way which made Parkins shudder as he had never in his life thought it possible. In a very few moments it seemed to know that the bed was empty, and then, moving forward into the area of light and facing the window, it showed for the first time what manner of thing it was.

Parkins, who very much dislikes being questioned about it, did once describe something of it in my hearing, and I gathered that what he chiefly remembers about it is a horrible, an intensely horrible, face *of crumpled linen*. What expression he read upon it he could not or would not tell, but that the fear of it went nigh to maddening him is certain.

But he was not at leisure to watch it for long. With formidable quickness it moved into the middle of the room, and, as it groped and waved, one corner of its draperies swept across Parkins's face. He could not – though he knew how perilous a sound was – he could not keep back a cry of disgust, and this gave the searcher an instant clue. It leapt towards him upon the instant, and the next moment he was halfway through the window backwards, uttering cry upon cry at the utmost pitch of his voice, and the linen face was thrust close into his own. At this, almost the last possible second, deliverance came, as you will have guessed: the colonel burst the door open, and was just in time to see the dreadful group at the window. When he reached the figures only one was left. Parkins sank forward into the room in a faint, and before him on the floor lay a tumbled heap of bedclothes.

Colonel Wilson asked no questions, but busied himself in keeping everyone else out of the room and in getting Parkins back to his bed; he himself, wrapped in a rug, occupied the other bed for the rest of the night. Early on the next day Rogers arrived, more welcome than he would have been a day before, and the three of them held a very long consultation in the professor's room. At the end of it the colonel left the hotel door carrying a small object between his finger and thumb, which he cast as far into the sea as a very brawny arm could send it. Later on the smoke of a bonfire ascended from the back premises of the Globe.

Exactly what explanation was patched up for the staff and visitors at the hotel I must confess I do not recollect. The professor was somehow cleared of the ready suspicion of delirium tremens, and the hotel of the reputation of a troubled house.

There is not much question as to what would have happened to Parkins if the colonel had not intervened when he did. He would either have fallen out of the window or else lost his wits. But it is not so evident what more the creature that came in answer to the whistle could have done than frighten. There seemed to be absolutely nothing material about it save the bed-clothes of which it had made itself a body. The colonel, who remembered a not very dissimilar occurrence in India, was of the opinion that if Parkins had closed with it it could really have done very little, and that its one power was that of frightening. The whole thing, he said, served to confirm his opinion of the Church of Rome.

There is really nothing more to tell, but, as you may imagine, the professor's views on certain points are less clear-cut than they used to be. His nerves, too, have suffered: he cannot even now see a surplice hanging on a door quite unmoved, and the spectacle of a scarecrow in a field late on a winter afternoon has cost him more than one sleepless night.

The Monkey's Paw

W. W. JACOBS

I

WITHOUT, THE NIGHT WAS COLD AND WET, but in the small parlour of Lakesnam Villa the blinds were drawn and the fire burned brightly. Father and son were at chess, the former, who possessed ideas about the game involving radical changes, putting his king into such sharp and unnecessary perils that it even provoked comment from the white-haired old lady knitting placidly by the fire.

'Hark at the wind,' said Mr White, who, having seen a fatal mistake after it was too late, was amiably desirous of preventing his son from seeing it.

'I'm listening,' said the latter, grimly surveying the board as he stretched out his hand. 'Check.'

'I should hardly think that he'd come tonight,' said his father, with his hand poised over the board.

'Mate,' replied the son.

'That's the worst of living so far out,' bawled Mr White, with sudden and unlooked-for violence; 'of all the beastly, slushy, out-of-the-way places to live in, this is the worst. Pathway's a bog and the road's a torrent. I don't know what people are thinking about. I suppose because only two houses on the road are let, they think it doesn't matter.'

'Never mind, dear,' said his wife soothingly; 'perhaps you'll win the next one.'

Mr White looked up sharply, just in time to intercept a knowing glance between mother and son. The words died away on his lips, and he hid a guilty grin in his thin grey beard.

'There he is,' said Herbert White, as the gate banged to loudly and heavy footsteps came towards the door.

The old man rose with hospitable haste, and opening the door, was heard condoling with the new arrival. The new arrival also condoled with himself, so that Mrs White said, 'Tut, tut!' and coughed gently as her husband entered the room, followed by a tall burly man, beady of eye and rubicund of visage.

'Sergeant-Major Morris,' he said, introducing him.

The sergeant-major shook hands, and taking the proffered seat by the fire, watched contentedly while his host got out whisky and tumblers and stood a small copper kettle on the fire.

At the third glass his eyes got brighter, and he began to talk, the little family circle regarding with eager interest this visitor from distant parts, as he squared his broad shoulders in the chair and spoke of strange scenes and doughty deeds, of wars and plagues and strange peoples.

'Twenty-one years of it,' said Mr White, nodding at his wife and son. 'When he went away he was a slip of a youth in the warehouse. Now look at him.'

'He don't look to have taken much harm,' said Mrs White politely.

'I'd like to go to India myself,' said the old man, 'just to look round a bit, you know.'

'Better where you are,' said the sergeant-major, shaking his head. He put down the empty glass, and sighing softly, shook it again.

'I should like to see those old temples and fakirs and jugglers,' said the old man. 'What was that you started telling me the other day about a monkey's paw or something, Morris?'

'Nothing,' said the soldier hastily. 'Leastways, nothing worth hearing.'

'Monkey's paw?' said Mrs White curiously.

'Well, it's just a bit of what you might call magic, perhaps,' said the sergeant-major off-handedly.

His three listeners leaned forward eagerly. The visitor absent-mindedly put his empty glass to his lips and then set it down again. His host filled it for him.

'To look at,' said the sergeant-major, fumbling in his pocket, 'it's just an ordinary little paw, dried to a mummy.'

He took something out of his pocket and proffered it. Mrs White drew back with a grimace, but her son, taking it, examined it curiously.

'And what is there special about it?' inquired Mr White, as he took it from his son, and having examined it, placed it upon the table.

'It had a spell put on it by an old fakir,' said the sergeant-major, 'a very holy man. He wanted to show that fate ruled people's lives, and that those who interfered with it did so to their sorrow. He put a spell on it so that three separate men could each have three wishes from it.'

His manner was so impressive that his hearers were conscious that their light laughter jarred somewhat.

'Well, why don't you have three, sir?' said Herbert White cleverly.

The soldier regarded him in the way that middle age is wont to regard presumptuous youth. 'I have,' he said quietly, and his blotchy face whitened.

'And did you really have the three wishes granted?' asked Mrs White.

'I did,' said the sergeant-major, and his glass tapped against his strong teeth.

'And has anybody else wished?' enquired the old lady.

'The first man had his three wishes, yes,' was the reply. 'I don't know what the first two were, but the third was for death. That's how I got the paw.'

His tones were so grave that a hush fell upon the group.

'If you've had your three wishes, it's no good to you now, then, Morris,' said the old man at last. 'What do you keep it for?'

The soldier shook his head. 'Fancy, I suppose,' he said slowly. 'I did have some idea of selling it, but I don't think I will. It has caused enough mischief already. Besides, people won't buy. They think it's a fairy tale, some of them, and those who do think anything of it want to try it first and pay me afterwards.'

'If you could have another three wishes,' said the old man, eyeing him keenly, 'would you have them?'

'I don't know,' said the other. 'I don't know.'

He took the paw, and dangling it between his front finger and thumb, suddenly threw it upon the fire. White, with a slight cry, stooped down and snatched it off.

'Better let it burn,' said the soldier solemnly.

'If you don't want it, Morris,' said the old man, 'give it to me.'

'I won't,' said his friend doggedly. 'I threw it on the fire. If you keep it, don't blame me for what happens. Pitch it on the fire again, like a sensible man.'

The other shook his head and examined his new possession closely. 'How do you do it?' he inquired.

'Hold it up in your right hand and wish aloud,' said the sergeant-major, 'but I warn you of the consequences.'

'Sounds like *The Arabian Nights*,' said Mrs White, as she rose and began to set the supper. 'Don't you think you might wish for four pairs of hands for me?'

Her husband drew the talisman from his pocket, and then all three burst into laughter as the sergeant-major, with a look of alarm on his face, caught him by the arm.

'If you must wish,' he said gruffly, 'wish for something sensible.'

Mr White dropped it back into his pocket, and placing chairs, motioned his friend to the table. In the business of supper the talisman was partly forgotten, and afterward the three sat listening in an enthralled fashion to a second instalment of the soldier's adventures in India.

'If the tale about the monkey paw is not more truthful than those he has been telling us,' said Herbert, as the door closed behind their guest, just in time for him to catch the last train, 'we shan't make much out of it.'

'Did you give him anything for it, father?' inquired Mrs White, regarding her husband closely.

'A trifle,' said he, colouring slightly. 'He didn`t want it, but I made him take it. And he pressed me again to throw it away.'

'Likely,' said Herbert, with pretended horror. 'Why, we're going to be rich, and famous, and happy. Wish to be an emperor, father, to begin with; then you can't be henpecked.'

He darted round the table, pursued by the maligned Mrs White armed with an antimacassar.

Mr White took the paw from his pocket and eyed it dubiously. 'I don't know what to wish for, and that's a fact,' he said slowly. 'It seems to me I've got all I want.'

'If you only cleared the house, you'd be quite happy, wouldn't you?' said Herbert, with his hand on his shoulder. 'Well, wish for two hundred pounds, then; that'll just do it.'

His father, smiling shamefacedly at his own credulity, held up the talisman, as his son, with a solemn face somewhat marred by a wink at his mother, sat down at the piano and struck a few impressive chords.

'I wish for two hundred pounds!' said the old man distinctly.

A fine crash from the piano greeted the words, interrupted by a shuddering cry from the old man. His wife and son ran to him.

'It moved,' he cried, with a glance of disgust at the object as it lay on the floor. 'As I wished, it twisted in my hands like a snake.'

'Well, I don't see the money,' said his son, as he picked it up and placed it on the table, 'and I bet I never shall.'

'It must have been your fancy, father,' said his wife, regarding him anxiously.

He shook his head. 'Never mind, though; there's no harm done, but it gave me a shock all the same.'

They sat down by the fire again while the two men finished their pipes. Outside, the wind was higher than ever, and the old man started nervously at the sound of a door banging upstairs. A silence unusual and depressing settled upon all three, which lasted until the old couple rose to retire for the night.

'I expect you'll find the cash tied up in a big bag in the middle of your bed,' said Herbert, as he bade them good-night, 'and something horrible squatting up on top of the wardrobe watching you as you pocket your ill-gotten gains.'

II

In the brightness of the wintry sun next morning as it streamed over the breakfast table Herbert laughed at his fears. There was an air of prosaic wholesomeness about the room which it had lacked on the previous night, and the dirty, shrivelled little paw was pitched on the sideboard with a carelessness which betokened no great belief in its virtues.

'I suppose all old soldiers are the same,' said Mrs White. 'The idea of our listening to such nonsense! How could wishes be granted in these days? And if they could, how could two hundred pounds hurt you, father?'

'Might drop on his head from the sky,' said the frivolous Herbert.

'Morris said the things happened so naturally,' said his father, 'that you might if you so wished attribute it to coincidence.'

'Well, don't break into the money before I come back,' said Herbert, as he rose from the table. 'I'm afraid it'll turn you into a mean, avaricious man, and we shall have to disown you.'

His mother laughed, and following him to the door, watched him down the road, and returning to the breakfast table, was very happy at the expense of her husband's credulity. All of which did not prevent her from scurrying to the door at the postman's knock, nor prevent her from referring somewhat shortly to retired sergeant-majors of bibulous habits when she found that the post brought a tailor's bill.

'Herbert will have some more of his funny remarks, I expect, when he comes home,' she said, as they sat at dinner.

'I dare say,' said Mr White, pouring himself out some beer; 'but for all that, the thing moved in my hand; that I'll swear to.'

'You thought it did,' said the old lady soothingly.

'I say it did,' replied the other. 'There was no thought about it; I had just – What's the matter?'

His wife made no reply. She was watching the mysterious movements of a man outside, who, peering in an undecided fashion at the house appeared to be trying to make up his mind to enter. In mental connection with the two hundred pounds, she noticed that the stranger was well dressed and wore a silk hat of glossy newness. Three times he paused at the gate, and then walked on again. The fourth time he stood with his hand upon it, and then with sudden resolution flung it open and walked up the path. Mrs White at the same moment placed her hands behind her, and hurriedly unfastening the strings of her apron, put that useful article of apparel beneath the cushion of her chair.

She brought the stranger, who seemed ill at ease, into the room. He gazed furtively at Mrs White, and listened in a preoccupied fashion as the old lady apologised for the appearance of the room, and her husband's coat, a garment which he usually reserved for the garden. She then waited as patiently as her sex would permit for him to broach his business, but he was at first strangely silent.

'I – was asked to call,' he said at last, and stooped and picked a piece of cotton from his trousers. 'I come from Maw and Meggins.'

The old lady started. 'Is anything the matter?' she asked breathlessly. 'Has anything happened to Herbert? What is it? What is it?'

Her husband interposed. 'There, there, mother,' he said hastily. 'Sit down, and don't jump to conclusions. You've not brought bad news, I'm sure, sir,' and he eyed the other wistfully.

'I'm sorry – ' began the visitor.

'Is he hurt?' demanded the mother.

The visitor bowed in assent. 'Badly hurt,' he said quietly, 'but he is not in any pain.'

'Oh, thank God!' said the old woman, clasping her hands. 'Thank God for that! Thank – '

She broke off suddenly as the sinister meaning of the assurance dawned upon her and she saw the awful confirmation of her fears in the other's averted face. She caught her breath, and turning to her slower-witted husband, laid her trembling old hand upon his. There was a long silence.

'He was caught in the machinery,' said the visitor at length, in a low voice.

'Caught in the machinery,' repeated Mr White, in a dazed fashion, 'yes.'

He sat staring blankly out at the window, and taking his wife's hand between his own, pressed it as he had been wont to do in their old courting days nearly forty years before.

'He was the only one left to us,' he said, turning gently to the visitor. 'It is hard.'

The other coughed, and rising, walked slowly to the window. 'The firm wished me to convey their sincere sympathy with you in your great loss,' he said, without looking round. 'I beg that you will understand I am only their servant and merely obeying orders.'

There was no reply; the old woman's face was white, her eyes staring, and her breath inaudible; on the husband's face was a look such as his friend the sergeant might have carried into his first action.

'I was to say that Maw and Meggins disclaim all responsibility,' continued the other. 'They admit no liability at all, but in consideration of your son's services they wish to present you with a certain sum as compensation.'

Mr White dropped his wife's hand, and rising to his feet, gazed with a look of horror at his visitor. His dry lips shaped the words, 'How much?'

'Two hundred pounds,' was the answer.

Unconscious of his wife's shriek, the old man smiled faintly, put out his hands like a sightless man, and dropped, a senseless heap, to the floor.

III

In the huge new cemetery, some two miles distant, the old people buried their dead, and came back to a house steeped in shadow and silence. It was all over so quickly that at first they could hardly realise it, and remained in a state of expectation as though of something else to happen – something else which was to lighten this load, too heavy for old hearts to bear.

But the days passed, and expectation gave place to resignation – the hopeless resignation of the old, sometimes miscalled apathy. Sometimes they hardly exchanged a word, for now they had nothing to talk about, and their days were long to weariness.

It was about a week after that that the old man, waking suddenly in the night, stretched out his hand and found himself alone. The room was in darkness, and the sound of subdued weeping came from the window. He raised himself in bed and listened.

'Come back,' he said tenderly. 'You will be cold.'

'It is colder for my son,' said the old woman, and wept afresh.

The sound of her sobs died away on his ears. The bed was warm, and his eyes heavy with sleep. He dozed fitfully, and then slept until a sudden wild cry from his wife awoke him with a start.

'The monkey's paw!' she cried wildly. 'The monkey's paw!'

He started up in alarm. 'Where? Where is it? What's the matter?'

She came stumbling across the room toward him. 'I want it,' she said quietly. 'You've not destroyed it?'

'It's in the parlour, on the bracket,' he replied, marvelling. 'Why?'

She cried and laughed together, and bending over, kissed his cheek.

'I only just thought of it,' she said hysterically. 'Why didn't I think of it before? Why didn't you think of it?'

'Think of what?' he questioned.

'The other two wishes,' she replied rapidly. 'We've only had one.'

'Was not that enough?' he demanded fiercely.

'No,' she cried triumphantly; 'we'll have one more. Go down and get it quickly, and wish our boy alive again.'

The man sat up in bed and flung the bedclothes from his quaking limbs. 'Good God, you are mad!' he cried, aghast.

'Get it,' she panted; 'get it quickly, and wish – Oh, my boy, my boy!'

Her husband struck a match and lit the candle. 'Get back to bed,' he said unsteadily. 'You don't know what you are saying.'

'We had the first wish granted,' said the old woman feverishly; 'why not the second?'

'A coincidence,' stammered the old man.

'Go and get it and wish,' cried the old woman, and dragged him towards the door.

He went down in the darkness, and felt his way to the parlour, and then to the mantelpiece. The talisman was in its place, and a horrible fear that the unspoken wish might bring his mutilated son before him ere he could escape from the room seized upon him, and he caught his breath as he found that he had lost the direction of the door. His brow cold with sweat, he felt his way round the table, and groped along the wall until he found himself in the small passage with the unwholesome thing in his hand.

Even his wife's face seemed changed as he entered the room. It was white and expectant, and to his fears seemed to have an unnatural look upon it. He was afraid of her.

'Wish!' she cried, in a strong voice.

'It is foolish and wicked,' he faltered.

'Wish!' repeated his wife.

He raised his hand. 'I wish my son alive again.'

The talisman fell to the floor, and he regarded it shudderingly. Then he sank trembling into a chair as the old woman, with burning eyes, walked to the window and raised the blind.

He sat until he was chilled with the cold, glancing occasionally at the figure of the old woman peering through the window. The candle end, which had burnt below the rim of the china candlestick, was throwing pulsating shadows on the ceiling and walls, until, with a flicker larger than the rest, it expired. The old man, with an unspeakable sense of relief at the failure of the talisman, crept back to his bed, and a minute or two afterwards the old woman came silently and apathetically beside him.

Neither spoke, but both lay silently listening to the ticking of the clock. A stair creaked, and a squeaky mouse scurried noisily through the wall. The darkness was oppressive, and after lying for some time screwing up his courage, the husband took the box of matches, and striking one, went downstairs for a candle.

At the foot of the stairs the match went out, and he paused to strike another, and at the same moment a knock, so quiet and stealthy as to be scarcely audible, sounded on the front door.

The matches fell from his hand. He stood motionless, his breath suspended until the knock was repeated. Then he turned and fled swiftly back to the bedroom, and closed the door behind him. A third knock sounded through the house.

'*What's that?*' cried the old woman, starting up.

'A rat,' said the old man, in shaking tones – 'a rat. It passed me on the stairs.'

His wife sat up in bed listening. A loud knock resounded through the house.

'It's Herbert!' she screamed. 'It's Herbert!'

She ran to the door, but her husband was before her, and catching her by the arm, held her tightly.

'What are you going to do?' he whispered hoarsely.

'It's my boy; it's Herbert!' she cried, struggling mechanically. 'I forgot it was two miles away. What are you holding me for? Let go. I must open the door.'

'For God's sake, don't let it in,' cried the old man, trembling.

'You're afraid of your own son,' she cried, struggling. 'Let me go. I'm coming, Herbert; I'm coming.'

There was another knock, and another. The old woman with a sudden wrench broke free and ran from the room. Her husband followed to the landing, and called after her appealingly as she hurried downstairs. He heard the chain rattle back and the bottom bolt drawn slowly and stiffly from the socket. Then the old woman's voice, strained and panting.

'The top bolt,' she cried loudly. 'Come down. I can't reach it.'

But her husband was on his hands and knees groping wildly on the floor in search of the paw. If he could only find it before the thing outside got in. A perfect fusillade of knocks reverberated through the house, and he heard the scraping of a chair as his wife put it down in the passage against the door. He heard the creaking of the bolt as it came slowly back, and at the same moment he found the monkey's paw, and frantically breathed his third and last wish.

The knocking ceased suddenly, although the echoes of it were still in the house. He heard the chair drawn back and the door opened. A cold wind rushed up the staircase, and a long loud wail of disappointment and misery from his wife gave him courage to run down to her side, and then to the gate beyond. The street lamp flickering opposite shone on a quiet and deserted road.

The Mark of the Beast

RUDYARD KIPLING

Your gods and my gods – do you
or I know which are the stronger?
Native proverb

EAST OF SUEZ, some hold, the direct control of providence ceases, man being there handed over to the power of the gods and devils of Asia, and the Church of England providence only exercising an occasional and modified supervision in the case of Englishmen.

This theory accounts for some of the more unnecessary horrors of life in India; it may be stretched to explain my story.

My friend Strickland of the police, who knows as much of natives of India as is good for any man, can bear witness to the facts of the case. Dumoise, our doctor, also saw what Strickland and I saw. The inference which he drew from the evidence was entirely incorrect. He is dead now; he died in a rather curious manner, which has been elsewhere described.

When Fleete came to India he owned a little money and some land in the Himalayas, near a place called Dharmsala. Both properties had been left him by an uncle, and he came out to finance them. He was a big, heavy, genial and inoffensive man. His knowledge of natives was, of course, limited, and he complained of the difficulties of the language.

He rode in from his place in the hills to spend New Year in the station, and he stayed with Strickland. On New Year's Eve there was a big dinner at the club, and the night was excusably wet. When men foregather from the uttermost ends of the Empire they have a right to be riotous. The Frontier had sent down a contingent o' Catch-'em-Alive-Os who had not seen twenty white faces for a year, and were used to ride fifteen miles to dinner at the next fort at the risk of a Khyberee bullet where their drinks should lie. They profited by their new security, for they tried to play pool with a curled-up hedgehog found in the garden, and one of them carried the marker round the room in his teeth. Half a dozen planters had come in from the south and were talking 'horse' to the Biggest Liar in Asia, who was trying to cap all their stories at once. Everybody was there, and there was a general closing up of ranks and taking stock of our losses in dead or disabled that had fallen during the past year. It was a very wet night, and I remember that we sang 'Auld Lang Syne' with our feet in the Polo Championship Cup and our heads among the stars, and swore that we were all dear friends. Then some of us went away and annexed Burma, and some tried to open up the Sudan and were opened up by fuzzies in that cruel scrub outside Suakim, and some found stars and medals, and some were married, which was bad, and some did other things which were worse, and the others of us stayed in our chains and strove to make money on insufficient experiences.

Fleete began the night with sherry and bitters, drank champagne steadily up to dessert, then raw, rasping Capri with all the strength of whisky, took Benedictine with his coffee, four or five whiskies and sodas to improve his pool strokes, beer and bones at half-past two, winding up with old brandy. Consequently, when he came out, at half-past three in the morning, into fourteen degrees of frost, he was very angry with his horse for coughing, and tried to leapfrog into the saddle. The horse broke away and went to his stables; so Strickland and I formed a guard of dishonour to take Fleete home.

Our road lay through the bazaar, close to a little temple of Hanuman, the monkey-god, who is a leading divinity worthy of respect. All gods have good points, just as have all priests. Personally, I attach much importance to Hanuman, and am kind to his people – the great grey apes of the hills. One never knows when one may want a friend.

There was a light in the temple, and as we passed we could hear voices of men chanting hymns. In a native temple the priests rise at all hours of the night to do honour to their god. Before we could stop him, Fleete dashed up the steps, patted two priests on the back, and was gravely grinding the ashes of his cigar-butt into the forehead of the red stone image of Hanuman.

Strickland tried to drag him out, but he sat down and said solemnly: 'Shee that? 'Mark of the B–beasht! *I* made it. Ishn't it fine?'

In half a minute the temple was alive and noisy, and Strickland, who knew what came of polluting gods, said that things might occur. He, by virtue of his official position, long residence in the country and weakness for going among the natives, was known to the priests and he felt unhappy. Fleete sat on the ground and refused to move. He said that 'good old Hanuman' made a very soft pillow.

Then, without any warning, a Silver Man came out of a recess behind the image of the god. He was perfectly naked in that bitter, bitter cold, and his body shone like frosted silver, for he was what the Bible calls 'a leper as white as snow'. Also he had no face, because he was a leper of some years' standing, and his disease was heavy upon him. We two stooped to haul Fleete up, and the temple was filling and filling with folk who seemed to spring from the earth, when the Silver Man ran in under our arms, making a noise exactly like the mewing of an otter, caught Fleete round the body and dropped his head on Fleete's breast before we could wrench him away. Then he retired to a corner and sat mewing while the crowd blocked all the doors.

The priests were very angry until the Silver Man touched Fleete. That nuzzling seemed to sober them.

At the end of a few minutes' silence one of the priests came to Strickland and said, in perfect English, 'Take your friend away. He has done with Hanuman but Hanuman has not done with him.' The crowd gave room and we carried Fleete into the road.

Strickland was very angry. He said that we might all three have been knifed, and that Fleete should thank his stars that he had escaped without injury.

Fleete thanked no one. He said that he wanted to go to bed. He was gorgeously drunk.

We moved on, Strickland silent and wrathful, until Fleete was taken with violent shivering fits and sweating. He said that the smells of the bazaar were overpowering, and he wondered why slaughterhouses were permitted so near English residences. 'Can't you smell the blood?' said Fleete.

We put him to bed at last, just as the dawn was breaking, and Strickland invited me to have another whisky and soda. While we were drinking he talked of the trouble in the temple, and admitted that it baffled him completely. Strickland hates being mystified by natives, because his business in life is to overmatch them with their own weapons. He has not yet succeeded in doing this, but in fifteen or twenty years he will have made some small progress.

'They should have mauled us,' he said, 'instead of mewing at us. I wonder what they meant. I don't like it one little bit.'

I said that the managing committee of the temple would in all probability bring a criminal action against us for insulting their religion. There was a section of the Indian Penal Code which exactly met Fleete's offence. Strickland said he only hoped and prayed that they would do this. Before I left I looked into Fleete's room, and saw him lying on his right side, scratching his left breast. Then I went to bed, cold, depressed and unhappy, at seven o'clock in the morning.

At one o'clock I rode over to Strickland's house to inquire after Fleete's head. I imagined that it would be a sore one. Fleete was breakfasting and seemed unwell. His temper was gone, for he was abusing the cook for not supplying him with an underdone chop. A man who can eat raw meat after a wet night is a curiosity. I told Fleete this and he laughed.

'You breed queer mosquitoes in these parts,' he said. 'I've been bitten to pieces, but only in one place.

'Let's have a look at the bite,' said Strickland. 'It may have gone down since this morning.'

While the chops were being cooked, Fleete opened his shirt and showed us, just over his left breast, a mark, the perfect double of the black rosettes –

the five or six irregular blotches arranged in a circle – on a leopard's hide. Strickland looked and said, 'It was only pink this morning. It's grown black now.'

Fleete ran to a glass.

'By Jove!' he said, 'this is nasty. What is it?'

We could not answer. Here the chops came in, all red and juicy, and Fleete bolted three in a most offensive manner. He ate on his right grinders only, and threw his head over his right shoulder as he snapped the meat. When he had finished, it struck him that he had been behaving strangely, for he said apologetically, 'I don't think I ever felt so hungry in my life. I've bolted like an ostrich.'

After breakfast Strickland said to me, 'Don't go. Stay here, and stay for the night.'

Seeing that my house was not three miles from Strickland's, this request was absurd. But Strickland insisted, and was going to say something, when Fleete interrupted by declaring in a shamefaced way that he felt hungry again. Strickland sent a man to my house to fetch over my bedding and a horse, and we three went down to Strickland's stables to pass the hours until it was time to go out for a ride. The man who has a weakness for horses never wearies of inspecting them; and when two men are killing time in this way they gather knowledge and lies the one from the other.

There were five horses in the stables, and I shall never forget the scene as we tried to look them over. They seemed to have gone mad. They reared and screamed and nearly tore up their pickets; they sweated and shivered and lathered and were distraught with fear. Strickland's horses used to know him as well as his dogs; which made the matter more curious. We left the stable for fear of the brutes throwing themselves in their panic. Then Strickland turned back and called me. The horses were still frightened, but they let us 'gentle' and make much of them, and put their heads in our bosoms.

'They aren't afraid of *us*,' said Strickland. 'D'you know, I'd give three months' pay if Outrage here could talk.'

But Outrage was dumb, and could only cuddle up to his master and blow out his nostrils, as is the custom of horses when they wish to explain things but can't. Fleete came up when we were in the stalls, and as soon as the horses saw him, their fright broke out afresh. It was all that we could do to escape from the place unkicked. Strickland said, 'They don't seem to love you, Fleete.'

'Nonsense,' said Fleete; 'my mare will follow me like a dog.' He went to her; she was in a loose-box; but as he slipped the bars she plunged, knocked him down, and broke away into the garden. I laughed, but Strickland was not amused. He took his moustache in both fists and pulled at it till it nearly came out. Fleete, instead of going off to chase his property, yawned, saying that he felt sleepy. He went to the house to lie down, which was a foolish way of spending New Year's Day.

Strickland sat with me in the stables and asked if I had noticed anything peculiar in Fleete's manner. I said that he ate his food like a beast; but that this might have been the result of living alone in the hills, out of the reach of society as refined and elevating as ours for instance. Strickland was not amused. I do not think that he listened to me, for his next sentence referred to the mark on Fleete's breast, and I said that it might have been caused by blister-flies, or that it was possibly a birthmark newly born and now visible for the first time. We both agreed that it was unpleasant to look at, and Strickland found occasion to say that I was a fool.

'I can't tell you what I think now,' said he, 'because you would call me a madman; but you must stay with me for the next few days, if you can. I want you to watch Fleete, but don't tell me what you think till I have made up my mind.'

'But I am dining out tonight,' I said.

'So am I,' said Strickland, 'and so is Fleete. At least if he doesn't change his mind.'

We walked about the garden smoking, but saying nothing – because we were friends, and talking spoils good tobacco – till our pipes were out. Then we went to wake up Fleete. He was wide awake and fidgeting about his room.

'I say, I want some more chops,' he said. 'Can I get them?'

We laughed and said, 'Go and change. The ponies will be round in a minute.'

'All right,' said Fleete. 'I'll go when I get the chops – underdone ones, mind.'

He seemed to be quite in earnest. It was four o'clock, and we had had breakfast at one; still, for a long time, he demanded those underdone chops. Then he changed into riding clothes and went out into the veranda. His pony – the mare had not been caught – would not let him come near. All three horses were unmanageable – mad with fear – and finally Fleete said that he would stay at home and get something to eat. Strickland and I rode out wondering. As we passed the temple of Hanuman, the Silver Man came out and mewed at us.

'He is not one of the regular priests of the temple,' said Strickland. 'I think I should peculiarly like to lay my hands on him.'

There was no spring in our gallop on the racecourse that evening. The horses were stale, and moved as though they had been ridden out.

'The fright after breakfast has been too much for them,' said Strickland.

That was the only remark he made through the remainder of the ride. Once or twice, I think, he swore to himself; but that did not count.

We came back in the dark at seven o'clock, and saw that there were no lights in the bungalow. 'Careless ruffians my servants are!' said Strickland.

My horse reared at something on the carriage drive, and Fleete stood up under its nose.

'What are you doing, grovelling about the garden?' said Strickland.

But both horses bolted and nearly threw us. We dismounted by the stables and returned to Fleete, who was on his hands and knees under the orange-bushes.

'What the devil's wrong with you?' said Strickland .

'Nothing, nothing in the world,' said Fleete, speaking very quickly and thickly. 'I've been gardening – botanising, you know. The smell of the earth is delightful. I think I'm going for a walk – a long walk– all night.'

Then I saw that there was something excessively out of order somewhere, and I said to Strickland, 'I am not dining out.'

'Bless you!' said Strickland. 'Here, Fleete, get up. You'll catch fever there. Come in to dinner and let's have the lamps lit. We'll all dine at home.'

Fleete stood up unwillingly, and said, 'No lamps – no lamps. It's much nicer here. Let's dine outside and have some more chops – lots of 'em and underdone – bloody ones with gristle.'

Now a December evening in Northern India is bitterly cold, and Fleete's suggestion was that of a maniac.

'Come in,' said Strickland sternly. 'Come in at once.'

Fleete came, and when the lamps were brought, we saw that he was literally plastered with dirt from head to foot. He must have been rolling in the garden. He shrank from the light and went to his room. His eyes were horrible to look at. There was a green light behind them, not in them, if you understand, and the man's lower lip hung down.

Strickland said, 'There is going to be trouble – big trouble – tonight. Don't you change your riding-things.'

We waited and waited for Fleete's reappearance, and ordered dinner in the meantime. We could hear him moving about his own room, but there was no light there. Presently from the room came the long-drawn howl of a wolf.

People write and talk lightly of blood running cold and hair standing up, and things of that kind. Both sensations are too horrible to be trifled with. My heart stopped as though a knife had been driven through it, and Strickland turned as white as the tablecloth.

The howl was repeated, and was answered by another howl far across the fields.

That set the gilded roof on the horror. Strickland dashed into Fleete's room. I followed, and we saw Fleete getting out of the window. He made beast-noises in the back of his throat. He could not answer us when we shouted at him. He spat.

I don't quite remember what followed, but I think that Strickland must have stunned him with the long bootjack, or else I should never have been able to sit on his chest. Fleete could not speak, he could only snarl, and his snarls were those of a wolf, not of a man. The human spirit must have been giving way all day and have died out with the twilight. We were dealing with a beast that had once been Fleete.

The affair was beyond any human and rational experience. I tried to say 'hydrophobia', but the word wouldn't come, because I knew that I was lying.

We bound this beast with leather thongs of the punkah-rope, and tied its thumbs and big toes together, and gagged it with a shoe-horn, which makes a very efficient gag if you know how to arrange it. Then we carried it into the dining room, and sent a man to Dumoise, the doctor, telling him to come over at once. After we had dispatched the messenger and were drawing breath, Strickland said, 'It's no good. This isn't any doctor's work.' I, also, knew that he spoke the truth.

The beast's head was free, and it threw it about from side to side. Anyone entering the room would have believed that we were curing a wolf's pelt. That was the most loathsome accessory of all.

Strickland sat with his chin in the heel of his fist, watching the beast as it wriggled on the ground, but saying nothing. The shirt had been torn open in the scuffle and showed the black rosette mark on the left breast. It stood out like a blister. :

In the silence of the watching we heard something without, mewing like a she-otter. We both rose to our feet, and, I answer for myself, not Strickland, felt sick actually and physically sick. We told each other, as did the men in *Pinafore*, that it was the cat.

Dumoise arrived, and I never saw a little man so unprofessionally shocked. He said that it was a heart-rending case of hydrophobia, and that nothing could be done. At least any palliative measures would only prolong the agony. The beast was foaming at the mouth. Fleete, as we told Dumoise, had been bitten by dogs once or twice. Any man who keeps half a dozen terriers must expect a nip now and again. Dumoise could offer no help. He could only certify that Fleete was dying of hydrophobia. The beast was then howling, for it had managed to spit out the shoehorn. Dumoise said that he would be ready to certify to the cause of death, and that the end was certain. He was a good little man, and he offered to remain with us; but Strickland refused the kindness. He did not wish to poison Dumoise's New Year. He would only ask him not to give the real cause of Fleete's death to the public.

So Dumoise left, deeply agitated; and as soon as the noise of the cartwheels had died away Strickland told me, in a whisper, his suspicions. They were so wildly improbable that he dared not say them out aloud; and I, who entertained all Strickland's beliefs, was so ashamed of owning to them that I pretended to disbelieve.

'Even if the Silver Man had bewitched Fleete for polluting the image of Hanuman, the punishment could not have fallen so quickly.'

As I was whispering this the cry outside the house rose again, and the beast fell into a fresh paroxysm of struggling till we were afraid that the thongs that held it would give way.

'Watch!' said Strickland. 'If this happens six times I shall take the law into my own hands. I order you to help me.'

He went into his room and came out in a few minutes with the barrels of an old shotgun, a piece of fishing-line, some thick cord, and his heavy wooden bedstead. I reported that the convulsions had followed the cry by two seconds in each case, and the beast seemed perceptibly weaker.

Strickland muttered, 'But he can't take away the life! He can't take away the life!'

I said, though I knew that I was arguing against myself. 'It may be a cat. It must be a cat. If the Silver Man is responsible, why does he dare to come here?'

Strickland arranged the wood on the hearth, put the gun-barrels into the glow of the fire, spread the twine on the table and broke a walking stick in two. There was one yard of fishing line, gut lapped with wire, such as is used for *mahseer*-fishing, and he tied the two ends together in a loop.

Then he said, 'How can we catch him? He must be taken alive and unhurt.'

I said that we must trust in providence, and go out softly with polo-sticks into the shrubbery at the front of the house. The man or animal that made the cry was evidently moving round the house as regularly as a night-watchman. We could wait in the bushes till he came by and knock him over.

Strickland accepted this suggestion, and we slipped out from a bathroom window into the front veranda and then across the carriage drive into the bushes.

In the moonlight we could see the leper coming round the corner of the house. He was perfectly naked, and from time to time he mewed and stopped to dance with his shadow. It was an unattractive sight, and thinking of poor Fleete, brought to such degradation by so foul a creature, I put away all my doubts and resolved to help Strickland from the heated gun-barrels to the loop of twine – from the loins to the head and back again – with all tortures that might be needful.

The leper halted in the front porch for a moment and we jumped out on him with the sticks. He was wonderfully strong, and we were afraid that he might escape or be fatally injured before we caught him. We had an idea that lepers were frail creatures, but this proved to be incorrect. Strickland knocked his legs from under him and I put my foot on his neck. He mewed hideously, and even through my riding-boots I could feel that his flesh was not the flesh of a clean man.

He struck at us with his hand- and feet-stumps. We looped the lash of a dog-whip round him, under the armpits, and dragged him backwards into the hall and so into the dining-room where the beast lay. There we tied him with trunkstraps. He made no attempt to escape, but mewed.

When we confronted him with the beast the scene was beyond descrip-tion. The beast doubled backwards into a bow as though he had been poisoned with strychnine, and moaned in the most pitiable fashion. Several other things happened also, but they cannot be put down here.

'I think I was right,' said Strickland. 'Now we will ask him to cure this case.'

But the leper only mewed. Strickland wrapped a towel round his hand and took the gun-barrels out of the fire. I put the half of the broken walking stick through the loop of fishing-line and buckled the leper comfortably to Strickland's bedstead. I understood then how men and women and little children can endure to see a witch burnt alive; for the beast was moaning on the floor, and though the Silver Man had no face, you could see horrible feelings passing through the slab that took its place, exactly as waves of heat play across red-hot iron – gun-barrels for instance.

Strickland shaded his eyes with his hands for a moment and we got to work. This part is not to be printed.

The dawn was beginning to break when the leper spoke. His mewings had not been satisfactory up to that point. The beast had fainted from exhaustion and the house was very still. We unstrapped the leper and told him to take away the evil spirit. He crawled to the beast and laid his hand upon the left breast. That was all. Then he fell face down and whined, drawing in his breath as he did so.

We watched the face of the beast, and saw the soul of Fleete coming back into the eyes. Then a sweat broke out on the forehead and the eyes – they were human eyes – closed. We waited for an hour, but Fleete still slept. We carried him to his room and bade the leper go, giving him the bedstead, and the sheet on the bedstead to cover his nakedness, the gloves and the towels with which we had touched him, and the whip that had been hooked round his body. He put the sheet about him and went out into the early morning without speaking or mewing.

Strickland wiped his face and sat down. A night-gong, far away in the city, made seven o'clock.

'Exactly four-and-twenty hours!' said Strickland. 'And I've done enough to ensure my dismissal from the service, besides permanent quarters in a lunatic asylum. Do you believe that we are awake?'

The red-hot gun-barrel had fallen on the floor and was singeing the carpet. The smell was entirely real.

That morning at eleven we two together went to wake up Fleete. We looked and saw that the black leopard-rosettes on his chest had disappeared. He was very drowsy and tired, but as soon as he saw us, he said, 'Oh! Confound you fellows. Happy New Year to you. Never mix your liquors. I'm nearly dead.'

'Thanks for your kindness, but you're over time,' said Strickland. 'Today is the morning of the second. You've slept the clock round with a vengeance.'

The door opened, and little Dumoise put his head in. He had come on foot, and fancied that we were laying out Fleete.

'I've brought a nurse,' said Dumoise. 'I suppose that she can come in for . . . what is necessary.'

'By all means,' said Fleete cheerily, sitting up in bed. 'Bring on your nurses.'

Dumoise was dumb. Strickland led him out and explained that there must have been a mistake in the diagnosis. Dumoise remained dumb and left the house hastily. He considered that his professional reputation had been injured, and was inclined to make a personal matter of the recovery. Strickland went out too. When he came back, he said that he had been to call on the temple of Hanuman to offer redress for the pollution of the god, and had been solemnly assured that no white man had ever touched the idol, and that he was an incarnation of all the virtues labouring under a delusion. 'What do you think?' said Strickland.

I said, ' "There are more things . . ." '

But Strickland hates that quotation. He says that I have worn it threadbare.

One other curious thing happened which frightened me as much as anything in all the night's work. When Fleete was dressed he came into the dining-room and sniffed. He had a quaint trick of moving his nose when he sniffed. 'Horrid doggy smell, here,' said he. 'You should really keep those terriers of yours in better order. Try sulphur, Strick.'

But Strickland did not answer. He caught hold of the back of a chair, and, without warning, went into an amazing fit of hysterics. It is terrible to see a strong man overtaken with hysteria. Then it struck me that we had fought for Fleete's soul with the Silver Man in that room, and had disgraced ourselves as Englishmen for ever, and I laughed and gasped and gurgled just as shamefully as Strickland, while Fleete thought that we had both gone mad. We never told him what we had done.

Some years later, when Strickland had married and was a churchgoing member of society for his wife's sake, we reviewed the incident dispassionately and Strickland suggested that I should put it before the public.

I cannot myself see that this step is likely to clear up the mystery; because, in the first place, no one will believe a rather unpleasant story, and, in the second, it is well known to every right-minded man that the gods of the heathen are stone and brass, and any attempt to deal with them otherswise is justly condemned.

The Prayer

VIOLET HUNT

It is but giving over of a game,
That must be lost. PHILASTER

I

'COME, MRS ARNE – come, my dear, you must not give way like this! You can't stand it – you really can't! Let Miss Kate take you away – now do!' urged the nurse, with her most motherly of intonations.

'Yes, Alice, Mrs Joyce is right. Come away – do come away – you are only making yourself ill. It is all over; you can do nothing! Oh, oh, do come away!' implored Mrs Arne's sister, shivering with excitement and nervousness.

A few moments ago Dr Graham had relinquished his hold on the pulse of Edward Arne with the hopeless movement of the eyebrows that meant – the end.

The nurse had made the little gesture of resignation that was possibly a matter of form with her. The young sister-in-law had hidden her face in her hands. The wife had screamed a scream that had turned them all hot and cold – and flung herself on the bed over her dead husband. There she lay; her cries were terrible, her sobs shook her whole body.

The three gazed at her pityingly, not knowing what to do next. The nurse, folding her hands, looked towards the doctor for directions, and the doctor drummed with his fingers on the bedpost. The young girl timidly stroked the shoulder that heaved and writhed under her touch.

'Go away! Go away!' her sister reiterated continually, in a voice hoarse with fatigue and passion.

'Leave her alone, Miss Kate,' whispered the nurse at last; 'she will work it off best herself, perhaps.'

She turned down the lamp, as if to draw a veil over the scene. Mrs Arne raised herself on her elbow, showing a face stained with tears and purple with emotion.

'What! Not gone?' she said harshly. 'Go away, Kate, go away! It is my house. I don't want you, I want no one – I want to speak to my husband. Will you go away – all of you. Give me an hour, half an hour – five minutes!'

She stretched out her arms imploringly to the doctor.

'Well . . .' said he, almost to himself

He signed to the two women to withdraw, and followed them out into the passage. 'Go and get something to eat,' he said peremptorily, 'while you can. We shall have trouble with her presently I'll wait in the dressing-room.'

He glanced at the twisting figure on the bed, shrugged his shoulders, and passed into the adjoining room, without, however, closing the door of communication. Sitting down in an armchair drawn up to the fire, he stretched himself and closed his eyes. The professional aspects of the case of Edward Arne rose up before him in all its interesting forms of complication . . .

It was just this professional attitude that Mrs Arne unconsciously resented, both in the doctor and in the nurse. Through all their kindness she had realised and resented their scientific interest in her husband, for to them he had been no more than a curious and complicated case; and now that the blow had fallen, she regarded them both in the light of executioners. Her one desire, expressed with all the shameless sincerity of blind and thought-less misery, was to be free of their hateful presence and alone – alone with her dead!

She was weary of the doctor's subdued manly tones – of the nurse's commonplace motherliness, too habitually adapted to the needs of all to be appreciated by the individual – of the childish consolation of the young sister, who had never loved, never been married, did not know what sorrow was! Their expressions of sympathy struck her like blows, the touch of their hands on her body, as they tried to raise her, stung her in every nerve.

With a sigh of relief she buried her head in the pillow, pressed her body more closely against that of her husband, and lay motionless.

Her sobs ceased.

The lamp went out with a gurgle. The fire leaped up, and died. She raised her head and stared about her helplessly, then sinking down again she put her lips to the ear of the dead man.

'Edward – dear Edward!' she whispered, 'why have you left me? Darling, why have you left me? I can't stay behind – you know I can't. I am too young to be left. It is only a year since you married me. I never thought it was only for a year. "Till death us do part!" Yes, I know that's in it, but nobody ever thinks of that! I never thought of living without you! I meant to die with you.

'No – no – I can't die – I must not – till my baby is born. You will never see it. Don't you want to see it? Don't you? Oh, Edward, speak! Say something, darling, one word – one little word! Edward! Edward! are you there? Answer me for God's sake, answer me!

'Darling, I am so tired of waiting. Oh, think, dearest. There is so little time. They only gave me half an hour. In half an hour they will come and take you away from me – take you where I can't come to you – with all my love I can't come to you! I know the place – I saw it once. A great lonely place full of graves, and little stunted trees dripping with dirty London rain . . . and gas lamps flaring all round . . . but quite, quite dark where the grave is . . . a long grey stone just like the rest. How could you stay there? – all alone – all alone – without me?

'Do you remember, Edward, what we once said – that whichever of us died first should come back to watch over the other, in the spirit? I promised you, and you promised me. What children we were! Death is not what we thought. It comforted us to say that then.

'Now, it's nothing – nothing – worse than nothing! I don't want your spirit – I can't see it – or feel it – I want you, you, your eyes that looked at me, your mouth that kissed me – '

She raised his arms and clasped them round her neck, and lay there very still, murmuring, 'Oh, hold me, hold me! Love me if you can. Am I hateful? This is me! These are your arms . . .'

The doctor in the next room moved in his chair. The noise awoke her from her dream of contentment, and she unwound one dead arm from her neck, and, holding it up by the wrist, considered it ruefully.

'Yes, I can put it round me, but I have to hold it there. It is quite cold – it doesn't care. Ah, my dear, you don't care! You are dead. I kiss you, but you don't kiss me. Edward! Edward! Oh, for heaven's sake kiss me once. Just once!

'No, no, that won't do – that's not enough! that's nothing! worse than nothing! I want you back, you, all of you . . . What shall I do? . . . I often pray . . . Oh, if there be a God in heaven, and if He ever answered a prayer, let Him answer mine – my only prayer – I'll never ask another – and give you back to me! As you were – as I loved you – as I adored you! He must listen. He must! My God, my God, he's mine – he's my husband, he's my lover – give him back to me!'

'Left alone for half an hour or more with the corpse! It's not right!'

The muttered expression of the nurse's revolted sense of professional decency came from the head of the staircase, where she had been waiting for the last few minutes. The doctor joined her.

'Hush, Mrs Joyce! I'll go to her now.'

The door creaked on its hinges as he gently pushed it open and went in.

'What's that? What's that?' screamed Mrs Arne. 'Doctor! Doctor! Don't touch me! Either I am dead or he is alive!'

'Do you want to kill yourself, Mrs Arne?' said Dr Graham, with calculated sternness, coming forward; 'come away!'

'Not dead! Not dead!' she murmured.

'He is dead, I assure you. Dead and cold an hour ago! Feel!' He took hold of her, as she lay face downwards, and in so doing he touched the dead man's cheek – it was not cold! Instinctively his finger sought a pulse.

'Stop! Wait!' he cried in his intense excitement. 'My dear Mrs Arne, control yourself!'

But Mrs Arne had fainted, and fallen heavily off the bed on the other side. Her sister, hastily summoned, attended to her, while the man they had all given over for dead was, with faint gasps and sighs and reluctant moans, pulled, as it were, hustled and dragged back over the threshold of life.

II

'Why do you always wear black, Alice?' asked Esther Graham. 'You are not in mourning that I know of.'

She was Dr Graham's only daughter and Mrs Arne's only friend. She sat with Mrs Arne in the dreary drawing-room of the house in Chelsea. She had come to tea. She was the only person who ever did come to tea.

She was brusque, kind and blunt, and had a talent for making inappropriate remarks. Six years ago Mrs Arne had been a widow for an hour! Her husband had succumbed to an apparently mortal illness, and for the space of an hour had lain dead. When suddenly and inexplicably he had revived from his trance, the shock, combined with six weeks' nursing, had nearly killed his wife. All this Esther had heard from her father. She herself had only come to know Mrs Arne after her child was born, and all the tragic circumstances of her husband's illness put aside, and it was hoped forgotten. And when her idle question received no answer from the pale absent woman who sat opposite, with listless lack-lustre eyes fixed on the green and blue flames dancing in the fire, she hoped it had passed unnoticed. She waited for five minutes for Mrs Arne to resume the conversation, then her natural impatience got the better of her.

'Do say something, Alice!' she implored.

'Esther, I beg your pardon!' said Mrs Arne. 'I was thinking.'

'What were you thinking of?'

'I don't know.'

'No, of course you don't. People who sit and stare into the fire never do think, really. They are only brooding and making themselves ill, and that is what you are doing. You mope, you take no interest in anything, you never go out – I am sure you have not been out of doors today?'

'No – yes – I believe not. It is so cold.'

'You are sure to feel the cold if you sit in the house all day, and sure to get ill! Just look at yourself!'

Mrs Arne rose and looked at herself in the Italian mirror over the chimney-piece. It reflected faithfully enough her even pallor, her dark hair and eyes, the sweeping length of her eyelashes, the sharp curves of her nostrils and the delicate arch of her eyebrows, forming a thin sharp black line, so clear as to seem almost unnatural.

'Yes I do look ill,' she said with conviction

'No wonder. You choose to bury yourself alive.'

'Sometimes I do feel as if I lived in a grave. I look up at the ceiling and fancy it is my coffin-lid.'

'Don't please talk like that!' expostulated Miss Graham, pointing to Mrs Arne's little girl. 'If only for Dolly's sake, I think you should not give way to such morbid fancies. It isn't good for her to see you like this always.'

'Oh, Esther,' the other exclaimed, stung into something like vivacity, 'don't reproach me! I hope I am a good mother to my child!'

'Yes, dear, you are a model mother – and model wife too. Father says the way you look after your husband is something wonderful, but don't you think for your own sake you might try to be a little gayer? You encourage these moods, don't you? What is it? Is it the house?'

She glanced around her – at the high ceiling, at the heavy damask portières, the tall cabinets of china, the dim oak panelling – it reminded her of a neglected museum. Her eye travelled into the farthest corners, where the faint filmy dusk was already gathering, lit only by the bewildering cross-lights of the glass panels of cabinet doors – to the tall narrow windows – then back again to the woman in her mourning dress, cowering by the fire.

She said sharply, 'You should go out more.'

'I do not like to – leave my husband.'

'Oh, I know that he is delicate and all that, but still, does he never permit you to leave him? Does he never go out by himself?'

'Not often!'

'And you have no pets! It is very odd of you. I simply can't imagine a house without animals!'

'We did have a dog once,' answered Mrs Arne plaintively, 'but it howled so we had to give it away. It would not go near Edward . . . But please don't imagine that I am dull! I have my child.' She laid her hand on the flaxen head at her knee.

Miss Graham rose, frowning.

'Ah, you are too bad!' she exclaimed. 'You are like a widow exactly, with one child, stroking its orphan head and saying, "Poor fatherless darling." '

Voices were heard outside. Miss Graham stopped talking quite suddenly, and sought her veil and gloves on the mantelpiece.

'You need not go, Esther,' said Mrs Arne. 'It is only my husband.'

'Oh, but it is getting late,' said the other, crumpling up her gloves in her muff, and shuffling her feet nervously.

'Come!' said her hostess, with a bitter smile, 'put your gloves on properly – if you must go – but it is quite early still.'

'Please don't go, Miss Graham,' put in the child.

'I must. Go and meet your papa, like a good girl.'

'I don't want to.'

'You mustn't talk like that, Dolly,' said the doctor's daughter absently, still looking towards the door.

Mrs Arne rose and fastened the clasps of the big fur cloak for her friend. The wife's white, sad, oppressed face came very close to the girl's cheerful one as she murmured in a low voice – 'You don't like my husband, Esther? I can't help noticing it. Why don't you?'

'Nonsense!' retorted the other, with the emphasis of one who is repelling an overtrue accusation. 'I do, only – '

'Only what?'

'Well, dear, it is foolish of me, of course, but I am – a little afraid of him.'

'Afraid of Edward!' said his wife slowly. 'Why should you be?'

'Well, dear – you see – I – I suppose women can't help being a little afraid of their friends' husbands – they can spoil their friendships with their wives in a moment, if they choose to disapprove of them. I really must go! Goodbye, child; give me a kiss! Don't ring, Alice. Please don't! I can open the door for myself – '

'Why should you?' said Mrs Arne. 'Edward is in the hall; I heard him speaking to Foster.'

'No; he has gone into his study. Goodbye, you apathetic creature!' She gave Mrs Arne a brief kiss and dashed out of the room. The voices outside had ceased, and she had reasonable hopes of reaching the door without being intercepted by Mrs Arne's husband. But he met her on the stairs. Mrs Arne, listening intently from her seat by the fire, heard her exchange a few shy sentences with him, the sound of which died away as they went downstairs together. A few moments after, Edward Arne came into the room and dropped into the chair just vacated by his wife's visitor.

He crossed his legs and said nothing. Neither did she.

His nearness had the effect of making the woman look at once several years older. Where she was pale he was well-coloured; the network of little filmy wrinkles that, on a close inspection, covered her face, had no parallel on his smooth skin. He was handsome; soft, well-groomed flakes of auburn hair lay over his forehead, and his steely blue eyes shone equably, a contrast to the sombre fire of hers, and the masses of dark crinkly hair that shaded her brow. The deep lines of permanent discontent furrowed that brow as she sat with her chin propped on her hands, and her elbows resting on her knees. Neither spoke. When the hands of the clock over Mrs Arne's head pointed to seven, the white-aproned figure of the nurse appeared in the doorway, and the little girl rose and kissed her mother very tenderly.

Mrs Arne's forehead contracted. Looking uneasily at her husband, she said to the child tentatively, yet boldly, as one grasps a nettle, 'Say good-night to your father!'

The child obeyed, saying, 'Good-night,' indifferently in her father's direction.

'Kiss him!'

'No, please – please not.'

Her mother looked down on her curiously, sadly . . .

'You are a naughty, spoilt child!' she said, but without conviction. 'Excuse her, Edward.'

He did not seem to have heard.

'Well, if you don't care – ' said his wife bitterly. 'Come, child!' She caught the little girl by the hand and left the room.

At the door she half turned and looked fixedly at her husband. It was a strange ambiguous gaze; in it passion and dislike were strangely combined. Then she shivered and closed the door softly after her.

The man in the armchair sat with no perceptible change of attitude, his unspeculative eyes fixed on the fire, his hands clasped idly in front of him. The pose was obviously habitual. The servant brought lights and closed the shutters, drew the curtains and made up the fire noisily, without, however, eliciting any reproof from his master.

Edward Arne was an ideal master, as far as Foster was concerned. He kept cases of cigars, but never smoked them, although the supply had often to be renewed. He did not care what he ate or drank, although he kept as good a cellar as most gentlemen – Foster knew that. He never interfered, he counted for nothing, he gave no trouble. Foster had no intention of ever leaving such an easy place. True, his master was not cordial; he very seldom addressed him or seemed to know whether he was there, but then neither did he grumble if the fire in the study was allowed to go out, or interfere with Foster's liberty in any way. He had a better place of it than Annette, Mrs Arne's maid, who would be called up in the middle of the night to bathe her mistress's forehead with eau-de-Cologne, or made to brush her long hair for hours together to soothe her. Naturally enough Foster and Annette compared notes as to their respective situations, and drew unflattering parallels between this capricious wife and model husband.

III

Miss Graham was not a demonstrative woman. On her return home she somewhat startled her father, as he sat by his study table, deeply interested in his diagnosis book, by the sudden violence of her embrace.

'Why this excitement?' he asked, smiling and turning round He was a young-looking man for his age; his thin wiry figure and clear colour belied the evidence of his hair, tinged with grey, and the tired wrinkles that gave value to the acuteness and brilliancy of the eyes they surrounded.

'I don't know!' she replied, 'only you are so nice and alive somehow. I always feel like this when I come back from seeing the Arnes.'

'Then don't go to see the Arnes.'

'I'm so fond of her, father, and she will never come here to me as you know. Or else nothing would induce me to enter her tomb of a house, and talk to that walking funeral of a husband of hers. I managed to get away today without having to shake hands with him. I always try to avoid it. But, father, I do wish you would go and see Alice.'

'Is she ill?'

'Well, not exactly ill, I suppose, but her eyes make me quite uncomfortable, and she says such odd things! I don't know if it is you or the clergyman she wants, but she is all wrong somehow! She never goes out except to church; she never pays a call, or has anyone to call on her! Nobody ever asks the Arnes to dinner, and I'm sure I don't blame them – the sight of that man at one's table would spoil any party – and they never entertain. She is always alone. Day after day I go in and find her sitting over the fire, with that same brooding expression. I shouldn't be surprised in the least if she were to go mad some day. Father, what is it? What is the tragedy of the house? There is one I am convinced. And yet, though I have been the intimate friend of that woman for years, I know no more about her than the man in the street.'

'She keeps her skeleton safe in the cupboard,' said Dr Graham. 'I respect her for that. And please don't talk nonsense about tragedies. Alice Arne is only morbid – the malady of the age. And she is a very religious woman.'

'I wonder if she complains of her odious husband to Mr Bligh. She is always going to his services.'

'Odious?'

'Yes, odious!' Miss Graham shuddered. 'I cannot stand him! I cannot bear the touch of his cold froggy hands, and the sight of his fishy eyes! That inane smile of his simply makes me shrivel up. Father, honestly, do you like him yourself?'

'My dear, I hardly know him! It is his wife I have known ever since she was a child, and I a boy at college. Her father was my tutor. I never knew her husband till six years ago, when she called me in to attend him in a very serious illness. I suppose she never speaks of it? No? A very odd affair. For the life of me I cannot tell how he managed to recover. You needn't tell people, for it affects my reputation, but I didn't save him! Indeed I have never been able to account for it. The man was given over for dead!'

'He might as well be dead for all the good he is,' said Esther scornfully. 'I have never heard him say more than a couple of sentences in my life.'

'Yet he was an exceedingly brilliant young man; one of the best men of his year at Oxford – a good deal run after – poor Alice was wild to marry him!'

'In love with that spiritless creature? He is like a house with someone dead in it, and all the blinds down!'

'Come, Esther, don't be morbid – not to say silly! You are very hard on the poor man! What's wrong with him? He is the ordinary, commonplace, cold-blooded specimen of humanity, a little stupid, a little selfish – people who have gone through a serious illness like that are apt to be – but on the whole, a good husband, a good father, a good citizen.'

'Yes, and his wife is afraid of him, and his child hates him!' exclaimed Esther.

'Nonsense!' said Dr Graham sharply. 'The child is spoilt. Only children are apt to be – and the mother wants a change or a tonic of some kind. I'll go and talk to her when I have time. Go along and dress. Have you forgotten that George Graham is coming to dinner?'

After she had gone the doctor made a note on the corner of his blotting-pad, *Mem. – to go and see Mrs Arne*, and dismissed the subject of the memorandum entirely from his mind.

George Graham was the doctor's nephew, a tall, weedy, cumbrous young man, full of fads and fallacies, with a gentle manner that somehow inspired confidence. He was several years younger than Esther, who loved to listen to his semi-scientific, semi-romantic stories of things met with in the course of his profession.

'Oh, I come across very queer things!' he would say mysteriously. 'There's a queer little widow!'

'Tell me about your little widow?' asked Esther that day after dinner, when, her father having gone back to his study, she and her cousin sat together as usual.

He laughed.

'You like to hear of my professional experiences? Well, she certainly interested me,' he said thoughtfully. 'She is an odd psychological study in her way. I wish I could come across her again.'

'Where did you come across her, and what is her name?'

'I don't know her name, I don't want to; she is not a personage to me, only a case. I hardly know her face even. I have never seen it except in the twilight. But I gathered that she lived somewhere in Chelsea, for she came out on to the Embankment with only a kind of lacy thing over her head; she can't live far off, I fancy.'

Esther became instantly attentive. 'Go on,' she said.

'It was three weeks ago,' said George Graham. 'I was coming along the Embankment about ten o'clock. I walked through that little grove, you know, just between Cheyne Walk and the river, and I heard in there someone sobbing very bitterly. I looked and saw a woman sitting on a seat, with her head in her hands, crying. I was most awfully sorry, of course, and I thought I could perhaps do something for her, get her a glass of water, or salts, or something. I took her for a woman of the people – it was quite dark, you know. So I asked her very politely if I could do anything for her, and then I noticed her hands – they were quite white and covered with diamonds.'

'You were sorry you spoke, I suppose,' said Esther.

'She raised her head and said – I believe she laughed – "Are you going to tell me to move on?" '

'She thought you were a policeman?'

'Probably – if she thought at all – but she was in a semi-dazed condition. I told her to wait till I came back, and dashed round the corner to the chemist's and bought a bottle of salts. She thanked me, and made a little effort to rise and go away. She seemed very weak. I told her I was a medical man. I started in and talked to her.'

'And she to you?'

'Yes, quite straight. Don't you know that women always treat a doctor as if he were one step removed from their father confessor – not human – not in the same category as themselves? It is not complimentary to one as a man, but one hears a good deal one would not otherwise hear. She ended by telling me all about herself – in a veiled way, of course. It soothed her – relieved her – she seemed not to have had an outlet for years!'

'To a mere stranger!'

'To a doctor. And she did not know what she was saying half the time. She was hysterical, of course. Heavens! what nonsense she talked! She spoke of herself as a person somehow haunted, cursed by some malign fate, a victim of some fearful spiritual catastrophe, don't you know? I let her run on. She was convinced of the reality of a sort of "doom" that she fancied had befallen her. It was quite pathetic. Then it got rather chilly – she shivered – I suggested her going in. She shrank back; she said, "If you only knew what a relief it is, how much less miserable I am out here! I can breathe; I can live – it is my only glimpse of the world that is alive – I live in a grave – oh, let me stay!" She seemed positively afraid to go home.'

'Perhaps someone bullied her at home.'

'I suppose so, but then – she had no husband. He died, she told me, years ago. She had adored him, she said – '

'Is she pretty?'

'Pretty! Well, I hardly noticed. Let me see! Oh, yes, I suppose she was pretty – no, now I think of it, she would be too worn and faded to be what you call pretty.'

Esther smiled.

'Well, we sat there together for quite an hour, then the clock of Chelsea church struck eleven, and she got up and said, "Goodbye," holding out her hand quite naturally, as if our meeting and conversation had been nothing out of the common. There was a sound like a dead leaf trailing across the walk and she was gone.'

'Didn't you ask if you should see her again?'

'That would have been a mean advantage to take.'

'You might have offered to see her home.'

'I saw she did not mean me to.'

'She was a lady, you say,' pondered Esther. 'How was she dressed?'

'Oh, all right, like a lady – in black – mourning, I suppose. She has dark crinkly hair, and her eyebrows are very thin and arched – I noticed that in the dusk.'

'Does this photograph remind you of her?' asked Esther suddenly, taking him to the mantelpiece.

'Rather!'

'Alice! Oh, it couldn't be – she is not a widow, her husband is alive – has your friend any children?'

'Yes, one, she mentioned it.'

'How old?'

'Six years old, I think she said. She talks of the "responsibility of bringing up an orphan".'

'George, what time is it?' Esther asked suddenly.

'About nine o'clock.'

'Would you mind coming out with me?'

'I should like it. Where shall we go?'

'To St Adhelm's! It is close by here. There is a special late service tonight, and Mrs Arne is sure to be there.'

'Oh, Esther – curiosity!'

'No, not mere curiosity. Don't you see if it is my Mrs Arne who talked to you like this, it is very serious? I have thought her ill for a long time; but as ill as that! – '

At St Adhelm's Church, Esther Graham pointed out a woman who was kneeling beside a pillar in an attitude of intense devotion and abandonment. She rose from her knees, and turned her rapt face up towards the pulpit whence the Reverend Ralph Bligh was holding his impassioned discourse. George Graham touched his cousin on the shoulder, and motioned to her to leave her place on the outermost rank of worshippers.

'That is the woman!' said he.

IV

'*Mem. – to go and see Mrs Arne.* The doctor came across this note on his blotting-pad one day six weeks later. His daughter was out of town. He had heard nothing of the Arnes since her departure. He had promised to go and see her. He was a little conscience-stricken. Yet another week elapsed before he found time to call upon the daughter of his old tutor.

At the corner of Tite Street he met Mrs Arne's husband, and stopped. A doctor's professional kindliness of manner is, or ought to be, independent of his personal likings and dislikings, and there was a pleasant cordiality about his greeting which should have provoked a corresponding fervour on the part of Edward Arne.

'How are you, Arne?' Graham said. 'I was on my way to call on your wife.'

'Ah – yes!' said Edward Arne, with the ascending inflection of polite acquiescence. A ray of blue from his eyes rested transitorily on the doctor's face, and in that short moment the latter noted its intolerable vacuity, and for the first time in his life felt a sharp pang of sympathy for the wife of such a husband.

'I suppose you are off to your club? – er – goodbye!' he wound up abruptly. With the best will in the world he somehow found it almost impossible to carry on a conversation with Edward Arne, who raised his hand to his hat-brim in token of salutation, smiled sweetly, and walked on.

'He really is extraordinarily good-looking,' reflected the doctor, as he watched him down the street and safely over the crossing with a certain degree of solicitude for which he could not exactly account. 'And yet one feels one's vitality ebbing out at the fingerends as one talks to him. I shall begin to believe in Esther's absurd fancies about him soon. Ah, there's the little girl!' he exclaimed, as he turned into Cheyne Walk and caught sight of her with her nurse, making violent demonstrations to attract his attention. 'She is alive, at any rate. How is your mother, Dolly?' he asked.

'Quite well, thank you,' was the child's reply. She added, 'She's crying. She sent me away because I looked at her. So I did. Her cheeks are quite red.'

'Run away – run away and play!' said the doctor nervously. He ascended the steps of the house, and rang the bell very gently and neatly.

'Not at – ' began Foster, with the intonation of polite falsehood, but stopped on seeing the doctor, who, with his daughter, was a privileged person. 'Mrs Arne will see you, sir.'

'Mrs Arne is not alone?' he said interrogatively.

'Yes, sir, quite alone. I have just taken tea in.'

Dr Graham's doubts were prompted by the low murmur as of a voice, or voices, which came to him through the open door of the room at the head of the stairs. He paused and listened while Foster stood by, merely remarking, 'Mrs Arne do talk to herself sometimes, sir.'

It was Mrs Arne's voice – the doctor recognised it now. It was not the voice of a sane or healthy woman. He at once mentally removed his visit from the category of a morning call, and prepared for a semi-professional enquiry.

'Don't announce me,' he said to Foster, and quietly entered the back drawing-room, which was separated by a heavy tapestry portière from the room where Mrs Arne sat, with an open book on the table before her, from which she had been apparently reading aloud. Her hands were now clasped tightly over her face, and when, presently, she removed them and began feverishly to turn page after page of her book, the crimson of her cheeks was seamed with white where her fingers had impressed themselves.

The doctor wondered if she saw him, for though her eyes were fixed in his direction, there was no apprehension in them. She went on reading, and it was the text, mingled with passionate interjections and fragmentary utterances, of the burial service that met his ears.

' "For as in Adam all die!" ' All die! It says all! For he must reign . . . The last enemy that shall be destroyed is Death. What shall they do if the dead rise not at all! . . . I die daily . . . ! Daily! No, no, better get it over . . . dead and buried . . . out of sight, out of mind . . . under a stone. Dead men don't come back. . . . Go on! Get it over. I want to hear the earth rattle on the coffin, and then I shall know it is done. "Flesh and blood cannot inherit!" Oh, what did I do? What have I done? Why did I wish it so fervently? Why did I pray for it so earnestly? God gave me my wish – '

'Alice! Alice!' groaned the doctor.

She looked up. ' "When this corruptible shall have put on incorruption – " "Dust to dust, ashes to ashes, earth to earth – " Yes, that is it. "After death, though worms destroy this body – " ' She flung the book aside and sobbed. 'That is what I was afraid of. My God! My God! Down there – in the dark – for ever and ever and ever! I could not bear to think of it! My Edward! And so I interfered . . . and prayed . . . and prayed till . . . Oh! I am punished. Flesh and blood could not inherit! I kept him there – I would not let him go . . . I kept him . . . I prayed . . . I denied him Christian burial . . . Oh, how could I know . . . '

'Good heavens, Alice!' said Dr Graham, coming sensibly forward, 'what does this mean? I have heard of schoolgirls going through the marriage service by themselves, but the burial service – '

He laid down his hat and went on severely, 'What have you to do with such things? Your child is flourishing – your husband alive and here – '

'And who kept him here?' interrupted Alice Arne fiercely, accepting the fact of his appearance without comment.

'You did,' he answered quickly, 'with your care and tenderness. I believe the warmth of your body, as you lay beside him for that half-hour, maintained the vital heat during that extraordinary suspension of the heart's action which made us all give him up for dead. You were his best doctor, and brought him back to us.'

'Yes, it was I – it was I – you need not tell me it was I!'

'Come, be thankful!' he said cheerfully. 'Put that book away, and give me some tea. I'm very cold.'

'Oh, Dr Graham, how thoughtless of me!' said Mrs Arne, rallying at the slight imputation on her politeness he had purposely made. She tottered to the bell and rang it before he could anticipate her.

'Another cup,' she said quite calmly to Foster, who answered it. Then she sat down quivering all over with the suddenness of the constraint put upon her.

'Yes, sit down and tell me all about it,' said Dr Graham good-humouredly, at the same time observing her with the closeness he gave to difficult cases.

'There is nothing to tell,' she said simply, shaking her head, and futilely altering the position of the teacups on the tray. 'It all happened years ago. Nothing can be done now. Will you have sugar?'

He drank his tea and made conversation. He talked to her of some Dante lectures she was attending; of some details connected with her child's kindergarten classes. These subjects did not interest her. There was a subject she wished to discuss, he could see that a question trembled on her tongue, and tried to lead up to it.

She introduced it herself, quite quietly, over a second cup. 'Sugar, Dr Graham? I forget. Dr Graham, tell me, do you believe that prayers – wicked, unreasonable prayers – are granted?'

He helped himself to another slice of bread and butter before answering.

'Well,' he said slowly, 'it seems hard to believe that every fool who has a voice to pray with and a brain to conceive idiotic requests with should be permitted to interfere with the economy of the universe. As a rule, if people were long-sighted enough to see the result of their petitions, I fancy very few of us would venture to interfere.'

Mrs Arne groaned.

She was a good churchwoman, Graham knew, and he did not wish to sap her faith in any way, so he said no more, but inwardly wondered if a too rigid interpretation of some of the religious dogmas of the vicar of St Adhelm's, her spiritual adviser, was not the clue to her distress. Then she put another question –

'Eh! What?' he said. 'Do I believe in ghosts? I will believe you if you will tell me you have seen one.'

'You know, doctor,' she went on, 'I was always afraid of ghosts – of spirits – things unseen. I couldn't ever read about them. I could not bear the idea of someone in the room with me that I could not see. There was a text that always frightened me that hung up in my room: "Thou, God, seest me!" It frightened me when I was a child, whether I had been doing wrong or not. But now,' shuddering, 'I think there are worse things than ghosts.'

'Well, now, what sort of things?' he asked good-humouredly. 'Astral bodies?'

She leaned forward and laid her hot hand on his.

'Oh, doctor, tell me, if a spirit – without the body we know it by – is terrible, what of a body' – her voice sank to a whisper, 'a body – senseless – lonely – stranded on this earth – without a spirit?'

She was watching his face anxiously. He was divided between a morbid inclination to laugh and the feeling of intense discomfort provoked by this wretched scene. He longed to give the conversation a more cheerful turn, yet did not wish to offend her by changing it too abruptly.

'I have heard of people not being able to keep body and soul together,' he replied at last, 'but I am not aware that practically such a division of forces has ever been achieved. And if we could only accept the theory of the de-spiritualised body, what a number of antipathetic people now wandering about in the world it would account for!'

The piteous gaze of her eyes seemed to seek to ward off the blow of his misplaced jocularity. He left his seat and sat down on the couch beside her.

'Poor child! poor girl! you are ill, you are over-excited. What is it? Tell me,' he asked her as tenderly as the father she had lost in early life might have done. Her head sank on his shoulder.

'Are you unhappy?' he asked her gently.

'Yes!'

'You are too much alone. Get your mother or your sister to come and stay with you.'

'They won't come,' she wailed. 'They say the house is like a grave. Edward has made himself a study in the basement. It's an impossible room – but he has moved all his things in, and I can't – I won't go to him there . . .'

'You're wrong. For it's only a fad,' said Dr Graham, 'he'll tire of it. And you must see more people somehow. It's a pity my daughter is away. Had you any visitors today?'

'Not a soul has crossed the threshold for eighteen days.'

'We must change all that,' said the doctor vaguely. 'Meantime you must cheer up. Why, you have no need to think of ghosts and graves – no need to be melancholy – you have your husband and your child – '

'I have my child – yes.'

The doctor took hold of Mrs Arne by the shoulder, and held her a little away from him. He thought he had found the cause of her trouble – a more commonplace one than he had supposed.

'I have known you, Alice, since you were a child,' he said gravely. 'Answer me! You love your husband, don't you?'

'Yes.' It was as if she were answering futile prefatory questions in the witness-box. Yet he saw by the intense excitement in her eyes that he had come to the point she feared and yet desired to bring forward.

'And he loves you?'

She was silent.

'Well, then, if you love each other, what more can you want? Why do you say you have only your child in that absurd way?'

She was still silent, and he gave her a little shake.

'Tell me, have you and he had any difference lately? Is there any – coldness – any – temporary estrangement between you?'

He was hardly prepared for the burst of foolish laughter that proceeded from the demure Mrs Arne as she rose and confronted him, all the blood in her body seeming for the moment to rush to her usually pale cheeks.

'Coldness! Temporary estrangement! If that were all! Oh, is everyone blind but me? There is all the world between us! – all the difference between this world and the next!'

She sat down again beside the doctor and whispered in his ear, and her words were like a breath of hot wind from some Gehenna of the soul.

'Oh, doctor, I have borne it for six years, and I must speak. No other woman could bear what I have borne, and yet be alive! And I loved him so; you don't know how I loved him! That was it – that was my crime – '

'Crime?' repeated the doctor.

'Yes, crime! It was impious, don't you see? But I have been punished. Oh, doctor, you don't know what my life is! Listen! Listen! I must tell you. To live with a – At first, before I guessed, when I used to put my arms round him, and he merely submitted – and then it dawned on me what I was kissing! It is enough to turn a living woman into stone – for I am living, though sometimes I forget it. Yes, I am a live woman, though I live in a grave. Think what it is! – to wonder every night if you will be alive in the morning, to lie down every night in an open grave – to smell death in every corner – every room – to breathe death – to touch it . . . '

The portière in front of the door shook, a hoopstick parted it, a round white-clad bundle supported on a pair of mottled red legs peeped in, pushing a hoop in front of her. The child made no noise. Mrs Arne seemed to have heard her, however. She slewed round violently as she sat on the sofa beside Dr Graham, leaving her hot hands clasped in his.

'You ask Dolly,' she exclaimed. 'She knows it, too – she feels it.'

'No, no, Alice, this won't do!' the doctor adjured her very low. Then he raised his voice and ordered the child from the room. He had managed to lift Mrs Arne's feet and lay her full length on the sofa by the time the maid reappeared. She had fainted.

He pulled down her eyelids and satisfied himself as to certain facts he had up till now dimly apprehended. When Mrs Arne's maid returned, he gave her mistress over to her care and proceeded to Edward Arne's new study in the basement.

'Morphia!' he muttered to himself, as he stumbled and faltered through gaslit passages, where furtive servants eyed him and scuttled to their burrows.

'What is he burying himself down here for?' he thought. 'Is it to get out of her way? They *are* a nervous pair of them!'

Arne was sunk in a large armchair drawn up before the fire. There was no other light, except a faint reflection from the gas-lamp in the road, striking down past the iron bars of the window that was sunk below the level of the street. The room was comfortless and empty, there was little furniture in it except a large bookcase at Arne's right hand and a table with a Tantalus on it standing some way off. There was a faded portrait in pastel of Alice Arne over the mantelpiece, and beside it, a poor pendant, a pen-and-ink sketch of the master of the house. They were quite discrepant, in size and medium, but they appeared to look at each other with the stolid attentiveness of newly married people.

'Seedy, Arne?' Graham said.

'Rather, today. Poke the fire for me, will you?'

'I've known you quite seven years,' said the doctor cheerfully, 'so I presume I can do that. . . . There, now! . . . And I'll presume further – What have we got here?'

He took a small bottle smartly out of Edward Arne's fingers and raised his eyebrows. Edward Arne had rendered it up agreeably; he did not seem upset or annoyed.

'Morphia. It isn't a habit. I only got hold of the stuff yesterday – found it about the house. Alice was very jumpy all day, and communicated her nerves to me, I suppose. I've none as a rule, but do you know, Graham, I seem to be getting them – feel things a good deal more than I did, and want to talk about them.'

'What, are you growing a soul?' said the doctor carelessly, lighting a cigarette.

'Heaven forbid!' Arne answered equably. 'I've done very well without one all these years. But I'm fond of old Alice, you know, in my own way. When I was a young man, I was quite different. I took things hardly and got excited about them. Yes, excited. I was wild about Alice, wild! Yes, by Jove! though she has forgotten all about it.'

'Not that, but still it's natural she should long for some little demonstration of affection now and then . . . and she'd be awfully distressed if she saw you fooling with that bottle of morphia! You know, Arne, after that narrow squeak you had of it five years ago, Alice and I have a good right to consider that your life belongs to us!'

Edward Arne settled in his chair and replied, rather fretfully –

'All very well, but you didn't manage to do the job thoroughly. You didn't turn me out lively enough to please Alice. She's annoyed because when I take her in my arms, I don't hold her tight enough. I'm too quiet, too

languid! . . . Hang it all, Graham, I believe she'd like me to stand for
Parliament! . . . Why can't she let me just go along my own way? Surely a
man who's come through an illness like mine can be let off parlour tricks?
All this worry – it culminated the other day when I said I wanted to colonise
a room down here! and did, with a spurt that took it out of me horribly – all
this worry, I say, seeing her upset and so on, keeps me low, and so I feel as if
I wanted to take drugs to soothe me.'

'Soothe!' said Graham. 'This stuff is more than soothing if you take
enough of it. I'll send you something more like what you want, and I'll take
this away, by your leave.'

'I really can't argue!' replied Arne . . . 'If you see Alice tell her you find me
fairly comfortable and don't put her off this room. I really like it best. She
can come and see me here. I keep a good fire, tell her . . . I feel as if I wanted
to sleep . . . .' he added brusquely.

'You have been indulging already,' said Graham softly. Arne had begun to
doze off. His cushion had sagged down, the doctor stooped to rearrange it,
carelessly laying the little phial for the moment in a crease of the rug
covering the man's knees.

Mrs Arne in her mourning dress was crossing the hall as he came to the top
of the basement steps and pushed open the swing door. She was giving some
orders to Foster the butler, who disappeared as the doctor advanced.

'You're about again,' he said, 'good girl!'

'Too silly of me,' she said, 'to be hysterical! After all these years! One
should be able to keep one's own counsel. But it is over now, I promise I will
never speak of it again.'

'We frightened poor Dolly dreadfully. I had to order her out like a
regiment of soldiers.'

'Yes, I know. I'm going to her now.'

On his suggestion that she should look in on her husband first she looked
askance.

'Down there!'

'Yes, that's his fancy. Let him be. He is a good deal depressed about
himself and you. He notices a great deal more than you think. He isn't quite
as apathetic as you describe him to be . . . Come here!' He led her into the
unlit dining-room a little way. 'You expect too much, my dear. You do
really! You make too many demands on the vitality you saved.'

'What did one save him for?' she asked fiercely. She continued more
quietly, 'I know. I am going to be different.'

'Not you,' said Dr Graham fondly. He was very partial to Alice Arne in
spite of her silliness. 'You'll worry about Edward till the end of the chapter.
I know you. And – ' he turned her round by the shoulder so that she fronted
the light in the hall – 'you elusive thing, let me have a good look at you . . .
Hum! Your eyes, they're a bit starey . . . '

He let her go again with a sigh of impotence. Something must be done . . .
soon . . . he must think . . . He got hold of his coat and began to get into it . . .

Mrs Arne smiled, buttoned a button for him and then opened the front
door, like a good hostess, a very little way. With a quick flirt of his hat he
was gone, and she heard the clap of his brougham door and the order,
'Home.'

'Been saying goodbye to that thief Graham?' said her husband gently, when
she entered his room, her pale eyes staring a little, her thin hand busy at the
front of her dress . . .

'Thief? Why? One moment! Where's your switch?'

She found it and turned on a blaze of light from which her husband
seemed to shrink.

'Well, he carried off my drops. Afraid of my poisoning myself, I suppose?'

'Or acquiring the morphia habit,' said his wife in a dull level voice, 'as I
have.'

She paused. He made no comment. Then, picking up the little phial Dr
Graham had left in the crease of the rug, she spoke –

'You are the thief, Edward, as it happens, this is mine.'

'Is it? I found it knocking about: I didn't know it was yours. Well, will you
give me some?'

'I will, if you like.'

'Well, dear, decide. You know I am in your hands and Graham's. He was
rubbing that into me today.'

'Poor lamb!' she said derisively; 'I'd not allow my doctor, or my wife
either, to dictate to me whether I should put an end to myself, or not.'

'Ah, but you've got a spirit, you see!' Arne yawned. 'However, let me have
a go at the stuff and then you put it on top of a wardrobe or a shelf, where I
shall know it is, but never reach out to get it, I promise you.'

'No, you wouldn't reach out a hand to keep yourself alive, let alone kill
yourself,' said she. 'That is you all over, Edward.'

'And don't you see that is why I did die,' he said, with earnestness
unexpected by her. 'And then, unfortunately, you and Graham bustled up
and wouldn't let nature take its course . . . I rather wish you hadn't been so
officious.'

'And let you stay dead,' said she carelessly. 'But at the time I cared for you
so much that I should have had to kill myself, or commit suttee like a Hindu
widow. Ah, well!'

She reached out for a glass half-full of water that stood on the low ledge of
the bookcase close by the arm of his chair . . . 'Will this glass do? What's in
it? Only water? How much morphia shall I give you? An overdose?'

'I don't care if you do, and that's a fact.'

'It was a joke, Edward,' she said piteously.

'No joke to me. This fag end of life I've clawed hold of doesn't interest me. And I'm bound to be interested in what I'm doing or I'm no good. I'm no earthly good now. I don't enjoy life, I've nothing to enjoy it with – in here' – he struck his breast. 'It's like a dull party one goes to by accident. All I want to do is to get into a cab and go home.'

His wife stood over him with the half-full glass in one hand and the little bottle in the other. Her eyes dilated . . . her chest heaved . . .

'Edward!' she breathed. 'Was it all so useless?'

'Was what useless? Yes, as I was telling you, I go as one in a dream – a bad, bad dream, like the dreams I used to have when I overworked at college. I was brilliant, Alice, brilliant, do you hear? At some cost, I expect! Now I hate people – my fellow creatures. I've left them. They come and go – jostling me and pushing me on the pavements as I go along avoiding them. Do you know where they should be, really, in relation to me?'

He rose a little in his seat – she stepped nervously aside, made as if to put down the bottle and the glass she was holding, then thought better of it and continued to extend them mechanically.

'They should be over my head. I've already left them and their petty nonsense of living. They mean nothing to me, no more than if they were ghosts walking. Or perhaps it's I who am a ghost to them? . . . You don't understand it. It's because I suppose you have no imagination. You just know what you want and do your best to get it. You blurt out your blessed petition to your deity and the idea that you're irrelevant never enters your head, soft, persistent, high-church thing that you are! . . '

Alice Arne smiled, and balanced the objects she was holding. He motioned her to pour out the liquid from one to the other, but she took no heed; she was listening with all her ears. It was the nearest approach to the language of compliment, to anything in the way of loverlike personalities that she had heard fall from his lips since his illness. He went on, becoming as it were lukewarm to his subject –

'But the worst of it is that once break the cord that links you to humanity – it can't be mended. Man doesn't live by bread alone . . . or lives to disappoint you. What am I to you, without my own poor personality? . . . Don't stare so, Alice! I haven't talked so much or so intimately for ages, have I? Let me try and have it out . . . Are you in any sort of hurry?'

'No, Edward.'

'Pour that stuff out and have done . . . Well, Alice, it's a queer feeling, I tell you. One goes about with one's looks on the ground like a man who eyes the bed he is going to lie down in, and longs for. Alice, the crust of the earth seems a barrier between me and my own place. I want to scratch the boardings with my nails and shriek something like this: "Let me get down to you all, there where I belong!" It's a horrible sensation, like a vampire reversed! . . . '

'Is that why you insisted on having this room in the basement?' she asked breathlessly.

'Yes, I can't bear being upstairs, somehow. Here, with these barred windows and stone-cold floors . . . I can see the people's feet walking above there in the street . . . one has some sort of illusion . . .'

'Oh!' She shivered and her eyes travelled like those of a caged creature round the bare room and fluttered when they rested on the sombre windows imperiously barred. She dropped her gaze to the stone flags that showed beyond the oasis of Turkey carpet on which Arne's chair stood . . . Then to the door, the door that she had closed on entering. It had heavy bolts, but they were not drawn against her, though by the look of her eyes it seemed she half imagined they were . . .

She made a step forward and moved her hands slightly. She looked down on them and what they held . . . then changed the relative positions of the two objects and held the bottle over the glass . . .

'Yes, come along!' her husband said. 'Are you going to be all day giving it me?'

With a jerk, she poured the liquid out into a glass and handed it to him. She looked away – towards the door . . .

'Ah, your way of escape!' said he, following her eyes. Then he drank, painstakingly.

The empty bottle fell out of her hands. She wrung them, murmuring – 'Oh, if I had only known!'

'Known what? That I should go near to cursing you for bringing me back?' He fixed his cold eyes on her, as the liquid passed slowly over his tongue . . . 'Or that you would end by taking back the gift you gave?'

Sredni Vashtar

SAKI (H. H. MUNRO)

CONRADIN WAS TEN YEARS OLD, and the doctor had pronounced his professional opinion that the boy would not live another five years. The doctor was silky and effete, and counted for little, but his opinion was endorsed by Mrs De Ropp, who counted for nearly everything. Mrs De Ropp was Conradin's cousin and guardian, and in his eyes she represented those three-fifths of the world that are necessary and disagreeable and real; the other two-fifths, in perpetual antagonism to the foregoing, were summed up in himself and his imagination. One of these days Conradin supposed he would succumb to the mastering pressure of wearisome necessary things – such as illnesses and coddling restrictions and drawn-out dullness. Without his imagination, which was rampant under the spur of loneliness, he would have succumbed long ago.

Mrs De Ropp would never, in her honestest moments, have confessed to herself that she disliked Conradin, though she might have been dimly aware that thwarting him 'for his good' was a duty which she did not find particularly irksome. Conradin hated her with a desperate sincerity which he was perfectly able to mask. Such few pleasures as he could contrive for himself gained an added relish from the likelihood that they would be displeasing to his guardian, and from the realm of his imagination she was locked out – an unclean thing, which should find no entrance.

In the dull, cheerless garden, overlooked by so many windows that were ready to open with a message not to do this or that, or a reminder that medicines were due, he found little attraction. The few fruit-trees that it contained were set jealously apart from his plucking, as though they were rare specimens of their kind blooming in an arid waste; it would probably have been difficult to find a market-gardener who would have offered ten shillings for their entire yearly produce. In a forgotten corner, however, almost hidden behind a dismal shrubbery, was a disused toolshed of respectable proportions, and within its walls Conradin found a haven, something that took on the varying aspects of a playroom and a cathedral. He had peopled it with a legion of familiar phantoms, evoked partly from fragments of history and partly from his own brain, but it also boasted two inmates of flesh and blood. In one corner lived a ragged-plumaged Houdan hen, on which the boy lavished an affection that had scarcely another outlet. Further back in the gloom stood a large hutch, divided into two compart-ments, one of which was fronted with close iron bars. This was the abode of a large polecat-ferret, which a friendly butcher-boy had once smuggled, cage and all, into its present quarters, in exchange for a long-secreted hoard of small silver. Conradin was dreadfully afraid of the lithe, sharp-fanged beast, but it was his most treasured possession. Its very presence in the tool-shed was a secret and fearful joy, to be kept scrupulously from the knowledge of the Woman, as he privately dubbed his cousin. And one day, out of heaven knows what material, he spun the beast a wonderful name, and from that moment it grew into a god and a religion. The Woman indulged in religion once a week at a church near by, and took Conradin with her, but to him the church service was an alien rite in the House of Rimmon. Every Thursday, in the dim and musty silence of the toolshed, he worshipped with mystic and elaborate ceremonial before the wooden hutch where dwelt Sredni Vashtar, the great ferret. Red flowers in their season and scarlet berries in the wintertime were offered at his shrine, for he was a god who laid some special stress on the fierce impatient side of things, as opposed to the Woman's religion, which, as far as Conradin could observe, went to great lengths in the contrary direction. And on great festivals powdered nutmeg was strewn in front of his hutch, an important feature of the offering being that the nutmeg had to be stolen. These festivals were of irregular occurrence, and were chiefly appointed to celebrate some passing event. On one occasion, when Mrs De Ropp suffered from acute toothache for three days, Conradin kept up the festival during the entire three days, and almost succeeded in persuading himself that Sredni Vashtar was personally responsible for the toothache. If the malady had lasted for another day the supply of nutmeg would have given out.

The Houdan hen was never drawn into the cult of Sredni Vashtar. Conradin had long ago settled that she was an Anabaptist. He did not pretend to have the remotest knowledge as to what an Anabaptist was, but he privately hoped that it was dashing and not very respectable. Mrs De Ropp was the ground plan on which he based and detested all respectability.

After a while Conradin's absorption in the toolshed began to attract the notice of his guardian. 'It is not good for him to be pottering down there in all weathers,' she promptly decided, and at breakfast one morning she announced that the Houdan hen had been sold and taken away overnight. With her short-sighted eyes she peered at Conradin, waiting for an outbreak of rage and sorrow, which she was ready to rebuke with a flow of excellent precepts and reasoning. But Conradin said nothing: there was nothing to be said. Something perhaps in his white set face gave her a momentary qualm, for at tea that afternoon there was toast on the table, a delicacy which she usually banned on the ground that it was bad for him; also because the making of it 'gave trouble', a deadly offence in the middle-class feminine eye.

'I thought you liked toast,' she exclaimed, with an injured air, observing that he did not touch it.

'Sometimes,' said Conradin.

In the shed that evening there was an innovation in the worship of the hutch-god. Conradin had been wont to chant his praises, tonight he asked a boon.

'Do one thing for me, Sredni Vashtar.'

The thing was not specified. As Sredni Vashtar was a god he must be supposed to know. And choking back a sob as he looked at that other empty corner, Conradin went back to the world he so hated.

And every night, in the welcome darkness of his bedroom, and every evening in the dusk of the toolshed, Conradin's bitter litany went up: 'Do one thing for me, Sredni Vashtar.'

Mrs De Ropp noticed that the visits to the shed did not cease, and one day she made a further journey of inspection.

'What are you keeping in that locked hutch?' she asked. 'I believe it's guinea-pigs. I'll have them all cleared away.'

Conradin shut his lips tight, but the Woman ransacked his bedroom till she found the carefully hidden key, and forthwith marched down to the shed to complete her discovery. It was a cold afternoon, and Conradin had been bidden to keep to the house. From the furthest window of the dining-room the door of the shed could just be seen beyond the corner of the shrubbery, and there Conradin stationed himself. He saw the Woman enter, and then he imagined her opening the door of the sacred hutch and peering down with her short-sighted eyes into the thick straw bed where his god lay hidden. Perhaps she would prod at the straw in her clumsy impatience. And Conradin fervently breathed his prayer for the last time. But he knew as he prayed that he did not believe. He knew that the Woman would come out presently with that pursed smile he loathed so well on her face, and that in an hour or two the gardener would carry away his wonderful god, a god no longer, but a simple brown ferret in a hutch. And he knew that the Woman would triumph always as she triumphed now and that he would grow ever more sickly under her pestering and domineering and superior wisdom, till one day nothing would matter much more with him, and the doctor would be proved right. And in the sting and misery of his defeat, he began to chant loudly and defiantly the hymn of his threatened idol: Sredni Vashtar went forth, His thoughts were red thoughts and his teeth were white. His enemies called for peace, but he brought them death. Sredni Vashtar the Beautiful.

And then of a sudden he stopped his chanting and drew closer to the window-pane. The door of the shed still stood ajar as it had been left, and the minutes were slipping by. They were long minutes, but they slipped by nevertheless. He watched the starlings running and flying in little parties across the lawn; he counted them over and over again, with one eye always on that swinging door. A sour-faced maid came in to lay the table for tea, and still Conradin stood and waited and watched. Hope had crept by inches into his heart, and now a look of triumph began to blaze in his eyes that had only known the wistful patience of defeat. Under his breath, with a furtive exultation, he began once again the paean of victory and devastation. And presently his eyes were rewarded: out through that doorway came a long, low, yellow-and-brown beast, with eyes a-blink at the waning daylight, and dark wet stains around the fur of jaws and throat. Conradin dropped on his knees. The great polecat-ferret made its way down to a small brook at the foot of the garden, drank for a moment, then crossed a little plank bridge and was lost to sight in the bushes. Such was the passing of Sredni Vashtar.

'Tea is ready,' said the sour-faced maid; 'where is the mistress?'

'She went down to the shed some time ago,' said Conradin.

And while the maid went to summon her mistress to tea, Conradin fished a toasting-fork out of the sideboard drawer and proceeded to toast himself a piece of bread. And during the toasting of it and the buttering of it with much butter and the slow enjoyment of eating it, Conradin listened to the noises and silences which fell in quick spasms beyond the dining-room door. The loud foolish screaming of the maid, the answering chorus of wondering ejaculations from the kitchen region, the scuttering footsteps and hurried embassies for outside help, and then, after a lull, the scared sobbings and the shuffling tread of those who bore a heavy burden into the house.

'Whoever will break it to the poor child? I couldn't for the life of me!' exclaimed a shrill voice. And while they debated the matter among themselves, Conradin made himself another piece of toast.

Aylmer Vance and the Vampire

A. AND C. ASKEW

AYLMER VANCE had rooms in Dover Street, Piccadilly, and now that I had decided to follow in his footsteps and to accept him as my instructor in matters psychic, I found it convenient to lodge in the same house. Aylmer and I quickly became close friends, and he showed me how to develop that faculty of clairvoyance which I had possessed without being aware of it. And I may say at once that this particular faculty of mine proved of service on several important occasions.

At the same time I made myself useful to Vance in other ways, not the least of which was that of acting as recorder of his many strange adventures. For himself, he never cared much about publicity, and it was some time before I could persuade him, in the interests of science, to allow me to give any detailed account of his experiences to the world.

The incidents which I will now narrate occurred very soon after we had taken up our residence together, and while I was still, so to speak, a novice.

It was about ten o'clock in the morning that a visitor was announced. He sent up a card which bore upon it the name of Paul Davenant.

The name was familiar to me, and I wondered if this could be the same Mr Davenant who was so well known for his polo playing and for his success as an amateur rider, especially over the hurdles? He was a young man of wealth and position, and I recollected that he had married, about a year ago, a girl who was reckoned the greatest beauty of the season. All the illustrated papers had given their portraits at the time, and I remember thinking what a remarkably handsome couple they made.

Mr Davenant was ushered in, and at first I was uncertain as to whether this could be the individual whom I had in mind, so wan and pale and ill did he appear. A finely built, upstanding man at the time of his marriage, he had now acquired a languid droop of the shoulders and a shuffling gait, while his face, especially about the lips, was bloodless to an alarming degree.

And yet it was the same man, for behind all this I could recognise the shadow of the good looks that had once distinguished Paul Davenant.

He took the chair which Aylmer offered him – after the usual preliminary civilities had been exchanged – and then glanced doubtfully in my direction. 'I wish to consult you privately, Mr Vance,' he said. 'The matter is of considerable importance to myself, and, if I may say so, of a somewhat delicate nature.'

Of course I rose immediately to withdraw from the room, but Vance laid his hand upon my arm.

'If the matter is connected with research in my particular line, Mr Davenant,' he said, 'if there is any investigation you wish me to take up on your behalf, I shall be glad if you will include Mr Dexter in your confidence. Mr Dexter assists me in my work. But, of course – '

'Oh, no,' interrupted the other, 'if that is the case, pray let Mr Dexter remain. I think,' he added, glancing at me with a friendly smile, 'that you are an Oxford man, are you not, Mr Dexter? It was before my time, but I have heard of your name in connection with the river. You rowed at Henley, unless I am very much mistaken.'

I admitted the fact, with a pleasurable sensation of pride. I was very keen upon rowing in those days, and a man's prowess at school and college always remain dear to his heart.

After this we quickly became on friendly terms, and Paul Davenant proceeded to take Aylmer and myself into his confidence.

He began by calling attention to his personal appearance. 'You would hardly recognise me for the same man I was a year ago,' he said. 'I've been losing flesh steadily for the last six months. I came up from Scotland about a week ago, to consult a London doctor. I've seen two – in fact, they've held a sort of consultation over me – but the result, I may say, is far from satisfactory. They don't seem to know what is really the matter with me.'

'Anaemia – heart,' suggested Vance. He was scrutinising his visitor keenly, and yet without any particular appearance of doing so. 'I believe it not infrequently happens that you athletes overdo yourselves – put too much strain upon the heart – '

'My heart is quite sound,' responded Davenant. 'Physically it is in perfect condition. The trouble seems to be that it hasn't enough blood to pump into my veins. The doctors wanted to know if I had met with an accident involving a great loss of blood – but I haven't. I've had no accident at all, and as for anaemia, well, I don't seem to show the ordinary symptoms of it. The inexplicable thing is that I've lost blood without knowing it, and apparently this has been going on for some time, for I've been getting steadily worse. It was almost imperceptible at first – not a sudden collapse, you understand, but a gradual failure of health.'

'I wonder,' remarked Vance slowly, 'what induced you to consult me? For you know, of course, the direction in which I pursue my investigations. May I ask if you have reason to consider that your state of health is due to some cause which we may describe as superphysical?'

A slight colour came to Davenant's white cheeks.

'There are curious circumstances,' he said in a low and earnest tone of voice. 'I've been turning them over in my mind, trying to see light through them. I dare say it's all the sheerest folly – and I must tell you that I'm not in the least a superstitious sort of man. I don't mean to say that I'm absolutely incredulous, but I've never given thought to such things – I've led too active a life. But, as I have said, there are curious circumstances about my case, and that is why I decided upon consulting you.'

'Will you tell me everything without reserve?' said Vance. I could see that he was interested. He was sitting up in his chair, his feet supported on a stool, his elbows on his knees, his chin in his hands – a favourite attitude of his. 'Have you,' he suggested, slowly, 'any mark upon your body, anything that you might associate, however remotely, with your present weakness and ill-health?'

'It's a curious thing that you should ask me that question,' returned Davenant, 'because I have got a curious mark, a sort of scar, that I can't account for. But I showed it to the doctors, and they assured me that it could have nothing whatever to do with my condition. In any case, if it had, it was something altogether outside their experience I think they imagined it to be nothing more than a birthmark, a sort of mole, for they asked me if I'd had it all my life. But that I can swear I haven't. I only noticed it for the first time about six months ago, when my health began to fail. But you can see for yourself.'

He loosened his collar and bared his throat. Vance rose and made a careful scrutiny of the suspicious mark. It was situated a very little to the left of the central line, just above the clavicle, and, as Vance pointed out, directly over the big vessels of the throat. My friend called to me so that I might examine it, too. Whatever the opinion of the doctors may have been, Aylmer was obviously deeply interested.

And yet there was very little to show. The skin was quite intact, and there was no sign of inflammation. There were two red marks, about an inch apart, each of which was inclined to be crescent in shape. They were more visible than they might otherwise have been owing to the peculiar whiteness of Davenant's skin.

'It can't be anything of importance,' said Davenant, with a slightly uneasy laugh. 'I'm inclined to think the marks are dying away.'

'Have you ever noticed them more inflamed than they are at present?' enquired Vance. 'If so, was it at any special time?'

Davenant reflected. 'Yes,' he replied slowly, 'there have been times, usually, I think perhaps invariably, when I wake up in the morning, that I've noticed them larger and more angry looking. And I've felt a slight sensation of pain – a tingling – oh, very slight, and I've never worried about it. Only now you suggest it to my mind, I believe that those same mornings I have felt particularly tired and done up – a sensation of lassitude absolutely unusual to me. And once, Mr Vance, I remember quite distinctly that there was a stain of blood close to the mark. I didn't think anything of it at the time, and just wiped it away.'

'I see.' Aylmer Vance resumed his seat and invited his visitor to do the same. 'And now,' he resumed, 'you said, Mr Davenant, that there are certain peculiar circumstances you wish to acquaint me with. Will you do so?'

And so Davenant readjusted his collar and proceeded to tell his story. I will tell it as far as I can, without any reference to the occasional interruptions of Vance and myself.

Paul Davenant, as I have said, was a man of wealth and position, and so, in every sense of the word, he was a suitable husband for Miss Jessica MacThane, the young lady who eventually became his wife. Before coming to the incidents attending his loss of health, he had a great deal to recount about Miss MacThane and her family history

She was of Scottish descent, and although she had certain characteristic features of her race, she was not really Scotch in appearance. Hers was the beauty of the far south rather than that of the Highlands in which she had her origin. Names are not always suited to their owners, and Miss MacThane's was peculiarly inappropriate. She had, in fact, been christened Jessica in a sort of pathetic effort to counteract her obvious departure from normal type. There was a reason for this which we were soon to learn.

Miss MacThane was especially remarkable for her wonderful red hair, hair such as one hardly ever sees outside of Italy – not the Celtic red – and it was so long that it reached to her feet, and it had an extraordinary gloss upon it so that it seemed almost to have individual life of its own. Then she had just the complexion that one would expect with such hair, the purest ivory white, and not in the least marred by freckles, as is so often the case with red-haired girls. Her beauty was derived from an ancestress who had been brought to Scotland from some foreign shore – no one knew exactly whence.

Davenant fell in love with her almost at once and he had every reason to believe, in spite of her many admirers, that his love was returned. At this time he knew very little about her personal history. He was aware only that she was very wealthy in her own right, an orphan, and the last representative of a race that had once been famous in the annals of history – or rather infamous, for the MacThanes had distinguished themselves more by cruelty and lust of blood than by deeds of chivalry. A clan of turbulent robbers in the past, they had helped to add many a bloodstained page to the history of their country.

Jessica had lived with her father, who owned a house in London, until his death when she was about fifteen years of age. Her mother had died in Scotland when Jessica was still a tiny child. Mr MacThane had been so affected by his wife's death that, with his little daughter, he had abandoned his Scotch estate altogether – or so it was believed – leaving it to the management of a bailiff – though, indeed, there was but little work for the bailiff to do, since there were practically no tenants left. Blackwick Castle had borne for many years a most unenviable reputation.

After the death of her father, Miss MacThane had gone to live with a certain Mrs Meredith, who was a connection of her mother's – on her father's side she had not a single relation left. Jessica was absolutely the last of a clan once so extensive that intermarriage had been a tradition of the family, but which for the last two hundred years had been gradually dwindling to extinction.

Mrs Meredith took Jessica into society – which would never have been her privilege had Mr MacThane lived, for he was a moody, self-absorbed man, and prematurely old – one who seemed worn down by the weight of a great grief.

Well, I have said that Paul Davenant quickly fell in love with Jessica, and it was not long before he proposed for her hand. To his great surprise, for he had good reason to believe that she cared for him, he met with a refusal; nor would she give any explanation, though she burst into a flood of pitiful tears.

Bewildered and bitterly disappointed, he consulted Mrs Meredith, with whom he happened to be on friendly terms, and from her he learnt that Jessica had already had several proposals all from quite desirable men, but that one after another had been rejected.

Paul consoled himself with the reflection that perhaps Jessica did not love them, whereas he was quite sure that she cared for himself. Under these circumstances he determined to try again.

He did so, and with better result. Jessica admitted her love, but at the same time she repeated that she would not marry him. Love and marriage were not for her. Then, to his utter amazement, she declared that she had been born under a curse – a curse which, sooner or later, was bound to show itself in her, and which, moreover, must react cruelly, perhaps fatally, upon anyone with whom she linked her life. How could she allow a man she loved to take such a risk? Above all since the evil was hereditary, there was one point upon which she had quite made up her mind: no child should ever call her mother – she must be the last of her race indeed.

Of course, Davenant was amazed and inclined to think that Jessica had got some absurd idea into her head which a little reasoning on his part would dispel. There was only one other possible explanation. Was it lunacy she was afraid of?

But Jessica shook her head. She did not know of any lunacy in her family. The ill was deeper, more subtle than that. And then she told him all that she knew.

The curse – she made use of that word for want of a better – was attached to the ancient race from which she had her origin. Her father had suffered from it, and his father and grandfather before him. All three had taken to themselves young wives who had died mysteriously, of some wasting disease, within a few years. Had they observed the ancient family tradition of intermarriage this might possibly not have happened, but in their case, since the family was so near extinction, this had not been possible.

For the curse – or whatever it was – did not kill those who bore the name of MacThane. It only rendered them a danger to others. It was as if they absorbed from the blood-soaked walls of their fatal castle a deadly taint, which reacted terribly upon those with whom they were brought into contact, especially their nearest and dearest.

'Do you know what my father said we have it in us to become?' said Jessica with a shudder. 'He used the word vampires. Paul, think of it – vampires – preying upon the life blood of others.'

And then, when Davenant was inclined to laugh, she checked him. 'No,' she cried out, 'it is not impossible. Think. We are a decadent race. From the earliest times our history has been marked by bloodshed and cruelty. The walls of Blackwick Castle are impregnated with evil – every stone could tell its tale of violence, pain, lust and murder. What can one expect of those who have spent their lifetime within its walls?'

'But you have not done so,' exclaimed Paul. 'You have been spared that, Jessica. You were taken away after your mother died, and you have no recollection of Blackwick Castle, none at all. And you need never set foot in it again.'

'I'm afraid the evil is in my blood,' she replied sadly, 'although I am unconscious of it now. And as for not returning to Blackwick – I'm not sure I can help myself. At least, that is what my father warned me of. He said there is something there, some compelling force, that will call me to it in spite of myself. But, oh, I don't know – I don't know, and that is what makes it so difficult. If I could only believe that all this is nothing but an idle superstition, I might be happy again, for I have it in me to enjoy life, and I'm young, very young; but my father told me these things when he was on his deathbed.' She added the last words in a low, awestricken tone.

Paul pressed her to tell him all that she knew, and eventually she revealed another fragment of family history which seemed to have some bearing upon the case. It dealt with her own astonishing likeness to that ancestress of a couple of hundred years ago, whose existence seemed to have presaged the gradual downfall of the clan of the MacThanes.

A certain Robert MacThane, departing from the traditions of his family, which demanded that he should not marry outside his clan, brought home a wife from foreign shores, a woman of wonderful beauty, who was possessed of glowing masses of red hair and a complexion of ivory whiteness – such as had more or less distinguished since then every female of the race born in the direct line.

It was not long before this woman came to be regarded in the neighbourhood as a witch. Queer stories were circulated abroad as to her doings, and the reputation of Blackwick Castle became worse than ever before.

And then one day she disappeared. Robert MacThane had been absent upon some business for twenty-four hours, and it was upon his return that he found her gone. The neighbourhood was searched, but without avail, and then Robert, who was a violent man and who had adored his foreign wife, called together certain of his tenants whom he suspected, rightly or wrongly, of foul play, and had them murdered in cold blood. Murder was easy in those days, yet such an outcry was raised that Robert had to take to flight, leaving his two children in the care of their nurse, and for a long while Blackwick Castle was without a master.

But its evil reputation persisted. It was said that Zaïda, the witch, though dead, still made her presence felt. Many children of the tenantry and young people of the neighbourhood sickened and died – possibly of quite natural causes; but this did not prevent a mantle of terror settling upon the countryside, for it was said that Zaïda had been seen – a pale woman clad in white – flitting about the cottages at night, and where she passed sickness and death were sure to supervene.

And from that time the fortune of the family gradually declined. Heir succeeded heir, but no sooner was he installed at Blackwick Castle than his nature, whatever it may previously have been, seemed to undergo a change. It was as if he absorbed into himself all the weight of evil that had stained his family name – as if he did, indeed, become a vampire, bringing blight upon any not directly connected with his own house.

And so, by degrees, Blackwick was deserted of its tenantry. The land around it was left uncultivated – the farms stood empty. This had persisted to the present day, for the superstitious peasantry still told their tales of the mysterious white woman who hovered about the neighbourhood, and whose appearance betokened death – and possibly worse than death.

And yet it seemed that the last representatives of the MacThanes could not desert their ancestral home. Riches they had, sufficient to live happily upon elsewhere, but, drawn by some power they could not contend against, they had preferred to spend their lives in the solitude of the now half-ruined castle, shunned by their neighbours, feared and execrated by the few tenants that still clung to their soil.

So it had been with Jessica's grandfather and great-grandfather. Each of them had married a young wife, and in each case their love story had been all too brief. The vampire spirit was still abroad, expressing itself – or so it seemed – through the living representatives of bygone generations of evil, and young blood had been demanded as the sacrifice.

And to them had succeeded Jessica's father. He had not profited by their example, but had followed directly in their footsteps. And the same fate had befallen the wife whom he passionately adored. She had died of pernicious anaemia – so the doctors said – but he had regarded himself as her murderer.

But, unlike his predecessors, he had torn himself away from Blackwick – and this for the sake of his child. Unknown to her, however, he had returned year after year, for there were times when the passionate longing for the gloomy, mysterious halls and corridors of the old castle, for the wild stretches of moorland and the dark pinewoods, would come upon him too strongly to be resisted. And so he knew that for his daughter, as for himself, there was no escape, and he warned her, when the relief of death was at last granted to him, of what her fate must be.

This was the tale that Jessica told the man who wished to make her his wife, and he made light of it, as such a man would, regarding it all as foolish superstition, the delusion of a mind overwrought. And at last – perhaps it was not very difficult, for she loved him with all her heart and soul – he succeeded in inducing Jessica to think as he did, to banish morbid ideas, as he called them, from her brain and to consent to marry him at an early date.

'I'll take any risk you like,' he declared. 'I'll even go and live at Blackwick if you should desire it. To think of you, my lovely Jessica, a vampire! Why, I never heard such nonsense in my life.'

'Father said I'm very like Zaida, the witch,' she protested, but he silenced her with a kiss.

And so they were married and spent their honeymoon abroad, and in the autumn Paul accepted an invitation to a house party in Scotland for the grouse shooting, a sport to which he was absolutely devoted, and Jessica agreed with him that there was no reason why he should forgo his pleasure.

Perhaps it was an unwise thing to do, to venture to Scotland, but by this time the young couple, more deeply in love with each other than ever, had got quite over their fears. Jessica was redolent with health and spirits, and more than once she declared that if they should be anywhere in the neighbourhood of Blackwick she would like to see the old castle out of curiosity – and just to show how absolutely she had got over the foolish terrors that used to assail her.

This seemed to Paul to be quite a wise plan, and so one day, since they were actually staying at no great distance, they motored over to Blackwick, and finding the bailiff, got him to show them over the castle.

It was a great castellated pile, grey with age, and in places falling into ruin. It stood on a steep hillside, with the rock of which it seemed to form part, and on one side of it there was a precipitous drop to a mountain stream a hundred feet below. The robber MacThanes of the old days could not have desired a better stronghold.

At the back, climbing up the mountainside, were dark pinewoods, from which, here and there, rugged crags protruded, and these were fantastically shaped, some like gigantic and misshapen human forms, which stood up as if they mounted guard over the castle and the narrow gorge by which alone it could be approached.

This gorge was always full of weird, uncanny sounds. It might have been a storehouse for the wind, which, even on calm days, rushed up and down as if seeking an escape, and it moaned among the pines and whistled in the crags and shouted derisive laughter as it was tossed from side to side of the rocky heights. It was like the plaint of lost souls – that is the expression Davenant made use of – the plaint of lost souls.

The road, little more than a track now, passed through this gorge, and then, after skirting a small but deep lake, which hardly knew the light of the sun so shut in was it by overhanging trees, climbed the hill to the castle.

And the castle! Davenant used but a few words to describe it, yet somehow I could see the gloomy edifice in my mind's eye, and something of the lurking horror that it contained communicated itself to my brain. Perhaps my clairvoyant sense assisted me, for when he spoke of them I seemed already acquainted with the great stone halls, the long corridors, gloomy and cold even on the brightest and warmest of days, the dark, oak-panelled rooms, and the broad central staircase up which one of the early MacThanes had once led a dozen men on horseback in pursuit of a stag which had taken refuge within the precincts of the castle. There was the keep, too, its walls so thick that the ravages of time had made no impression upon them, and beneath the keep were dungeons which could tell terrible tales of ancient wrong and lingering pain.

Well Mr and Mrs Davenant visited as much as the bailiff could show them of this ill-omened edifice, and Paul, for his part, thought pleasantly of his own Derbyshire home, the fine Georgian mansion, replete with every modern comfort, where he proposed to settle with his wife. And so he received something of a shock when, as they drove away, she slipped her hand into his and whispered: 'Paul, you promised, didn't you, that you would refuse me nothing?'

She had been strangely silent till she spoke those words. Paul, slightly apprehensive, assured her that she only had to ask – but the speech did not come from his heart, for he guessed vaguely what she desired.

She wanted to go and live at the castle – oh, only for a little while, for she was sure she would soon tire of it. But the bailiff had told her that there were papers, documents, which she ought to examine, since the property was now hers – and, besides, she was interested in this home of her ancestors, and wanted to explore it more thoroughly. Oh, no, she wasn't in the least influenced by the old superstition – that wasn't the attraction – she had quite got over those silly ideas. Paul had cured her, and since he himself was so convinced that they were without foundation he ought not to mind granting her her whim.

This was a plausible argument, not easy to controvert. In the end Paul yielded, though it was not without a struggle. He suggested amendments. Let him at least have the place done up for her – that would take time; or let them postpone their visit till next year – in the summer – not move in just as the winter was upon them.

But Jessica did not want to delay longer than she could help, and she hated the idea of redecoration. Why, it would spoil the illusion of the old place, and, besides, it would be a waste of money since she only wished to remain there for a week or two. The Derbyshire house was not quite ready yet; they must allow time for the paper to dry on the walls.

And so, a week later, when their stay with their friends was concluded, they went to Blackwick, the bailiff having engaged a few raw servants and generally made things as comfortable for them as possible. Paul was worried and apprehensive, but he could not admit this to his wife after having so loudly proclaimed his theories on the subject of superstition.

They had been married three months at this time; nine had passed since then, and they had never left Blackwick for more than a few hours – till now; Paul had come to London – alone.

'Over and over again,' he declared, 'my wife has begged me to go. With tears in her eyes, almost upon her knees, she has entreated me to leave her, but I have steadily refused unless she will accompany me. But that is the trouble, Mr Vance, she cannot; there is something, some mysterious horror, that holds her there as surely as if she were bound with fetters. It holds her more strongly even than it held her father – we found out that he used to spend six months at least of every year at Blackwick – months when he pretended that he was travelling abroad. You see the spell – or whatever the accursed thing may be – never really relaxed its grip on him.'

'Did you never attempt to take your wife away?' asked Vance.

'Yes, several times; but it was hopeless. She would become so ill as soon as we were beyond the limit of the estate that I invariably had to take her back. Once we got as far as Dorekirk – that is the nearest town, you know – and I thought I should be successful, if only I could get through the night. But she escaped me, she climbed out of a window – she meant to go back on foot, at night, all those long miles. Then I have had doctors down; but it is I who wanted the doctors, not she. They have ordered me away, but I have refused to obey them till now.'

'Is your wife changed at all – physically?' interrupted Vance.

Davenant reflected. 'Changed,' he said, 'yes, but so subtly that I hardly know how to describe it. She is more beautiful than ever – and yet it isn't the same beauty, if you can understand me. I have spoken of her white complexion, well, one is more than ever conscious of it now because her lips have become so red – they are almost like a splash of blood upon her face. And the upper one has a peculiar curve that I don't think it had before, and when she laughs she doesn't smile – do you know what I mean? Then her hair – it has lost its wonderful gloss. Of course, I know she is fretting about me; but that is so peculiar, too, for at times, as I have told you, she will implore me to go and leave her, and then, perhaps only a few minutes later, she will wreathe her arms round my neck and say she cannot live without me. And I feel that there is a struggle going on within her, that she is only yielding slowly to the horrible influence – whatever it is – that she is herself when she begs me to go, but when she entreats me to stay – and it is then that her fascination is most intense – oh, I can't help remembering what she told me before we were married, and that word' – he lowered his voice – 'the word "vampire" – '

He passed his hand over a brow that was wet with perspiration. 'But that's absurd, ridiculous,' he muttered; 'these fantastic beliefs have been exploded years ago. We live in the twentieth century.'

A pause ensued, then Vance said quietly, 'Mr Davenant, since you have taken me into your confidence, since you have found doctors of no avail, will you let me try to help you? I think I may be of some use, if it is not already too late. Should you agree, Mr Dexter and I will accompany you, as you have suggested, to Blackwick Castle as early as possible – by tonight's mail north. Under ordinary circumstances I should tell you, as you value your life, not to return – '

Davenant shook his head. 'That is advice which I should never take,' he declared. 'I had already decided, under any circumstances, to travel north tonight. I am glad that you both will accompany me.'

And so it was decided. We settled to meet at the station, and presently Paul Davenant took his departure. Any other details that remained to be told he would put us in possession of during the course of the journey.

'A curious and most interesting case,' remarked Vance when we were alone. 'What do you make of it, Dexter?'

'I suppose,' I replied cautiously, 'that there is such a thing as vampirism even in these days of advanced civilisation? I can understand the evil influence that a very old person may have upon a young one, if they happen to be in constant intercourse – the worn-out tissue sapping healthy vitality for their own support. And there are certain people – I could think of several myself – who seem to depress one and undermine one's energies, quite unconsciously, of course, but one feels somehow that vitality has passed from oneself to them. And in this case, when the force is centuries old, expressing itself, in some mysterious way, through Davenant's wife, is it not feasible to believe that he may be physically affected by it, even though the whole thing is sheerly mental?'

'You think, then,' demanded Vance, 'that it is sheerly mental? Tell me, if that is so, how do you account for the marks on Davenant's throat?'

This was a question to which I found no reply, and though I pressed him for his views, Vance would not commit himself further just then.

Of our long journey to Scotland I need say nothing. We did not reach Blackwick Castle till late in the afternoon of the following day. The place was just as I had conceived it – as I have already described it. And a sense of gloom settled upon me as our car jolted us over the rough road that led through the Gorge of the Winds – a gloom that deepened when we penetrated into the vast cold hall of the castle.

Mrs Davenant, who had been informed by telegram of our arrival, received us cordially. She knew nothing of our actual mission, regarding us merely as friends of her husband's. She was most solicitous on his behalf, but there was something strained about her tone, and it made me feel vaguely uneasy. The impression that I got was that the woman was impelled to everything that she said or did by some force outside herself – but, of course, this was a conclusion that the circumstances I was aware of might easily have conduced to. In every other aspect she was charming, and she had an extraordinary fascination of appearance and manner that made me readily understand the force of a remark made by Davenant during our journey.

'I want to live for Jessica's sake. Get her away from Blackwick, Vance, and I feel that all will be well. I'd go through hell to have her restored to me as she was.'

And now that I had seen Mrs Davenant I realised what he meant by those last words. Her fascination was stronger than ever, but it was not a natural fascination – not that of a normal woman, such as she had been. It was the fascination of a Circe, of a witch, of an enchantress – and as such was irresistible.

We had a strong proof of the evil within her soon after our arrival. It was a test that Vance had quietly prepared. Davenant had mentioned that no flowers grew at Blackwick, and Vance declared that we must take some with us as a present for the lady of the house. He purchased a bouquet of pure white roses at the little town where we left the train, for the motor car had been sent to meet us.

Soon after our arrival he presented these to Mrs Davenant. She took them it seemed to me nervously, and hardly had her hand touched them before they fell to pieces, in a shower of crumpled petals, to the floor.

'We must act at once,' said Vance to me when we were descending to dinner that night. 'There must be no delay.'

'What are you afraid of?' I whispered.

'Davenant has been absent a week,' he replied grimly. 'He is stronger than when he went away, but not strong enough to survive the loss of more blood. He must be protected. There is danger tonight.'

'You mean from his wife?' I shuddered at the ghastliness of the suggestion.

'That is what time will show.' Vance turned to me and added a few words with intense earnestness. 'Mrs Davenant, Dexter, is at present hovering between two conditions. The evil thing has not yet completely mastered her – you remember what Davenant said, how she would beg him to go away and the next moment entreat him to stay? She has made a struggle, but she is gradually succumbing, and this last week, spent here alone, has strengthened the evil. And that is what I have got to fight, Dexter – it is to be a contest of will, a contest that will go on silently till one or the other obtains the mastery. If you watch, you may see. Should a change show itself in Mrs Davenant you will know that I have won.'

Thus I knew the direction in which my friend proposed to act. It was to be a war of his will against the mysterious power that had laid its curse upon the house of MacThane. Mrs Davenant must be released from the fatal charm that held her.

And I, knowing what was going on, was able to watch and understand. I realised that the silent contest had begun even while we ate dinner. Mrs Davenant ate practically nothing and seemed ill at ease; she fidgeted in her chair, talked a great deal, and laughed – it was the laugh without a smile, as Davenant had described it. And as soon as she was able to she withdrew.

Later, as we sat in the drawing-room, I could feel the clash of wills. The air in the room felt electric and heavy, charged with tremendous but invisible forces. And outside, round the castle, the wind whistled and shrieked and moaned – it was as if all the dead and gone MacThanes, a grim army, had collected to fight the battle of their race.

And all this while we four in the drawing-room were sitting and talking the ordinary commonplaces of after-dinner conversation! That was the extraordinary part of it – Paul Davenant suspected nothing and I, who knew, had to play my part. But I hardly took my eyes from Jessica's face. When would the change come, or was it, indeed, too late!

At last Davenant rose and remarked that he was tired and would go to bed. There was no need for Jessica to hurry. He would sleep that night in his dressing-room and did not want to be disturbed.

And it was at that moment, as his lips met hers in a good-night kiss, as she wreathed her enchantress arms about him, careless of our presence, her eyes gleaming hungrily, that the change came.

It came with a fierce and threatening shriek of wind, and a rattling of the casement, as if the horde of ghosts without was about to break in upon us. A long quivering sigh escaped from Jessica's lips, her arms fell from her husband's shoulders, and she drew back, swaying a little from side to side.

'Paul,' she cried, and somehow the whole timbre of her voice was changed, 'what a wretch I've been to bring you back to Blackwick, ill as you are! But we'll go away, dear; yes, I'll go, too. Oh, will you take me away – take me away tomorrow?' She spoke with an intense earnestness – unconscious all the time of what had been happening to her. Long shudders were convulsing her frame. 'I don't know why I've wanted to stay here,' she kept repeating. 'I hate the place, really – it's evil – evil.'

Having heard these words I exulted, for surely Vance's success was assured. But I was to learn that the danger was not yet past.

Husband and wife separated, each going to their own room. I noticed the grateful if mystified glance that Davenant threw at Vance, vaguely aware, as he must have been, that my friend was somehow responsible for what had happened. It was settled that plans for departure were to be discussed on the morrow.

'I have succeeded,' Vance said hurriedly, when we were alone, 'but the change may be transitory. I must keep watch tonight. Go to bed, Dexter, there is nothing that you can do.'

I obeyed – though I would sooner have kept watch, too – watch against a danger of which I had no understanding. I went to my room, a gloomy and sparsely furnished apartment, but I knew that it was quite impossible for me to think of sleeping. And so, dressed as I was, I went and sat by the open window, for now the wind that had raged round the castle had died down to a low moaning in the pine trees – a whimpering of timeworn agony.

And it was as I sat thus that I became aware of a white figure that stole out from the castle by a door that I could not see, and, with hands clasped, ran swiftly across the terrace to the wood. I had but a momentary glance, but I felt convinced that the figure was that of Jessica Davenant.

And instinctively I knew that some great danger was imminent. It was, I think, the suggestion of despair conveyed by those clasped hands. At any rate, I did not hesitate. My window was some height from the ground, but the wall below was ivy-clad and afforded good foothold. The descent was quite easy. I achieved it, and was just in time to take up the pursuit in the right direction, which was into the thickness of the wood that clung to the slope of the hill.

I shall never forget that wild chase. There was just sufficient room to enable me to follow the rough path, which, luckily, since I had now lost sight of my quarry, was the only possible way that she could have taken; there were no intersecting tracks, and the wood was too thick on either side to permit of deviation.

And the wood seemed full of dreadful sounds – moaning and wailing and hideous laughter: the wind, of course, and the screaming of night birds – once I felt the fluttering of wings in close proximity to my face. But I could not rid myself of the thought that I, in my turn, was being pursued, that the forces of hell were combined against me.

The path came to an abrupt end on the border of the sombre lake that I have already mentioned. And now I realised that I was indeed only just in time, for before me, plunging knee deep in the water, I recognised the white-clad figure of the woman I had been pursuing. Hearing my footsteps, she turned her head, and then threw up her arms and screamed. Her red hair fell in heavy masses about her shoulders, and her face, as I saw it in that moment, was hardly human for the agony of remorse that it depicted.

'Go!' she screamed. 'For God's sake, let me die!'

But I was by her side almost as she spoke She struggled with me – sought vainly to tear herself from my clasp – implored me, with panting breath, to let her drown.

'It's the only way to save him!' she gasped. 'Don't you understand that I am a thing accursed? For it is I – I – who have sapped his life blood! I know it now, the truth has been revealed to me tonight! I am a vampire, without hope in this world or the next, so for his sake – for the sake of his unborn child – let me die – let me die!'

Was ever so terrible an appeal made? Yet I – what could I do? Gently I overcame her resistance and drew her back to shore. By the time I reached it, she was lying a dead weight upon my arm. I laid her down upon a mossy bank, and, kneeling by her side, gazed intently into her face.

And then I knew that I had done well. For the face I looked upon was not that of Jessica the vampire, as I had seen it that afternoon, it was the face of Jessica, the woman whom Paul Davenant had loved.

And later Aylmer Vance had his tale to tell.

'I waited,' he said, 'until I knew that Davenant was asleep, and then I stole into his room to watch by his bedside. And presently she came, as I guessed she would, the vampire, the accursed thing that has preyed upon the souls of her kin, making them like to herself when they too have passed into Shadowland, and gathering sustenance for her horrid task from the blood of those who are alien to her race. Paul's body and Jessica's soul – it is for one and the other, Dexter, that we have fought.'

'You mean,' I hesitated, 'Zaïda the witch?'

'Even so,' he agreed. 'Hers is the evil spirit that has fallen like a blight upon the house of MacThane. But now I think she may be exorcised for ever.'

'Tell me.'

'She came to Paul Davenant last night, as she must have done before, in the guise of his wife. You know that Jessica bears a strong resemblance to her ancestress. He opened his arms, but she was foiled of her prey, for I had taken my precautions; I had placed that upon Davenant's breast while he slept which robbed the vampire of her power of ill. She sped wailing from the room – a shadow – she who a minute before had looked at him with Jessica's eyes and spoken to him with Jessica's voice. Her red lips were Jessica's lips, and they were close to his when his eyes were opened and he saw her as she was – a hideous phantom of the corruption of the ages. And so the spell was removed, and she fled away to the place whence she had come – '

He paused. 'And now?' I enquired.

'Blackwick Castle must be rased to the ground,' he replied. 'That is the only way. Every stone of it, every brick, must be ground to powder and burnt with fire, for therein is the cause of all the evil. Davenant has consented.'

'And Mrs Davenant?'

'I think,' Vance answered cautiously, 'that all may be well with her. The curse will be removed with the destruction of the castle. She has not – thanks to you – perished under its influence. She was less guilty than she imagined – herself preyed upon rather than preying. But can't you understand her remorse when she realised, as she was bound to realise, the part she had played? And the knowledge of the child to come – its fatal inheritance – '

'I understand,' I muttered with a shudder. And then, under my breath, I whispered, 'Thank God!'

The Gateway of the Monster

W. H. HODGSON

IN RESPONSE TO Carnacki's usual card of invitation to have dinner and listen to a story, I arrived promptly at Cheyne Walk, to find the three others who were always invited to these happy little times there before me. Five minutes later, Carnacki, Arkright, Jessop, Taylor and I were all engaged in the 'pleasant occupation' of dining.

'You've not been long away this time,' I remarked as I finished my soup, forgetting, momentarily, Carnacki's dislike of being asked even to skirt the borders of his story until such time as he was ready. Then he would not stint words.

'No,' he replied with brevity and I changed the subject, remarking that I had been buying a new gun, to which piece of news he gave an intelligent nod and a smile, which I think showed a genuinely good-humoured appreciation of my intentional changing of the conversation.

Later, when dinner was finished, Carnacki snugged himself comfortably down in his big chair, along with his pipe, and began his story, with very little circumlocution.

'As Dodgson was remarking just now, I've only been away a short time, and for a very good reason too – I've only been away a short distance. The exact locality I am afraid I must not tell you; but it is less than twenty miles from here; rest assured, except for meaning a change of name, that won't spoil the story. And it *is* a story too! One of the most extraordinary things I have ever run against.

'I received a letter a fortnight ago from a man I will call Anderson, asking for an appointment. I arranged a time and when he turned up I found that he wished me to look into, and see whether I could not clear up, a long-standing and well-authenticated case of what he termed "haunting". He gave me very full particulars and, finally, as the thing seemed to present something unique, I decided to take it up.

'Two days later I drove up to the house in question late in the afternoon and discovered it a very old place, standing quite alone in its own grounds. Anderson had left a letter with the butler, I found, pleading excuses for his absence, and leaving the whole house at my disposal for my investigations.

'The butler evidently knew the object of my visit and I questioned him pretty thoroughly during dinner, which I had in rather lonely state. He is an elderly and privileged servant, and had the history of the Grey Room exact in detail. From him I learned more particulars regarding two things that Anderson had mentioned in but a casual manner. The first was that the door of the Grey Room would be heard in the dead of night to open, and slam heavily, and this even when the butler knew it was locked and the key on the bunch in his pantry. The second was that the bedclothes would always be found torn off the bed and hurled in a heap into a corner.

'But it was the door slamming that chiefly bothered the old butler. Many and many a time, he told me, had he lain awake and just shivered with fright, listening; for at night the door would be slammed time after time – thud! thud! thud! so that sleep was impossible.

'From Anderson, I knew already that the room had a history extending back over a hundred and fifty years. Three people had been strangled in it – an ancestor of his and his wife and child. This is authentic, as I had taken very great pains to make sure, so that you can imagine it was with a feeling that I had a striking case to investigate, that I went upstairs after dinner to have a look at the Grey Room.

'Peters, the butler, was in rather a state about my going, and assured me with much solemnity that in all the twenty years of his service, no one had ever entered that room after nightfall. He begged me in quite a fatherly way to wait till the morning when there could be no danger and then he could accompany me himself.

'Of course, I told him not to bother. I explained that I should do no more than look around a bit and perhaps fix a few seals. He need not fear, I was used to that sort of thing. But he shook his head when I said that.

' "There isn't many ghosts like ours, sir," he assured me with mournful pride. And by Jove! he was right, as you will see.

'I took a couple of candles and Peters followed with his bunch of keys. He unlocked the door, but would not come inside with me. He was evidently in quite a fright and renewed his request that I would put off my examination until daylight. Of course I laughed at him, and told him he could stand sentry at the door and catch anything that came out.

' "It never comes outside, sir," he said, in his funny old solemn manner. Somehow he managed to make me feel as if I were going to have the creeps right away. Anyway, it was one to him, you know.

'I left him there and examined the room. It is a big apartment and well furnished in the grand style, with a huge four-poster which stands with its head to the end wall. There were two candles on the mantelpiece and two on each of the three tables that were in the room. I lit the lot and after that the room felt a little less inhumanly dreary, though, mind you, it was quite fresh and well kept in every way.

'After I had taken a good look round I sealed lengths of narrow ribbon across the windows, along the walls, over the pictures, and over the fireplace and the wall-closets. All the time, as I worked, the butler stood just without the door and I could not persuade him to enter, though I jested with him a little as I stretched the ribbon and went here and there about my work. Every now and again he would say: "You'll excuse me, I'm sure, sir; but I do wish you would come out, sir. I'm fair in a quake for you."

'I told him he need not wait, but he was loyal enough in his way to what he considered his duty. He said he could not go away and leave me all alone there. He apologised, but made it very clear that I did not realise the danger of the room; and I could see, generally, that he was getting into a really frightened state. All the same I had to make the room so that I should know if anything material entered it, so I asked him not to bother me unless he really heard something. He was beginning to fret my nerves and the "feel" of the room was bad enough already, without making things any nastier.

'For a time further I worked, stretching ribbons across a little above the floor and sealing them so that the merest touch would break the seals were anyone to venture into the room in the dark with the intention of playing the fool.

'All this had taken me far longer than I had anticipated and, suddenly, I heard a clock strike eleven. I had taken off my coat soon after commencing work; now however, as I had practically made an end of all that I intended to do, I walked across to the settee and picked it up. I was in the act of getting into it when the old butler's voice (he had not said a word for the last hour) came sharp and frightened: "Come out, sir, quick! There's something going to happen!" Jove! but I jumped, and then in the same moment, one of the candles on the table to the left of the bed went out. Now whether it was the wind, or what, I do not know; but just for a moment I was enough startled to make a run for the door; though I am glad to say that I pulled up before I reached it. I simply could not bunk out with the butler standing there after having, as it were, read him a sort of lesson on "bein' brave, y'know". So I just turned right round, picked up the two candles off the mantelpiece, and walked across to the table near the bed. Well, I saw nothing. I blew out the candle that was still alight; then I went to those on the two other tables and blew them out. Then, outside the door, the old man called again: "Oh! sir, do be told! Do be told!"

' "All right, Peters," I said, and by Jove, my voice was not as steady as I should have liked! I made for the door and had a bit of work not to start running. I took some thundering long strides, though, as you can imagine. Near the entrance I had a sudden feeling that there was a cold wind in the room. It was almost as if the window had been suddenly opened a little. I got to the door and the old butler gave back a step, in a sort of instinctive way.

' "Collar the candles, Peters!" I said, pretty sharply, and shoved them into his hands. I turned and caught the handle and slammed the door shut with a crash. Somehow, do you know, as I did so I thought I felt something pull back on it, but it must have been only fancy. I turned the key in the lock, and then again, double-locking the door.

'I felt easier then and set to and sealed the door. In addition I put my card over the keyhole and sealed it there, after which I pocketed the key and went downstairs – with Peters who was nervous and silent, leading the way. Poor old beggar! It had not struck me until that moment that he had been enduring a considerable strain during the last two or three hours.

'About midnight I went to bed. My room lay at the end of the corridor upon which opens the door of the Grey Room. I counted the doors between it and mine and found that five rooms lay between. And I am sure you can understand that I was not sorry.

'Just as I was beginning to undress an idea came to me and I took my candle and sealing-wax and sealed the doors of all the five rooms. If any door slammed in the night, I should know just which one.

'I returned to my room, locked myself in and went to bed. I was woken suddenly from a deep sleep by a loud crash somewhere out in the passage. I sat up in bed and listened, but heard nothing. Then I lit my candle. I was in the very act of lighting it when there came the bang of a door being violently slammed along the corridor.

'I jumped out of bed and got my revolver. I unlocked the door and went out into the passage, holding my candle high and keeping the pistol ready. Then a queer thing happened. I could not go a step towards the Grey Room. You all know I am not really a cowardly chap. I've gone into too many cases connected with ghostly things to be accused of that; but I tell you I funked it, simply funked it, just like any blessed kid. There was something precious unholy in the air that night. I backed into my bedroom and shut and locked the door. Then I sat on the bed all night and listened to the dismal thudding of a door up the corridor. The sound seemed to echo through all the house.

'Daylight came at last and I washed and dressed. The door had not slammed for about an hour, and I was getting back my nerve again. I felt ashamed of myself, though in some ways it was silly, for when you're meddling with that sort of thing your nerve is bound to go, sometimes. And you just have to sit quiet and call yourself a coward until the safety of the day comes. Sometimes it is more than just cowardice, I fancy. I believe at times it is something warning you and fighting *for* you. But all the same, I always feel mean and miserable after a time like that.

'When the day came properly I opened my door, and keeping my revolver handy, went quietly along the passage. I had to pass the head of the stairs on the way, and who should I see coming up but the old butler, carrying a cup of coffee. He had merely tucked his nightshirt into his trousers and had an old pair of carpet slippers on.

' "Hullo, Peters!" I said, feeling suddenly cheerful, for I was as glad as any lost child to have a live human being close to me. "Where are you off to with the refreshments?"

'The old man gave a start and slopped some of the coffee. He stared up at me and I could see that he looked white and done-up. He came on up the stairs and held out the little tray to me.

' "I'm very thankful indeed, sir, to see you safe and well," he said. "I feared one time you might risk going into the Grey Room, sir. I've lain awake all night, with the sound of the door. And when it came light I thought I'd make you a cup of coffee. I knew you would want to look at the seals – and somehow it seems safer if there's two, sir."

' "Peters," I said, "you're a brick. This is very thoughtful of you." And I drank the coffee. "Come along," I told him, and handed him back the tray. "I'm going to have a look at what the brutes have been up to. I simply hadn't the pluck to in the night."

' "I'm very thankful, sir," he replied. "Flesh and blood can do nothing, sir, against devils, and that's what's in the Grey Room after dark."

'I examined the seals on all the doors as I went along and found them right, but when I got to the Grey Room, the seal was broken, though the visiting-card over the keyhole was untouched. I ripped it off and unlocked the door and went in, rather cautiously as you can imagine; but the whole room was empty of anything to frighten one; and there was heaps of light. I examined all my seals, and not a single one was disturbed. The old butler had followed me in, and suddenly he said, 'The bedclothes, sir!'

'I ran up to the bed and looked over, and sure enough, they were lying in the corner to the left of the bed. Jove! you can imagine how queer I felt. Something *had* been in the room. I stared for a while from the bed to the clothes on the floor. I had a feeling that I did not want to touch either. Old Peters, though, did not seem to be affected that way. He went over to the bed-coverings and was going to pick them up, as doubtless he had done every day these twenty years back, but I stopped him. I wanted nothing touched until I had finished my examination. This I must have spent a full hour over and then I let Peters straighten up the bed, after which we went out and I locked the door, for the room was getting on my nerves.

'I had a short walk and then breakfast, which made me feel more my own man. Then to the Grey Room again, and with Peters' help and that of one of the maids, I had everything taken out except the bed, even the very pictures.

'I examined the walls, floor and ceiling then, with probe, hammer and magnifying glass, but found nothing unusual. I can assure you I began to realise in very truth that some incredible thing had been loose in the room during the past night.

'I sealed up everything again and went out, locking and sealing the door as before.

'After dinner that night, Peters and I unpacked some of my stuff and I fixed up my camera and flashlight opposite to the door of the Grey Room with a string from the trigger of the flashlight to the door. You see, if the door really opened, the flashlight would blare out and there would be, possibly, a very queer picture to examine in the morning.

'The last thing I did before leaving was to uncap the lens and after that I went off to my bedroom and to bed, for I intended to be up at midnight, and to ensure this, I set my little alarm to call me; also I left my candle burning.

'The clock woke me at twelve and I got up and into my dressing-gown and slippers. I shoved my revolver into my right side-pocket and opened my door. Then I lit my darkroom lamp and withdrew the slide so that it would give a clear light. I carried it up the corridor about thirty feet and put it down on the floor, with the open side away from me, so that it would show me anything that might approach along the dark passage. Then I went back and sat in the doorway of my room, with my revolver handy, staring up the passage towards the place where I knew my camera stood outside the door of the Grey Room.

'I should think I had watched for about an hour and a half when suddenly I heard a faint noise away up the corridor. I was immediately conscious of a queer prickling sensation about the back of my head and my hands began to sweat a little. The following instant the whole end of the passage flicked into sight in the abrupt glare of the flashlight. Then came the succeeding darkness and I peered nervously up the corridor, listening tensely, and trying to find what lay beyond the faint, red glow of my dark-lamp, which now seemed ridiculously dim by contrast with the tremendous blaze of the flash-powder . . . And then, as I stooped forward, staring and listening, there came the crashing thud of the door of the Grey Room. The sound seemed to fill the whole of the large corridor and go echoing hollowly through the house. I tell you, I felt horrible – as if my bones were water. Simply beastly. Jove! how I did stare and how I listened. And then it came again, thud, thud, thud, and then a silence that was almost worse than the noise of the door, for I kept fancying that some brutal thing was stealing upon me along the corridor.

'Suddenly, my lamp was put out, and I could not see a yard before me. I realised all at once that I was doing a very silly thing, sitting there, and I jumped up. Even as I did so, I thought I heard a sound in the passage, quite near to me. I made one backward spring into my room and slammed and locked the door.

'I sat on my bed and stared at the door. I had my revolver in my hand, but it seemed an abominably useless thing. Can you understand? I felt that there was something the other side of my door. For some unknown reason, I *knew* it was pressed up against the door, and it was soft. That was just what I thought. Most extraordinary thing to imagine, when you come to think of it!

'Presently I got hold of myself a bit and marked out a pentacle hurriedly with chalk on the polished floor and there I sat in it until it was almost dawn. And all the time, away up the corridor, the door of the Grey Room thudded at solemn and horrid intervals. It was a miserable, brutal night.

'When the day began to break, the thudding of the door came gradually to an end, and at last I grabbed together my courage and went along the corridor in the half-light, to cap the lens of my camera. I can tell you, it took some doing; but if I had not gone my photograph would have been spoilt, and I was tremendously keen to save it. I got back to my room and then set to and rubbed out the five-pointed star in which I had been sitting.

'Half an hour later there was a tap at my door. It was Peters, with my coffee. When I had drunk it we both walked along to the Grey Room. As we went, I had a look at the seals on the other doors, but they were untouched. The seal on the door of the Grey Room was broken, as also was the string from the trigger of the flashlight, but the visiting-card over the keyhole was still there. I ripped it off and opened the door. Nothing unusual was to be seen, until we came to the bed; then I saw that, as on the previous day, the bedclothes had been torn off and hurled into the left-hand corner, exactly where I had seen them before. I felt very queer, but I did not forget to look at the seals – only to find that not one had been broken.

'Then I turned and looked at old Peters and he looked at me, nodding his head.

' "Let's get out of here!" I said. "It's no place for any living human to enter without proper protection."

'We went out then and I locked and sealed the door, again.

'After breakfast I developed the negative, but it showed only the door of the Grey Room, half opened. Then I left the house, as I wanted to get certain matters and implements that might be necessary to life and perhaps to the spirit, for I intended to spend the coming night in the Grey Room.

'I got back in a cab about half-past five with my apparatus, and this Peters and I carried up to the Grey Room where I piled it carefully in the centre of the floor. When everything was in the room, including a cat which I had brought, I locked and sealed the door and went towards my bedroom, telling Peters I should not be down to dinner. He said, "Yes, sir," and went downstairs, thinking that I was going to turn in, which was what I wanted him to believe, as I knew it would have worried both himself and me if he had known what I intended.

'But I merely got my camera and flashlight from my bedroom and hurried back to the Grey Room. I entered and locked and sealed myself in and set to, for I had a lot to do before it got dark.

'First I cleared away all the ribbons across the floor; then I carried the cat, still fastened in its basket, over towards the far wall and left it. I returned then to the centre of the room and measured out a space twenty-one feet in diameter, which I swept with a broom of hyssop. About this I drew a circle of chalk, taking care never to step over the circle.

'Beyond this I smudged, with a bunch of garlic, a broad belt right around the chalked circle, and when this was complete I took from among my stores in the centre a small jar of a certain water. I broke away the parchment and withdrew the stopper. Then, dipping my left forefinger in the little jar, I went round the circle again, making upon the floor, just within the line of chalk, the second sign of the Saaamaaa Ritual, and joining each sign most carefully with the left-handed crescent. I can tell you, I felt easier when this was done and the "water-circle" complete.

'Then I unpacked some more of the stuff that I had brought and placed a lighted candle in the "valley" of each crescent. After that I drew a pentacle so that each of the five points of the defensive star touched the chalk circle. In the five points of the star I placed five portions of a certain bread, each wrapped in linen; and in the five "vales", five opened jars of the water I had used to make the water-circle. And now I had my first protective barrier complete.

'Now anyone, except you who know something of my methods of investigation, might consider all this a piece of useless and foolish superstition; but you all remember the Black Veil case, in which I believe my life was saved by a very similar form of protection, whilst Aster, who sneered at it and would not come inside, died.

'I got the idea from the Sigsand manuscript, written, so far as I can make out, in the fourteenth century. At first, naturally, I imagined it was just an expression of the superstition of his time, and it was not until long after my first reading that it occurred to me to test his "defence", which I did, as I've just said, in that horrible Black Veil business. You know how *that* turned out. Later I used it several times and always I came through safe, until that Noving Fur case. It was only a partial defence there and I nearly died in the pentacle.

'After that I came across Professor Garder's *Experiments with a Medium*. When they surrounded the medium with a current of a certain number of vibrations in vacuum, he lost his position – almost as if it cut him off from the immaterial. That made me think, and led eventually to the electric pentacle, which is a most marvellous defence against manifestations. I used the shape of the defensive star for this protection because I have, personally, no doubt at all but that there is some extraordinary virtue in the old magic figure. Curious thing for a twentieth-century man to admit, is it not? But then, as you all know, I never did, and never will allow myself to be blinded by a little cheap laughter. I ask questions and keep my eyes open!

'In this last case I had little doubt that I had run up against an abnatural monster, and I meant to take every possible care, for the danger is abominable.

'I turned now to fit the electric pentacle, setting it so that each of its points and vales coincided exactly with the points and vales of the drawn pentagram upon the floor. Then I connected up the battery and the next instant the pale blue glare from the intertwining vacuum tubes shone out.

'I glanced about me then, with something of a sigh of relief, and realised suddenly that the dusk was upon me, for the window was grey and unfriendly. Then I stared round at the big, empty room, over the double-barrier of electric and candle light, and had an abrupt, extraordinary sense of weirdness thrust upon me – in the air, you know, it seemed; as it were a sense of something inhuman impending. The room was full of the stench of bruised garlic, a smell I hate.

'I turned now to my camera, and saw that it and the flashlight were in order. Then I tested the action of my revolver carefully, though I had little thought that it would be needed. Yet, to what extent materialisation of an abnatural creature is possible, given favourable conditions, no one can say, and I had no idea what horrible thing I was going to see or feel the presence of. I might, in the end, have to fight with a material thing. I did not know and could only be prepared. You see, I never forgot that three people had been strangled in the bed close to me, and the fierce slamming of the door I had heard myself. I had no doubt that I was investigating a dangerous and ugly case.

'By this time the night had come (though the room was very light with the burning candles), and I found myself glancing behind me constantly and then all round the room. It was nervy work waiting for that thing to come into the room.

'Suddenly I was aware of a little, cold wind sweeping over me, coming from behind. I gave one great nerve-thrill and a prickly feeling went all over the back of my head. Then I hove myself round with a sort of stiff jerk and stared straight against that queer wind. It seemed to come from the corner of the room to the left of the bed – the place where both times I had found the heap of tossed bedclothes. Yet I could see nothing unusual, no opening – nothing! . . .

'Abruptly I was aware that the candles were all a-flicker in that unnatural wind . . . I believe I just squatted there and stared in a horribly frightened, wooden way for some minutes. I shall never be able to let you know how disgustingly horrible it was sitting in that vile, cold wind! And then – flick! flick! flick! all the candles round the outer barrier went out, and there was I, locked and sealed in that room and with no light beyond the weakish blue glare of the electric pentacle.

'A time of abominable tenseness passed and still that wind blew upon me, and then suddenly I knew that something stirred in the corner to the left of the bed. I was made conscious of it rather by some inward, unused sense, than by either sight or sound, for the pale, short-radius glare of the pentacle gave but a very poor light for seeing by. Yet, as I stared, something began slowly to grow upon my sight – a moving shadow, a little darker than the surrounding shadows. I lost the thing amid the vagueness and for a moment or two I glanced swiftly from side to side with a fresh, new sense of impending danger. Then my attention was directed to the bed. All the coverings were being drawn steadily off, with a hateful, stealthy sort of motion. I heard the slow, dragging slither of the clothes, but I could see nothing of the thing that pulled. I was aware in a funny, subconscious, introspective fashion that the "creep" had come upon me, prickling all over my head, yet I was cooler mentally than I had been for some minutes – sufficiently so to feel that my hands were sweating coldly and to shift my revolver, half-consciously, whilst I rubbed my right hand dry upon my knee, though never for an instant taking my gaze or my attention from those moving clothes.

'The faint noises from the bed ceased once and there was a most intense silence, with only the dull thudding of the blood beating in my head. Yet immediately afterwards I heard again the slurring sound of the bedclothes being dragged off the bed. In the midst of my nervous tension I remembered the camera and teached out for it, but without looking away from the bed. And then, you know, all in a moment, the whole of the bed-coverings were torn off with extraordinary violence and I heard the flump they made as they were hurled into the corner.

'There was a time of absolute quietness then for perhaps a couple of minutes and you can imagine how horrible I felt. The bedclothes had been thrown with such savageness! And then again the abominable unnaturalness of the thing that had just been done before me!

'Suddenly, over by the door, I heard a faint noise – a sort of crickling sound – and then a pitter or two upon the floor. A great nervous thrill swept over me, seeming to run up my spine and over the back of my head, for the seal that secured the door had just been broken. Something was there. I could not see the door; at least, I mean to say that it was impossible to say how much I actually saw and how much my imagination supplied. I made it out only as a continuation of the grey walls . . . And then it seemed to me that something dark and indistinct moved and wavered there among the shadows.

'Abruptly I was aware that the door was opening and with an effort I reached again for my camera; but before I could aim it, the door was slammed with a terrific crash that filled the whole room with a sort of hollow thunder. I jumped like a frightened child. There seemed such a power behind the noise, as if a vast, wanton force were "out". Can you understand?

'The door was not touched again; but, directly afterwards I heard the basket in which the cat lay creak. I tell you, I fairly pringled all along my back. I knew that I was going to learn definitely whether what was abroad was dangerous to life. From the cat there rose suddenly a hideous caterwaul that ceased abruptly, and then – too late – I snapped on the flashlight. In the great glare I saw that the basket had been overturned and the lid was wrenched open, with the cat lying half in and half out upon the floor. I saw nothing else, but I was full of the knowledge that I was in the presence of some being or thing that had power to destroy.

'During the next two or three minutes there was an odd, noticeable quietness in the room, and you must remember I was half-blinded for the time because of the flashlight, so that the whole place seemed to be pitchy dark just beyond the shine of the pentacle. I tell you it was most horrible. I just knelt there in the star and whirled round on my knees, trying to see whether anything was coming at me.

'My power of sight came gradually and I got a little hold of myself, and abruptly I saw the thing I was looking for, close to the water-circle. It was big and indistinct and wavered curiously as though the shadow of a vast spider hung suspended in the air, just beyond the barrier. It passed swiftly round the circle and seemed to probe ever towards me, but only to draw back with extraordinary jerky movements, as might a living person who touched the hot bar of a grate.

'Round and round it moved and round and round I turned. Then just opposite to one of the vales in the pentacles it seemed to pause, as though as a preliminary to a tremendous effort. It retired almost beyond the glow of the vacuum light and then came straight towards me, appearing to gather form and solidity as it came. There seemed a vast malign determination behind the movement that must succeed. I was on my knees and I jerked back, falling on to my left hand and hip, in a wild endeavour to get back from the advancing thing. With my right hand I was grabbing madly for my revolver which I had let slip. The brutal thing came with one great sweep straight over the garlic and the water-circle, almost to the vale of the pentacle. I believe I yelled. Then, just as suddenly as it had swept over, it seemed to be hurled back by some mighty, invisible force.

'It must have been some moments before I realised that I was safe, and then I got myself together in the middle of the pentacles, feeling horribly done and shaken and glancing round and round the barrier, but the thing had vanished. Yet I had learnt something, for I knew now that the Grey Room was haunted by a monstrous hand.

'Suddenly, as I crouched there, I saw what had so nearly given the monster an opening through the barrier. In my movements within the pentacle I must have touched one of the jars of water, for just where the thing had made its attack the jar that guarded the "deep" of the vale had been moved to one side and this had left one of the "five doorways" unguarded. I put it back quickly and felt almost safe again, for I had found the cause and the defence was still good. I began to hope again that I should see the morning come in. When I saw that thing so nearly succeed I'd had an awful, weak, overwhelming feeling that the barriers could never bring me safe through the night against such a force. You can understand?

'For a long time I could not see the hand; but presently I thought I saw, once or twice, an odd wavering over among the shadows near the door. A little later, as though in a sudden fit of malignant rage, the dead body of the cat was picked up and beaten with dull, sickening blows against the solid floor. That made me feel rather queer.

'A minute afterwards the door was opened and slammed twice with tremendous force. The next instant the thing made one swift, vicious dart at me from out of the shadows. Instinctively I started sideways from it and so plucked my hand from upon the electric pentacle, where – for a wickedly careless moment – I had placed it. The monster was hurled off from the neighbourhood of the pentacles, though – owing to my inconceivable foolishness – it had been enabled for a second time to pass the outer barriers. I can tell you I shook for a time with sheer funk. I moved right to the centre of the pentacles again and knelt there, making myself as small and compact as possible.

'As I knelt, I began to have, presently, a vague wonder at the two "accidents" which had so nearly allowed the brute to get at me. Was I being influenced to unconscious voluntary actions that endangered me? The thought took hold of me and I watched my every movement. Abruptly I stretched a tired leg and knocked over one of the jars of water. Some was spilled, but because of my suspicious watchfulness, I had it upright and back within the vale while yet some of the water remained. Even as I did so the vast, black half-materialised hand beat up at me out of the shadows and seemed to leap almost into my face, so nearly did it approach, but for the third time it was thrown back by some altogether enormous, over-mastering force. Yet, apart from the dazed fright in which it left me, I had for a moment that feeling of spiritual sickness, as if some delicate, beautiful, inward grace had suffered, which is felt only upon the too near approach of the abhuman and is more dreadful in a strange way than any physical pain that can be suffered. I knew by this more of the extent and closeness of the danger, and for a long time I was simply cowed by the butt-headed brutality of that force upon my spirit. I can put it no other way.

'I knelt again in the centre of the pentacles, watching myself with as much fear, almost, as the monster, for I knew now that unless I guarded myself from every sudden impulse that came to me I might simply work my own destruction. Do you see how horrible it all was?

'I spent the rest of the night in a haze of sick fright and so tense that I could not make a single movement naturally – I was in such fear that any desire for action that came to me might be prompted by the influence that I knew was at work on me. And outside of the barrier that ghastly thing went, round and round, grabbing and grabbing in the air at me. Twice more was the body of the dead cat molested. The second time I heard every bone in its body scrunch and crack. And all the time the horrible wind was blowing upon me from the corner of the room to the left of the bed.

'Then, just as the first touch of dawn came into the sky the unnatural wind ceased in a single moment and I could see no sign of the hand. The dawn came slowly and presently the wan light filled all the room and made the pale glare of the electric pentacle look more unearthly. Yet it was not until the day had fully come that I made any attempt to leave the barrier, for I did not know but that there was some method abroad in the sudden stopping of that wind to entice me from the pentacles.

'At last, when the dawn was strong and bright, I took one last look round and ran for the door. I got it unlocked in a nervous, clumsy fashion; then locked it hurriedly and went to my bedroom where I lay on the bed and tried to steady my nerves. Peters came presently with the coffee and when I had drunk it I told him I meant to have a sleep, as I had been up all night. He took the tray and went out quietly, and after I had locked my door I turned in properly and at last got to sleep.

'I woke about midday and after some lunch went up to the Grey Room. I switched off the current from the pentacle, which I had left on in my hurry; also, I removed the body of the cat. You can understand, I did not want anyone to see the poor brute.

'After that I made a very careful search of the corner where the bedclothes had been thrown. I made several holes through the woodwork and probed, but found nothing. Then it occurred to me to try with my instrument under the skirting. I did so and heard my wire ring on metal. I turned the hook-end of the probe that way and fished for the thing. At the second go I got it. It was a small object and I took it to the window. I found it to be a curious ring made of some greyish metal. The curious thing about it was that it was made in the form of a pentagon; that is, the same shape as the inside of the magic pentacle, but without the "mounts" which form the points of the defensive star. It was free from all chasing or engraving.

'You will understand that I was excited when I tell you that I felt sure I held in my hand the famous Luck Ring of the Anderson family which, indeed, was of all things the most intimately connected with the history of the haunting. This ring had been handed on from father to son through generations, and always – in obedience to some ancient family tradition – each son had to promise never to wear the ring. The ring, I may say, was brought home by one of the Crusaders under very peculiar circumstances, but the story is too long to go into here.

'It appears that young Sir Hulbert, an ancestor of Anderson's, made a bet one evening, in drink, you know, that he would wear the ring that night. He did so, and in the morning his wife and child were found strangled in the bed in the very room in which I stood. Many people, it would seem, thought young Sir Hulbert was guilty of having done the thing in drunken anger and he, in an attempt to prove his innocence, slept a second night in the room. He also was strangled.

'Since then no one had spent a night in the Grey Room until I did so. The ring had been lost so long that its very existence had become almost a myth, and it was most extraordinary to stand there with the actual thing in my hand, as you can understand.

'It was while I stood there looking at the ring that I got an idea. Supposing that it were, in a way, a doorway – you see what I mean? A sort of gap in the world-hedge, if I may so phrase my idea. It was a queer thought, I know, and possibly was not my own, but one of those mental nudgings from the Outside.

'You seen the wind had come from that part of the room where the ring lay. I pondered the thought a lot. Then the shape – the inside of a pentacle. It had no mounts, and as the Sigsand manuscript has it: "Thee mownts are thee Five Hills of safetie. To lack is to gyve pow'r to thee daemon; and surlie to fayvor thee Evill Thynge." You see, the very shape of the ring was significant. I determined to test it.

'I unmade my pentacle, for it must be "made" afresh *and around* the one to be protected. Then I went out and locked the door, after which I left the house to get certain items, for neither "yarbs nor fyre nor water" must be used a second time. I returned about seven-thirty and, as soon as the things I had brought had been carried up to the Grey Room, I dismissed Peters for the night, just as I had done the evening before. When he had gone downstairs I let myself into the room and locked and sealed the door. I went to the place in the centre of the room where all the stuff had been packed and set to work with all my speed to construct a barrier about me and the ring.

'I do not remember whether I explained to you, but I had reasoned that if the ring were in any way a "medium of admission", and it were enclosed with me in the electric pentacle, it would be, to express it loosely, insulated. Do you see? The force which had visible expression as a hand would have to stay beyond the barrier which separates the ab from the normal, for the "gateway" would be removed from accessibility.

'As I was saying, I worked with all my speed to get the barrier completed about me and the ring for it was already later than I cared to be in that room unprotected. Also, I had a feeling that there would be a vast effort made that night to regain the use of the ring. For I had the strongest conviction that the ring was a necessity to materialisation. You will see whether I was right.

'I completed the barriers in about an hour and you can imagine something of the relief I felt when I saw the pale glare of the electric pentacle once more all about me. From then onwards, for about two hours, I sat quietly facing the corner from which the wind came.

'About eleven o'clock I had a queer knowledge that something was near to me, yet nothing happened for a whole hour after that. Then suddenly I felt the cold, queer wind begin to blow upon me. To my astonishment it seemed now to come from behind me and I whipped round with a hideous quake of fear. The wind met me in the face. It was flowing up from the floor close to me. I stared in a sickening maze of new frights. What on earth had I done now! The ring was there, close beside me, where I had put it. Suddenly, as I stared, bewildered, I was aware that there was something queer about the ring – funny shadowy movements and convolutions. I looked at them stupidly. And then, abruptly, I knew that the wind was blowing up at me from the ring. A queer indistinct smoke became visible to me, seeming to pour upwards through the ring and mix with the moving shadows. Suddenly I realised that I was in more than any mortal danger, for the convoluting shadows about the ring were taking shape and the deathhand was forming within the pentacle. My goodness, do you realise it? I had brought the gateway into the pentacles and the brute was coming through – pouring into the material world, as gas might pour out from the mouth of a pipe.

'I should think that I knelt for a couple of moments in a sort of stunned fright. Then with a mad, awkward movement I snatched at the ring, intending to hurl it out of the pentacles. Yet, it eluded me as though some invisible, living thing jerked it hither and thither. At last I gripped it, but in the same instant it was torn from my grasp with incredible and brutal force. A great black shadow covered it and rose into the air and came at me. I saw that it was the hand, vast and nearly perfect in form. I gave one crazy yell and jumped over the pentacles and the ring of burning candles and ran despairingly for the door. I fumbled idiotically and ineffectually with the key, and all the time I stared, with a fear that was like insanity, towards the barriers. The hand was plunging towards me; yet, even as it had been unable to pass into the pentacles when the ring was without; so, now that the ring was within, it had no power to pass out. The monster was chained, as surely as any beast would be, were chains riveted upon it.

'Even then, in that moment, I got a flash of this knowledge, but I was too utterly shaken with fright to reason and the instant I managed to get the key turned I sprang into the passage and slammed the door with a crash. I locked it and got to my room, somehow; for I was trembling so that I could hardly stand, as you can imagine. I locked myself in and managed to get the candle lit; then I lay down on the bed and kept quiet for an hour or two, and so I grew steadier.

'I got a little sleep later, but woke when Peters brought my coffee. When I had drunk it I felt altogether better and took the old man along with me to have a look into the Grey Room. I opened the door and peeped in. The candles were still burning wan against the daylight and behind them was the pale, glowing star of the electric pentacle. And there in the middle was the ring – the gateway of the monster, lying demure and ordinary.

'Nothing in the room was touched and I knew that the brute had never managed to cross the pentacles. Then I went out and locked the door.

'After a further sleep of some hours I left the house. I returned in the afternoon in a cab. I had with me an oxyhydrogen jet and two cylinders, containing the gases. I carried the things to the Grey Room and there, in the centre of the electric pentacle, I erected the little furnace. Five minutes later the Luck Ring, once the luck but now the bane of the Anderson family, was no more than a little splash of hot metal.'

Carnacki felt in his pocket and pulled out something wrapped in tissue paper. He passed it to me. I opened it and found a small circle of greyish metal something like lead, only harder and rather brighter.

'Well,' I asked, at length, after examining it and handing it round to the others, 'did that stop the haunting?'

Carnacki nodded. 'Yes,' he said. 'I slept three nights in the Grey Room before I left. Old Peters nearly fainted when he knew that I meant to, but by the third night he seemed to realise that the house was just safe and ordinary. And you know, I believe in his heart he hardly approved.'

Carnacki stood up and began to shake hands. 'Out you go!' he said, genially.

And, presently, we went pondering to our various homes.

Tarnhelm

HUGH WALPOLE

I

I WAS, I SUPPOSE, at that time a peculiar child, peculiar a little by nature, but also because I had spent so much of my young life in the company of people very much older than myself.

After the events that I am now going to relate, some quite indelible mark was set on me. I became then, and have always been since, one of those persons, otherwise insignificant, who have decided, without possibility of change, about certain questions.

Some things, doubted by most of the world, are for these people true and beyond argument; this certainty of theirs gives them a kind of stamp, as though they lived so much in their imagination as to have very little assurance as to what is fact and what fiction. This 'oddness' of theirs puts them apart. If now, at the age of fifty, I am a man with very few friends, very much alone, it is because, if you like, my Uncle Robert died in a strange manner forty years ago and I was a witness of his death.

I have never until now given any account of the strange proceedings that occurred at Faildyke Hall on the evening of Christmas Eve in the year 1890. The incidents of that evening are still remembered very clearly by one or two people, and a kind of legend of my Uncle Robert's death has been carried on into the younger generation. But no one still alive was a witness of them as I was, and I feel it is time that I set them down upon paper.

I write them down without comment. I extenuate nothing; I disguise nothing. I am not, I hope, in any way a vindictive man, but my brief meeting with my Uncle Robert and the circumstances of his death gave my life, even at that early age, a twist difficult for me very readily to forgive.

As to the so-called supernatural element in my story, everyone must judge for himself about that. We deride or we accept according to our natures. If we are built of a certain solid practical material the probability is that no evidence, however definite, however first-hand, will convince us. If dreams are our daily portion, one dream more or less will scarcely shake our sense of reality.

However, to my story.

My father and mother were in India from my eighth to my thirteenth years. I did not see them, except on two occasions when they visited England. I was an only child, loved dearly by both my parents, who, however, loved one another yet more. They were an exceedingly sentimental couple of the old-fashioned kind. My father was in the Indian civil service, and wrote poetry. He even had his epic, *Tantalus: A Poem in Four Cantos*, published at his own expense.

This, added to the fact that my mother had been considered an invalid before he married her made my parents feel that they bore a very close resemblance to the Brownings, and my father even had a pet name for my mother that sounded curiously like the famous and hideous 'Ba'.

I was a delicate child, was sent to Mr Ferguson's Private Academy at the tender age of eight, and spent my holidays as the rather unwanted guest of various relations

'Unwanted' because I was, I imagine, a difficult child to understand. I had an old grandmother who lived at Folkestone, two aunts who shared a little house in Kensington, an aunt, uncle and a brood of cousins inhabiting Cheltenham, and two uncles who lived in Cumberland. All these relations, except the two uncles, had their proper share of me and for none of them had I any great affection.

Children were not studied in those days as they are now. I was thin, pale and bespectacled, aching for affection but not knowing at all how to obtain it; outwardly undemonstrative but inwardly emotional and sensitive, playing games, because of my poor sight, very badly, reading a great deal more than was good for me, and telling myself stories all day and part of every night

All of my relations tired of me, I fancy, in turn and at last it was decided that my uncles in Cumberland must do their share. These two were my father's brothers, the eldest of a long family of which he was the youngest. My Uncle Robert, I understood, was nearly seventy, my Uncle Constance some five years younger. I remember always thinking that Constance was a funny name for a man.

My Uncle Robert was the owner of Faildyke Hall, a country house between the lake of Wastwater and the little town of Seascale on the sea coast. Uncle Constance had lived with Uncle Robert for many years. It was decided, after some family correspondence, that the Christmas of this year, 1890, should be spent by me at Faildyke Hall.

I was at this time just eleven years old, thin and skinny, with a bulging forehead, large spectacles and a nervous, shy manner. I always set out, I remember, on any new adventure with mingled emotions of terror and anticipation. Maybe *this* time the miracle would occur: I should discover a friend or a fortune, should cover myself with glory in some unexpected way; be at last what I always longed to be, a hero.

I was glad that I was not going to any of my other relations for Christmas, and especially not to my cousins at Cheltenham, who teased and persecuted me and whose vicinity was never free of ear-splitting noises. What I wanted most in life was to be allowed to read in peace. I understood that at Faildyke there was a glorious library.

My aunt saw me into the train. I had been presented by my uncle with one of the most gory of Harrison Ainsworth's romances, *The Lancashire Witches*, and I had five bars of chocolate cream, so that that journey was as blissfully happy as any experience could be to me at that time. I was permitted to read in peace, and I had just then little more to ask of life.

Nevertheless, as the train puffed its way north, this new country began to force itself on my attention. I had never before been in the North of England, and I was not prepared for the sudden sense of space and freshness that I received

The naked, unsystematic hills, the freshness of the wind on which the birds seemed to be carried with especial glee, the stone walls that ran like grey ribbons about the moors, and, above all, the vast expanse of sky upon whose surface clouds swam, raced, eddied and extended as I had never anywhere witnessed . . .

I sat, lost and absorbed, at my carriage window, and when at last, long after dark had fallen, I heard 'Seascale' called by the porter, I was still staring in a sort of romantic dream. When I stepped out on to the little narrow platform and was greeted by the salt tang of the sea wind, my first real introduction to the North Country may be said to have been completed. I am writing now in another part of that same Cumberland country, and beyond my window the line of the fell runs strong and bare against the sky, while below it the lake lies, a fragment of silver glass at the feet of Skiddaw.

It may be that my sense of the deep mystery of this country had its origin in this same strange story that I am now relating. But again perhaps not, for I believe that that first evening arrival at Seascale worked some change in me, so that since then none of the world's beauties – from the crimson waters of Kashmir to the rough glories of our own Cornish coast – can rival for me the sharp, peaty winds and strong, resilient turf of the Cumberland hills.

That was a magical drive in the pony-trap to Faildyke that evening. It was bitterly cold, but I did not seem to mind it. Everything was magical to me.

From the first I could see the great slow hump of Black Combe jet against the frothy clouds of the winter night, and I could hear the sea breaking and the soft rustle of the bare twigs in the hedgerows.

I made, too, the friend of my life that night, for it was Bob Armstrong who was driving the trap. He has often told me since (for although he is a slow man of few words he likes to repeat the things that seem to him worth while) that I struck him as 'pitifully lost' that evening on the Seascale platform. I looked, I don't doubt, pinched and cold enough. In any case it was a lucky appearance for me, for I won Armstrong's heart there and then, and he, once he gave it, could never bear to take it back again.

He, on his side, seemed to me gigantic that night. He had, I believe, one of the broadest chests in the world: it was a curse to him, he said, because no ready-made shirts would ever fit him.

I sat in close to him because of the cold; he was very warm, and I could feel his heart beating like a steady clock inside his rough coat. It beat for me that night, and it has beaten for me, I'm glad to say, ever since.

In truth, as things turned out, I needed a friend. I was nearly asleep and stiff all over my little body when I was handed down from the trap and at once led into what seemed to me an immense hall crowded with the staring heads of slaughtered animals and smelling of straw.

I was so sadly weary that my uncles, when I met them in a vast billiard-room in which a great fire roared in a stone fireplace like a demon, seemed to me to be double.

In any case, what an odd pair they were! My Uncle Robert was a little man with grey untidy hair and little sharp eyes hooded by two of the bushiest eyebrows known to humanity. He wore (I remember as though it were yesterday) shabby country clothes of a faded green colour, and he had on one finger a ring with a thick red stone.

Another thing that I noticed at once when he kissed me (I detested to be kissed by anybody) was a faint scent that he had, connected at once in my mind with the caraway-seeds that there are in seed-cake. I noticed, too, that his teeth were discoloured and yellow.

My Uncle Constance I liked at once. He was fat, round, friendly and clean. Rather a dandy was Uncle Constance. He wore a flower in his buttonhole and his linen was snowy white in contrast with his brother's.

I noticed one thing, though, at that very first meeting, and that was that before he spoke to me and put his fat arm around my shoulder he seemed to look towards his brother as though for permission. You may say that it was unusual for a boy of my age to notice so much, but in fact I noticed everything at that time. Years and laziness, alas! have slackened my observation.

II

I had a horrible dream that night; it woke me screaming, and brought Bob Armstrong in to quiet me.

My room was large, like all the other rooms that I had seen, and empty, with a great expanse of floor and a stone fireplace like the one in the billiard-room. It was, I afterwards found, next to the servants' quarters. Armstrong's room was next to mine, and Mrs Spender's, the housekeeper's, beyond his.

Armstrong was then, and is yet, a bachelor. He used to tell me that he loved so many women that he never could bring his mind to choose any one of them. And now he has been too long my personal bodyguard and is too lazily used to my ways to change his condition. He is, moreover, seventy years of age.

Well, what I saw in my dream was this. They had lit a fire for me (and it was necessary; the room was of an icy coldness) and I dreamt that I awoke to see the flames rise to a last vigour before they died away. In the brilliance of that illumination I was conscious that something was moving in the room. I heard the movement for some little while before I saw anything.

I sat up, my heart hammering, and then to my horror discerned, slinking against the farther wall, the evillest-looking yellow mongrel of a dog that you can fancy.

I find it difficult, I have always found it difficult, to describe exactly the horror of that yellow dog. It lay partly in its colour, which was vile, partly in its mean and bony body, but for the most part in its evil head – flat, with sharp little eyes and jagged yellow teeth.

As I looked at it, it bared those teeth at me and then began to creep, with an indescribably loathsome action, in the direction of my bed. I was at first stiffened with terror. Then, as it neared the bed, its little eyes fixed upon me and its teeth bared, I screamed again and again.

The next I knew was that Armstrong was sitting on my bed, his strong arm about my trembling little body. All I could say over and over was, 'The dog! the dog! the dog!'

He soothed me as though he had been my mother.

'See, there's no dog there! There's no one but me! There's no one but me!'

I continued to tremble, so he got into bed with me, held me close to him, and it was in his comforting arms that I fell asleep.

III

In the morning I woke to a fresh breeze and a shining sun and the chrysanthemums, orange, crimson and dun, blowing against the grey stone wall beyond the sloping lawns. So I forgot about my dream. I only knew that I loved Bob Armstrong better than anyone else on earth.

Everyone during the next days was very kind to me. I was so deeply excited by this country, so new to me, that at first I could think of nothing else. Bob Armstrong was Cumbrian from the top of his flaxen head to the thick nails under his boots, and, in grunts and monosyllables, as was his way, he gave me the colour of the ground.

There was romance everywhere: smugglers stealing in and out of Drigg and Seascale, the ancient cross in Gosforth churchyard, Ravenglass, with all its seabirds, once a port of splendour. Muncaster Castle and Broughton and black Wastwater with the grim Screes, Black Combe, upon whose broad back the shadows were always dancing – even the little station at Seascale, naked to the sea-winds, at whose bookstall I bought a publication entitled the *Weekly Telegraph* that contained, week by week, instalments of the most thrilling story in the world.

Everywhere romance – the cows moving along the sandy lanes, the sea thundering along the Drigg beach, Gable and Scafell pulling their cloud-caps about their heads, the slow voices of the Cumbrian farmers calling their animals, the little tinkling bell of the Gosforth church – everywhere romance and beauty.

Soon, though, as I became better accustomed to the country, the people immediately around me began to occupy my attention, stimulate my restless curiosity, and especially my two uncles. They were, in fact, queer enough.

Faildyke Hall itself was not queer, only very ugly. It had been built about 1830, I should imagine, a square white building, like a thick-set, rather conceited woman with a very plain face. The rooms were large, the passages innumerable; and everything covered with a very hideous whitewash. Against this whitewash hung old photographs, yellowed with age, and faded, bad watercolours. The furniture was strong and ugly.

One romantic feature, though, there was – and that was the little grey tower where my Uncle Robert lived. This tower was at the end of the garden and looked out over a sloping field to the Scafell group beyond Wastwater. It had been built hundreds of years ago as a defence against the Scots. Robert had had his study and bedroom there for many years and it was his domain; no one was allowed to enter it save his old servant Hucking, a bent, wizened, grubby little man who spoke to no one and, so they said in the kitchen, managed to go through life without sleeping. He looked after my Uncle Robert, cleaned his rooms, and was supposed to clean his clothes.

I, being both an inquisitive and romantic-minded boy, was soon as eagerly excited about this tower as was Bluebeard's wife about the forbidden room. Bob told me that whatever I did I was never to set foot inside.

And then I discovered another thing – that Bob Armstrong hated, feared and was proud of my Uncle Robert. He was proud of him because he was head of the family, and because, so he said, he was the cleverest old man in the world.

'Nothing he can't seemingly do,' said Bob, 'but he don't like you to watch him at it.'

All this only increased my longing to see the inside of the tower, although I couldn't be said to be fond of my Uncle Robert either.

It would be hard to say that I disliked him during those first days. He was quite kindly to me when he met me, and at mealtimes, when I sat with my two uncles at the long table in the big, bare, whitewashed dining-room, he was always anxious to see that I had plenty to eat. But I never liked him; it was perhaps because he wasn't clean. Children are sensitive to those things. Perhaps I didn't like the fusty, seed-caky smell that he carried about with him.

Then there came the day when he invited me into the grey tower and told me about Tarnhelm.

Pale slanting shadows of sunlight fell across the chrysanthemums and the grey stone walls, the long fields and the dusky hills. I was playing by myself by the little stream that ran beyond the rose garden, when Uncle Robert came up behind me in the soundless way he had and, tweaking me by the ear, asked me whether I would like to come with him inside his tower. I was, of course, eager enough; but I was frightened too, especially when I saw Hucking's motheaten old countenance peering at us from one of the narrow slits that pretended to be windows.

However, in we went, my hand in Uncle Robert's hot dry one. There wasn't, in reality, so very much to see when you were inside – all untidy and musty, with cobwebs over the doorways and old pieces of rusty iron and empty boxes in the corners, and the long table in Uncle Robert's study covered with a thousand things – books with the covers hanging on them, sticky green bottles, a looking-glass, a pair of scales, a globe, a cage with mice in it, a statue of a naked woman, an hour-glass – everything old and stained and dusty.

However, Uncle Robert made me sit down close to him, and told me many interesting stories – among others, the story about Tarnhelm.

Tarnhelm was something that you put over your head, and its magic turned you into any animal that you wished to be. Uncle Robert told me the story of a god called Wotan, and how he teased the dwarf who possessed Tarnhelm by saying that he couldn't turn himself into a mouse or some such animal; and the dwarf, his pride wounded, turned himself into a mouse, which the god easily captured and so stole Tarnhelm.

On the table, among all the litter, was a grey skull-cap.

'That's my Tarnhelm,' said Uncle Robert, laughing. 'Like to see me put it on?'

But I was suddenly frightened, terribly frightened. The sight of Uncle Robert made me feel quite ill. The room began to run round and round. The white mice in the cage twittered. It was stuffy in that room, enough to turn any boy sick.

That was the moment, I think, when Uncle Robert stretched out his hand towards his grey skull-cap – after that I was never happy again in Faildyke Hall. That action of his, simple and apparently friendly though it was, seemed to open my eyes to a number of things.

We were now within ten days of Christmas. The thought of Christmas had then – and, to tell the truth, still has – a most happy effect on me. There is the beautiful story, the geniality and kindliness, still, in spite of modern pessimists, much happiness and goodwill. Even now I yet enjoy giving presents and receiving them – then it was an ecstasy to me, the look of the parcel, the paper, the string, the exquisite surprise.

Therefore I had been anticipating Christmas eagerly. I had been promised a trip into Whitehaven for present-buying, and there was to be a tree and a dance for the Gosforth villagers. Then after my visit to Uncle Robert's tower, all my happiness of anticipation vanished. As the days went on and my observation of one thing and another developed, I would, I think, have run away back to my aunts in Kensington, had it not been for Bob Armstrong.

It was, in fact, Armstrong who started me on that voyage of observation that ended so horribly, for when he had heard that Uncle Robert had taken me inside his tower his anger was fearful. I had never before seen him angry; now his great body shook, and he caught me and held me until I cried out.

He wanted me to promise that I would never go inside there again. What? Not even with Uncle Robert? No, most especially not with Uncle Robert; and then, dropping his voice and looking around him to be sure that there was no one listening, he began to curse Uncle Robert. This amazed me, because loyalty to his masters was one of Bob's great laws. I can see us now, standing on the stable cobbles in the falling white dusk, while the horses stamped in their stalls and the little sharp stars appeared one after another, glittering between the driving clouds.

'I'll not stay,' I heard him say to himself. 'I'll be like the rest. I'll not be staying. To bring a child into it . . .'

From that moment he seemed to have me very specially in his charge. Even when I could not see him I felt that his kindly eye was upon me, and this sense of the necessity that I should be guarded made me yet more uneasy and distressed.

The next thing that I observed was that the servants were all fresh, had been there not more than a month or two. Then, only a week before

Christmas, the housekeeper departed. Uncle Constance seemed greatly upset at these occurrences; Uncle Robert did not seem in the least affected by them.

I come now to my Uncle Constance. At this distance of time it is strange with what clarity I still can see him – his stoutness, his shining cleanliness, his dandyism, the flower in his buttonhole, his little brilliantly shod feet, his thin, rather feminine voice. He would have been kind to me, I think, had he dared, but something kept him back. And what that something was I soon discovered; it was fear of my Uncle Robert.

It did not take me a day to discover that he was utterly subject to his brother. He said nothing without looking to see how Uncle Robert took it; suggested no plan until he first had assurance from his brother; was terrified beyond anything that I had before witnessed in a human being at any sign of irritation in my uncle.

I discovered after this that Uncle Robert enjoyed greatly to play on his brother's fears. I did not understand enough of their life to realise what were the weapons that Robert used, but that they were sharp and piercing I was neither too young nor too ignorant to perceive.

Such was our situation, then, a week before Christmas. The weather had become very wild, with a great wind. All nature seemed in an uproar. I could fancy when I lay in my bed at night and heard the shouting in my chimney that I could catch the crash of the waves upon the beach, see the black waters of Wastwater cream and curdle under the Screes. I would lie awake and long for Bob Armstrong – the strength of his arm and the warmth of his breast – but I considered myself too grown a boy to make any appeal.

I remember that now almost minute by minute my fears increased. What gave them force and power who can say? I was much alone, I had now a great terror of my uncle, the weather was wild, the rooms of the house large and desolate, the servants mysterious, the walls of the passages lit always with an unnatural glimmer because of their white colour, and although Armstrong had watch over me he was busy in his affairs and could not always be with me.

I grew to fear and dislike my Uncle Robert more and more. Hatred and fear of him seemed to be everywhere and yet he was always soft-voiced and kindly. Then, a few days before Christmas, occurred the event that was to turn my terror into panic.

I had been reading in the library Mrs Radcliffe's *Romance of the Forest*, an old book long forgotten, worthy of revival. The library was a fine room run to seed, bookcases from floor to ceiling, the windows small and dark, holes in the old faded carpet. A lamp burnt at a distant table. One stood on a little shelf at my side.

Something, I know not what, made me look up. What I saw then can even now stop my heart in its recollection. By the library door, not moving, staring across the room's length at me, was a yellow dog.

I will not attempt to describe all the pitiful fear and mad freezing terror that caught and held me. My main thought, I fancy, was that that other vision on my first night in the place had not been a dream. I was not asleep now; the book in which I had been reading had fallen to the floor, the lamps shed their glow, I could hear the ivy tapping on the pane. No, this was reality.

The dog lifted a long, horrible leg and scratched itself. Then very slowly and silently across the carpet it came towards me.

I could not scream; I could not move; I waited. The animal was even more evil than it had seemed before, with its flat head, its narrow eyes, its yellow fangs. It came steadily in my direction, stopped once to scratch itself again, then was almost at my chair.

It looked at me, bared its fangs, but now as though it grinned at me, then passed on. After it was gone there was a thick foetid scent in the air – the scent of caraway-seed.

IV

I think now on looking back that it was remarkable enough that I, a pale, nervous child who trembled at every sound, should have met the situation as I did. I said nothing about the dog to any living soul, not even to Bob Armstrong. I hid my fears – and fears of a beastly and sickening kind they were, too – within my breast. I had the intelligence to perceive – and *how I* caught in the air the awareness of this I can't, at this distance, understand – that I was playing my little part in the climax to something that had been piling up, for many a month, like the clouds over Gable.

Understand that I offer from first to last in this no kind of explanation. There is possibly – and to this day I cannot quite be sure – nothing to explain. My Uncle Robert died simply – but you shall hear.

What was beyond any doubt or question was that it was after my seeing the dog in the library that Uncle Robert changed so strangely in his behaviour to me. That may have been the merest coincidence. I only know that as one grows older one calls things coincidence more and more seldom.

In any case, that same night at dinner Uncle Robert seemed twenty years older. He was bent, shrivelled, would not eat, snarled at anyone who spoke to him and especially avoided even looking at me. It was a painful meal, and it was after it, when Uncle Constance and I were sitting alone in the old yellow-papered drawing-room – a room with two ticking clocks forever racing one another – that the most extraordinary thing occurred. Uncle Constance and I were playing draughts. The only sounds were the roaring of the wind down the chimney, the hiss and splutter of the fire, the silly ticking of the clocks. Suddenly Uncle Constance put down the piece that he was about to move and began to cry.

To a child it is always a terrible thing to see a grown-up person cry, and even to this day to hear a man cry is very distressing to me. I was moved desperately by poor Uncle Constance, who sat there, his head in his white plump hands, all his stout body shaking. I ran over to him and he clutched me and held me as though he would never let me go. He sobbed incoherent words about protecting me, caring for me . . . seeing that that monster . . .

At the word I remember that I too began to tremble. I asked my uncle what monster, but he could only continue to murmur incoherently about hate and not having the pluck, and if only he had the courage . . .

Then, recovering a little, he began to ask me questions. Where had I been? Had I been into his brother's tower? Had I seen anything that frightened me? If I did would I at once tell him? And then he muttered that he would never have allowed me to come had he known that it would go as far as this, that it would be better if I went away that night, and that if he were not afraid . . . Then he began to tremble again and to look at the door, and I trembled too. He held me in his arms; then we thought that there was a sound and we listened, our heads up, our two hearts hammering. But it was only the clocks ticking and the wind shrieking as though it would tear the house to pieces.

That night, however, when Bob Armstrong came up to bed he found me sheltering there. I whispered to him that I was frightened; I put my arms around his neck and begged him not to send me away; he promised me that I should not leave him and I slept all night in the protection of his strength.

How, though, can I give any true picture of the fear that pursued me now? For I knew from what both Armstrong and Uncle Constance had said that there was real danger, that it was no hysterical fancy of mine or ill-digested dream. It made it worse that Uncle Robert was now no more seen. He was sick; he kept within his tower, cared for by his old wizened manservant. And so, being nowhere, he was everywhere. I stayed with Armstrong when I could, but a kind of pride prevented me from clinging like a girl to his coat.

A deathly silence seemed to fall about the place. No one laughed or sang, no dog barked, no bird sang. Two days before Christmas an iron frost came to grip the land. The fields were rigid, the sky itself seemed to be frozen grey, and under the olive cloud Scafell and Gable were black.

Christmas Eve came.

On that morning, I remember, I was trying to draw – some childish picture of one of Mrs Radcliffe's scenes – when the double doors unfolded and Uncle Robert stood there. He stood there, bent, shrivelled, his long, grey locks falling over his collar, his bushy eyebrows thrust forward. He wore his old green suit and on his finger gleamed his heavy red ring. I was frightened, of course, but also I was touched with pity. He looked so old, so frail, so small in this large empty house.

I sprang up. 'Uncle Robert,' I asked timidly, 'are you better?'

He bent still lower until he was almost on his hands and feet; then he looked up at me, and his yellow teeth were bared, almost as an animal snarls. Then the doors closed again.

The slow, stealthy, grey afternoon came at last. I walked with Armstrong to Gosforth village on some business that he had. We said no word of any matter at the Hall. I told him, he has reminded me, of how fond I was of him and that I wanted to be with him always, and he answered that perhaps it might be so, little knowing how true that prophecy was to stand. Like all children I had a great capacity for forgetting the atmosphere that I was not at that moment in, and I walked beside Bob along the frozen roads, with some of my fears surrendered.

But not for long. It was dark when I came into the long, yellow drawing-room. I could hear the bells of Gosforth church pealing as I passed from the ante-room.

A moment later there came a shrill, terrified cry: 'Who's that? Who is it?'

It was Uncle Constance, who was standing in front of the yellow silk window curtains, staring at the dusk. I went over to him and he held me close to him.

Listen!' he whispered. 'What can you hear?'

The double doors through which I had come were half open. At first I could hear nothing but the clocks and the very faint rumble of a cart on the frozen road. There was no wind.

My uncle's fingers gripped my shoulder. 'Listen!' he said again. And now I heard. On the stone passage beyond the drawing-room was the patter of an animal's feet. Uncle Constance and I looked at one another. In that exchanged glance we confessed that our secret was the same. We knew what we should see.

A moment later it was there, standing in the double doorway, crouching a little and staring at us with a hatred that was mad and sick – the hatred of a sick animal crazy with unhappiness, but loathing us more than its own misery.

Slowly it came towards us, and to my reeling fancy all the room seemed to stink of caraway-seed.

'Keep back! Keep away!' my uncle screamed

I became oddly in my turn the protector.

'It shan't touch you! It shan't touch you, uncle!' I called.

But the animal came on.

It stayed for a moment near a little round table that contained a composition of dead waxen fruit under a glass dome. It stayed here, its nose down, smelling the ground. Then, looking up at us, it came on again.

Oh God! – even now as I write after all these years it is with me again, the flat skull, the cringing body in its evil colour and that loathsome smell. It slobbered a little at its jaw. It bared its fangs.

Then I screamed, hid my face in my uncle's breast and saw that he held, in his trembling hand, a thick, heavy, old-fashioned revolver.

Then he cried out: 'Go back, Robert . . . Go back!'

The animal came on. He fired. The detonation shook the room. The dog turned and, blood dripping from its throat, crawled across the floor.

By the door it halted, turned and looked at us. Then it disappeared into the other room.

My uncle had flung down his revolver; he was crying, sniffling; he kept stroking my forehead murmuring words.

At last, clinging to one another, we followed the splotches of blood, across the carpet, beside the door, through the doorway.

Huddled against a chair in the outer sitting-room, one leg twisted under him, was my Uncle Robert, shot through the throat.

On the floor, by his side, was a grey skull-cap.

The Rocking-Horse Winner

D. H. LAWRENCE

THERE WAS A WOMAN who was beautiful, who started with all the advantages, yet she had no luck. She married for love, and the love turned to dust. She had bonnie children, yet she felt they had been thrust upon her, and she could not love them. They looked at her coldly, as if they were finding fault with her. And hurriedly she felt she must cover up some fault in herself. Yet what it was that she must cover up she never knew. Nevertheless, when her children were present, she always felt the centre of her heart go hard. This troubled her, and in her manner she was all the more gentle and anxious for her children, as if she loved them very much. Only she herself knew that at the centre of her heart was a hard little place that could not feel love, no, not for anybody. Everybody else said of her: 'She is such a good mother. She adores her children.' Only she herself, and her children themselves, knew it was not so. They read it in each other's eyes.

There were a boy and two little girls. They lived in a pleasant house, with a garden, and they had discreet servants, and felt themselves superior to anyone in the neighbourhood.

Although they lived in style, they felt always an anxiety in the house. There was never enough money. The mother had a small income, and the father had a small income, but not nearly enough for the social position which they had to keep up. The father went into town to some office. But though he had good prospects, these prospects never materialised. There was always the grinding sense of the shortage of money, though the style was always kept up.

At last the mother said: 'I will see if *I* can't make something.' But she did not know where to begin. She racked her brains, and tried this thing and the other, but could not find anything successful. The failure made deep lines come into her face. Her children were growing up, they would have to go to school. There must be more money, there must be more money. The father, who was always very handsome and expensive in his tastes, seemed as if he never *would* be able to do anything worth doing. And the mother, who had a great belief in herself, did not succeed any better, and her tastes were just as expensive.

And so the house came to be haunted by the unspoken phrase: *There must be more money! There must be more money*! The children could hear it all the time, though nobody said it aloud. They heard it at Christmas, when the expensive and splendid toys filled the nursery. Behind the shining modern rocking-horse, behind the smart doll's house, a voice would start whispering: 'There *must* be more money! There *must* be more money!' And the children would stop playing, to listen for a moment. They would look into each other's eyes, to see if they had all heard. And each one saw in the eyes of the other two that they too had heard. 'There *must* be more money! There *must* be more money!'

It came whispering from the springs of the still-swaying rocking-horse, and even the horse, bending his wooden, champing head, heard it. The big doll, sitting so pink and smirking in her new pram¡ could hear it quite plainly, and seemed to be smirking all the more self-consciously because of it. The foolish puppy, too, that took the place of the teddy-bear, he was looking so extraordinarily foolish for no other reason but that he heard the secret whisper all over the house: 'There *must* be more money!'

Yet nobody ever said it aloud. The whisper was everywhere, and therefore no one spoke it. Just as no one ever says: 'We are breathing!' in spite of the fact that breath is coming and going all the time.

'Mother,' said the boy Paul one day, 'why don't we keep a car of our own? Why do we always use uncle's, or else a taxi?'

'Because we're the poor members of the family,' said the mother.

'But why *are* we, mother?'

'Well – I suppose,' she said slowly and bitterly, 'it's because your father has no luck.'

The boy was silent for some time.

'Is luck money, mother?' he asked, rather timidly.

'No, Paul. Not quite. It's what causes you to have money.'

'Oh!' said Paul vaguely. 'I thought when Uncle Oscar said *filthy lucker*, it meant money.'

'*Filthy lucre* does mean money,' said the mother. 'But it's lucre, not luck.'

'Oh!' said the boy. 'Then what *is* luck, mother?'

'It's what causes you to have money. If you're lucky you have money. That's why it's better to be born lucky than rich. If you're rich, you may lose your money. But if you're lucky, you will always get more money.'

'Oh! Will you? And is father not lucky?'

'Very unlucky, I should say,' she said bitterly.

The boy watched her with unsure eyes.

'Why?' he asked.

'I don't know. Nobody ever knows why one person is lucky and another unlucky.'

'Don't they? Nobody at all? Does *nobody* know?'

'Perhaps God. But He never tells.'

'He ought to, then. And aren't you lucky either, mother?'

'I can't be, if I married an unlucky husband.'

'But by yourself, aren't you?'

'I used to think I was, before I married. Now I think I am very unlucky indeed.'

'Why?'

'Well – never mind! Perhaps I'm not really,' she said.

The child looked at her to see if she meant it. But he saw, by the lines of her mouth, that she was only trying to hide something from him.

'Well, anyhow,' he said stoutly, 'I'm a lucky person.'

'Why?' said his mother, with a sudden laugh.

He stared at her. He didn't even know why he had said it. 'God told me,' he asserted, brazening it out.

'I hope He did, dear!' she said, again with a laugh, but rather bitter.

'He did, mother!'

'Excellent!' said the mother, using one of her husband's exclamations.

The boy saw she did not believe him; or rather, that she paid no attention to his assertion. This angered him somewhere, and made him want to compel her attention.

He went off by himself, vaguely, in a childish way, seeking for the clue to 'luck'. Absorbed, taking no heed of other people, he went about with a sort of stealth, seeking inwardly for luck. He wanted luck, he wanted it, he wanted it. When the two girls were playing dolls in the nursery, he would sit on his big rocking-horse, charging madly into space, with a frenzy that made the little girls peer at him uneasily. Wildly the horse careered, the waving dark hair of the boy tossed, his eyes had a strange glare in them. The little girls dared not speak to him.

When he had ridden to the end of his mad little journey, he climbed down and stood in front of his rocking-horse, staring fixedly into its lowered face. Its red mouth was slightly open, its big eye was wide and glassy-bright.

'Now!' he would silently command the snorting steed. 'Now, take me to where there is luck! Now take me!'

And he would slash the horse on the neck with the little whip he had asked Uncle Oscar for. He *knew* the horse could take him to where there was luck, if only he forced it. So he would mount again and start on his furious ride, hoping at last to get there. He knew he could get there.

'You'll break your horse, Paul!' said the nurse.

'He's always riding like that! I wish he'd leave off!' said his elder sister Joan.

But he only glared down on them in silence. Nurse gave him up. She could make nothing of him. Anyhow, he was growing beyond her.

One day his mother and his Uncle Oscar came in when he was on one of his furious rides. He did not speak to them.

'Hallo, you young jockey! Riding a winner?' said his uncle.

'Aren't you growing too big for a rocking-horse? You're not a very little boy any longer, you know,' said his mother.

But Paul only gave a blue glare from his big, rather close-set eyes. He would speak to nobody when he was in full tilt. His mother watched him with an anxious expression on her face.

At last he suddenly stopped forcing his horse into the mechanical gallop and slid down.

'Well, I got there!' he announced fiercely, his blue eyes still flaring, and his sturdy long legs straddling apart.

'Where did you get to?' asked his mother.

'Where I wanted to go,' he flared back at her.

'That's right, son!' said Uncle Oscar. 'Don't you stop till you get there. What's the horse's name?'

'He doesn't have a name,' said the boy.

'Gets on without all right?' asked the uncle.

'Well, he has different names. He was called Sansovino last week.'

'Sansovino, eh? Won the Ascot. How did you know this name?'

'He always talks about horse-races with Bassett,' said Joan.

The uncle was delighted to find that his small nephew was posted with all the racing news. Bassett, the young gardener, who had been wounded in the left foot in the war and had got his present job through Oscar Cresswell, whose batman he had been, was a perfect blade of the 'turf'. He lived in the racing events, and the small boy lived with him.

Oscar Cresswell got it all from Bassett.

'Master Paul comes and asks me, so I can't do more than tell him, sir,' said Bassett, his face terribly serious, as if he were speaking of religious matters.

'And does he ever put anything on a horse he fancies?'

'Well – I don't want to give him away – he's a young sport, a fine sport, sir. Would you mind asking him himself? He sort of takes a pleasure in it, and perhaps he'd feel I was giving him away, sir, if you don't mind.'

Bassett was serious as a church.

The uncle went back to his nephew and took him off for a ride in the car.

'Say, Paul, old man, do you ever put anything on a horse?' the uncle asked.

The boy watched the handsome man closely.

'Why, do you think I oughtn't to?' he parried.

'Not a bit of it! I thought perhaps you might give me a tip for the Lincoln.'

The car sped on into the country, going down to Uncle Oscar's place in Hampshire.

'Honour bright?' said the nephew.

'Honour bright, son!' said the uncle.

'Well, then, Daffodil.'

'Daffodil! I doubt it, sonny. What about Mirza?'

'I only know the winner,' said the boy. 'That's Daffodil.'

'Daffodil, eh?'

There was a pause. Daffodil was an obscure horse comparatively.

'Uncle!'

'Yes, son?'

'You won't let it go any further, will you? I promised Bassett.'

'Bassett be damned, old man! What's he got to do with it?'

'We're partners. We've been partners from the first. Uncle, he lent me my first five shillings, which I lost. I promised him, honour bright, it was only between me and him; only you gave me that ten-shilling note I started winning with, so I thought you were lucky. You won't let it go any further, will you?'

The boy gazed at his uncle from those big, hot, blue eyes, set rather close together. The uncle stirred and laughed uneasily.

'Right you are, son! I'll keep your tip private. Daffodil, eh? How much are you putting on him?'

'All except twenty pounds,' said the boy. 'I keep that in reserve.'

The uncle thought it a good joke.

'You keep twenty pounds in reserve, do you, you young romancer? What are you betting, then?'

'I'm betting three hundred,' said the boy gravely. 'But it's between you and me, Uncle Oscar! Honour bright?'

The uncle burst into a roar of laughter.

'It's between you and me all right, you young Nat Gould,' he said, laughing. 'But where's your three hundred?'

'Bassett keeps it for me. We're partners.'

'You are, are you! And what is Bassett putting on Daffodil?'

'He won't go quite as high as I do, I expect. Perhaps he'll go a hundred and fifty.'

'What, pennies?' laughed the uncle.

'Pounds,' said the child, with a surprised look at his uncle. 'Bassett keeps a bigger reserve than I do.'

Between wonder and amusement Uncle Oscar was silent. He pursued the matter no further, but he determined to take his nephew with him to the Lincoln races.

'Now, son,' he said, 'I'm putting twenty on Mirza, and I'll put five on for you on any horse you fancy. What's your pick?'

'Daffodil, uncle.'

'No, not the fiver on Daffodil!'

'I should if it was my own fiver,' said the child.

'Good! Good! Right you are! A fiver for me and a fiver for you on Daffodil.'

The child had never been to a race-meeting before, and his eyes were blue fire. He pursed his mouth tight and watched. A Frenchman just in front had put his money on Lancelot. Wild with excitement, he flayed his arms up and down, yelling '*Lancelot! Lancelot!*' in his French accent.

Daffodil came in first, Lancelot second, Mirza third. The child, flushed and with eyes blazing, was curiously serene. His uncle brought him four five-pound notes, four to one.

'What am I to do with these?' he cried, waving them before the boy's eyes.

'I suppose we'll talk to Bassett,' said the boy. 'I expect I have fifteen hundred now; and twenty in reserve; and this twenty.'

His uncle studied him for some moments.

'Look here, son!' he said. 'You're not serious about Bassett and that fifteen hundred, are you?'

'Yes, I am. But it's between you and me, uncle. Honour bright?'

'Honour bright all right, son! But I must talk to Bassett.'

'If you'd like to be a partner, uncle, with Bassett and me, we could all be partners. Only, you'd have to promise, honour bright, uncle, not to let it go beyond us three. Bassett and I are lucky, and you must be lucky, because it was your ten shillings I started winning with . . . '

Uncle Oscar took both Bassett and Paul into Richmond Park for an afternoon, and there they talked.

'It's like this, you see, sir,' Bassett said. 'Master Paul would get me talking about racing events, spinning yarns, you know, sir. And he was always keen on knowing if I'd made or if I'd lost. It's about a year since, now, that I put five shillings on Blush of Dawn for him: and we lost. Then the luck turned, with that ten shillings he had from you: that we put on Singhalese. And since that time, it's been pretty steady, all things considering. What do you say, Master Paul?'

'We're all right when we're sure,' said Paul. 'It's when we're not quite sure that we go down.'

'Oh, but we're careful then,' said Bassett.

'But when are you *sure*?' smiled Uncle Oscar.

'It's Master Paul, sir,' said Bassett in a secret, religious voice. 'It's as if he had it from heaven. Like Daffodil, now, for the Lincoln. That was as sure as eggs.'

'Did you put anything on Daffodil?' asked Oscar Cresswell.

'Yes, sir. I made my bit.'

'And my nephew?'

Bassett was obstinately silent, looking at Paul.

'I made twelve hundred, didn't I, Bassett? I told uncle I was putting three hundred on Daffodil.'

'That's right,' said Bassett, nodding.

'But where's the money?' asked the uncle.

'I keep it safe locked up, sir. Master Paul he can have it any minute he likes to ask for it.'

'What, fifteen hundred pounds?'

'And twenty! And *forty*, that is, with the twenty he made on the course.'

'It's amazing!' said the uncle.

'If Master Paul offers you to be partners, sir, I would, if I were you; if you'll excuse me,' said Bassett.

Oscar Cresswell thought about it.

'I'll see the money,' he said.

They drove home again, and, sure enough, Bassett came round to the garden-house with fifteen hundred pounds in notes. The twenty pounds reserve was left with Joe Glee, in the Turf Commission deposit.

'You see, it's all right, uncle, when I'm *sure*! Then we go strong, for all we're worth. Don't we, Bassett?'

'We do that, Master Paul.'

'And when are you sure?' said the uncle, laughing.

'Oh, well, sometimes I'm *absolutely* sure, like about Daffodil,' said the boy; 'and sometimes I have an idea; and sometimes I haven't even an idea, have I, Bassett? Then we're careful, because we mostly go down.'

'You do, do you! And when you're sure, like about Daffodil, what makes you sure, sonny?'

'Oh, well, I don't know,' said the boy uneasily. 'I'm sure, you know, uncle; that's all.'

'It's as if he had it from heaven, sir,' Bassett reiterated.

'I should say so!' said the uncle.

But he became a partner. And when the Leger was coming on Paul was 'sure' about Lively Spark, which was a quite inconsiderable horse. The boy insisted on putting a thousand on the horse, Bassett went for five hundred, and Oscar Cresswell two hundred. Lively Spark came in first, and the betting had been ten to one against him. Paul had made ten thousand.

'You see,' he said, 'I was absolutely sure of him.'

Even Oscar Cresswell had cleared two thousand.

'Look here, son,' he said, 'this sort of thing makes me nervous.'

'It needn't, uncle! Perhaps I shan't be sure again for a long time.'

'But what are you going to do with your money?' asked the uncle.

'Of course,' said the boy, 'I started it for mother. She said she had no luck, because father is unlucky, so I thought if *I* was lucky, it might stop whispering.'

'What might stop whispering?'

'Our house. I *hate* our house for whispering.'

'What does it whisper?'

'Why – why' – the boy fidgeted – 'why, I don't know. But it's always short of money, you know, uncle.'

'I know it, son, I know it.'

'You know people send mother writs, don't you, uncle?'

'I'm afraid I do,' said the uncle.

'And then the house whispers, like people laughing at you behind your back. It's awful, that is! I thought if I was lucky – '

'You might stop it,' added the uncle.

The boy watched him with big blue eyes that had an uncanny cold fire in them, and he said never a word.

'Well, then!' said the uncle. 'What are we doing?'

'I shouldn't like mother to know I was lucky,' said the boy.

'Why not, son?'

'She'd stop me.'

'I don't think she would.'

'Oh!' – and the boy writhed in an odd way – 'I *don't* want her to know, uncle.'

'All right, son! We'll manage it without her knowing.'

They managed it very easily. Paul, at the other's suggestion, handed over five thousand pounds to his uncle, who deposited it with the family lawyer, who was then to inform Paul's mother that a relative had put five thousand pounds into his hands, which sum was to be paid out a thousand pounds at a time, on the mother's birthday, for the next five years.

'So she'll have a birthday present of a thousand pounds for five successive years,' said Uncle Oscar. 'I hope it won't make it all the harder for her later.'

Paul's mother had her birthday in November. The house had been 'whispering' worse than ever lately, and, even in spite of his luck, Paul could not bear up against it. He was very anxious to see the effect of the birthday letter, telling his mother about the thousand pounds.

When there were no visitors, Paul now took his meals with his parents, as he was beyond the nursery control. His mother went into town nearly every day. She had discovered that she had an odd knack of sketching furs and dress materials, so she worked secretly in the studio of a friend who was the chief 'artist' for the leading drapers. She drew the figures of ladies in furs and ladies in silk and sequins for the newspaper advertisements. This young woman artist earned several thousand pounds a year, but Paul's mother only made several hundreds, and she was again dissatisfied. She so wanted to be first in something, and she did not succeed, even in making sketches for drapery advertisements.

She was down to breakfast on the morning of her birthday. Paul watched her face as she read her letters. He knew the lawyer's letter. As his mother read it, her face hardened and became more expressionless. Then a cold, determined look came on her mouth. She hid the letter under the pile of others, and said not a word about it.

'Didn't you have anything nice in the post for your birthday, mother?' said Paul.

'Quite moderately nice,' she said, her voice cold and absent.

She went away to town without saying more.

But in the afternoon Uncle Oscar appeared. He said Paul's mother had had a long interview with the lawyer, asking if the whole five thousand could not be advanced at once, as she was in debt.

'What do you think, uncle?' said the boy.

'I leave it to you, son.'

'Oh, let her have it, then! We can get some more with the other,' said the boy.

'A bird in the hand is worth two in the bush, laddie!' said Uncle Oscar.

'But I'm sure to *know* for the Grand National; or the Lincolnshire; or else the Derby. I'm sure to know for *one* of them,' said Paul.

So Uncle Oscar signed the agreement, and Paul's mother touched the whole five thousand. Then something very curious happened. The voices in the house suddenly went mad, like a chorus of frogs on a spring evening. There were certain new furnishings, and Paul had a tutor. He was *really* going to Eton, his father's school, in the following autumn. There were flowers in the winter, and a blossoming of the luxury Paul's mother had been used to. And yet the voices in the house, behind the sprays of mimosa and almond-blossom, and from under the piles of iridescent cushions, simply trilled and screamed in a sort of ecstasy: 'There *must* be more money! Oh-h-h; there *must* be more money. Oh, now, now—w! Now—w—w – there *must* be more money! – more than ever!'

More than ever?

It frightened Paul terribly. He studied away at his Latin and Greek with his tutor. But his intense hours were spent with Bassett. The Grand National had gone by; he had not 'known', and had lost a hundred pounds. Summer was at hand. He was in agony for the Lincoln. But even for the Lincoln he didn't 'know', and he lost fifty pounds. He became wild-eyed and strange, as if something were going to explode in him.

'Let it alone, son! Don't you bother about it!' urged Uncle Oscar. But it was as if the boy couldn't really hear what his uncle was saying.

'I've got to know for the Derby! I've got to know for the Derby!' the child reiterated, his big blue eyes blazing with a sort of madness.

His mother noticed how overwrought he was.

'You'd better go to the seaside. Wouldn't you like to go now to the seaside, instead of waiting? I think you'd better,' she said, looking down at him anxiously, her heart curiously heavy because of him.

But the child lifted his uncanny blue eyes.

'I couldn't possibly go before the Derby, mother!' he said. 'I couldn't possibly!'

'Why not?' she said, her voice becoming heavy when she was opposed. 'Why not? You can still go from the seaside to see the Derby with your Uncle Oscar, if that's what you wish. No need for you to wait here. Besides, I think you care too much about these races. It's a bad sign. My family has been a gambling family, and you won't know till you grow up how much damage it has done. But it has done damage. I shall have to send Bassett away, and ask Uncle Oscar not to talk racing to you, unless you promise to be reasonable about it; go away to the seaside and forget it. You're all nerves!'

'I'll do what you like, mother, so long as you don't send me away till after the Derby,' the boy said.

'Send you away from where? Just from this house?'

'Yes,' he said, gazing at her.

'Why, you curious child, what makes you care about this house so much, suddenly? I never knew you loved it.'

He gazed at her without speaking. He had a secret within a secret, something he had not divulged, even to Bassett or to his Uncle Oscar.

But his mother, after standing undecided and a little bit sullen for some moments, said: 'Very well, then! Don't go to the seaside till after the Derby, if you don't wish it. But promise me you won't let your nerves go to pieces. Promise you won't think so much about horse-racing, and *events*, as you call them!'

'Oh no,' said the boy casually. 'I won't think much about them, mother. You needn't worry. I wouldn't worry, mother, if I were you.'

'If you were me and I were you,' said his mother, 'I wonder what we *should* do!'

'But you know you needn't worry, mother, don't you?' the boy repeated.

'I should be awfully glad to know it,' she said wearily.

'Oh, well, you *can*, you know. I mean, you *ought* to know you needn't worry,' he insisted.

'Ought I? Then I'll see about it,' she said.

Paul's secret of secrets was his wooden horse, that which had no name. Since he was emancipated from a nurse and a nursery-governess, he had had his rocking-horse removed to his own bedroom at the top of the house.

'Surely you're too big for a rocking-horse!' his mother had remonstrated.

'Well, you see, mother, till I can have a *real* horse, I like to have *some* sort of animal about,' had been his quaint answer.

'Do you feel he keeps you company?' she laughed.

'Oh yes! He's very good, he always keeps me company when I'm there,' said Paul.

So the horse, rather shabby, stood in an arrested prance in the boy's bedroom.

The Derby was drawing near, and the boy grew more and more tense. He hardly heard what was spoken to him, he was very frail, and his eyes were really uncanny. His mother had sudden strange seizures of uneasiness about him. Sometimes, for half an hour, she would feel a sudden anxiety about him that was almost anguish. She wanted to rush to him at once, and know he was safe.

Two nights before the Derby, she was at a big party in town when one of her rushes of anxiety about her boy, her first-born, gripped her heart till she could hardly speak. She fought with the feeling, might and main, for she believed in common sense. But it was too strong. She had to leave the dance and go downstairs to telephone to the country. The children's nursery-governess was terribly surprised and startled at being rung up in the night.

'Are the children all right, Miss Wilmot?'

'Oh yes, they are quite all right.'

'Master Paul? Is he all right?'

'He went to bed as right as a trivet. Shall I run up and look at him?'

'No,' said Paul's mother reluctantly. 'No! Don't trouble. It's all right. Don't sit up. We shall be home fairly soon.' She did not want her son's privacy intruded upon.

'Very good,' said the governess.

It was about one o'clock when Paul's mother and father drove up to their house. All was still. Paul's mother went to her room and slipped off her white fur cloak. She had told her maid not to wait up for her. She heard her husband downstairs, mixing a whisky and soda.

And then, because of the strange anxiety at her heart, she stole upstairs to her son's room. Noiselessly she went along the upper corridor. Was there a faint noise? What was it?

She stood, with arrested muscles, outside his door, listening. There was a strange, heavy, and yet not loud noise. Her heart stood still. It was a soundless noise, yet rushing and powerful. Something huge, in violent, hushed motion. What was it? What in God's name was it? She ought to know. She felt that she knew the noise. She knew what it was.

Yet she could not place it. She couldn't say what it was. And on and on it went, like a madness.

Softly, frozen with anxiety and fear, she turned the door-handle.

The room was dark. Yet in the space near the window, she heard and saw something plunging to and fro. She gazed in fear and amazement.

Then suddenly she switched on the light, and saw her son in his green pyjamas, madly surging on the rocking-horse. The blaze of light suddenly lit him up, as he urged the wooden horse, and lit her up, as she stood, blonde, in her dress of pale green and crystal, in the doorway.

'Paul!' she cried. 'Whatever are you doing?'

'It's Malabar!' he screamed in a powerful, strange voice. 'It's Malabar!'

His eyes blazed at her for one strange and senseless second, as he ceased urging his wooden horse. Then he fell with a crash to the ground, and she, all her tormented motherhood flooding upon her, rushed to gather him up.

But he was unconscious and unconscious he remained, with some brain-fever. He talked and tossed, and his mother sat stonily by his side.

'Malabar! It's Malabar! Bassett, Bassett, I *know*! It's Malabar!'

So the child cried, trying to get up and urge the rocking-horse that gave him his inspiration.

'What does he mean by Malabar?' asked the heart-frozen mother.

'I don't know,' said the father stonily.

'What does he mean by Malabar?' she asked her brother Oscar.

'It's one of the horses running for the Derby,' was the answer.

And, in spite of himself, Oscar Cresswell spoke to Bassett, and himself put a thousand on Malabar: at fourteen to one.

The third day of the illness was critical: they were waiting for a change. The boy, with his rather long, curly hair, was tossing ceaselessly on the pillow. He neither slept nor regained consciousness, and his eyes were like blue stones. His mother sat, feeling her heart had gone, turned actually into a stone.

In the evening, Oscar Cresswell did not come, but Bassett sent a message, saying could he come up for one moment, just one moment? Paul's mother was very angry at the intrusion, but on second thoughts she agreed. The boy was the same. Perhaps Bassett might bring him to consciousness.

The gardener, a shortish fellow with a little brown moustache and sharp little brown eyes, tiptoed into the room, touched his imaginary cap to Paul's mother, and stole to the bedside, staring with glittering, smallish eyes at the tossing, dying child.

'Master Paul!' he whispered. 'Master Paul! Malabar came in first all right, a clean win. I did as you told me. You've made over seventy thousand pounds, you have; you've got over eighty thousand. Malabar came in all right, Master Paul.'

'Malabar! Malabar! Did I say Malabar, mother? Did I say Malabar? Do you think I'm lucky, mother? I knew Malabar, didn't I? Over eighty thousand pounds! I call that lucky, don't you, mother? Over eighty thousand pounds! I knew, didn't I know I knew? Malabar came in all right. If I ride my horse till I'm sure, then I tell you, Bassett, you can go as high as you like. Did you go for all you were worth, Bassett?'

'I went a thousand on it, Master Paul.'

'I never told you, mother, that if I can ride my horse, and *get there*, then I'm absolutely sure – oh, absolutely! Mother, did I ever tell you? I *am* lucky!'

'No, you never did,' said his mother.

But the boy died in the night.

And even as he lay dead, his mother heard her brother's voice saying to her: 'My God, Hester, you're eighty-odd thousand to the good, and a poor devil of a son to the bad. But, poor devil, poor devil, he's best gone out of a life where he rides his rocking-horse to find a winner.'

The Beast with Five Fingers

W. F. HARVEY

THE STORY, I suppose, begins with Adrian Borlsover, whom I met when I was a little boy and he an old man. My father had called to appeal for a subscription, and I was with him. Before we left, Mr Borlsover laid his right hand in blessing on my head. I shall never forget the awe in which I gazed up at his face and realised for the first time that eyes might be dark and beautiful and shining, and yet not able to see.

For Adrian Borlsover was blind.

He was an extraordinary man, who came of an eccentric stock. Borlsover sons for some reason always seemed to marry very ordinary women; which perhaps accounted for the fact that no Borlsover had been a genius, and only one Borlsover had been mad. But they were great champions of little causes, generous patrons of odd sciences, founders of querulous sects, trustworthy guides to the bypath meadows of erudition.

Adrian was an authority on the fertilisation of orchids. He had held at one time the family living at Borlsover Conyers, until a congenital weakness of the lungs obliged him to seek a less rigorous climate in the sunny south-coast watering-place where I had seen him. Occasionally he would relieve one or other of the local clergy. My father described him as a fine preacher, who gave long and inspiring sermons from what many men would have considered unprofitable texts. 'An excellent proof,' he would add, 'of the truth of the doctrine of direct verbal inspiration.'

Adrian Borlsover was exceedingly clever with his hands. His penmanship was exquisite. He illustrated all his scientific papers, made his own woodcuts, and carved the reredos that is at present the chief feature of interest in the church at Borlsover Conyers. He had an exceedingly clever knack in cutting silhouettes for young ladies and paper pigs and cows for little children, and made more than one complicated wind-instrument of his own devising

When he was fifty years old Adrian Borlsover lost his sight. In a wonderfully short time he adapted himself to the new conditions of life. He quickly learnt to read Braille. So marvellous indeed was his sense of touch that he was still able to maintain his interest in botany The mere passing of his long supple fingers over a flower was sufficient means for its identification, though occasionally he would use his lips. I have found several letters of his among my father's correspondence; in no case was there anything to show that he was afflicted with blindness and this in spite of the fact that he exercised undue economy in the spacing of lines. Towards the close of his life Adrian Borlsover was credited with powers of touch that seemed almost uncanny. It has been said that he could tell at once the colour of a ribbon placed between his fingers. My father would neither confirm nor deny the story.

Adrian Borlsover was a bachelor. His elder brother, Charles, had married late in life, leaving one son, Eustace, who lived in the gloomy Georgian mansion at Borlsover Conyers, where he could work undisturbed in collecting material for his great book on heredity.

Like his uncle, he was a remarkable man. The Borlsovers had always been born naturalists, but Eustace possessed in a special degree the power of systematising his knowledge. He had received his university education in Germany; and then, after post-graduate work in Vienna and Naples, had travelled for four years in South America and the East, getting together a huge store of material for a new study into the processes of variation.

He lived alone at Borlsover Conyers with Saunders, his secretary, a man who bore a somewhat dubious reputation in the district, but whose powers as a mathematician, combined with his business abilities, were invaluable to Eustace.

Uncle and nephew saw little of each other. The visits of Eustace were confined to a week in the summer or autumn – tedious weeks, that dragged almost as slowly as the bath-chair in which the old man was drawn along the sunny seafront. In their way the two men were fond of each other, though their intimacy would, doubtless, have been greater, had they shared the same religious views. Adrian held to the old-fashioned evangelical dogmas of his early manhood; his nephew for many years had been thinking of embracing Buddhism. Both men possessed, too, the reticence the Borlsovers had always shown, and which their enemies sometimes called hypocrisy. With Adrian it was a reticence as to the things he had left undone; but with Eustace it seemed that the curtain which he was so careful to leave undrawn hid something more than a half-empty chamber.

Two years before his death, Adrian Borlsover developed, unknown to himself, the not uncommon power of automatic writing. Eustace made the discovery by accident. Adrian was sitting reading in bed, the forefinger of his left hand tracing the Braille characters, when his nephew noticed that a pencil the old man held in his right hand was moving slowly along the opposite page. He had left his seat in the window and sat down beside the bed. The right hand continued to move, and now he could see plainly that they were letters and words which it was forming.

'Adrian Borlsover,' wrote the hand, 'Eustace Borlsover, Charles Borlsover, Francis Borlsover, Sigismund Borlsover, Adrian Borlsover, Eustace Borlsover, Saville Borlsover. B for Borlsover. Honesty is the Best Policy Beautiful Belinda Borlsover.'

'What curious nonsense!' said Eustace to himself.

'King George ascended the throne in 1760,' wrote the hand. 'Crowd, a noun of multitude; a collection of individuals. Adrian Borlsover, Eustace Borlsover.'

'It seems to me,' said his uncle, closing the book, 'that you had much better make the most of the afternoon sunshine and take your walk now.'

'I think perhaps I will,' Eustace answered as he picked up the volume. 'I won't go far, and when I come back I can read to you those articles in *Nature* about which we were speaking.'

He went along the promenade, but stopped at the first shelter, and, seating himself in the corner best protected from the wind, he examined the book at leisure. Nearly every page was scored with a meaningless jumble of pencil-marks; rows of capital letters, short words, long words complete sentences, copy-book tags. The whole thing, in fact, had the appearance of a copy-book, and, on a more careful scrutiny, Eustace thought that there was ample evidence to show that the handwriting at the beginning of the book, good though it was, was not nearly so good as the handwriting at the end.

He left his uncle at the end of October with a promise to return early in December. It seemed to him quite clear that the old man's power of automatic writing was developing rapidly, and for the first time he looked forward to a visit that would combine duty with interest.

But on his return he was at first disappointed. His uncle, he thought, looked older. He was listless, too, preferring others to read to him and dictating nearly all his letters. Not until the day before he left had Eustace an opportunity of observing Adrian Borlsover's new-found faculty.

The old man, propped up in bed with pillows, had sunk into a light sleep. His two hands lay on the coverlet, his left hand tightly clasping his right. Eustace took an empty manuscript book and placed a pencil within reach of the fingers of the right hand. They snatched at it eagerly, then dropped the pencil to loose the left hand from its restraining grasp.

'Perhaps to prevent interference I had better hold that hand,' said Eustace to himself, as he watched the pencil. Almost immediately it began to write.

'Blundering Borlsovers, unnecessarily unnatural, extraordinarily eccentric, culpably curious.'

'Who are you?' asked Eustace in a low voice.

'Never you mind,' wrote the hand of Adrian.

'Is it my uncle who is writing?'

'O my prophetic soul, mine uncle!'

'Is it anyone I know?'

'Silly Eustace, you'll see me very soon.'

'When shall I see you?'

'When poor old Adrian's dead.'

'Where shall I see you?'

'Where shall you not?'

Instead of speaking his next question, Eustace wrote it. 'What is the time?'

The fingers dropped the pencil and moved three or four times across the paper. Then, picking up the pencil, they wrote: 'Ten minutes before four. Put your book away, Eustace. Adrian mustn't find us working at this sort of thing. He doesn't know what to make of it, and I won't have poor old Adrian disturbed. Au revoir!'

Adrian Borlsover awoke with a start.

'I've been dreaming again,' he said; 'such queer dreams of leaguered cities and forgotten towns. You were mixed up in this one, Eustace, though I can't remember how. Eustace, I want to warn you. Don't walk in doubtful paths. Choose your friends well. Your poor grandfather . . .'

A fit of coughing put an end to what he was saying, but Eustace saw that the hand was still writing. He managed unnoticed to draw the book away. 'I'll light the gas,' he said, 'and ring for tea.' On the other side of the bedcurtain he saw the last sentence that had been written.

'It's too late, Adrian,' it said. 'We're friends already, aren't we, Eustace Borlsover?'

On the following day Eustace left. He thought his uncle looked ill when he said goodbye, and the old man spoke despondently of the failure his life had been.

'Nonsense, uncle,' said his nephew. 'You have got over your difficulties in a way not one in a hundred thousand would have done. Everyone marvels at your splendid perseverance in teaching your hand to take the place of your lost sight. To me it's been a revelation of the possibilities of education.'

'Education,' said his uncle dreamily, as if the word had started a new train of thought. 'Education is good so long as you know to whom and for what purpose you give it. But with the lower orders of men, the base and more sordid spirits, I have grave doubts as to its results. Well, goodbye, Eustace; I may not see you again. You are a true Borlsover, with all the Borlsover faults. Marry, Eustace. Marry some good, sensible girl. And if by any chance I don't see you again, my will is at my solicitors. I've not left you any legacy, because I know you're well provided for; but I thought you might like to have my books. Oh, and there's just another thing. You know, before the end, people often lose control over themselves and make absurd requests. Don't pay any attention to them, Eustace. Goodbye!' and he held out his hand. Eustace took it. It remained in his a fraction of a second longer than he had expected and gripped him with a virility that was surprising. There was, too, in its touch a subtle sense of intimacy.

'Why, uncle,' he said, 'I shall see you alive and well for many long years to come.'

Two months later Adrian Borlsover died.

Eustace Borlsover was in Naples at the time. He read the obituary notice in the *Morning Post* on the day announced for the funeral.

'Poor old fellow!' he said. 'I wonder whether I shall find room for all his books.'

The question occurred to him again with greater force when, three days later, he found himself standing in the library at Borlsover Conyers, a huge room built for use and not for beauty in the year of Waterloo by a Borlsover who was an ardent admirer of the great Napoleon. It was arranged on the plan of many college libraries, with tall projecting bookcases forming deep recesses of dusty silence, fit graves for the old hates of forgotten controversy, the dead passions of forgotten lives. At the end of the room, behind the bust of some unknown eighteenth-century divine, an ugly iron corkscrew stair led to a shelf-lined gallery. Nearly every shelf was full.

'I must talk to Saunders about it,' said Eustace. 'I suppose that we shall have to have the billiard-room fitted up with bookcases.'

The two men met for the first time after many weeks in the dining-room that evening.

'Hallo!' said Eustace, standing before the fire with his hands in his pockets. 'How goes the world, Saunders? Why these dress togs?' He himself was wearing an old shooting-jacket. He did not believe in mourning, as he had told his uncle on his last visit; and, though he usually went in for quiet-coloured ties, he wore this evening one of an ugly red, in order to shock Morton the butler, and to make them thrash out the whole question of mourning for themselves in the servants' hall. Eustace was a true Borlsover. 'The world,' said Saunders, 'goes the same as usual, confoundedly slow. The dress togs are accounted for by an invitation from Captain Lockwood to bridge.'

'How are you getting there?'

'There's something the matter with the car, so I've told Jackson to drive me round in the dogcart. Any objection?'

'Oh dear me, no! We've had all things in common for far too many years for me to raise objections at this hour of the day.'

You'll find your correspondence in the library,' went on Saunders. 'Most of it I've seen to. There are a few private letters I haven't opened. There's also a box with a rat or something inside it that came by the evening post. Very likely it's the six-toed beast Terry was sending us to cross with the four-toed albino. I didn't look because I didn't want to mess up my things; but I should gather from the way it's jumping about that it's pretty hungry.'

'Oh, I'll see to it,' said Eustace, 'while you and the captain earn an honest penny.'

Dinner over and Saunders gone, Eustace went into the library. Though the fire had been lit, the room was by no means cheerful.

'We'll have all the lights on, at any rate,' he said, as he turned the switches. 'And, Morton,' he added, when the butler brought the coffee, 'get me a screwdriver or something to undo this box. Whatever the animal is, he's kicking up the deuce of a row. What is it? Why are you dawdling?'

'If you please, sir, when the postman brought it, he told me that they'd bored the holes in the lid at the post office. There were no breathing holes in the lid, sir, and they didn't want the animal to die. That is all, sir.'

'It's culpably careless of the man, whoever he was,' said Eustace, as he removed the screws, 'packing an animal like this in a wooden box with no means of getting air. Confound it all! I meant to ask Morton to bring me a cage to put it in. Now I suppose I shall have to get one myself.'

He placed a heavy book on the lid from which the screws had been removed, and went into the billiard-room. As he came back into the library with an empty cage in his hand, he heard the sound of something falling, and then of something scuttling along the floor.

'Bother it! The beast's got out. How in the world am I to find it again in this library?'

To search for it did indeed seem hopeless. He tried to follow the sound of the scuttling in one of the recesses, where the animal seemed to be running behind the books in the shelves; but it was impossible to locate it. Eustace resolved to go on quietly reading. Very likely the animal might gain confidence and show itself. Saunders seemed to have dealt in his usual methodical manner with most of the correspondence. There were still the private letters.

What was that? Two sharp clicks and the lights in the hideous candelabras that hung from the ceiling suddenly went out.

'I wonder if something has gone wrong with the fuse,' said Eustace, as he went to the switches by the door. Then he stopped. There was a noise at the other end of the room, as if something was crawling up the iron corkscrew stair. 'If it's gone into the gallery,' he said, 'well and good.' He hastily turned on the lights, crossed the room, and climbed up the stair. But he could see nothing. His grandfather had placed a little gate at the top of the stair, so that children could run and romp in the gallery without fear of accident. This Eustace closed, and, having considerably narrowed the circle of his search, returned to his desk by the fire.

How gloomy the library was! There was no sense of intimacy about the room. The few busts that an eighteenth-century Borlsover had brought back from the Grand Tour might have been in keeping in the old library. Here they seemed out of place. They made the room feel cold in spite of the heavy red damask curtains and great gilt cornices.

With a crash two heavy books fell from the gallery to the floor; then, as Borlsover looked, another and yet another.

'Very well. You'll starve for this, my beauty!' he said. 'We'll do some little experiments on the metabolism of rats deprived of water. Go on! Chuck them down! I think I've got the upper hand.' He turned once more to his correspondence. One letter was from the family solicitor. It spoke of his uncle's death, and of the valuable collection of books that had been left to him in the will.

There was one request [he read] which certainly came as a surprise to me. As you know, Mr Adrian Borlsover had left instructions that his body was to be buried in as simple a manner as possible at Eastbourne. He expressed a desire that there should be neither wreaths nor flowers of any kind, and hoped that his friends and relatives would not consider it necessary to wear mourning. The day before his death we received a letter cancelling these instructions. He wished the body to be embalmed (he gave us the address of the man we were to employ – Pennifer, Ludgate Hill), with orders that his right hand should be sent to you, stating that it was at your special request. The other arrangements about the funeral remained unaltered.

'Good Lord,' said Eustace, 'what in the world was the old boy driving at? And what in the name of all that's holy is that?'

Someone was in the gallery. Someone had pulled the cord attached to one of the blinds, and it had rolled up with a snap. Someone must be in the gallery, for a second blind did the same. Someone must be walking round the gallery, for one after the other the blinds sprang up, letting in the moonlight.

'I haven't got to the bottom of this yet,' said Eustace, 'but I will do, before the night is very much older,' and he hurried up the corkscrew stair. He had just got to the top, when the lights went out a second time, and he heard again the scuttling along the floor. Quickly he stole on tiptoe in the dim moonshine in the direction of the noise, feeling, as he went, for one of the switches. His fingers touched the metal knob at last. He turned on the electric light.

About ten yards in front of him, crawling along the floor, was a man's hand. Eustace stared at it in utter amazement. It was moving quickly in the manner of a geometer caterpillar, the fingers humped up one moment, flattened out the next; the thumb appeared to give a crablike motion to the whole. While he was looking, too surprised to stir, the hand disappeared round the corner.

Eustace ran forward. He no longer saw it, but he could hear it as it squeezed its way behind the books on one of the shelves. A heavy volume had been displaced. There was a gap in the row of books, where it had got in. In his fear lest it should escape him again, he seized the first book that came to his hand and plugged it into the hole. Then, emptying two shelves of their contents, he took the wooden boards and propped them up in front to make his barrier doubly sure.

'I wish Saunders was back,' he said; 'one can't tackle this sort of thing alone.' It was after eleven, and there seemed little likelihood of Saunders returning before twelve. He did not dare to leave the shelf unwatched even to run downstairs to ring the bell. Morton, the butler, often used to come round about eleven to see that the windows were fastened, but he might not come tonight. Eustace was thoroughly unstrung. At last he heard steps down below.

'Morton!' he shouted. 'Morton!'

'Sir?'

'Has Mr Saunders got back yet?'

'Not yet, sir.'

'Well, bring me some brandy, and hurry up about it. I'm up in the gallery, you duffer.'

Morton fetched the brandy.

'Thanks,' said Eustace, as he emptied the glass. 'Don't go to bed yet, Morton. There are a lot of books that have fallen down by accident. Bring them up and put them back in their shelves.'

Morton had never seen Borlsover in so talkative a mood as on that night. 'Here,' said Eustace, when the books had been put back and dusted, 'you might hold up these boards for me, Morton. That beast in the box got out, and I've been chasing it all over the place.'

'I think I can hear it clawing at the books, sir. They're not valuable, I hope? I think that's the carriage, sir; I'll go and call Mr Saunders.'

It seemed to Eustace that he was away for five minutes but it could hardly have been more than one when he returned with Saunders. 'All right, Morton, you can go now. I'm up here, Saunders.'

'What's all the row?' asked Saunders, as he lounged forward with his hands in his pockets. The luck had been with him all the evening. He was completely satisfied, both with himself and with Captain Lockwood's taste in wines. 'What's the matter? You look to me to be in an absolutely blue funk.'

'That old devil of an uncle of mine,' began Eustace – 'Oh, I can't explain it all. It's his hand that's been playing Old Harry all the evening. But I've got it cornered behind these books. You've got to help me to catch it.'

'What's up with you, Eustace? What's the game?'

'It's no game, you silly idiot! If you don't believe me, take out one of those books and put your hand in and feel.'

'All right,' said Saunders; 'but wait till I've rolled up my sleeve. The accumulated dust of centuries, eh?' He took off his coat, knelt down, and thrust his arm along the shelf.

'There's something there right enough,' he said. 'It's got a funny, stumpy end to it, whatever it is, and nips like a crab. Ah! no, you don't!' He pulled his hand out in a flash. 'Shove in a book quickly. Now it can't get out.'

'What was it?' asked Eustace.

'Something that wanted very much to get hold of me. I felt what seemed like a thumb and forefinger. Give me some brandy.'

'How are we to get it out of there? What about a landing-net'

'No good. It would be too smart for us. I tell you, Saunders, it can cover the ground far faster than I can walk. But I think I see how we can manage it. The two books at the end of the shelf are big ones that go right back against the wall. The others are very thin. I'll take out one at a time, and you slide the rest along, until we have it squashed between the end two.'

It certainly seemed to be the best plan. One by one as they took out the books, the space behind grew smaller and smaller. There was something in it that was certainly very much alive. Once they caught sight of fingers feeling for a way of escape. At last they had it pressed between the two big books.

'There's muscle there, if there isn't warm flesh and blood,' said Saunders, as he held them together. 'It seems to be a hand right enough, too. I suppose this is a sort of infectious hallucination. I've read about such cases before.'

'Infectious fiddlesticks!' said Eustace, his face white with anger; 'bring the thing downstairs. We'll get it back into the box.'

It was not altogether easy, but they were successful at last. 'Drive in the screws,' said Eustace, 'we won't run any risks. Put the box in this old desk of mine. There's nothing in it that I want. Here's the key. Thank goodness there's nothing wrong with the lock.'

'Quite a lively evening,' said Saunders. 'Now let's hear more about your uncle.'

They sat up together until early morning. Saunders had no desire for sleep. Eustace was trying to explain and forget; to conceal from himself a fear that he had never felt before – the fear of walking alone down the long corridor to his bedroom

'Whatever it was,' said Eustace to Saunders on the following morning, 'I propose that we drop the subject. There's nothing to keep us here for the next ten days. We'll motor up to the Lakes and get some climbing.'

'And see nobody all day, and sit bored to death with each other every night. Not for me, thanks. Why not run up to town? Run's the exact word in this case, isn't it? We're both in such a blessed funk. Pull yourself together, Eustace, and let's have another look at the hand.'

'As you like,' said Eustace; 'there's the key.'

They went into the library and opened the desk. The box was as they had left it on the previous night.

'What are you waiting for?' asked Eustace.

'I am waiting for you to volunteer to open the lid. However, since you seem to funk it, allow me. There doesn't seem to be the likelihood of any rumpus this morning at all events.' He opened the lid and picked out the hand.

'Cold?' asked Eustace.

'Tepid. A bit below blood heat by the feel. Soft and supple too. If it's the embalming, it's a sort of embalming I've never seen before. Is it your uncle's hand?'

'Oh, yes, it's his all right,' said Eustace. 'I should know those long thin fingers anywhere. Put it back in the box, Saunders. Never mind about the screws. I'll lock the desk, so that there'll be no chance of its getting out. We'll compromise by motoring up to town for a week. If we can get off soon after lunch, we ought to be at Grantham or Stamford by night.'

'Right,' said Saunders, 'and tomorrow – oh, well, by tomorrow we shall have forgotten all about this beastly thing.'

If, when the morrow came, they had not forgotten, it was certainly true that at the end of the week they were able to tell a very vivid ghost-story at the little supper Eustace gave on Hallowe'en.

'You don't want us to believe that it's true, Mr Borlsover? How perfectly awful!'

'I'll take my oath on it, and so would Saunders here, wouldn't you, old chap?'

'Any number of oaths,' said Saunders. 'It was a long, thin hand, you know, and it gripped me just like that.'

'Don't, Mr Saunders! Don't! How perfectly horrid! Now tell us another one, do! Only a really creepy one, please.'

'Here's a pretty mess!' said Eustace on the following day, as he threw a letter across the table to Saunders. It's your affair, though. Mrs Merritt, if I understand it, gives a month's notice.'

'Oh, that's quite absurd on Mrs Merritt's part,' replied Saunders. 'She doesn't know what she's talking about. Let's see what she says.

> Dear Sir – This is to let you know that I must give you a month's notice as from Tuesday, the 13th. For a long time I've felt the place too big for me; but when Jane Parfit and Emma Laidlaw go off with scarcely as much as an 'If you please,' after frightening the wits out of the other girls, so that they can't turn out a room by themselves or walk alone down the stairs for fear of treading on half-frozen toads or hearing it run along the passages at night, all I can say is that it's no place for me. So I must ask you, Mr Borlsover, sir, to find a new housekeeper, that has no objection to large and lonely houses, which some people do say – not that I believe them for a minute, my poor mother always having been a Wesleyan – are haunted.
>
> Yours faithfully,
> Elizabeth Merritt

> PS – I should be obliged if you would give my respects to Mr Saunders. I hope that he won't run any risks with his cold.'

'Saunders,' said Eustace, 'you've always had a wonderful way with you in dealing with servants. You mustn't let poor old Merritt go.'

'Of course she shan't go,' said Saunders. 'She's probably only angling for a rise in salary. I'll write to her this morning.'

'No. There's nothing like a personal interview. We've had enough of town. We'll go back tomorrow, and you must work your cold for all it's worth. Don't forget that it's got on to the chest, and will require weeks of feeding up and nursing.'

'All right; I think I can manage Mrs Merritt.'

But Mrs Merritt was more obstinate than he had thought. She was very sorry to hear of Mr Saunders's cold, and how he lay awake all night in London coughing; very sorry indeed. She'd change his room for him gladly and get the south room aired, and wouldn't he have a hot basin of bread and milk last thing at night? But she was afraid that she would have to leave at the end of the month.

'Try her with an increase of salary,' was the advice of Eustace.

It was no use. Mrs Merritt was obdurate, though she knew of a Mrs Goddard, who had been housekeeper to Lord Gargrave, who might be glad to come at the salary mentioned.

'What's the matter with the servants, Morton?' asked Eustace that evening, when he brought the coffee into the library. 'What's all this about Mrs Merritt wanting to leave?'

'If you please, sir, I was going to mention it myself. I have a confession to make, sir. When I found your note, asking me to open that desk and take out the box with the rat, I broke the lock, as you told me, and was glad to do it, because I could hear the animal in the box making a great noise, and I thought it wanted food. So I took out the box, sir, and got a cage, and was going to transfer it, when the animal got away.'

'What in the world are you talking about? I never wrote any such note.'

'Excuse me, sir; it was the note I picked up here on the floor the day you and Mr Saunders left. I have it in my pocket now.'

It certainly seemed to be in Eustace's handwriting. It was written in pencil and began somewhat abruptly.

'*Get a hammer, Morton,*' he read, '*or some tool and break open the lock in the old desk in the library. Take out the box that is inside. You need not do anything else. The lid is already open. Eustace Borlsover.*'

'And you opened the desk?'

'Yes, sir; and, as I was getting the cage ready, the animal hopped out.'

'What animal?'

'The animal inside the box, sir.'

'What did it look like?'

'Well, sir, I couldn't tell you,' said Morton, nervously. 'My back was turned, and it was halfway down the room when I looked up.'

'What was its colour?' asked Saunders. 'Black?'

'Oh, no, sir; a greyish white. It crept along in a very funny way, sir. I don't think it had a tail.'

'What did you do then?'

'I tried to catch it; but it was no use. So I set the rat-traps and kept the library shut. Then that girl, Emma Laidlaw, left the door open when she was cleaning, and I think it must have escaped.'

'And you think it is the animal that's been frightening the maids?'

'Well, no, sir, not quite. They said it was – you'll excuse me, sir – a hand that they saw. Emma trod on it once at the bottom of the stairs. She thought then it was a half-frozen toad, only white. And then Parfit was washing up the dishes in the scullery. She wasn't thinking about anything in particular. It was close on dusk. She took her hands out of the water and was drying them absent-minded-like on the roller towel, when she found she was drying someone else's hand as well, only colder than hers.'

'What nonsense!' exclaimed Saunders.

'Exactly, sir; that's what I told her, but we couldn't get her to stop.'

'You don't believe all this?' said Eustace, turning suddenly towards the butler.

'Me, sir? Oh, no, sir! I've not seen anything.'

'Nor heard anything?'

'Well, sir, if you must know the bells do ring at odd times, and there's nobody there when we go; and when we go round to draw the blinds of a night, as often as not somebody's been there before us. But, as I says to Mrs Merritt, a young monkey might do wonderful things, and we all know that Mr Borlsover has had some strange animals about the place.'

'Very well, Morton, that will do.'

'What do you make of it?' asked Saunders, when they were alone. 'I mean of the letter he said you wrote.'

'Oh, that's simple enough,' said Eustace. 'See the paper it's written on? I stopped using that paper years ago, but there were a few odd sheets and envelopes left in the old desk. We never fastened up the lid of the box before locking it in. The hand got out, found a pencil, wrote this note, and shoved it through the crack on to the floor, where Morton found it. That's plain as daylight.'

'But the hand couldn't write!'

'Couldn't it? You've not seen it do the things I've seen.' And he told Saunders more of what had happened at Eastbourne.

'Well,' said Saunders, 'in that case we have at least an explanation of the legacy. It was the hand which wrote, unknown to your uncle, that letter to your solicitor bequeathing itself to you. Your uncle had no more to do with that request than I. In fact, it would seem that he had some idea of this automatic writing and feared it.'

'Then if it's not my uncle, what is it?'

'I suppose some people might say that a disembodied spirit had got your uncle to educate and prepare a little body for it. Now it's got into that little body and is off on its own.'

'Well, what are we to do?'

'We'll keep our eyes open,' said Saunders, 'and try to catch it. If we can't do that, we shall have to wait till the bally clockwork runs down. After all, if it's flesh and blood, it can't live for ever.'

For two days nothing happened. Then Saunders saw it sliding down the banister in the hall. He was taken unawares and lost a full second before he started in pursuit, only to find that the thing had escaped him. Three days later, Eustace, writing alone in the library at night, saw it sitting on an open book at the other end of the room. The fingers crept over the page, as if it were reading, but before he had time to get up from his seat, it had taken the alarm, and was pulling itself up the curtains. Eustace watched it grimly, as it hung on to the cornice with three fingers and flicked thumb and forefinger at him in an expression of scornful derision.

'I know what I'll do,' he said. 'If I only get it into the open, I'll set the dogs on to it.'

He spoke to Saunders of the suggestion.

'It's a jolly good idea,' he said; 'only we won't wait till we find it out of doors. We'll get the dogs. There are the two terriers and the under-keeper's Irish mongrel that's on to rats like a flash. Your spaniel has not got spirit enough for this sort of game.'

They brought the dogs into the house, and the keeper's Irish mongrel chewed up the slippers, and the terriers tripped up Morton, as he waited at table; but all three were welcome. Even false security is better than no security at all.

For a fortnight nothing happened. Then the hand was caught, not by the dogs, but by Mrs Merritt's grey parrot. The bird was in the habit of periodically removing the pins that kept his seed- and water-tins in place, and then escaping through the holes in the side of his cage. When once at liberty, Peter would show no inclination to return, and would often be about the house for days. Now, after six consecutive weeks of captivity, Peter had again discovered a new way of unloosing his bolts and was at large, exploring the tapestried forests of the curtains and singing songs in praise of liberty from cornice and picture-rail.

'It's no use your trying to catch him,' said Eustace to Mrs Merritt, as she came into the study one afternoon towards dusk with a stepladder. 'You'd much better leave Peter alone. Starve him into surrender, Mrs Merritt: and don't leave bananas and seed about for him to peck at when he fancies he's hungry. You're far too soft-hearted.'

'Well, sir, I see he's right out of reach now on that picture-rail; so, if you wouldn't mind closing the door, sir, when you leave the room, I'll bring his cage in tonight and put some meat inside it. He's that fond of meat, though it does make him pull out his feathers to suck the quills. They say that if you cook – '

'Never mind, Mrs Merritt,' said Eustace, who was busy writing; 'that will do; I'll keep an eye on the bird.'

For a short time there was silence in the room.

'Scratch poor Peter,' said the bird. 'Scratch poor old Peter!'

'Be quiet, you beastly bird!'

'Poor old Peter! Scratch poor Peter; do!'

'I'm more likely to wring your neck, if I get hold of you.' He looked up at the picture-rail, and there was the hand, holding on to a hook with three fingers, and slowly scratching the head of the parrot with the fourth. Eustace ran to the bell and pressed it hard; then across to the window, which he closed with a bang. Frightened by the noise, the parrot shook its wings preparatory to flight, and, as it did so, the fingers of the hand got hold of it by the throat. There was a shrill scream from Peter, as he fluttered across the room, wheeling round in circles that ever descended, borne down under the weight that clung to him. The bird dropped at last quite suddenly, and Eustace saw fingers and feathers rolled into an inextricable mass on the floor. The struggle abruptly ceased, as finger and thumb squeezed the neck; the bird's eyes rolled up to show the whites, and there was a faint, half-choked gurgle. But, before the fingers had time to loose their hold, Eustace had them in his own.

'Send Mr Saunders here at once,' he said to the maid who came in answer to the bell. 'Tell him I want him immediately.'

Then he went with the hand to the fire. There was a ragged gash across the back, where the bird's beak had torn it, but no blood oozed from the wound. He noted with disgust that the nails had grown long and discoloured.

'I'll burn the beastly thing,' he said. But he could not burn it. He tried to throw it into the flames, but his own hands, as if impelled by some old primitive feeling, would not let him. And so Saunders found him, pale and irresolute, with the hand still clasped tightly in his fingers.

'I've got it at last,' he said, in a tone of triumph.

'Good, let's have a look at it.'

'Not when it's loose. Get me some nails and a hammer and a board of some sort.'

'Can you hold it all right?'

'Yes, the thing's quite limp; tired out with throttling poor old Peter, I should say.'

'And now,' said Saunders, when he returned with the things, 'what are we going to do?'

'Drive a nail through it first, so that it can't get away. Then we can take our time over examining it.'

'Do it yourself,' said Saunders. 'I don't mind helping you with guinea-pigs occasionally, when there's something to be learned, partly because I don't fear a guinea-pig's revenge. This thing's different.'

'Oh, my aunt!' Eustace giggled hysterically, 'look at it now.' For the hand was writhing in agonised contortions, squirming and wriggling upon the nail like a worm upon the hook.

'Well,' said Saunders, 'you've done it now. I'll leave you to examine it.'

'Don't go, in heaven's name! Cover it up, man; cover it up! Shove a cloth over it! Here!' and he pulled off the antimacassar from the back of a chair and wrapped the board in it. 'Now get the keys from my pocket and open the safe. Chuck the other things out. Oh, Lord, it's getting itself into frightful knots! Open it quick!' He threw the thing in and banged the door.

'We'll keep it there till it dies,' he said. 'May I burn in hell, if I ever open the door of that safe again.'

Mrs Merritt departed at the end of the month. Her successor, Mrs Handyside, certainly was more successful in the management of the servants. Early in her rule she declared that she would stand no nonsense, and gossip soon withered and died.

'I shouldn't be surprised if Eustace married one of these days,' said Saunders. Well, I'm in no hurry for such an event. I know him far too well for the future Mrs Borlsover to like me. It will be the same old story again; a long friendship slowly made – marriage – and a long friendship quickly forgotten.'

But Eustace did not follow the advice of his uncle and marry. Old habits crept over and covered his new experience. He was, if anything, less morose, and showed a greater inclination to take his natural part in country society.

Then came the burglary. The men, it was said, broke into the house by way of the conservatory. It was really little more than an attempt, for they only succeeded in carrying away a few pieces of plate from the pantry. The safe in the study was certainly found open and empty, but, as Mr Borlsover informed the police inspector, he had kept nothing of value in it during the last six months.

'Then you're lucky in getting off so easily, sir,' the man replied. 'By the way they have gone about their business, I should say they were experienced cracksmen. They must have caught the alarm when they were just beginning their evening's work.'

'Yes,' said Eustace, 'I suppose I am lucky.'

'I've no doubt,' said the inspector, 'that we shall be able to trace the men. I've said that they must have been old hands at the game. The way they got in and opened the safe shows that. But there's one little thing that puzzles me. One of them was careless enough not to wear gloves, and I'm bothered if I know what he was trying to do. I've traced his fingermarks on the new varnish on the window-sashes in every one of the downstairs rooms. They are very distinctive ones too.'

'Right or left hand, or both?' asked Eustace.

'Oh, right every time. That's the funny thing. He must have been a foolhardy fellow, and I rather think it was him that wrote that.' He took out a slip of paper from his pocket. 'That's what he wrote, sir: *I've got out, Eustace Borlsover, but I'll be back before long*. Some jailbird just escaped, I suppose. It will make it all the easier for us to trace him. Do you know the writing, sir?'

'No,' said Eustace. 'It's not the writing of anyone I know.'

'I'm not going to stay here any longer,' said Eustace to Saunders at luncheon. 'I've got on far better during the last six months than I expected, but I'm not going to run the risk of seeing that thing again. I shall go up to town this afternoon. Get Morton to put my things together, and join me with the car at Brighton on the day after tomorrow. And bring the proofs of those two papers with you. We'll run over them together.'

'How long are you going to be away?'

'I can't say for certain, but be prepared to stay for some time. We've stuck to work pretty closely through the summer, and I for one need a holiday. I'll engage the rooms at Brighton. You'll find it best to break the journey at Hitchin. I'll wire to you there at the Crown to tell you the Brighton address.'

The house he chose at Brighton was in a terrace. He had been there before. It was kept by his old college gyp, a man of discreet silence, who was admirably partnered by an excellent cook. The rooms were on the first floor; the two bedrooms were at the back, and opened out of each other. 'Mr Saunders can have the smaller one, though it is the only one with a fireplace,' he said. 'I'll stick to the larger of the two, since it's got a bathroom adjoining. I wonder what time he'll arrive with the car.'

Saunders came about seven, cold and cross and dirty. 'We'll light the fire in the dining-room,' said Eustace, 'and get Prince to unpack some of the things while we are at dinner. What were the roads like?'

'Rotten. Swimming with mud, and a beastly cold wind against us all day. And this is July. Dear old England!'

'Yes,' said Eustace, 'I think we might do worse than leave old England for a few months.'

They turned in soon after twelve.

'You oughtn't to feel cold, Saunders,' said Eustace, 'when you can afford to sport a great fur-lined coat like this. You do yourself very well, all things considered. Look at those gloves, for instance. Who could possibly feel cold when wearing them?'

'They are far too clumsy, though, for driving. Try them on and see' – and he tossed them through the door on to Eustace's bed and went on with his unpacking. A minute later he heard a shrill cry of terror. 'Oh, Lord,' he heard, 'it's in the glove! Quick, Saunders, quick!' Then came a smacking thud. Eustace had thrown it from him. 'I've chucked it into the bathroom,' he gasped; 'it's hit the wall and fallen into the bath. Come now, if you want to help.' Saunders, with a lighted candle in his hand, looked over the edge of the bath. There it was, old and maimed, dumb and blind, with a ragged hole in the middle, crawling, staggering, trying to creep up the slippery sides, only to fall back helpless.

'Stay there,' said Saunders. 'I'll empty a collar-box or something, and we'll jam it in. It can't get out while I'm away.'

'Yes, it can,' shouted Eustace. 'It's getting out now; it's climbing up the plug-chain. No, you brute, you filthy brute, you don't! Come back, Saunders; it's getting away from me. I can't hold it; it's all slippery. Curse its claws! Shut the window, you idiot! It's got out.' There was the sound of something dropping on to the hard flagstones below, and Eustace fell back fainting.

For a fortnight he was ill.

'I don't know what to make of it,' the doctor said to Saunders. 'I can only suppose that Mr Borlsover has suffered some great emotional shock. You had better let me send someone to help you nurse him. And by all means indulge that whim of his never to be left alone in the dark. I would keep a light burning all night, if I were you. But he must have more fresh air. It's perfectly absurd, this hatred of open windows.'

Eustace would have no one with him but Saunders.

'I don't want the other man,' he said. 'They'd smuggle it in somehow. I know they would.'

'Don't worry about it, old chap. This sort of thing can't go on indefinitely. You know I saw it this time as well as you. It wasn't half so active. It won't go on living much longer, especially after that fall. I heard it hit the flags myself. As soon as you're a bit stronger, we'll leave this place, not bag and baggage, but with only the clothes on our backs, so that it won't be able to hide anywhere. We'll escape it that way. We won't give any address, and we won't have any parcels sent after us. Cheer up, Eustace! You'll be well enough to leave in a day or two. The doctor says I can take you out in a chair tomorrow.'

'What have I done?' asked Eustace. 'Why does it come after me? I'm no worse than other men. I'm no worse than you, Saunders; you know I'm not. It was you who was at the bottom of that dirty business in San Diego, and that was fifteen years ago.'

'It's not that, of course,' said Saunders. 'We are in the twentieth century, and even the parsons have dropped the idea of your old sins finding you out. Before you caught the hand in the library, it was filled with pure malevolence – to you and all mankind. After you spiked it through with that nail, it naturally forgot about other people and concentrated its attention on you. It was shut up in that safe, you know, for nearly six months. That gives plenty of time for thinking of revenge.'

Eustace Borlsover would not leave his room, but he thought there might be something in Saunders's suggestion of a sudden departure from Brighton. He began rapidly to regain his strength.

'We'll go on the 1st of September,' he said.

The evening of the 31st of August was oppressively warm. Though at midday the windows had been wide open, they had been shut an hour or so before dusk. Mrs Prince had long since ceased to wonder at the strange habits of the gentlemen on the first floor. Soon after their arrival she had been told to take down the heavy window curtains in the two bedrooms, and day by day the rooms had seemed to grow more bare. Nothing was left lying about.

'Mr Borlsover doesn't like to have any place where dirt can collect,' Saunders had said as an excuse. 'He likes to see into all the corners of the room.'

'Couldn't I open the window just a little?' he said to Eustace that evening. 'We're simply roasting in here, you know.'

'No, leave well alone. We're not a couple of boarding-school misses fresh from a course of hygiene lectures. Get the chessboard out.'

They sat down and played. At ten o'clock Mrs Prince came to the door with a note. 'I am sorry I didn't bring it before,' she said, 'but it was left in the letterbox.'

'Open it, Saunders, and see if it wants answering.'

It was very brief. There was neither address nor signature. *Will eleven o'clock tonight be suitable for our last appointment?*

'Who is it from?' asked Borlsover.

'It was meant for me,' said Saunders. 'There's no answer, Mrs Prince,' and he put the paper into his pocket. 'A dunning letter from a tailor; I suppose he must have got wind of our leaving.'

It was a clever lie, and Eustace asked no more questions. They went on with their game.

On the landing outside Saunders could hear the grandfather clock whispering the seconds, blurting out the quarter-hours.

'Check,' said Eustace. The clock struck eleven. At the same time there was a gentle knocking on the door; it seemed to come from the bottom panel.

'Who's there?' asked Eustace.

There was no answer.

'Mrs Prince, is that you?'

'She is up above,' said Saunders; 'I can hear her walking about the room.'

'Then lock the door; bolt it too. Your move, Saunders.'

While Saunders sat with his eyes on the chessboard, Eustace walked over to the window and examined the fastenings. He did the same in Saunders's room and the bathroom. There were no doors between the three rooms, or he would have shut and locked them too.

'Now, Saunders,' he said, 'don't stay all night over your move. I've had time to smoke one cigarette already. It's bad to keep an invalid waiting. There's only one possible thing for you to do. What was that?'

'The ivy blowing against the window. There, it's your move now, Eustace.'

'It wasn't the ivy, you idiot! It was someone tapping at the window,' and he pulled up the blind. On the outer side of the window, clinging to the sash, was the hand.

'What is that it's holding?'

'It's a pocketknife. It's going to try to open the window by pushing back the fastener with the blade.'

'Well, let it try,' said Eustace. 'Those fasteners screw down; they can't be opened that way. Anyhow, we'll close the shutters. It's your move, Saunders. I've played.'

But Saunders found it impossible to fix his attention on the game. He could not understand Eustace, who seemed all at once to have lost his fear. 'What do you say to some wine?' he asked. 'You seem to be taking things coolly, but I don't mind confessing that I'm in a blessed funk.'

'You've no need to be. There's nothing supernatural about that hand, Saunders. I mean, it seems to be governed by the laws of time and space. It's not the sort of thing that vanishes into thin air or slides through oaken doors. And since that's so, I defy it to get in here. We'll leave the place in the morning. I for one have bottomed the depths of fear. Fill your glass, man! The windows are all shuttered; the door is locked and bolted. Pledge me my Uncle Adrian! Drink, man! What are you waiting for?'

Saunders was standing with his glass half raised. 'It can get in,' he said hoarsely; 'it can get in! We've forgotten. There's the fireplace in my bedroom. It will come down the chimney.'

'Quick!' said Eustace, as he rushed into the other room; 'we haven't a minute to lose. What can we do? Light the fire, Saunders. Give me a match, quick!'

'They must be all in the other room. I'll get them.'

'Hurry, man, for goodness' sake! Look in the bookcase! Look in the bathroom! Here, come and stand here; I'll look.'

'Be quick!' shouted Saunders. 'I can hear something!'

'Then plug a sheet from your bed up the chimney. No, here's a match!' He had found one, at last, that had slipped into a crack in the floor.

'Is the fire laid? Good, but it may not burn. I know – the oil from that old reading-lamp and this cotton-wool. Now the match, quick! Pull the sheet away, you fool! We don't want it now.'

There was a great roar from the grate, as the flames shot up. Saunders had been a fraction of a second too late with the sheet. The oil had fallen on to it. It, too, was burning

'The whole place will be on fire!' cried Eustace, as he tried to beat out the flames with a blanket. 'It's no good! I can't manage it. You must open the door, Saunders, and get help.'

Saunders ran to the door and fumbled with the bolts. The key was stiff in the lock. 'Hurry,' shouted Eustace, 'or the heat will be too much for me.' The key turned in the lock at last. For half a second Saunders stopped to look back. Afterwards he could never be quite sure as to what he had seen, but at the time he thought that something black and charred was creeping slowly, very slowly, from the mass of flames towards Eustace Borlsover. For a moment he thought of returning to his friend; but the noise and the smell of the burning sent him running down the passage, crying: 'Fire! Fire!' He rushed to the telephone to summon help, and then back to the bathroom – he should have thought of that before – for water. As he burst into the bedroom there came a scream of terror which ended suddenly, and then the sound of a heavy fall.

This is the story which I heard on successive Saturday evenings from the senior mathematical master at a second-rate suburban school. For Saunders has had to earn a living in a way which other men might reckon less congenial than his old manner of life. I had mentioned by chance the name of Adrian Borlsover, and wondered at the time why he changed the conversation with such unusual abruptness. A week later Saunders began to tell me something of his own history; sordid enough, though shielded with a reserve I could well understand, for it had to cover not only his failings, but those of a dead friend. Of the final tragedy he was at first especially loath to speak; and it was only gradually that I was able to piece together the narrative of the preceding pages. Saunders was reluctant to draw any conclusions. At one time he thought that the fingered beast had been animated by the spirit of Sigismund Borlsover, a sinister eighteenth-century ancestor, who, according to legend, built and worshipped in the ugly pagan temple that overlooked the lake. At another time, Saunders believed the spirit to belong to a man whom Eustace had once employed as a laboratory assistant – 'A black-haired, spiteful little brute,' he said, 'who died cursing his doctor because the fellow couldn't help him to live to settle some paltry score with Borlsover.'

From the point of view of direct contemporary evidence, Saunders's story is practically uncorroborated. All the letters mentioned in the narrative were destroyed, with the exception of the last note which Eustace received, or rather, which he would have received, had not Saunders intercepted it. That I have seen myself. The handwriting was thin and shaky, the handwriting of an old man. I remember the Greek 'e' was used in 'appointment'. A little thing that amused me at the time was that Saunders seemed to keep the note pressed between the pages of his Bible.

I had seen Adrian Borlsover once. Saunders I learnt to know well. It was by chance, however, and not by design, that I met a third person of the story – Morton, the butler. Saunders and I were walking in the Zoological Gardens one Sunday afternoon, when he called my attention to an old man who was standing before the door of the Reptile House.

'Why, Morton,' he said, clapping him on the back, 'how is the world treating you?'

'Poorly, Mr Saunders,' said the old fellow, though his face lighted up at the greeting. 'The winters drag terribly nowadays. There don't seem to be no summers or springs.'

'You haven't found what you were looking for, I suppose?'

'No, sir, not yet; but I shall some day. I always told them that Mr Borlsover kept some queer animals.'

'And what is he looking for?' I asked, when we had parted from him.

'A beast with five fingers,' said Saunders. 'This afternoon, since he has been in the Reptile House, I suppose it will be a reptile with a hand. Next week it will be a monkey with practically no body. The poor old chap is a born materialist.'